FILMI
STORIES

Celebrating 35 Years of
Penguin Random House India

FILMI STORIES

KUNAL BASU

VINTAGE
An imprint of Penguin Random House

VINTAGE

USA | Canada | UK | Ireland | Australia
New Zealand | India | South Africa | China

Vintage is part of the Penguin Random House group of companies
whose addresses can be found at global.penguinrandomhouse.com

Published by Penguin Random House India Pvt. Ltd
4th Floor, Capital Tower 1, MG Road,
Gurugram 122 002, Haryana, India

Penguin
Random House
India

First published in Vintage by Penguin Random House India 2023

ISBN 9780670098392

Typeset in Dante MT Std by Manipal Technologies Limited, Manipal
Printed at Thomson Press India Ltd, New Delhi

www.penguin.co.in

MIX
Paper
FSC FSC® C010615

For
Eugene Datta

CONTENTS

PROLOGUE

Filmi Stories

In the fleeting spring of 2021, as the world was reeling from the pandemic, I thought to write a few stories to drive out the despair that was filling me up like smoke in a chimney stack. Once I'd made that decision, I reached, quite naturally, for the Havana cigar box that was stowed away for safekeeping. It held scraps of paper with scribbled notes—story ideas I had saved for the future. Born in different places, such as airports and toilets, they carried the whiff of their genesis, coated with the veneer of hand-rolled tobacco. I shall need them someday, I'd told myself. But in that breathless spring, the scraps failed to revive my spirit.

Inspiration comes unannounced—I'd read somewhere. Like a long-lost penny, it shows up at unexpected places. Away from my desk, there was a chance I might encounter it in the garden or the kitchen or—if I was lucky—in a dream. The first of the lot surprised me by crawling out of its box as I was on the verge of losing my shirt in a game of Monopoly. In a flash, I envisioned a sole passenger in an airplane flying from one deserted airport to another. I could sense the agitation of the flyer, and it filled me—in equal parts—with alarm and ardour. I understood then that it wasn't a story that I was after, but the thrill of its possibility. Once it had played its trick, it invited other truants to burst forth from mouldy suitcases, rusty urns and jingling piggy banks. It was time to get going.

There was something about them that made me think of these stories as films. Maybe it had to do with their dramatic appearance. In the aftermath of a novel that I'd just finished writing, they offered a delicious interlude full of light and shadow, sound and silence and the jerky movement of a camera desperate to catch all the action. Writing these felt like directing a bunch of unruly actors, keeping no more than an eye on the script that seemed to take on a life of its own.

I have always considered film and fiction to be ungainly cousins, each trying its best to cover up the imperfection of the other. Might there be a third cousin? A kinder one, the peacemaker, deft in weaving together the senses, making them seem to be one through a clever sleight of hand? Such thoughts went into the making of these tales as spring heralded both the beginning and the end of *Filmi Stories*.

Oxford/Kolkata   Kunal Basu
April 2022

OK TATA

The thought of killing someone occurred to Jaggi in his sleep. In his dream, the target appeared as clear as day, and he knew exactly what needed to be done. Once that unpleasant thought had passed, he slept soundly—as only truckers can, like babies after they'd had their fill of mother's milk.

Arriving at the highway eatery at dusk, Pavan, his helper, had rushed to order a super-cold beer for his master and an extra-sweet tea for himself, while Jaggi stretched out on a coir bed reserved for regulars. After 12 hours in the driver's cabin, his body felt like his truck: part aching, part numb. Diesel smoke choked his nose and blocked the smell of sweat. When he spoke, his voice, resembling a dog's growl, sent Pavan bounding to fetch ice for his not-so-cold beer. Around him, fellow truckers grunted, groaned and spat out tobacco. A man, who must've spent days on the road, snored, drawing a curse or two. Only the smell of food and the nagging thought of hitting the road again with a full stomach kept them alert.

Clearing his throat with tea, Pavan made a false start, trying to warm Jaggi up to a full conversation. His eyes, trained to spot trespassers into the truck's blind spot, were unblinking.

'If you care to listen, I'll tell you something important, something . . .'

Jaggi shook his head even before Pavan could finish. The scoundrel was about to beg him for his very first night drive, he thought. He'd be reminding Jaggi of the promise he'd made to him 2 years back—to make him a master one day—when he'd joined him as helper, cleaner, tyre changer, beer fetcher—the one who sang badly only to keep him awake at the wheel.

'You must get your eyes checked before I let you drive at night,' Jaggi spoke gruffly, watching the eatery's cook bake bread in the oven. Pavan had bad eyes, he was certain. They watered from the high beams of passing trucks at night. The boy might drive with his head turned away from the road and get them killed.

'It's not that.' Pavan stopped to clear his throat again. 'Something serious.'

Jaggi raised himself on the bed and belched.

'It has to do with you and Jhimli.'

Used to drivers making unexpected manoeuvres on the road, Jaggi frowned and waited for the situation to unfold.

'It's about Raju, the welder who comes to visit her in her sister's home when you are away. She belongs to him now—I've heard people say. Maybe you know what's with your wife or maybe you don't. Maybe you don't care. Maybe she has left you already and become his wife.' His eyes didn't blink as he muttered his final words, 'You must know how bad something is before it's broken—didn't you teach me that, Master?'

The iced beer tasted warm after that. The owner got an earful because the lentil smelled like piss. Truckers looked up from their food as Jaggi stumbled out of the eatery to relieve himself in the open. Fearing the aftermath, Pavan had wisely withdrawn to the kitchen to chit-chat with the help. Only the snoring man, who'd woken up by then, made the mistake of asking Jaggi for a smoke and received a blast of indecipherable words in return. Then, he stumbled back into his bed, overcome by the combined force of the beer and 12 hours in the truck.

A clear night suspended the stars right above his head, and Jaggi saw the brightest of them smirking at him. It was Raju. His face was radiating the arc of a welder's torch. Like the high beam of an approaching truck, it was daring him to lower his eyes and take evasive action. Raju, the man who frequented Jhimli's sister's home to be with his wife, while he was on the road. The shadowy figure that prowled the huts like a beast, the thief who'd robbed him while he slept on rotten beds, filled up with warm beer and bad food. Raju, his one and only true enemy, the one he'd kill—as he clearly saw at the onset of his dream—with his bare hands, like a demon, separating limbs from torso, till his victim resembled the wreckage of a truck torn asunder by some violent collision.

At midnight, the eatery that doubled as a rest stop for truckers was empty. The few remaining men slept on coir beds or in truck cabins, waiting for a mechanic to arrive and get them moving again. Dogs feasted on kitchen scraps, while rats awaited their turn. Shadowy forms lurked behind trees, and there was no telling if they were thieves who'd come to rob the truckers or a band of jackals simply passing through. Jaggi didn't feel sad leaving Pavan behind at the stop. The boy would wake up in the morning and find his master gone. He'd thrash about wildly, curse Jaggi for abandoning him after he'd promised him the world and then weep, drawing the attention of some kind trucker. He'd find his berth in a cabin once again, keep an eye on the blind spot and sing for his new master. That is the way of the world: You lose something you love only to find something better.

The night gave comfort as Jaggi drove along the divided highway. There was too much to think about during the day— from stray cattle on the road to vultures who lurked at every turn to extract blood from the truckers. He cursed the lot of policemen, always thirsty for bribes. Nothing else mattered at night but the road, coaxing arms and legs to follow the single-minded pull of an invisible hand. The road is their true lover, it was said of truckers, and, like others, Jaggi too preferred night over day.

He had found Jhimli on the road, driving through the night to deliver his load of tomatoes to a cold storage before they ripened and rotted under the sun. The bait of a bonus made him drive fast, racing the truck's dying engine well beyond its capacity. It was a stretch known for flashing torches. Pimps swung torchlights to alert truckers of prey—girls, willing to spend a few hours inside their cabins for a little cash. Keep your blinkers on and pull up by the side if you wished to follow the norm of restless truckers and gain some action off the road. The tomatoes plus the fear of bandits in the guise of girls, who made deals with the pimps to raid trucks, had kept Jaggi going. He'd been wise to bring his load home before stopping for action at the dance bar nearby.

The new girl had caught his eye. She danced badly, like a waddling donkey. Truckers booed her. Other dancers pushed her out of their way to the back to scoop up the money that rained down on the stage. She stood motionless, head down, like a schoolgirl who'd received a scolding. Normally, the truckers didn't care too much about dancing. After a month on the road, the mere sight of a girl was a gift from heaven. A girl who smiled, threw a kiss in the air, knew the regulars by their names, served beer at the table and struck deals to visit them in their cabins. The 'regulars' liked it that way—having a known girl who wouldn't land them in a hospital with the clap or bring over some home-cooked food even if they were lucky.

Jhimli, the new girl, drew Jaggi to the dance bar. In no time, he'd become a regular, taking on the cold storage run all month. Tomatoes, onions, mangoes and pineapples in season—his truck smelled fruity sweet and drew flies bothering his helper. He had surprised the dancers by giving her the largest tip. The two had exchanged numbers, and he'd refrained from inviting her to his truck's cabin. He lost his head whenever she messaged him, argued needlessly with the truck's owner over cargo load or late payment, lost his temper with policemen and received fines for no fault of his. 'You will kill yourself,' fellow trucker Avtar Singh counselled him when Jaggi felt low because he'd missed out on the cold storage run. 'Drink doesn't kill a trucker on the road. Women do.' He came close to dying, driving non-stop all night to reach the dance bar, stabbing his thigh with a cigarette butt just to stay awake.

'I don't want you to take *bhukki*,' Jhimli told him, meaning the opium powder that was a staple among truckers. You swallowed bhukki to stop feeling sad, stop feeling angry, stop missing home, stop feeling anything. After a while, it gave you bulging eyes and sunken cheeks.

'I don't want you to waste money on me; spend it on what you eat.'

There was this thing with Jhimli that he couldn't fully fathom. She spoke to him without uttering a word, told him her full story with nudges and gestures. With her, he didn't feel the need to explain, as she understood everything like why he'd overloaded his truck to earn something extra to buy her a smartphone just so he could see her face when he called from the road. She gave him a tiny stone idol to place on the truck's dashboard and light incense sticks at sundown.

'I have Shiva and Hanuman to guard against accidents,' Jaggi frowned. 'Why do I need Kali?'

'She'll protect you from yourself,' Jhimli said, rising from the roof of Jaggi's truck and clambering down.

'Marry her, Jaggi,' Avtar advised him, as did Santosh who'd lost his wife at childbirth. 'It'll settle your mind. Stop you from driving all night like a madman. A woman gives you trouble at first. Then she saves you from trouble.'

Jhimli hadn't said yes or no when he took Avtar and Santosh's proposal to her. Throwing down the empty earthen teacup, she had shrugged, meaning that the answer was as obvious as changing a tyre after a blowout.

It was already dawn when Jaggi pulled up at Jhimli's sister's home. The village was waking up to assorted cries of domestic pets and the rustle of ducks eager to jump into the pond. He pictured Jhimli sleeping inside the hut, her phone by her side to receive a message from him. He imagined she was sleeping alone, her sick sister curled up in the adjoining room. She wouldn't be expecting him to show up now, take her for a joyride on his truck before taking her home. She'd be expecting to spend a few more days with her sister till Jaggi finished his run. Unless . . .

Switching off the engine, he moved back from his seat to the cabin's bunk bed for a snooze, hoping for a rerun of the dream that had taken him off the highway and brought him here.

As the story goes, it was Jhimli who found Jaggi, before he could make his dramatic entry into her sister's home. She found him snoring, with a fruit fly perched on his moustache, enjoying the periodic blasts from the nostrils. Village urchins had clambered on top of the truck, which they'd taken for a mountain, hauling each other up and shrieking aloud when they reached the roof's summit. Those who could read, recited the words OK TATA painted over the tail lights, rhyming TATA with *mota*, pointing and giggling at Jaggi's bulging girth.

Her sister woke Jhimli up when neighbours announced the truck's arrival. 'He has returned early,' she told Jhimli, a cloud over her eyes. 'His truck is full of onions.'

She took her time straightening the bed, counting her sister's pills, making a morning tiffin for Raju before taking it out to the camp where builders had pitched tent for the bridge under construction. Then she came over to the truck and woke Jaggi up. She told him a few basics while he drank his favourite sweet tea, keeping his face averted: He'd need to fetch medicines for her sister, buy a light bulb for the kitchen, and cover the onions with a thick tarpaulin unless he wished everyone in the village to cry. She told him to bathe in the pond, while she washed his clothes, taking care not to trample over the ducks' freshly laid eggs in the reeds.

Villagers came by all day—some to visit Jhimli's sister, others to engage in gossip. Munna—a gangly boy, barely 15—pestered Jhimli to let him meet Jaggi, to beg him to take him on as his helper. Shooing him away, she told all her visitors to keep their voices down as Jaggi was sleeping after a long and hard drive.

Awake all day, Jaggi watched the ebb and flow of villagers. Straining his neck through the window slit, he caught Jhimli passing over a midday tiffin to Raju, who approached the hut like a prey, unruffled by the scent of the hunter. He saw them exchange a few words, the man offering her some money and Jhimli shaking her head. He saw him again, squatting on the dirt with the urchins and playing marbles, with the assurance of an outsider who's won the trust of the villagers.

She belongs to him now. Maybe you know what's with your wife or maybe you don't. Maybe you don't care. Maybe she has left you already and become his wife—Pavan's words returned to him as he dozed, resting his back on the earthen wall to catch the action outside. Raju, who loitered around the hut, seemed a poor replica of the man he'd seen in his dream: not tall and sturdy like Kashi, the wrestler, who'd hidden heroin inside his cargo and got him arrested. He had broken Kashi's skull with the iron wrench used to change tyres, giving him no chance to tie his girdle around his waist and assume a wrestler's stance. Beaten him till he was senseless, and Pavan had to grab Jaggi by the feet and wrestle him to the ground to prevent a murder.

Raju looked harmless. Like a college boy or a low-paid clerk who bicycled to work and scampered off the path of a truck. He resembled a helper, ready to flee if his master raised a slap for slacking off while loading cargo. Softies—they had no place on the highway, the kind that truckers paid a few rupees to massage their sore backs and sore feet.

He imagined Raju throwing money at the dance bar and Jhimli kneeling down before him to snap up the dirty notes. She was no longer hiding behind the other dancers and was fully visible under the glaring lights, making those moves that made the rascal take off his shirt and blow a whistle. He saw the two of them leave the bar and climb up a truck's cabin and, once again, sensed the wrath of the demon surging through him.

Jaggi woke with a start and found Jhimli had brought him his favourite laddu. The hut smelled invitingly of ghee. Her sister showed her smiling face before disappearing to fetch water. Jhimli stuffed his mouth with the sweet and kept her face down. Then she spoke quietly.

'I know why you've come. You want to kill Raju.'

Jaggi started and a piece of the laddu got stuck inside his throat. Jhimli kept on speaking, avoiding his gaze.

'But I am going to ask you not to kill him today. Wait for just a few days, then you can do what you want.'

Jaggi managed to swallow down the offending piece and asked, 'Why should I wait?'

'Because today marks the beginning of the annual worship of our goddess. It'll last just a week. Everyone in the village will be celebrating this evening. They'll give sweets to each other, build a fire and offer prayers. The children will play games.'

'I shall throw that scoundrel into the fire,' Jaggi spoke gruffly, finishing off the last of the laddus.

'Then he will return to the village and refuse to leave.' Jhimli sounded scared. 'A person who dies an unnatural death during the goddess's worship returns as a ghost.'

Jaggi was about to curse loudly and berate Jhimli for believing in such hocus-pocus when she grabbed hold of his hand and pleaded, 'You'll be away on your truck. He'll return to haunt me.'

In the week of the worship that followed, Jaggi saw enough of Raju to keep the demon inside him alive. Village elders entrusted the young man to build a pyre with firewood, sprinkle it with kerosene and set it ablaze.

'He's a welder; he knows everything about fire,' a man limped up to Jaggi and claimed to be Jhimli's uncle. 'We are lucky to have him.'

'Why is he here?' Jaggi challenged the talkative uncle. 'What makes him hang around the village when he's nobody's friend or relative?'

'Because he can't leave. Neither him nor his friends who came to build the bridge.'

Another man, who supplied sand to the bridge builders, knew more. 'A sickness is spreading in the towns and villages, and work on the bridge has been stopped. Those boys want to leave, but buses and trains aren't plying. The government has forbidden all travel. They are trapped here.'

Jaggi scoffed. He hadn't seen policemen stopping anyone on the road. It must be a lie made up by Raju.

The morning after the fire, he saw Raju dangling like a kite from a pole, with the urchins forming a ring underneath him. One of the little devils pulled on Jaggi's arm, 'Why don't you join us? If he falls you can catch him.' Jaggi waited for Raju to fall and break his neck, but he managed to fix the snapped wire on the electric pole and descend swiftly like a monkey to everyone's delight.

He has become a pet to every villager, Jaggi fumed privately—son, brother, nephew, lover.

Stories about the bridge builders blew through the village like oven smoke from the kitchen, invited an outpouring of warmth. At the teashops, men talked about their plight: poor sods left to rot without ration or pay, abandoned by an uncaring contractor. Their families must miss them, and at this rate, they might have to walk home. 'Walk!' There were collective gasps. 'Walk for 300 kilometres! 500! Even 1000?'

Then there was Jhimli's sister, suffering from a bad heart and a bad knee, who mumbled something about village families adopting one of each till these difficulties passed.

'Adopting!' Jaggi exploded. 'Adopting these men is no better than adopting wild beasts. They'll sneak in like lambs then leave dragging out man, woman or child by the neck.'

He kept a rusty iron rod under his truck's seat to fight off highway robbers. But, here in the village, it didn't fit his purpose. His dream had foretold the manner of killing: dismembering his enemy, tearing apart the limbs from the body, like that of a dead chicken. Jhimli saw the fire in his eyes and came over with a jerry can of hooch.

'I know what you'll ask me,' she spoke clearly, wetting her mouth with a sip, then spitting out the drink to check for dead ants in the fermented toddy. 'You won't ask me about Raju and me. Why he comes around, and why I give him food. If he's what a man is to a woman, if I am still the Jhimli you met at the dance bar or your wife.'

Jaggi grunted, unbothered by Jhimli's words or dead ants.

'You'll ask me if the time has now come, and . . .'

'Has it?' Jaggi stopped her from saying more. She sighed, then shook her head.

'Not today. Tomorrow, I won't stop you.' She explained as Jaggi threw up his hands and made a face.

'The chowkidar will come to the village today to collect his share of the offerings to the goddess. He'll inform the police if there was a murder. They'll come to arrest you. They keep prisoners in jail until they die, I'm told. They might not let me visit you, and I'll be forced to go back to the dance bar.'

That night, drunk on hooch, Jaggi spied on the builders, going up to the bridge. Creeping past the jumble of abandoned machinery, he saw the incomplete pillars standing upright like cenotaphs. Boulders blocked his path. A crane hung limp against the night sky. Three men were gathered around a fire, sharing food. He saw Raju empty Jhimli's tiffin on to a plate. The men gobbled it down and scraped the bowl to recover the remaining bits of morsel. Raju was the youngest of the three, and the other two were consoling him like elder brothers—patting his arms, whispering softly and taking out their phones to send messages. He didn't look like the brave fire setter or the pole-climbing ape but beaten to the bone.

They're getting him ready for the thrashing—Jaggi could barely suppress a laugh. Preparing him for the sacrifice. Jaggi's arrival must've scared them; they must know that their young friend would have to pay with his life for stealing a man's wife. It was his last night at the camp. Jhimli must've told him.

Once he was back in this truck, Jaggi stood on the roof, reeling from the drink. His head seemed tall enough to touch the stars, arms ready to pluck out the bridge's columns like wheat stalks. He felt the demon rising and his laugh rang through the heart of every villager—awake or asleep—making them shudder.

And so, it was said that when the day broke, Jaggi hunted Raju down at the teashop where he was regaling the villagers with stories about welders boring tunnels under the sea. Men and women, young and old, followed them as he dragged Raju down to the pond that would be the scene of the punishment. Peasants abandoned their ploughs in the field to join the crowd. Cowherds didn't bother with a calf or two that'd gone astray. Women left their kitchen in a hurry, letting pots to smoulder. Leaning on Jhimli's arm, her sister limped over and slumped on a tree trunk that afforded the best view of the pond.

Grabbing Raju by the neck, Jaggi ripped open his shirt to bare his skinny chest that barely sprouted a tuft of hair, ribs straining against skin to receive the first blow. Turning him to one side, he gave his arms the maximum arch to do his business in the best way he knew. Groans went up with every thud, the villagers keeping count of the strikes. Ducks streaked across the pond and sprayed a cloud of feathers. No one cheered or raised an alarm. Raju seemed resigned to the assault, making a weak gesture to cover his face, opening himself up to Jaggi to do as he wished. Without any sight of blood, there was no telling how much damage was already done, although the young man had started to convulse and sputter at the mouth.

Jhimli sat motionless, almost unmindful of the action, as if the pond were the dance bar's stage where things happened every night, and there was no way to prevent either the good or the bad. Like others, she didn't wince as Jaggi set himself up for the final strike of the demon: turning Raju around, grabbing his arms to flex his back and bear down on the torso with the might of his leg. Then, like the rest of the villagers, she held her breath and gasped as Raju shrieked, howled like an animal on the verge of dying, yelled—and yelled yet again—for his mother. In that defining moment, his enemy slipped out of Jaggi's hold, and drifted away—face down like a corpse—to the pond's far end, trailing a stream of bubbles.

After she'd found someone to help her carry Raju over to the bridge and bring him to his senses, Jhimli returned to the truck to tend to Jaggi. She bandaged his knuckles with a piece of cloth torn from an old sari. Like his victim, he too had suffered to overcome the resistance of the bones and bore his fair share of bruises. Then, even without prompting, she told him Raju's full story with a few simple gestures.

'He is sad because his mother is dying, and he can't be by her side in the hospital because no bus or train will take him to the big city, which is his home.' She waited to see if Jaggi was listening and then went on. 'He doesn't have a brother or sister to look after her. She is all alone.'

'He can hitch a ride with someone who's going that way,' Jaggi waved aside Raju's troubles. 'Must be a lazy fellow, crying like a baby for his mother.'

'No one will take him,' Jhimli persisted. 'Drivers don't want to take a stranger, who might pass on the disease to them. He has tried. He and his friends have stood by the highway for days.'

Jaggi turned over on his side for Jhimli to massage his sore back.

'He'll have to stay here, till you kill him,' Jhimli paused, 'Unless . . .'

Jaggi yawned. 'Unless what?'

'Unless a kind trucker took pity on him and took him home.'

Asleep in the truck after Jhimli had left, Jaggi woke at the cry of a lost bird looking for its nest. Propped up in the cabin, he watched the dance of fireflies, and the flight of an occasional moth diving to its death on the windshield. Reaching under the seat, he recovered a tattered envelope and from it his mother's photo among the jumble of road permits. It was the only one he had, taken in a studio at their home town, before mother and son had gone for a pilgrimage to the famous temple by the Ganges. She was smiling in the photograph, her gaze fixed on young Jaggi standing behind the photographer who was wearing a black hood. They'd had fun during the pilgrimage—eating his favourite sweets, buying toys and bathing in the river. Squinting at the photo, he recalled the bathers—among them his mother—and the sudden panic as a big wave came down flooding the banks, swallowing the buoys, swallowing everything. He had seen his mother drown and yelled calling for someone to save her.

When he came for Raju the following day, villagers expected a rerun of the drama by the pond, making their moves early to crowd the banks. But this time, Jaggi grabbed him by the collar and dragged him over to his truck and threw him a bucket, barking out his order to wash the tyres, sweep the windshield clean of dead insects and fill up the tank with water. Sensing something was happening, Jhimli rushed over and begged for a sack of onions, then stole two after she'd finished haggling with Jaggi. The urchins broke out into a chorus of OK TATA as he lumbered his way out of the village on to the highway with Raju as his helper to deliver the rascal to his mother.

He'd make a bad helper, Jaggi concluded within hours of riding with Raju. The fellow chattered non-stop when he wasn't sleeping. Like a teacher, he lectured Jaggi about welding. 'It's the most dangerous job in the world, far riskier than driving trucks,' he said, inviting a glare from Jaggi.

'Think about it like joining up two pieces that are broken. You must melt both of them by applying high heat,' he stopped to wipe his sweaty face, 'then match them up to soak in the flame. They'll be bonded together once they cool, and nothing can separate them again.' Raju gave a short laugh, 'It's like uniting two friends, or a man and his . . .' He broke off mid-sentence as Jaggi swerved rashly to overtake a slow-moving car out for a joyride.

'Driving a truck is risky,' Jaggi gave his own lecture to stop the imbecile from bragging. 'A brake fail will land you in the bushes with no one to rescue you. Dogs will drag out your body and feast on your flesh.' He glanced sideways to check Raju's reaction then went into gorier stuff. 'If there was a short circuit, you might burn inside the cabin. When you drive through disturbed territories, rebels could shoot bullets at you, killing you on your seat.'

'Yes,' Raju smiled, as if he was the teacher indulging his young student's feeble arguments. 'But these things don't happen often, do they? For us welders, dangers come every day. Burns, electric shocks, blindings, gas poisoning. Look,' stretching out his left arm, he showed Jaggi an ugly scar. 'The contractor gives us nothing, no gloves, no goggles, nothing.'

'Just like us stupid drivers,' Jaggi mumbled. 'No shoes, no spectacles, no woollen clothes in the winter, nothing.'

That was the other thing with Raju, he made no mention of the thrashing, behaved as if it hadn't happened or happened only in Jaggi's dream. Their hands touched when Raju passed him the light, cupping his palm around the flame, or exchanged a water bottle across the gearbox. Unlike Pavan, who didn't sleep a wink on the road, Raju tucked up his feet on the seat whenever he ran out of words and dozed off, resting this head on Jaggi's shoulder.

The boy must have a short memory, Jaggi thought. Perhaps, he's accepted his punishment, made peace with his ugly past and expected Jaggi to do so. The gnashing together of flesh and bones had cancelled the heart's unrest. The brawl by the pond had turned them into driver and helper. When they bathed under the tap in a rest stop, lathering themselves thoroughly to get rid of the grime of the road, Jaggi saw the marks he'd left on Raju. An angry welt showed on his chest, where he'd struck; his jaw was bruised from the punches. It was hard to miss the swelling of the chin under the lather. Raju smiled shyly, catching Jaggi eyeing the damage. Did the welder's mind see the two of them as once broken pieces now joined together by the heat of the blows?

'Where did you find your new helper?' Trilok Singh asked Jaggi at the rest stop. He was carrying a load of marble, twice the maximum limit permitted by law. He had enough cash on him to pay off the police and crawled to his destination lest the truck should topple over under excessive weight. 'Your Pavan has been going around telling everyone that you've lost your mind and landed up in jail after killing someone.'

Jaggi cursed Pavan. A helper should never spread rumours about his master, even if he forced him to swallow shit.

'What will you do with the onions?' the eatery owner asked. The sacks let off a frowsy smell from lying under the sun much longer than intended.

'Eat them,' Jaggi replied, then spread himself out on a coir bed.

Jhimli called after he'd had his snooze and asked if he felt any pain inside his head for which he took pills from the same doctor who checked her sister's heart once every month.

'Why should I feel any pain?' he asked back.

'Because you left your pills behind. And you have someone with you who might trouble your head.'

Did she call to check up on him, or for Raju? Did she fear that Jaggi might keep his promise after all, finish Raju off and dump him on the highway? Why hadn't she stopped him at the pond? He wondered. The villagers must've known the reason, expected the two men to fight over a woman. They thought not to interfere in a matter of honour, but why hadn't Jhimli? Did she want one of them dead? Which one? The cold beer played tricks on his mind, and Jaggi saw her dancing at the bar, with both Raju and he vying for her attention, throwing down money, gesturing with their eyes for her to come over and spend the evening in the truck's cabin.

Maybe she missed being at the bar. Missed all the attention, happy to take on the danger like a trucker or a welder.

'There are ghosts everywhere,' Trilok Singh was telling stories to the truckers between burps after their nightly meal. Word had come about the mystery disease. Migrant workers weren't allowed to move from one state to another, with trucks checked for stowaways. Tollbooths and weigh stations reported long queues, and the bribery rate had doubled. Used to floods and riots, the truckers were happy to wait out the troubles till the flow resumed. Meanwhile, there were stories to tell, and Trilok had the knack of keeping the sleepiest of them awake.

'My friend Shabir visited a dargah on his Bombay–Nagpur run. Then he stopped to eat, took his nightly dose of bhukki and hit the road. Suddenly, a figure appeared out of nowhere and stood in the middle of the road. Must be some nutcase, Shabir thought. Or a crook who'd demand money to move out of the way.'

'Might've been a trucker too, who'd had an accident and wanted some help,' Ananth, who'd survived a near-fatal crash not long ago, added grimly.

'This man, dressed fully in white, claimed to be the Sufi saint's disciple and requested Shabir to help him reach the dargah. Reluctantly, he agreed. Turning back, he made the journey to the dargah, as it is a sin to deny someone who wishes to visit a saintly shrine. Then he hit the road again.'

'What's ghostly about . . .' Raju started to say, but Jaggi quietened him. Trilok went on.

'Again, he found a man in white in the middle of the road, at the very same spot as before. He too wanted to go to the dargah and Shabir, cursing his luck, agreed again.' Trilok Singh paused to swallow his dose of bhukki with a gulp of water, then picked up the thread of his story.

'He is said to have made ten trips back and forth between the dargah and the cursed spot all night, till his truck's tank ran empty. By then, of course, he had lost his mind totally.'

'Where is he now?' Ananth asked.

'In an asylum in Nagpur, where he claims to be the saint of the dargah and lies still on his back all day pretending to be dead.'

In the silence that followed, only Bundi, the owner of the rest stop's eatery who'd heard Trilok's story a dozen times, could be heard singing as he stacked up the plates for the morning meal and fed scraps to his pet dog. Then he cleared his throat and threw out his words to the truckers.

'These are just stories. If you want to see real ghosts, go to Manhar Palace. Like truckers, they come there during night-time, have their feast and tell stories to each other.'

Raju was keen to know more, and Bundi pointed with his arm towards the rolling mist, 'Just 5 kilometres from here, you'll see the ruins from the highway. If you can see the faint glow of a lamp, you'll know the ghosts have arrived.'

'Let's go to Manhar!' Raju shook Jaggi by the shoulders to wake him up after the truckers had fallen asleep. Jerking himself free, Jaggi went back to sleep.

'This is our best chance to see a ghost. Once we leave, there'll only be stories to listen to, all those lies made up by Trilok.' Raju's voice was choking with excitement.

Too tired to curse him properly, Jaggi managed nevertheless to utter a few. 'Why do we need ghosts?'

'Because then we'll know what'll happen to us when we die.'

Now woken up, Jaggi tried unsuccessfully to remember the very worst of curses. But Raju seemed to be beyond abuse.

'When you were about to kill me at that pond, I was thinking what'll I be when I wake up after my death. Will I become a duck—the last living thing I'd seen?'

'You'll become a snake if you go to that ruin. They'll bite you, and the poison will turn you into a hatchling inside a mother snake's egg,' Jaggi snorted.

'Welders are snake-proof. We live and work in camps near forests. Snakes don't mind us, nor we them.' Raju wasn't deterred, and it took a dozen pleas for Jaggi to finally give in.

Raju spoke non-stop during those 5 kilometres, but the sight of Manhar Palace silenced him. Leaving the truck, the two approached the ruins, Jaggi following Raju, as he stomped the ground with the iron rod, the truck's sole weapon, and made a clucking sound with his tongue.

'Snakes will think we are a pack of mongoose. They'll slither away from our path.'

It was a palace of arched doorways, about a score of them, each in a worse state of disrepair than the other. Moss covered the latticework that must've decorated the windows meant for sentries to look out from their watch towers. Gaping holes replaced the entrances to grand halls. A crushed column was all that remained as support for a scenic balcony suspended magically upon it. In the darkness of its surroundings, the ruins resembled a hillock mangled out of proportion by a miner's ballast.

Jaggi pulled on Raju's arm, urging him to turn back. 'Forget snakes; there might be jackals and jungle cats who aren't afraid of mongoose. Why would ghosts choose such a godforsaken place?'

'Look!' Raju pointed to what appeared to be a shrine inside the anteroom. A flame was burning, casting its shadow on the cobwebs suspended from the chandelier. 'The ghosts have come! They must know we are here as well.'

As they inched their way in, a brick fell from the ceiling, barely missing Jaggi. He let out a curse. Raju hushed him, 'Shh . . . ghosts have ears too!'

'To hell with ghosts.' Collecting himself, Jaggi thought aloud, 'Must be a den of criminals, amusing themselves while hiding from sight. Maybe this is where they come to share the loot and torture their victims. They might shoot at us, taking us to be the police.'

Raju ignored him, his gaze fixed at the flickering flame. He nudged Jaggi sharply with his elbow, 'Not criminals. Girls!'

'What! Where?' Leaving Raju's side, Jaggi took a few bold steps forward, standing at the entrance of what might've been a grand ballroom. The shadow on the wall appeared to undulate and grow in size till there wasn't one but many forms swaying and merging like well-choreographed dancers at a dance bar. They stood transfixed, barely breathing, then Raju cried aloud, 'They're coming for us!' and stumbled in the excitement of the moment, falling on the marble floor, dragging Jaggi down with him. Quite suddenly, the palace came alive with screeches. Dark forms appeared out of nowhere flying madly over their heads, crashing against the chandelier, banging against doorways and splintering the windowpanes. A sickening smell spread all around. Shielding themselves with their arms, Jaggi and Raju fought the onslaught, clinging on to each other like drowning sailors, guarding themselves against the devilish creatures diving down and poking their eyes, drilling holes into their skulls, striking mortal blows with their giant wings.

Then, both of them bolted out of the palace, escaping the manic flight of bats, shaken to the bone.

During the days of forced idleness, the truckers dealt in news about the sickness that was rapidly spreading. Nandiyal messaged Jaggi about troubles in the South. Depressing news came from Punjab: Mohandas, the oldest among the truckers, had lost his wife. Problems of food and water had arisen, with wheels coming to a grinding halt. There was no point blaming the police, who were just as clueless as anybody else. 'As long as I've flour, I'll bake bread,' even a jovial Bundi seemed worried. 'Then you'll have to get grass.'

Migrant workers marched in a silent file on the highway in a bid to reach home before the roads were closed to all forms of traffic. Bricklayers, carpenters, stonecutters, cleaners, blacksmiths; a few women among their rank, who'd gone to work the hardest of jobs—carrying loads on their heads at building sites or quarries. The lucky ones pedalled their cycles, the rest bore the full load of their possessions on their shoulders. The truckers watched them march all day under the sun, like an army of ghosts.

Trilok readied his truck to return to the road, while cursing the mother of the owner and the mother of her mother. 'They only care about profit. Doesn't matter if the driver dies or becomes an invalid. Who cares about marble when people are dying like flies!'

Qasim, who was carrying expensive TV sets imported from Japan, stayed awake most nights to guard his cargo and was in a hurry to leave. Phones kept ringing all day—owners hassling the drivers to move on and deliver their load, threatening to withhold salaries in case of delay. Everyone pulled Ananth's leg. He was the only one among them on his way home to attend the birth of his child.

'It'll be his tenth child!' Kundan, who was yet unmarried, announced amidst great merriment.

'No, seventh.' Ananth corrected him, smiling sheepishly.

'He's the busiest man in India, busier than the President,' Kundan wasn't the one to let go easily. 'He goes home just once in 3 months and spends less than half a day. Our Ananth has to work harder when he's at home than when he's driving his truck!'

'Soon he'll need his own truck to carry all his children!' Even Trilok found a reason to forget his owner's mother and laugh.

It was decided that they'd hold a party the night before they left the rest stop. Luckily, the kitchen had an extra supply of cooking oil and flour for bread. The ever-resourceful Bundi managed to catch a young goat that had strayed from its flock. But the truckers would have to do with local hooch as the supply of beer had run dry. Trilok announced that the grand feast will be followed by fireworks and ordered his friends to bring out their stash of rockets, sparklers and crackers, which the truckers kept ready to celebrate grand occasions when they were on the road far from home.

Kundan was first to light the fuse of the twinkling stars. Speeding off into the dark night, the rocket burst into a shower of glimmering stars. The truckers broke into a roar as his helper Mahi set off firecrackers—a garland of fifty, going off like rapid machine-gun fire. It didn't take much prodding for Ananth to bring out his booty that he'd saved for the birth of his child. His stock was the best of them all, as his village was a famous hub for fireworks. Sparklers, the dancing fountain, the ground spinner—the men danced and cheered, hugged one another, slurped on the hooch and kept Bundi busy at the oven.

Then Trilok brought out the mother of all crackers—the atom bomb. 'Keep your distance,' he warned everyone, 'if you don't wish to have your head blown off!' Jaggi took charge of setting a circle around the bomb. Bundi shut his ears with both hands; Kundan chanted a hymn to Hanuman, the God of all explosions. Lighting the end of a stick, Trilok stretched his arm to strike the fuse. It took several tries to light the flame, which sputtered and died out a few times before inching its way down to the bomb's core. Everyone waited with bated breath for a whole minute, then two, but the atom bomb refused to burst.

'Must be the damp gunpowder,' Ananth, who knew a thing or two about crackers, said.

In the habit of pulling everyone's leg, Kundan made everyone laugh, 'It's like Trilok's belly—full of gas, but no bang!'

'The bloody shopkeeper has cheated me,' Trilok fumed, then kicked the atom bomb away like a football.

Unmindful of the fireworks, Raju sat on the bed of Jaggi's truck, wedged between the onion sacks. His sight was set on the night sky.

'Your helper is drunk,' Mahi told Jaggi. 'Must be the first time for him drinking hooch.'

Coming over to Raju, Jaggi grabbed his neck and peered into his eyes. It was a master's job to teach his helper to drink properly. To get him drunk and make a fool of himself. Clean up his vomit even, just so he'd learn to care for his drunken master.

'She was everything to me,' Raju mumbled. His breath didn't smell of hooch. 'She was like a queen who'd taken pity on a poor welder like me. She knew what I needed, gave me everything and wanted nothing in return.'

Squatting beside Raju, Jaggi listened.

'There were days when she didn't come to the bridge even once. It was painful. It felt like an arc lamp stinging your arm. She didn't

wish to join up the parts like a welder, brought them close enough
simply to blind you. She was deadlier than fire.'

Jaggi could see tears in his helper's eyes. Raju rested his head on
Jaggi's shoulder and sighed. Away from the other truckers, Jaggi's
head swam, jumbling up his thoughts. What must he do? Strangle
Raju, now that he'd admitted his affair with Jhimli? Comfort his
wife's lover as if he were his son?

Later, as he sat in the cabin by himself, he thought about
Jhimli. With him, her husband, she'd joined up easily. There was
no giving and taking, only asking. She asked for money for her
sister, told him to keep account of his expenses on the road. Asked
him—in a roundabout way—about having children; scolded him
when he yelled at the urchins clambering all over his truck: 'Let
them play. Your kids would've done the same on their papa's
truck, if you had any.' He and Jhimli were joined-up pieces,
wanting nothing more from each other, felt no need for the white
heat of the welder's torch.

She was Raju's queen. Who was she really? Jaggi searched his
mind for an answer. Bar girl, wife, lover? Could she be the ghost of
his very own story?

The godown owner made no fuss unloading the onion sacks, then
made an offer to Jaggi. He could carry a load of explosives for a
mining company for the same fare as the onions. Seeing Jaggi scowl,
he made a counteroffer. 'If you're worried about explosives, you can
carry a load of dry fish. It's safe but will pay you less.' Before Jaggi
could answer, Raju said, 'Yes, we'll take it.'

'Are you mad?' Jaggi raised his hand to slap Raju as the loading
started. 'How will I explain to the owner that he'll have to do with
half the profit from the run? Plus, do you know what dry fish smells
like? It smells of shit. No, shit that has rotted for 200 years!'

Raju smirked, saying nothing more than, 'I have a plan.'

Faces covered with two layers of cloth to beat the stink, they drove for a few miles before Raju forced the truck to a stop. A small group of workers had gathered by the roadside looking for a lift.

'Their village is 25 kilometres away, and they'll pay us to take them there,' Raju looked triumphant, like a businessman who'd struck a good deal. 'They'll hide among the fish sacks.'

'And what about the police? What shall we tell them if they stop us for carrying people? Who'll pay when then confiscate the truck, and my driving licence?' Jaggi waved aside Raju's stupid plan.

'Well, first of all, the police won't catch us because we shall avoid the highway and travel by dirt tracks and village roads. If they do catch us, they won't search the cargo repelled by the fishy smell.'

'So, you want the truck to become a taxi?' It seemed like an outlandish plan.

'As long as it makes money,' Raju said, and waved the workers aboard.

For the next few days, they made the hard run over tracks that were roads only in name, rather dirt paths beaten down by bullock carts. Large craters filled with rainwater called for impossible manoeuvres. A journey of an hour took five. The truck's axle groaned as they rolled from side to side, making Jaggi curse Raju for his imbecile plan. For the most part, they travelled unnoticed, except when they approached their destination to let off passengers. More workers joined them and villagers too, pleading for a place to bring a sick patient to a hospital or to allow a bride to return to her in-laws after a visit to her parental home. Everyone trusted truckers who were well-versed in the map of the land. Like an expert agent, Raju managed the flow, counted the fare, returned change, wrote everything down in a notebook. 'We'll make more from our passengers than our cargo,' he pointed at the numbers, running his finger down the columns. 'You can share some of it with the owner and keep the rest for yourself.' There were times when he forced Jaggi to stop and pick up workers who'd lost everything and couldn't pay for their ride. 'Think of them as good luck charms,' he explained to Jaggi. 'Kindness pays back in kindness.' Their passengers paid them back in more ways than one. Regular travellers among them knew of secret roads no police could ever discover, offered to clear a path run over by thorny barbs. When they did encounter the police, everyone kept still and held their breath. The constables came around the back to examine the cargo, lifted up the covers with their baton then screwed up their noses before hurrying off.

There were times when Jaggi's legs felt like dead logs. 'A driver is no more than a machine,' he remembered Avtar Singh saying. 'You must take help when you have a broken part.' Using the trucker's own manual, he placed a brick on the accelerator and steered his truck while resting his feet up on the seat. Raju got one of the workers to massage his legs when they stopped for the night. His passengers rushed out of their hiding places like birds released from their cage. They bathed in a pond, laid out a meagre meal to share, told stories, dropped down exhausted and slept like the dead.

The smell of dry fish didn't bother him anymore and sitting apart from the rest, Jaggi observed the travellers. A trucker is nobody's friend—he'd learnt on the road. His family is his cargo, that he'd have to carry for as long as the road kept him alive. Like his truck, he lives to move, and he dies when he stops. He'd heard of truckers who'd been hale and hearty drop down dead when they quit the road to live a quiet life at home.

Raju called aloud to have him join the men, but he kept to himself. When Jhimli called, he told her to look after her sister and to keep away from those that were falling sick. A woman—a worker's wife—brought him his meal, waited till he finished eating, kept looking at him without saying a word. In the light of the moon, she resembled a star—queen of the stars.

Nearing the big city, a police convoy blocked their path and brought their run of luck to an end. It was Jaggi's fault. He'd tried to speed through, unnerved by the roadblock. A big officer banged on the cabin door and asked him to alight. Constables ran around the truck and pulled down the covers. The passengers poked their heads out like ducks from their coops. Barking out a sharp command, the officer ordered everyone to get down on the road, hunched on their knees, hands behind their back.

'I'm the driver, I'll tell the police. You are my helper,' Raju whispered to Jaggi.

'Don't be stupid,' Jaggi whispered back. 'You don't have a licence even.'

'Exactly!' Raju was breathless. 'They'll know I am the culprit. I've broken the law, not you. They can thrash me as much as they like. Put me in jail. That way, you can return to Jhimli. She won't be alone.'

Raju jumped out of the truck before Jaggi could protest and went up to the officer with a big smile on his face. The slap landed him on the ground.

Squatting with the rest of the passengers, Jaggi watched the beating: half a dozen constables taking their turn, putting their batons to good use. Raju cowered, face down. Each strike dented his frail frame, as the officer encouraged his men to teach the rascal the hardest of life's lessons. Unable to bear Raju's pain, Jaggi struggled to break free from the grasp of fellow passengers who held him down from both sides. He wished to scream, but one of the men had him in a firm lock around the neck. Wincing from the blows, Raju kept this gaze on Jaggi, seemed to speak to him in a continuous stream, just as he would inside the cabin. *Didn't you wish to punish me? Look! I am getting my due. This is my real punishment.* He appeared to smile as he writhed at the feet of the policemen. *You wanted to kill me, didn't you? They might kill me now. But you won't be the one responsible. You can be free. You can drive your truck, load cargo, go wherever you want or go to Jhimli if you like.* Managing to break free of his hold, Jaggi lunged at the policemen and screamed— the cry bottled up inside him bursting out in a horrible groan.

The passengers helped him, as Jaggi carried Raju to a flowing stream by the highway. Passed out from the beating, he was still breathing.

Limbs hung loose, and there were signs of a few broken bones. A cut on the back of the head was bleeding in trickles. Jaggi took off his shirt and soaked it in the stream. Then, cradling Raju, he pressed down on the wounds, soothing them with the cold cloth. Holding back the blood with the tip of his finger, he gazed at Raju's face, like a father at the son that he'd never had. For the first time ever, he felt the presence of none between the two of them, not even that of Jhimli.

They drove to the crematorium from Raju's home, where neighbours had taken his mother after her death. She was alive just hours before they'd managed to free the truck with bribes and reach the city. The burning was well under way when the two of them arrived, and Raju circled the pyre reciting a prayer taught by the priest.

Sitting on the truck's roof, Jaggi watched the proceedings. The wind had stirred up the smoke, curdling upwards in a thick column. A troop of vultures hovered above. The sun was halfway down in its dip under the horizon. He'll ask Raju to become his helper, he thought. A trucker's life was less dangerous than a welder's. He'll become a master soon, and Jaggi could become his helper, or he might simply stay home and let him carry load.

'Will you join me?' he asked Raju once the business at the crematorium was over. Raju shook his head. He offered Jaggi a piece of sweet that was a customary part of the ritual. Then, like a real helper, he picked up the bucket and washed down the tyres, cleaned the windshield, filled up the tank with water and set Jaggi down on his way but not before he'd given him a box of incense to light for the goddess at dusk to save him from himself.

JAILBIRDS

'If you annoy God, he'll send you to hell. But if you annoy the inspector general, he'll send you to Bazipur.'

Pankaj Jha recalled his senior's words as he stood on his office terrace and took in the sights of Bazipur Jail, renamed Bazipur District Correctional Home. As the newly appointed warden, it would be his kingdom for 2 years at least, or till the God of state prisons forgave him and appointed him as jailer in a town that didn't smell of dead animals. He could well imagine the relief of the departing warden who'd handed over charge to him and offered his consolation: 'Enjoy our garden while you're here. You won't find better flowers in an Indian prison.'

Gazing ahead, he saw clumps of dirty greenery that rubbed shoulders with thatched huts used as prison cells. High walls guarded the inmates' yard; cracks ran on cement, giving the jailer's quarter the appearance of an earthquake victim. The kitchen was no more than a hovel with giant clay ovens fencing it around like sentries. Even from a distance, he spotted a small forest: ripe jackfruit hanging from branches, the wayward growth of guava and hog plum along with an ancient banyan, its trunk painted red. Barbed wire blocked trespassers from entering the male and female wards. The prisoners were indoors, and a sickly horse munching hay made up the only living form.

'The British built the jail after the Mutiny.' Uddhav Pandey, the assistant warden, had crept up behind Pankaj and spoke in his barely audible voice. His wiry frame carried the long years he'd spent in the prison, having entered the service barely in his teens.

Turning around and facing the rear of the compound, Pankaj spotted the British quarters. At a safe distance from the convicts' enclosure, whitewashed buildings with tall wooden shutters and tiled roofs maximized the play of light and shadows. A chapel with a comical turret peeked behind them. Geometric stalls of the stable—abandoned half a century ago—residences of the constabulary and the warden's villa came into view.

'They used to hang terrorists here.' Trousers frayed and collars scuffed on his khaki prison uniform, Uddhav peppered his speech lightly with English, learnt from the Anglo-Indians who ran the affairs of Bazipur after the British had left.

'You mean freedom fighters,' Pankaj corrected him.

'You must get used to mosquitos, leaky roofs and mad convicts yelling in the middle of the night,' seniors had warned Pankaj. Prisons fell within the ambit of hell, but Bazipur lay at its abandoned edge. 'Don't expect the glamour of a high-security prison, just the grind of a rotting pigpen.'

'Most of our inmates are civil prisoners, with few convicts.'

'How many are civil?' Pankaj asked his deputy.

'I'd say 70 per cent, Sir.'

Pankaj gulped down the very same question that had landed him in Bazipur. 'Why are our jails full of innocent inmates, Sir?' he'd asked Mr Rishikesh Jadav, the inspector general of police, during a routine briefing of prison officers. 'Why crowd up the jails with civil prisoners who are just waiting to stand trial for years? Why not let them free?' Interrupted in his speech, Mr Jadav had given him a hard stare and shut him down, 'That's for the courts to decide, not wardens.'

'But everyone should be presumed innocent until proven guilty, isn't that so?' he had persisted, without realizing that Bazipur loomed in his destiny.

'We have a few 302s, 304s, 363s and 376s.' Uddhav tried bravely to shore up the prestige of Bazipur. He meant convicts sentenced for murder, culpable homicide, kidnapping and rape. As keeper of the jail's records, he smiled like a wolf with fang-like molars, used to feasting on the files. 'And we have the Ox Man here.'

Pankaj had heard about the Ox Man before arriving in Bazipur. It was one of many sordid tales that made its rounds among jailers, breaking the monotony of pointless custodianship. Ox Man was the landlord who'd demanded that his serf hand over his wife's pet ox. The poor man had refused and paid the price—lost ox and wife, both to the same knife.

'He's the king of the convicts,' Uddhav closed the criminal's file in his mind and drew Pankaj's attention to the garden separating the offices from the walled compound housing the warden's villa. 'Here's the real jewel of our jail.'

Pankaj saw the much-admired garden of Bazipur District Correctional Home. The splendour of the flowers took his breath away. The decaying walls had been turned into a delicately textured backdrop by the riot of colours, with the beds lined up neatly along them and offsetting the green lawn. For the first time since arriving at his new post, his nostrils felt completely free of the slaughterhouse smell that greets every visitor to Bazipur.

'It flowers all year,' Uddhav added, brimming with pride.

Pankaj watched a young man tending the garden, wielding his sickle rhythmically as he sat hunched on his heels.

'That's Bukka. The jewel of our jewel.'

Over the next week, Pankaj made enough rounds of the jail, drawing up an accurate mental map of his kingdom. Out on inspection with Pandey, he visited the wards after the morning bell had been sounded, heralding the hour for emptying bowels and bladders before prayers and yoga. The prison diet of soggy rice with watery lentil made him screw up his nose, inviting a sheepish remark from his deputy, 'They're given goat meat on Independence Day.' Spending less than a minute inside the cells that held 40–50 inmates in a windowless hall, he grasped the real meaning of a rotting pigpen. Uddhav banged on the hatches of the 'solitary' to wake up the condemned prisoners—the most dangerous of the lot—but failed to awaken them from their stupor. He was led to the jail's least protected area, which was also the most sacred: the gallows. Pankaj hesitated to step up on the platform that supported the crossbeam on two upright logs, but Uddhav insisted. The old Long Drop design was more than effective in breaking the neck cleanly, he remembered reading in some manual, but it resembled more a children's play swing in a park. Prisoners had left their offerings on the platform—garlands, rice pudding, cantaloupe.

Dressed in loose-fitting drawers and half-sleeved smocks, the inmates milled about the yard or lay curled up in the shade, like resting dogs with flies perched safely on their noses. Sidestepping them, he invited glances as the men checked out their new warden. Some joined their palms, others muttered a curse or landed a dollop of spit yards from his feet. It didn't take him long to meet the jail's notable characters.

The most pleasant of the lot, the Ox Man enquired about his hometown and confessed to Pankaj that his first love hailed from the very same place. He regretted not marrying her before her father bundled her off to a worthless groom in Agra. 'I should've fought for her.' He gave the forlorn look of a jilted lover. The Buffalo Man was tamer in comparison. 'He stole his neighbour's buffalo and got 10 years,' Uddhav whispered. 'He has refused to petition for a remission of his sentence.' He met the Magic Man, the trickster, the Train Man, caught travelling ticketless, the SIM Man, the shopkeeper charged with hoarding SIM cards, and the under-trial prisoner whom everyone called Gurudev, the astrologer who'd been accused of selling fake gemstones to his clients.

'Wait till you visit the female ward!' Uddhav Pandey warned Pankaj. 'Each day is a different story there.'

A troop of rhesus monkeys had descended upon the female ward on the day of Pankaj's visit across the barbed wire wall. They'd come to loot the hog plum but strayed over to the living quarters to harass the women. The inmates chased them with sticks as they snatched green mango and tamarind drying in the sun and entered the halls to scare those that were sleeping and steal clothes from the clothes lines. Nothing was spared in the battlefield, including curses and rocks landing close to Pankaj, making him hurry towards the exit.

'I won't let you escape like the monkeys!' Shanti Devi blocked his path, raising her voice over the din. 'Living in the villa like a prince, while we rot in hell.' She pointed towards the overflowing toilets and presented her complaint with full force: 'Ask your wife to use our beautiful shithole, then see if she can escape the germs. Make her sleep under a roof that drips all night, then hope she's able to sing your favourite song. Ask her to eat the rat poison that we're served.'

'She's a 302, serving a life sentence,' Uddhav spoke under his breath.

'All wardens are vultures. They pick our bones clean, then leave. Will you be a vulture too?'

Gathering a small crowd around her, Shanti Devi kept up her rant as Uddhav recited a summary of her case to his boss. 'She was convicted of a crime she hadn't committed. Her husband murdered a moneylender then laid the blame on her, claiming that the dead man was her lover and she had killed him in a fit of jealousy. She was heavily pregnant when she arrived in jail but delivered a dead foetus. Now, after 25 years, the prison has become her home.' He begged Shanti Devi to let Mr Jha pass and give him some time to settle down before he could apply his mind to the toilets.

Back in his office, Pankaj went through the files but couldn't find copies of petitions that might've gone out from his predecessors, asking the authorities to solve the problems of the female ward.

Recently married, Pankaj had warned Kavita about Bazipur. He had told her not to expect a pleasure palace, but his wife took to the warden's villa at first sight. 'Inside, it feels like a foreign country,'

she said, pointing at the high ceiling, the louvered windows and the expansive patio, befitting the home of a dignitary. But most of all, she loved the retinue of domestics—the civil prisoners from the female ward—who were pressed into her service. For sweeping and cleaning, she had Rekha; Lata for washing and ironing; Madhu for massage and beauty treatments, and Indu to mind the kitchen.

'I feel like a queen living in a harem!'

Drinking his evening glass of lassi, served with an extra topping of cream, Pankaj reminded Kavita of the downsides of Bazipur, but it failed to dampen her mood.

'So what if we can't go shopping in a mall or watch movies in a multiplex, our villa can be our own pleasure dome. We can do as we like here, without in-laws and nosy neighbours.' She winked at Pankaj, 'We can make our Baby Jha here!'

Pankaj's heart warmed at his wife's infinite capacity to see good in bad, although the thought of ushering in their first-born inside a prison made him frown.

'You can become the state's best warden. Buy sewing machines for the Bazipur girls or teach them to make jams and jellies. They can become rich in the prison, and you can win a promotion even!'

Even without the sewing machine, Kavita kept her retinue on their toes all day. If it wasn't the arduous business of sprinkling carbolic acid to ward off snakes, her staff was kept busy rearranging things to erase all signs of the previous resident. It included getting rid of the leopard skin rug on the floor of the living room. 'I don't wish to see a dead animal inside my home,' she said, despite being reminded by Uddhav that it was a prison relic—the remnant of a female leopard that'd sneaked into the male ward through a secret tunnel dug out by prisoners planning an escape. It was young and hungry and raided the store making a rattling sound with her paws. All hell broke loose after a convict-guard spotted the animal. Managing to trap it, the prisoners finished it off. The poachers among them picked the carcass clean like vultures, saving the skin for the warden.

Over time, Pankaj grew accustomed to Kavita's harem. Especially, Indu. Cooking wasn't a prominent feature among his wife's many charms, and he had resigned himself to a lifetime of khichdi. But Indu saved his taste buds from withering away. Returning home, he smelled the inviting aroma of onions frying in oil with young ginger and chillies, heard the sizzle of tender chicken thrown into that mix. The delicate whiff of stuffed pakoras and mint chutney made him doubly hungry even after a sizeable lunch; the tang of spicy curries lingered in the villa long after mealtime. He grew fond of Indu.

'Our poor Indu is an orphan. She was sent to a rich trader's home to work in the kitchen. She learnt everything about cooking from an elderly man who hailed from Kashmir. When he died, she took over his job.'

'Who brought her here?' Pankaj found it hard to square such an innocent past with the harsh life of the female ward.

'The trader's daughter-in-law hated Indu. She prided herself as a great cook and harassed her constantly. Our Indu was blamed for spoiling the dishes, even stealing from the larder. She was tortured daily, till one day she picked up the pestle and threw it at the daughter-in-law.'

'Then?' Pankaj was alarmed by the kitchen skirmish.

'It missed her target, but she was booked for assault and sent away. Even after 3 years, she's still awaiting trial.'

They sat silently in the patio, listening to Indu cleaning up in the kitchen. All wardens left Bazipur a little rounder, Pankaj recalled his seniors telling him. Rounder and wiser about life's cruelties.

'There's so much talent here,' Kavita mused, admiring the vase of fresh flowers that came from the prison every day to adorn the warden's villa. Hand-picked by Bukka, they dressed up the drab scenery and complimented the kitchen's aroma with the garden's fragrance. Like Indu's, the gardener's palette varied from day to day, swung between the extreme white of lilies and the unabashedly bold carnations.

Pankaj agreed with Kavita, admiring the bouquet that had arrived in the morning.

'He has sent a purple rose as well,' Kavita spoke fondly.

'Where have you put it? In our bedroom?'

Kavita shook her head. 'It's not for us.'

Pankaj frowned. 'Who is it for?'

'For Indu.' Kavita sighed.

'Why her?' he felt puzzled.

'Because it's the only way he can show his feelings for her.' Turning towards her husband, Kavita chided him, 'Didn't you know about the two of them? The whole jail knows.'

He spent boring hours in his office adding and subtracting. As warden, maintaining discipline and meting out punishment to offending inmates fell under his charge, along with keeping an eye on expenditures. He left the disciplining and punishment business to his deputy, didn't question Uddhav's judgement when he put a prisoner in irons for starting a fight, or condemned him to solitary for owning a knife, which was a prohibited item. He took solace in the fact that nobody took any notice of prisons anyway, a suicide or riot or jailbreak needed to draw the attention of the inspector general. Bringing out Bukka and Indu's prison files, he found his to be fat, hers thin. True to Kavita's account, Indu had been charged under Section 352 for assault or use of criminal force without grave provocation. Hearings had been postponed for various reasons, and the state had appointed a counsel since she couldn't afford a lawyer to argue her case.

Bukka's file carried allegations for which he could be charged under Section 435 for arson, Section 506 for criminal intimidation, Section 144A for carrying illegal weapons and many more making him a habitual offender. And yet, each time he spent just a few months in custody before receiving bail. Leaning back on his chair, Pankaj reached his conclusion about Bukka: He was a criminal by profession, in the service of some powerful man. His master bribed the police to prevent them from pursuing charges against Bukka, making him eligible for bail.

'Who takes care of the garden when he is out?' Pankaj asked Uddhav Pandey. His deputy made a face. 'He's never gone for too long. His master keeps him busy, and he's back here in no time.' Smiling, he added, 'He feeds extra water and fertilizers before he is released on bail, sad to leave his garden behind.'

Sad to leave his garden or leave Indu behind? Pankaj wondered.

A bulge showed on his forehead. Flared nostrils and a sharp jaw stood out from an ordinary face that'd be easy to miss among the six hundred or so inmates. Called into Pankaj's office, Bukka stood listlessly, answering the warden's questions with nods and shrugs.

'How many more days will you be here this time?' Pankaj asked.

'He has a few more weeks remaining,' Uddhav answered for him.

'Can't you find a job as a gardener and stop doing what you do?'

Bukka didn't answer; he kept staring at the vase of plastic flowers on Pankaj's desk.

'What'll happen if the police do file serious charges against you, and you're locked up for a very long time?'

The gardener shrugged. Uddhav raised his voice to scold him, 'Answer Sir's question.' Pankaj lifted his hand to calm his deputy. Then asked a final question, 'How do you choose which flowers to send to the warden's villa?'

Bukka's eyes came alive, a faint smile passed over his face. 'It depends on what I feel,' he said with the assurance of an artist.

Returning to his office after his afternoon rounds, Pankaj found the plastic flowers gone, replaced by a bunch of fresh daisies set amidst sprigs of mint.

Since good fortune never lasts forever, Pankaj found his favourite lassi replaced by an evil-smelling and vile-tasting potion. 'It'll stop your hair from falling, stop you from getting bald before your child is born,' Kavita said and urged him to finish it in one go. 'Indu has prepared it just for you. People of Bazipur swear by it.'

'It's of no use.' Screwing up his nose after a sip, Pankaj protested. 'My grandfather turned bald in his early 30s. My father followed suit when he was 38. The Jhas have an enmity with hair.'

Kavita showed no such remorse, drinking her potion with relish. 'Mine is for women who want to conceive. It makes them fertile.'

'How would Indu know about falling hair and becoming a mother?' Managing somehow to finish his drink, Pankaj was prepared to challenge his wife. But Kavita was unmoved. 'Don't underestimate the female ward. The women there aren't fools. Many have given birth eight to ten times.'

The worried look on Pankaj's face distracted Kavita from potions, and she pressed him to reveal the cause. 'Is it something to do with the inspector general again?'

Pankaj shook his head and decided to tell her about the afternoon's events.

Uddhav Pandey had entered the warden's office without knocking. He looked helpless. Maybe the female ward has revolted over toilets, Pankaj thought, but his deputy shook his head. 'A team of visitors will be arriving, Sir, to check on the health of our jail.'

Pankaj offered him some tea from his flask, then asked gently, 'Who are the members of the team?'

Uddhav made a face, 'the district magistrate's wife, a retired judge and a poet who has made a name for himself.' It was a move designed by the inspector general for the public to engage with the prisons and offer their valuable advice.

'So, let them give their advice, what's there to worry?' Pankaj tried to calm Uddhav down. He appeared unconvinced.

'It's a clever ploy, Sir, to expose our weaknesses. No one likes jails. The team will be upset with what they see . . . prisoners in iron, the solitary, the gallows. Plus, Shanti Devi will tell them about the toilets. They will write a bad report about their visit.'

'Are you worried about the visit too?' Kavita asked. Pankaj sighed. Setting aside the additions and subtractions, he explained the plight of wardens. 'The state doesn't want to spend money on jails. It's better to build roads and schools. Meanwhile, the courts keep sending over droves of innocents and convicts to rot inside. We are here to supervise disease and death.'

Kavita listened silently, then spoke up cheerfully, 'But you have two trump cards up your sleeve that'll surely charm the visitors.'

'Which two?' Pankaj asked, confused.

'You have Bukka's garden, which'll impress them, and Indu's cooking, which they'll be in love with when they come over to our villa for lunch!'

Bazipur Jail hummed with activity leading up to the team's visit. Pressed into urgent service, civil prisoners swept yards, patched up the cells' thatched roofs, dug a pit to burn down the rubbish accumulated over a decade. From the funds released by the warden, Raghu, a plumber by profession who was serving time for petty household theft, sealed the waste pipes. Shanti Devi, hand on her hips, supervised the repairs and ordered fellow inmates to leave the toilet doors open after use to drive off the malodorous gas. Discovering his voice amidst the crisis, Uddhav Pandey pestered his boss to take action before things got out of hand.

'I recommend holding Shanti Devi in solitary during the visit. That'll stop her from creating a scene.'

Pankaj admonished him. 'That'd be wrong. She's the Prison Mother. It might lead to a riot even.'

Then he brought over Abdul, the prison's long-bearded cook, to meet Pankaj. 'Tell Sir how you wish to prepare a feast for the visiting dignitaries,' he put the meek man in a spot.

'I'll start with kebabs, then mutton curry and biryani.'

Uddhav looked pleased, and the two of them got into a lengthy discussion about the merits of a young goat or a castrated adult till Pankaj brought matters to a close.

'Abdul will cook a feast for the prisoners, not for our visitors. They'll be served a special meal at the warden's villa, prepared by Mrs Jha's staff.'

Later, he explained to his agitated deputy, 'Abdul is used to cooking for convicts. His job is to please their demanding bellies not refined tongues. He deals in quantity not quality. Plus, some of our visitors might be vegetarians, and the sight of so much meat might turn their stomachs.'

Privately, he thought of a plan to distract his guests from the overcrowded cells and called upon Uddhav to arrange a private meeting with the Ox Man.

'Why must you meet with a murderer?' Kavita was sceptical of Pankaj's plan.

'Because I'm his warden.'

'What if he refuses to obey you?'

'Then we'll put him in solitary.'

The Ox Man's eyes lit up when Pankaj described his proposal to him.

'I want your help in finding the most talented actors among our inmates to perform a short play in front of our guests. Only you can bring out the best in them. Maybe you can lead the cast as the main actor.'

The murderer's eyes turned misty. Grasping Pankaj's arm, he launched into a family secret, his voice choking, 'My father was the greatest actor Bazipur had ever seen. He used to act in *nautankis*, and the audience loved him just as they loved Dilip Kumar or Dev Anand. He wished to leave this shitty place and go to Bombay and become a film star. But my grandfather held him back.' The Ox Man sighed. 'He'd have become a star if he'd disobeyed his father and gone. As his son, I'd have become a star too.'

Later, waiting for Kavita to join him in the patio, Pankaj went over the details of his plan. The visitors must see his jail as a lively place. Smelly, but happy.

Everyone expected the district magistrate's wife or the retired judge to play the key role, but the poet stole the show from them. Flagging off the play at the makeshift stage in the male ward's yard, Pankaj spoke briefly about the state's intention to reform the prisoners, not simply punish them. 'Otherwise, it'd be better to let them loose in a forest,' he said and received a moderate applause. Marshalling his troops, the Ox Man made his appearance as the bandit Valmiki, dazzling the guests by his costume, and took aim at an imaginary bird on the banyan tree with his bow and arrow. A hush fell over the convicts. The SIM Man sang a plaintive song as the arrow felled the bird. The Magic Man appeared magically from thin air to play the role of Narada, the sage. A couple of young convicts performed a tableau to enact the story of the fiery bandit falling prey to guilt and his rebirth as a saintly poet.

The plot was well managed, Pankaj was pleased to see. Female prisoners led into the male ward, but held at a distance from the male audience, cheered the loudest. Even Uddhav seemed to relax and let out the breath that he'd held back since the arrival of the guests.

Jumping up on the stage vacated by the actors, the poet—a middle-aged man dressed in old-fashioned dhoti-kurta—began reciting poems much to the bewilderment of the convicts. His love poems drew cheers from the female prisoners, while their male counterparts sat gazing through vacant eyes.

'He's a winner of many awards but was fired from his teaching job for pestering his girl pupils,' Uddhav, who knew everything about everybody, informed Pankaj.

From the yard, they moved into the garden. It was time for the retired judge—himself an avid gardener—to take over. With an arm over Bukka's shoulder, they went over the flower beds, exclaiming frequently. 'You have a genius here,' he confided to Pankaj later. 'Bazipur's rotten soil is only good for wildflowers and marigold at best. This fellow must know some magic to grow four varieties of lilies, five types of roses, camellias and carnations!'

Maybe the retired judge would take Bukka into his service, releasing him from his criminal tricks, Pankaj mused.

The garden party was startled by the commotion from the prison yards. 'It's the kebabs, the goat curry and the biryani,' Uddhav settled Pankaj's nerves.

As expected, Kavita had laid out a full spread, waiting for the guests. Her staff were dressed in identical sarees, and all had received Madhu's beauty treatment. They looked like waitresses of a five-star hotel. Hovering in the background, Indu behaved like the nervous chef, signalling her co-workers with her eyes to bring over refills of the dishes that were disappearing fast.

Finishing off the last of the samosas stuffed with cauliflower, the district magistrate's wife—a pure vegetarian—wiped her lips with a smile of satisfaction. In what appeared to be the definitive proof of the success of the team visit, she hugged Kavita before leaving, whispering into her ear, 'You must be so proud of your husband!'

'You must give Bukka a fat baksheesh,' Kavita told Pankaj after the guests had left.

He pretended not to have heard his wife.

'After all, he saved the day for you. He, Indu and that murderer.'

'He did.' Pankaj agreed with her, adding, 'But I can't give him any money.'

'Why not?' Kavita frowned.

'Because,' Pankaj recited verbatim from the Prison Act of 1894, written by the British, that was still the Bible of prison officials, one he'd had to memorize when he entered the service. 'No officer of a prison shall have any money or business dealings directly or indirectly with any prisoner.'

Kavita sat sulking, then left with her final words, 'But still, you must give him something.'

The two of them went to Roop Sagar. Clearing the slaughterhouses and the jumble of shops, the journey to the lake atop the hillocks neighbouring Bazipur took Kavita and Pankaj less than an hour. The road was frequented by pilgrims, eager to visit the temple of a local goddess on the banks of the lake. She had the power to grant the boon of a child. Devotees waded into the waters to pluck lotuses that bloomed by the shore to give as offering.

Sitting by the lake, Kavita tried to cheer Pankaj up, 'You haven't broken any rules, so stop worrying.'

He had in fact broken the rules at Kavita's insistence. She had harped on about granting a special favour to Bukka and suggested the best option. 'Let Indu and Bukka spend a bit of time by themselves,' she'd pleaded with her husband. 'They have no chance to meet, not with your ghastly British laws that prohibit all exchange between the two wards. I can see she is sad; her mind isn't inside the kitchen anymore.'

'How do you know she's missing him when they've hardly ever met each other?' he countered her.

'That's obvious,' Kavita made a face implying that Pankaj was overlooking the truth. 'And it must be the same with Bukka too. Have you noticed the flowers he's been sending her lately? Pink camellia—meaning longing and heartache.'

'But where can they meet?' Pankaj thought to press Kavita for a practical answer.

'Here, in our villa.' She had hastened to calm his consternation, 'I mean while we are away. We could go on a short trip somewhere, and you can tell the guards to let him in just for a few hours.' She took Pankaj's silence for approval, and went on to expand, 'Just imagine how happy Indu would be to cook a full meal for her man! That's what every woman wants.'

That was the 'something' that Kavita wanted him to grant his gardener and cook. And Pankaj had agreed more out of indulgence towards Kavita than sound judgement. Perhaps he was overthinking, he'd reasoned with himself. Prison laws were flouted as a matter of course. For a small bribe, prisoners could get whatever they wished—drugs, extra visits from families, a whole leg of mutton from the kitchen. Passing notes between the cells was easy. Gang members routinely called their contacts using smuggled phones with illegal SIMs. Big leaders even had their mistresses visit them under the noses of the wardens.

'How did the two of them meet?' Pankaj asked Kavita.

She giggled. 'Just like we'd met. Remember how you used to wait at the bus stop for me, then catch the one I was in? How you wiggled your way through the crowd to get close and pass me a note?'

'You mean they met on a bus in Bazipur?'

'Don't be silly! They met inside the prison van that takes inmates to the district court for case and bail hearings. Bukka would wait for her to board then find a seat next to her, Indu told me. If she didn't have a court date, he'd feign sickness and cancel his. They chatted inside the courthouse. He bribed the guards to let them have tea together in the huts that cater to visitors. He bought her gifts from his prison savings.'

'Is that why he returned frequently to the jail despite getting bail?' The picture of Bukka's periodic absences started to clear up in Pankaj's mind.

'Exactly!' Kavita was almost euphoric. 'Once he was free, he begged his boss for an assignment that would bring him back quickly.'

'You mean an assignment to commit a crime?'

'You can say that,' Kavita replied, then fell silent.

The lotus flowers were tantalizingly within reach, and Pankaj was tempted to reach out and pluck some for Kavita.

'He'd come back to the prison knowing full well that they'd never get a chance to meet each other except for an occasional visit to the courts?' Pankaj wanted a bit more of the Indu–Bukka story.

'Well . . .' Kavita waited, then went ahead to spill her secret. 'They do meet inside the jail, but they have to be careful.'

'What!' Pankaj exclaimed. 'How can they meet when the rules prohibit it?'

'It has to do with the British.'

'The British left India more than 70 years ago,' Pankaj was ready to dismiss Kavita's stories as pure illusion.

'Yes, but they left their jails behind. This one has secret passages. One can reach the kitchen from both the male and the female side. No guards are posted at the entry points. Plus, on days of family visits, male and female prisoners are allowed inside the same hall. Every Sunday, the women visit the male ward's yard to watch the football match between inmates. Once she's in, Shanti Devi stands guard outside the storeroom while Indu and Bukka meet inside. Then there is . . .'

Pankaj didn't wish to hear anymore. So, the British were no different than the Indians. The clauses of the Prison Act held sacred in principle but allowed to be violated in practice.

'How can you stop lovers from meeting?' Kavita opined. 'My family couldn't stop us, could they, from finding our own ways?'

Back to the villa, they carried on with Indu and Bukka at the patio. Kavita disappeared into the kitchen and returned with a glowing report. 'Indu is all flushed. She's never looked so happy before. Bukka, apparently, loved her cooking. It was the best meal he'd ever had, he told her.'

Privately, Pankaj felt happy. This small and illegal act has pleased Kavita; she has found the sort of deep satisfaction that can only come from helping others. Maybe this was meant to be, as his seniors had told him; his time in the pigpen was teaching him to rise above petty rules to reign over his kingdom in the manner of kings.

'What will Indu do now that she has a Prison Mother and a Prison Lover?'

'Bukka isn't her lover,' Kavita shot back.

'Then what is he?'

'Husband to be.'

They sat musing over that prospect. Strangely enough, their personal story of courtship and marriage expanded to take in that of their cook and gardener, giving them the impression that they were all part of the same story, an endless saga of secrets that took their time to come to light.

'Which flower did he bring for her?' Pankaj asked.

'A pink rose, meaning happiness, what else?'

A blue-throated thrush sat on the wall between the male and female wards, waiting for its partner. Straining its neck, it peeked at the other side, cooing a courting song. Then flew away together when the other one arrived. Without saying a word, Pankaj understood what Kavita was thinking, and she him.

In the dreary monsoon that followed, Bazipur was eventless except for the expected remission of the Ox Man's sentence. His followers carried him away on their shoulders and distributed sweets among the inmates. 'I'll become an actor now!' He beamed at Pankaj. 'You'll find me on screen, not inside a prison.' Bukka too left after receiving bail, and the garden showed early signs of decay.

The nemesis of the inspector general kept on haunting Pankaj with Mr Jadav demanding a progress report on his latest brainchild—the computerization of prison records. 'The day of the ledger is gone,' his voice boomed through the phone, forcing Pankaj to hold it at arm's length. 'Get Uddhav to create a databank.' Poor Uddhav could barely manage the ledgers, let alone a computer—Pankaj fumed. Bazipur was no Patna, not even a Munger. There was none among his civil prisoners who could be drafted in to do the job.

Sitting glumly in the patio and listening to the chatter of rain, he missed Kavita's silent arrival and her silent sigh. Then she let out a bombshell.

'Indu is pregnant.'

'What! How?' Pankaj was jolted away from Mr Jadav.

'What do you mean how?' Kavita sounded miffed.

'I mean . . . where?' His mind ran over his kingdom as Pankaj scanned the location of the 'how'.

'It could've happened anywhere,' Kavita shrugged. 'In the small yard behind the kitchen or . . .'

'Here in our villa, while we were at Roop Sagar?' Pankaj ventured aloud.

Kavita didn't answer him directly. 'It doesn't matter where it might have happened, the problem is what do we do now.'

Both sat silently, while their brains worked overtime. Recovering his composure, Pankaj led the next round of questioning: 'Does she plan to keep the baby?'

Kavita nodded. 'She has always wanted a child, she told me, and her Prison Mother is all in favour.'

'But the father won't be around.'

'Exactly.' Kavita agreed with him. 'That's the real problem. What if he denies being the father. Indu has suffered a lot already. Now she'll have to suffer as an unwed mother.'

'Why would Bukka deny?' Pankaj found her hard to follow. 'I thought they were planning to get married.'

'Yes, but he is free now, and she's not. He could simply brush her off.' She added an afterthought, 'Men can be like that.'

Pankaj wondered how he'd manage to explain to higher authorities if the word got out that a female prisoner has become pregnant under his charge. He'd be blamed for negligence of duty. It seemed a far greater problem than Bukka's absence. What if the inspector general found out? What punishment posting would he assign to Pankaj Jha? As such, Bazipur was at the bottom of the pile. How much further could he sink?

'Bukka must be brought back to the jail soon before he has a chance to disappear,' Kavita rose to leave. Then she turned towards Pankaj to make her final plea, 'You must do what you can. We owe it to our Indu.'

The evening's counting bell had stopped by the time he was alone in the patio, but it kept on ringing inside Pankaj's head, jarring every nerve, muscle and bone.

His first impulse was to summon Uddhav Pandey. His deputy looked crestfallen after he'd fired off his question: 'Why is Bukka taking so long to return to the jail?' Crime was a matter of daily life in Bazipur, he understood, and his gardener was a regular participant.

'It's the monsoon,' Uddhav sighed. 'Now the peasants are busy reaping seeds. No one has the time to fight over land. Property developers are sitting idle with the roads waterlogged. Residents of Bazipur are at home watching TV. They have no urge to come out into the streets where they could be robbed or raped.'

Pankaj felt depressed. It might be nature's way of applying a brake to human impulse, but without crime there'd be no Bukka.

Fidgeting with his files, Uddhav Pandey hesitated before offering his advice: 'You can ask the Ox Man to help, Sir.'

'Help how?'

'He could draw Bukka's master into some sort of dispute that will engage him once again.'

Ignoring the distraction of the clacking fan, Pankaj measured the worth of Uddhav's idea. By asking the Ox Man to encourage a criminal act, he'd become a party to the same. He'd find it hard to defend himself in court. Why couldn't the genius gardener hatch his own plan to return to the jail to be close to Indu?

The mood at the villa had shifted, and an air of tragedy hung over the patio as Pankaj sipped his lassi by himself. It tasted sour. Maybe the milk had spoilt in the heat, he thought, or perhaps Kavita had made it herself, allowing Indu to rest. Now the kitchen smell seemed less inviting than before, accompanied with darker thoughts. He felt trapped by the silly game the two of them had played, pretending to be Cupid to a pair of jailbirds. 'You must be careful with criminals,' he recalled his seniors advising him during his early days of training. 'They are psychologists in disguise. It's dead easy for them to discover your weaknesses, giving them the chance to turn from an innocent servant to a dangerous predator.'

Had Indu preyed on Kavita's desire to become a mother? She and Bukka trapped them into a vicious cycle of crime?

'I'll have to let Indu go if it goes on like this,' Kavita sulked during dinner. 'I can't bear to see her suffer like this. It's best if she doesn't come to the villa from the female ward. I can take over the cooking.'

When Pankaj called the Ox Man, he was both surprised and delighted. He had settled matters with his serf, whom he'd wronged, inspired by the example of Valmiki. 'You have changed me!' he confessed, then listened patiently as Pankaj asked for his favour.

'You are missing your gardener, aren't you?' The Ox Man laughed heartily. 'You can't bear to see the roses die before your eyes!' Accepting Pankaj's request would return him to the life of crime he'd left behind, but he promised to help the warden who'd changed its very course. 'I'll deliver you Bukka faster than Valmiki's arrow!'

As days passed without Bukka, both became restless. News of Indu's pregnancy would spread fast in the jail, he knew, rumour about the possible father even faster. The warden too might feature in the gossip—the only man she could've met inside the prison. It might shift from being a legal matter to a scandal.

'If your murderer can't help us, then we must find another way,' Kavita frowned at the flowers sent over by a jail staff. The wilting marigold reflected her mood of despondence.

'What other way is left?' Pankaj too sounded low.

Kavita shut her eyes, which meant she was thinking hard, then spoke about her new plan lucidly. 'Indu has Bukka's brother's number. He is still in Bazipur, and she has spoken to him a few times. He knows that she's carrying his baby. You must speak to him.'

'And say what? To commit a crime?'

'No. Tell him to meet Indu when she leaves the jail and take her to a marriage register. Order him to marry her without delay, as soon as possible. Once she's married, no one here will bat an eyelid; otherwise they'd take Indu to be a loose woman.'

'But even if they were married, won't people question how she managed to conceive a child when her husband was locked away from her in the male ward?'

Kavita gave him the look one reserves for a novice. 'A wife can always meet her husband inside the prison, everyone knows.'

Pankaj looked deeply into his wife's eyes then asked, 'And how will she be able to leave the jail in order to meet Bukka and get married?'

Kavita didn't think it was such a big deal. 'You have this system whereby a prisoner can leave and stay outside for a few days, don't you?'

Pankaj nodded. 'It's called parole.'

'Well, send her out on parole then.'

Pankaj yawned before taking his time to explain to Kavita: 'Only a court can award her parole, not me.'

'Why not?' Kavita seemed genuinely upset. 'You are the boss here. Surely you can decide to give her a few days' leave.'

'My job is to keep her safe, and out of harm's way while she is inside. That's all.' Preparing to retire for the night, he tried to stroke her arm, but she pushed him away.

'Then I'll take her out. She can accompany me when I go shopping.'

'The guards will stop you,' he spoke wearily, wishing to bring an end to her wild plan.

'I am the warden's wife. No one will dare.'

'True,' Pankaj nodded. 'But they'll stop Indu.'

'Then, she'll leave by herself without anyone finding out. You can help her do that, can't you?' Kavita made it sound as if it was the very smallest of favours that he could grant without any fuss.

Pankaj took in the full weight of Kavita's words. He restrained himself before replying, 'That will be a jailbreak. Are you asking me as her warden to help her escape?'

He could've recited to Kavita a full list of violations that would come into play if anything remotely resembling her plan came into effect. But he crumpled up the list even before writing it down. His wife wouldn't understand. She lived in the real world where laws mattered less than basic human needs. There was no reasonable reason to accept her plan, but he toyed with it all afternoon nevertheless having nothing better to do.

How could an inmate escape unnoticed from Bazipur Jail? Pankaj wondered. Opening up the prison's map in his mind, he ruled out the obvious route. Although convicts had tried in the past to mix in with visitors and sneak past the main gate, it was nearly impossible given the large presence of jail guards and the state's police force that checked everyone's badge before letting them out. Beautified by Madhu, Indu could try to pass herself off as a well-to-do lady, but her nervous eyes would give her away.

Bribery was the second route. She could borrow money from Kavita and tempt the supplier who brought trucks of half-rotten vegetables to the jail's kitchen to hide her in the empty baskets on his way out. But then, the supplier would want more from her than money.

'Has anyone ever escaped from our jail?' Pankaj asked Uddhav who was still struggling with the computer.

'The terrorists, I mean freedom fighters, had, I was told, Sir,' Uddhav stuck out his tongue in embarrassment. 'They fired twenty rounds from their country-made guns, before scaling the walls.'

A gun was out of the question, and Pankaj turned pages in his mind reading through scintillating stories of jailbreak. Indu, if she was willing, would have to rely on her guile in evading the guards and exit by the jail's weakest spot.

'Do you know the western gate of the jail, the one that everyone calls Butcher's Gate?' Pankaj asked Kavita during dinner.

She screwed up her nose. 'You mean the one facing the slaughterhouse? My girls call it the Gate to Hell!'

Hell might be her pathway to freedom—Pankaj mused.

'Fortunately, it's located in the male ward, and there's no way for female prisoners to reach it. The girls pass it by whenever they go on the van for their court dates. The slaughterhouse smell makes their toilets seem like perfume factories!'

Back in his office, Pankaj asked Uddhav about Butcher's Gate.

'It's a problem,' he screwed up his nose too. Our guards refuse to do duty there complaining of the smell, the flies and the rats that swarm the place hunting for slaughterhouse scraps.' He dropped his voice, 'There are nights when not even a single guard does duty there. You can say it's our weak spot.'

Pankaj smiled to himself. Even the most well-guarded prisons had their weak spots. Like Alcatraz, Britain's Maze Prison, and the nation's very own Tihar—the stage for the Bikini Killer Charles Sobhraj's daring escape.

Like a seasoned conspirator, he pondered over the other problem. Not only would Indu need to leave the prison for her registry marriage to Bukka, but she'd also have to return, undetected. Otherwise, her absence would be noted during the prison's roll call, and the police will begin a manhunt to capture her.

He came to the conclusion that he'd need a co-conspirator. But who?

'Indu would need a friend, another female prisoner, to help her, a friend who can keep her lips sealed. If she fails,' Pankaj started to spell out his thoughts to Kavita as they lay in bed, each gazing up at the fan, but she stopped him.

'You have to tell me the whole plan if you want my help.'

Turning to her, he spoke softly, fearing that the walls would overhear him. 'It's the roll call. If she's absent from the ward, then a friend must lie for her, make up some excuse.'

'That's easy.' Kavita dismissed his worry. 'Shanti Devi will say Indu is on her period and is changing in the toilet.'

It was a reasonable answer, Pankaj thought. Their jail still observed the primitive practice of demanding all prisoners, including sick ones, to assemble at the yard for roll call. But surely, no one would hassle a woman on her period.

'But how will she make herself absent?' Kavita pressed on.

Then Pankaj had no choice but to tell her about his plan for Indu's grand escape.

Uddhav Pandey listened to his boss in silence. His eyes twitched, showing that he was nervous.

'I want you to take over the duty of manning Butcher's Gate for a full day, starting at the crack of dawn to midnight. You, alone, will have charge of guarding it, and managing exits and entries. No guard will accompany you.'

'Why me alone?' Uddhav managed to ask.

'Because two events will occur during your charge that must be kept secret. A prisoner will leave the jail through Butcher's Gate before the morning bell and return through it after the night bell. After that you'll be free to leave.'

Uddhav took a few moments to recover from shock, then raised his eyes from the floor to Pankaj. He spoke in an even fainter whisper, 'That will be a jailbreak, Sir. It's a grave offence under the Prison Act. Indian Penal Code Section 129 under chapter VI deems any prison official found to help an escapee to be fit for imprisonment up to 3 years and a fine.'

His deputy was a lawyer in disguise, Pankaj concluded. Then assumed an official tone, 'Not technically a jailbreak. The prisoner will be absent for a few hours only. You can think of it as a casual leave.'

'And what if the inmate doesn't return? What will happen then?'

Pankaj chose to answer with silence.

Uddhav's eyes twitched even more. Creeping closer to the warden's table, he spoke haltingly, 'You will get transferred, Sir, if there is an enquiry. But I will lose my job.'

Everyone in a prison believes in give and take—Pankaj remembered one of his first lessons as a trainee. If you sweeten the give, then you can take everything.

'I have decided to recommend to the inspector general that you take over the duty of warden of Bazipur Jail when my term is up. Think of this as your last test, and our last job together.'

'Call Indu from the kitchen,' Pankaj told Kavita soon after reaching home. She came, wiping her hands in the folds of her sari. She smelled of raw fish, and a few scales dropped down as she stood facing him.

'I want you to call Bukka. I want to speak to him.'

She stood uncomprehending till he repeated his order. 'Call him now.'

Pankaj heard the sound of hammer hitting metal in the background when he finally managed to speak with Bukka after several tries. The broken connection made his voice sound squeaky. As usual he answered in grunts as Pankaj laid out his instructions.

'You will come to meet Indu at 5 tomorrow morning in front of Butcher's Gate. Do you understand?'

A grunt came in response.

'You will take her to the marriage registrar's office in Bazipur town. You two will marry tomorrow.'

There was a grunt again.

'Then you will bring her back to Butcher's Gate latest by 8 p.m. Do you understand, Bukka?'

There was silence this time. Pankaj repeated his words, more than a touch irritated. 'I can't see your face, so you must speak now.'

There was echo in the line when he replied, sounding in multiples, 'Yes, yes, yes.'

Pankaj lay in bed drenched in cold sweat, unable to sleep. Beside him, Kavita was tense too, he could sense. This could be the biggest mistake of his life, he worried. A game taken too far has landed him into a nightmare. What if the plan failed? He'd have to live the rest of his life with fellow wardens cracking jokes behind his back or, worse, he might lose his job even. He'd fallen victim to boredom, he concluded. His mind had searched fruitlessly for adventure amidst the utter drabness of Bazipur and latched on to a crazy one. He felt he was standing at a fork in the road—with the Prison Act of 1894 at one end and Kavita on the other.

'Wear your tracksuit and sneakers,' Kavita advised him as Pankaj jumped out of bed at the strike of the alarm clock. It was already 4.30 a.m., and he had to play his part in the plan. 'It'll make it seem as if you were out for your morning run.'

'How will she make her way from the female to the male ward?' Uddhav had asked Pankaj after he'd laid bare his plan to him, mentioning Indu by name.

'She will come to the kitchen, which is connected to her ward, and wait in its back yard till dawn. Abdul, our drunkard cook, won't be awake at that hour.'

'But how will she cross the male ward to reach Butcher's Gate?' Uddhav betrayed the legitimate concern of having a lone woman make her way through the males.

'I'll accompany her from the kitchen to the gate.' Pankaj had replied. 'No one will trouble her in the warden's presence. And you will bring her back to the female ward when she returns at night.'

Leaving the villa, he smelled the rains, and the freshness of leaves washed clean of summer's dust. The prison appeared not as dull as before but full of surprises. Saplings had grown overnight into creepers, and criss-crossed the walls, lending a pleasing geometry grafted on the bricks. Even the imposing ramparts seemed kinder under the monsoon clouds, pathetic witnesses to years of pain and longing, guarding the breath of all prisoners and wardens who'd inhabited Bazipur Jail.

Swinging his torch from side to side, he strode confidently past the gate of the male ward, returning the guard's salute with a polite nod. Indu was waiting for him outside the kitchen. She was drenched from the rain and carried a small bundle under her arm. It must be a dress she'd want to wear during the signing—Pankaj thought. Walking a few paces ahead of her, they left for Butcher's Gate.

Keeping the prison map open in his mind, Pankaj passed the cells that looked identical in the darkness. The passages between them seemed unreasonably narrow, forcing them to pass quite close to the huts. Crossings sprung up from nowhere, forcing him to hesitate before taking uncertain turns. Glancing back over his shoulder, he urged Indu to quicken her pace as sunrise was imminent. Their destination was close he could sense but shrouded mysteriously behind the prison quarters. Whoever had thought to design the damn place like a maze! he fumed, blaming the British. It took him quite some time to realize that they were lost inside the male ward.

The drizzle, which had steadily risen to a downpour, was their saviour. Normally, the inmates would be up and about at that hour, but the rains kept them indoors. Nobody was witness to the warden accompanied by a smallish frame, charging through the lanes between the cells then retracing their steps in even greater speed, helplessly stranded, frozen to their feet, at the crossings. Not even the ward dogs, more vigilant than the guards, barked their disapproval of the intruders.

Quite suddenly, they reached an opening. A gust of wind pummelled them towards a platform holding a wooden frame. It was swaying, at risk of collapsing in the wind. Garlands lay strewn on the platform alongside upturned earthen lamps. It was the gallows. Pankaj shivered. The image of a freedom fighter hanging by his neck flashed through his mind. Quite suddenly, Indu let out a start and lunged towards him, grabbing him and hiding her face in his arms.

'What is it, Indu?' He clasped her neck and looked into her eyes.

'My father,' she spoke between sobs. 'He was hung here.' She read the puzzled look in Pankaj's eyes and managed to say, 'He had gone mad. Killed my mother and my little brother. Only I was saved by a neighbour.'

Clearing skies brought them within sight of Butcher's Gate. Uddhav Pandey sat as the lone sentry under an umbrella and opened the locks without a word. Indu disappeared outside, into the hazy morning, without looking back.

'I don't want you to go to your office today,' Kavita said once Pankaj had returned after his morning mission. 'Let's treat today as Sunday!' There was more work in the house than usual, she declared, hustling Rekha and Lata around.

'What's special today?' Pankaj asked.

'Don't you know?' She frowned at him. 'It's Indu's wedding! When she returns this evening, she'll be a married lady. Too bad we can't have a proper wedding feast for her with guests, but I've decided to cook a special meal in her honour.'

He spent the day lazing around the house, checking his watch from time to time. Perhaps Bukka, given his reputation as a toughie, has managed to coerce the poor marriage registrar to complete the formalities early, and Indu would return sooner than planned. Who'd be witnesses at the signing? Maybe he'd invite his crime boss and fellow toughies. Do criminals have normal people as friends? He wondered.

Passage into the evening didn't worry Kavita or Pankaj unduly. 'These things take time,' Kavita reassured her husband when she saw him checking his watch. She winked at him, 'Maybe Bukka has taken her to a friend's house, just to be alone with her!' Shuffling back and forth from the kitchen, Kavita was nothing short of a live wire, and it pleased Pankaj to see her that way.

It was almost 9 p.m. when Uddhav Pandey arrived, looking like a wet crow.

'Where's Indu?' Kavita asked as soon as he folded his umbrella. Pankaj's deputy called his boss aside to give him the bad news. Indu, he said, had waited by Butcher's Gate braving the slaughterhouse smell the whole day, but the person she was waiting for hadn't arrived. She had paced that dirty street impatiently before the police arrived to pick her up. 'They thought she was a streetwalker,' Uddhav said, and made a sad face. 'They'd taken her away to the police station, where she had confessed everything.'

'What do you mean confessed?' Pankaj asked.

His sources within the police had given Uddhav the full report of her interrogation. 'They asked her where she was from, and Indu told them she lived in Bazipur Jail. How did she manage to come out if she was a prisoner, they pressed her. She said she didn't know. Are you a ghost? They teased her, and ultimately, she told them how you, the warden, had led her out of the gates without anyone finding out.'

'Where is she now?' Kavita asked, all her excitement gone.

'At the police station, Madam. Tomorrow, they'll shift her to the jail.'

The dinner turned cold on the table as Kavita and Pankaj sat speechless in the patio. A phone rang as they were on the verge of retiring for the night. It was from the Ox Man. He sounded just as excited as before. 'I've done your job, Sir,' he told Pankaj. 'I've poked Bukka's master and staged a fight between his men and mine. Bukka was among his troops and the police have arrested him early at dawn and taken him away. He should be reporting to your garden soon!'

Mr Rishikesh Jadav chewed the toasts slowly, moving them from one side of his mouth to the other, then back, taking care not to strain his false teeth. He had arrived at the jail early and held a full briefing with Uddhav Pandey, following the police complaint of a jailbreak. Kavita had invited him for breakfast, sending in her request through a jail staff, and he'd postponed his meeting with Pankaj at the warden's office to come over to the villa.

They ate in silence. Kavita kept her eyes on her untouched fruit bowl, while Pankaj nibbled at his portion. She waited to serve the inspector general another plate of toasts then started her confession, beginning with the conclusion, 'It's all my fault. My husband is innocent.' As Mr Jadav listened in rapt attention, she returned to the very beginning of the tale, with the arrival of flowers from the prison garden to the villa. She spoke about the star-crossed lovers who couldn't meet across the wall between the male and female wards and about their tryst here while she and her husband were visiting Roop Sagar. A calm descended over Pankaj listening to his wife's report, which made it seem as if the two of them were mere actors playing their part in some tragic saga. Finishing her account, Kavita sighed. Looking into Mr Jadav's eyes, she made her final deposition, 'So there we are, back to where we had started. Indu and Bukka will return to their wards, with no harm done except the flouting of laws.'

The inspector general kept silent for a full minute, then turned to Kavita. His voice sounded extraordinarily mellow. 'That's a love story. A real one, not the filmi type.' He kept shaking his head, then scolded her mildly like a loving uncle, 'But you could've invited Bukka to come over and got them married off here in your villa. There was no need for all this drama.'

'Married here, Sir?' Pankaj was astonished.

'Why not? Is there anything in the Prison Act of 1894 that prevents it?' Now assuming the tone of a senior lecturing a trainee he expounded on his proposal, 'This is the twenty-first century, Jha. We are talking about computerizing our records, making our prisons friendly places for the community. In Punjab and Haryana, they are even granting leave to convicts to go home and do their business with their spouses.' He glanced sharply at Kavita, then went on, 'We could be setting an example by holding the marriage inside the prison. It'll tell Bazipur and the world that a correctional home is open to the best of human emotions, including love.'

Tea arrived to relax all three of them. Pankaj fidgeted with the spoon, expecting to hear from Mr Jadav what awaited his fate, if his conduct would be deemed punishable under Section 129 of the Indian Penal Code.

'You, Jha, will have to pay a price,' Mr Jadav returned to official matters once he'd downed two cups. 'You'll have to move from Bazipur to Patna as head of our computerization programme for the state's correctional homes. There, you won't have as big a villa as this, but you'll be gainfully employed as a state servant, not some failed nautanki director.'

The wedding, as granted by the inspector general and planned by Kavita, was far easier to conduct than the escape. The groom and his party didn't have to travel far, simply pass through the gate of the male ward to the warden's villa. The sickly horse was pressed into service and riding it, Bukka appeared to shed his brooding form. Dressed up as bride by Madhu, Indu looked breathtaking. Kavita and Pankaj glowed with pride as they watched over their wards— she for Indu and he for Bukka—during the ceremony conducted by Gurudev, the fake gems seller. Shanti Devi blessed them both and then bride and groom touched the feet of all elders, starting with Kavita and Pankaj.

The Magic Man kept everyone enthralled with his tricks. Convicts sang and danced, the Ox Man's team performed a tableau and throughout the celebrations no one thought to escape from the prison although the guards were horribly drunk by midnight.

Exhausted afterwards, Kavita confided her secret to Pankaj. She had managed to win a final concession from the inspector general after the breakfast. He had promised to arrange a quick bail for Indu and parole for Bukka so that the couple could usher in their child outside the jail's walls.

'They can come with us to Patna, not as convicts but as our gardener and cook!' she exclaimed.

After he'd handed over his charge to Uddhav, the new warden, Pankaj stood on the terrace of his office and gazed out at the jail. Leaving Bazipur, he felt like a true warden—one who'd been guilty of breaking the law like the inmates, sharing with them the true spirit of the prison. Deep within, he understood the mission of jails and the role of laws in a world where everything was punishable and yet nothing was beyond pardon. Like all previous wardens, he too wondered what memory he'd carry forth from here, concurring finally with his predecessor. It had to be the flowers, he was certain.

STRUGGLER

Each day of the week, Abhilash Shukla wore a different watch from his prized collection, but the one he wore on Sundays was his favourite.

On Mondays, he brought out the Rolex Daytona 6263 Oyster Albino from the felt-lined box. It was the most expensive, a twenty-fifth anniversary gift from his wife. Manisha and he had travelled to London to mark the occasion and purchased it from Harrods. 'It's perfect for your broad wrist, Sir,' the English salesgirl had said. 'Not many can carry it off well.' It was a sales pitch, Abhilash Shukla knew, but it had made Manisha proud.

The Patek Philippe that he sported on Tuesdays was a gift from his older son Sumit. He had left it on his office desk the day he'd joined his father's business—Shukla & Sons Bathroom Supplies.

'How come you're giving gifts even before receiving your first pay cheque?' Abhilash asked him next morning at breakfast. His newly married wife Sreya answered for her husband, 'Because sons must pay respect to their fathers when they enter the workforce—it's our culture.'

'It's not a gift to you, but to himself!' Manisha commented wryly afterwards.

'How do you mean?' Abhilash was confused, turning his wrist to examine the exquisite timepiece.

'Because, as the company's ad says—*You never really own a Patek Philippe. You merely look after it for the next generation.*'

Wednesdays were reserved for the Piaget, the day he and his sons—Sumit and Sagar—met their most valued customers. The diamond, set at the dial's centre, signalled the solidity of the company.

On Thursday, when the family fasted till noon following Manisha's dictate, he picked his Rado. It was elegant, but not showy—befitting the austerity of the day.

But by Friday, he was back to flashier pieces, and at Sreya's insistence, he fastened the Cartier to his wrist. She had seen Shah Rukh Khan—no less—wear one at an award show and picked up an identical piece for her father-in-law.

On Saturdays, Abhilash played golf or pretended to do so, with other gentlemen of commensurate stature, although he worried about spraining his arm by a wild swing of the club. All his friends wore Tag Heuer Chronographs, and he did not wish to be the exception.

The family gathered for breakfast on Sundays, and although there was a prohibition on business talk, Sumit and Sagar used that hour to brief their father about pending company matters of strategic importance. Manisha withdrew after the meal had been served to join her Art of Life friends at a neighbour's home, while Sreya dashed off to the gym to wear off the week's indulgence.

Later, after he'd taken his afternoon nap, Abhilash strolled on the lawn and quite out of habit wore a watch—his favourite. It was an HMT Janata. It needed to be wound daily and sent for oiling, cleaning once every year. His father had taken it off his wrist when Abhilash had left Raipur, his hometown, for Bombay to test his fortunes. He remembered well the company's newspaper ad: *This Diwali give an HMT watch*. But his family couldn't afford to buy a new watch for their son.

'Why do you keep wearing such an old watch?' Sagar, his younger son who was keener than his older sibling to know about his father's early days, had asked him. 'Even Makkhan doesn't wear a mechanical watch.'

Makkhan was the family driver, who came into Abhilash's employment the day he was rich enough to buy his first car—a Premier Padmini.

'Because it reminds me of who I really am,' Abhilash had said, failing to supply a satisfactory answer.

Thinking deeply about Sagar's question, he realized that the HMT and Makkhan were the last remnants of his youth. And of course, the notebook full of handwritten poems he'd brought with him to Bombay in the dream of becoming a lyricist in films. It wasn't an empty dream, but one built on his reputation as a budding poet who'd won several college competitions and charmed a legion of young women. The family, hesitant at the risky prospect, had agreed to let him go, convinced that he'd soon return with his tail between his legs and find a suitable career as bank officer. But, Abhilash, never one to think small, had managed to expand his circle of friends in the city quickly enough to acquire the phone number of his boyhood idol—Dev Anand.

As he'd later describe many times to his friends, he hadn't expected the superstar to answer the phone. But in those days, stars orbited closer to earth, and he was struck speechless by Dev Anand's voice. 'Yes, young fellow. Let's meet at 6 p.m. tomorrow at Sun & Sand.'

The magic of that unexpected invitation had so enraptured Abhilash Shukla that he'd forgotten to wind up his HMT Janata and by the time he realized that it had stopped, he was already two hours late for the appointment.

In those days, Sun & Sand was the closest one could get to Paradise. Everyone in the lobby, including the waiters, resembled film stars. Reporters crowded the parking lot, and the smell of glamour drowned the smell of exquisite wines that flowed at the bar. Abhilash Shukla had waited 3 hours in the lobby, drawing the suspicion of every waiter and the doorman till the weight of his bad luck forced him to crumble. Dev Anand of his dreams, he was certain, had arrived sharply at 6, waited for 10 minutes then left, taking him for a joker.

'In life, accidents matter more than plans,' Mr Shukla lectured his staff frequently, drawing on that defining accident of his life. It had drained the ambition that'd brought him to Bombay but opened the door to another accident: his maternal uncle co-opting him

as a junior partner of his business. As it turned out, Bombay was
experiencing the biggest building boom of the generation, and he
had discovered the tiniest secret of so many buildings that sprouted
overnight: bathrooms.

Once the meeting with the Johnson Group—Bombay's largest
property developer—had gotten under way, Abhilash excused
himself and left the boardroom for the executive toilet. Turning
on the faucet, he examined his face in the mirror, tilting his cheek
from side to side to check his beard trimmed by his personal barber
who attended on him once a week. There was really no need for
such a frequent grooming as his facial hair had practically stopped
growing, but his philosophy of life didn't permit the interruption of
a habit. Taking off the Piaget from his left wrist, he wore it on his
right, examined the movement of the arms, then fastened the clasp
back again on the left. Taking his time in the toilet allowed him to
get through most of the meeting without his presence in the room,
and when he returned, the business was practically over save the
customary handshakes.

Later, while eating their home-cooked lunch in the boardroom,
Sumit and Sagar went over the details of the deal that had landed,
as expected, in their favour. Abhilash Shukla pretended to listen and
nodded from time to time. Then, at the strike of 4, he promptly
left the office with Makkhan in his Mercedes S class sedan bound
for home.

The Sons of Shukla & Sons were now firmly in charge of the
business he'd created 25 years ago, Abhilash noted, reflecting on
the day's meeting. Sumit had a knack for selling and Sagar for
technical details. Plus, Manohar Shah, his chief designer, was also
in attendance to calm the client's concerns. The bathrooms too
had changed from the time when he'd instal ceramic commodes
with wooden seats that frequently rattled and threatened to
topple the squatter over. Now there were toilets made from non-
toxic metals, offering dual flush, automatic seat warming and

self-cleaning facilities. Like the Piaget, his presence was merely ceremonial, Abhilash concluded, his role in the office reduced to enquiring about an employee's mother who'd recently had an operation to admonishing the doorman for wearing shoes without socks.

There were days when he asked Makkhan to stop at Chowpatty. Makkhan knew his master was in his Raipur mood and parked cautiously at the beachfront away from the pack of bikes that might scrape the expensive paint of the S class. Following a dozen or so feet behind, he squatted on the sand keeping a respectful distance from Abhilash. Chowpatty would be busy at that hour. Tourists jostled with lovers at the edge of the surf, children kicked empty cans around like footballs and hassled stall owners. The smell of food kept humans and animals engaged.

'Have I ever told you that I was once a poet?' Abhilash threw his words over his shoulder at Makkhan.

'No, Sir . . .' Makkhan knew very well, but shook his head.

'I was, what you'd say, a budding star,' Abhilash eyed a pair of lovers who'd ventured farther out into the sea than the others. 'Some compared me to the great Dinkar, even Kamal Amrohi.'

Makkhan waited till the Raipur mood had gained full strength, then chose his words carefully. 'Why don't you recite one of your poems, Sir? I am sure it is nothing short of a masterpiece.'

That was just the prompt Abhilash needed. Clearing his throat, he checked to see if there were any eavesdroppers nearby, then started, 'Let me see . . .'

It saddened Makkhan to think what would follow, every time they stopped at Chowpatty Beach. His master would begin to recite a poem then stop after a few lines. Brows furrowed, he'd try to remember the rest, correct himself after making a false start. Like a child who'd memorized a poem but forgotten it, he'd look helpless, trying to pluck out the lines from the mind's secret chamber. As the sea darkened and the tourists left, as business in the stalls quietened and the lovers had the beach all to themselves, as the last of the balloons left behind by a child flirted with the waves before drowning, Abhilash Shukla would abandon his poem and leave, striding up to the Mercedes and slumping back on the leather seat.

'Each member of a couple has his or her own sacred moment. It comes at night, and one must be alone to experience it.' Manisha had convinced her husband to sleep in separate bedrooms connected by a door that was left open at night to guard against any medical emergency. Sitting in the balcony adjoining his private bedroom, Abhilash purveyed his empire—the sumptuous gardens overseen by his wife, the largish cage that housed a peacock and a peahen that were Sreya's pets and the neighbours' mansions shielded by strategically planted trees. The older you get, the more difficulty you have falling asleep—Abhilash Shukla knew too well. Peering through the branches, he saw Mr Kukreja reclining on his easy chair, his servant massaging his legs. Mr Balbir Sawant—barely older than him—paced his balcony. His golf partner Sebastian, whom everyone called Johnny because of his resemblance to Johnny Walker, was reading the Bible. They were old like him with no more houses to build, no business to worry over, no children to raise and no wives to share a bed with. Old, comfortable and waiting to die.

At breakfast, Sreya spotted her father-in-law's vacant look and summoned the house physician. The series of tests that followed showed a healthy prostrate, a marginal rise in blood sugar level, no thyroid condition and normal blood pressure. It was an occasion to celebrate, and she ordered his favourite cheesecake with a generous caramel twirl.

Abhilash Shukla had everything. But deep down, he lacked something, not quite knowing what that missing part was. When he tried bringing it up with Manisha, she brushed it off. 'It's nothing but boredom. It comes from the fact that you've achieved everything you'd hoped for in life.'

'Now what?' he asked her.

'Now nothing,' she was dismissive of his discomfort. 'Keep doing what you've always done. Did Ravi Shankar stop playing the sitar after he'd been awarded the Padma Bhushan?'

It failed to comfort Abhilash Shukla.

Because even luxury cars aren't immune from defects, the Mercedes broke down one morning when Abhilash Shukla was on his way to office. A crowd formed around the wonder machine as Makkhan raised the bonnet and scratched his head. Unlike the Premier Padmini that he knew like his wife, the German miracle was an alien from another planet.

'I'll call Mrs Gupta and ask her to send over an office car,' Makkhan said and shut the bonnet before onlookers could touch the gleaming interiors or some mischief maker spit inside.

Beginning to sweat inside the car, Abhilash gazed around and spotted the Mumbai Suburban Railways station brimming with office goers. On an impulse, he left the car and made a move towards it, making his intentions clear to Makkhan.

'I'll take the train to work. You stay here, get the car fixed and then come over.'

Running after his master, Makkhan protested, 'No, Sir, please don't take the train. It's crowded and dangerous. Just wait for a few minutes.' He took a quick look at Hotel Adarsh—a three-star property that was nearby—and bolstered his plea, 'You can wait at the hotel's coffee shop, Sir. I'll come and fetch you when the office car arrives.'

'Nonsense!' Abhilash Shukla kept on walking resolutely, 'How many times have I told you that I am a Raipur boy? That I am not afraid of crowds. I used to travel by the train every day when I came to Bombay 25 years ago. A half-hour ride won't kill me.'

Jumping into the crowded compartment and elbowing his way inwards, Abhilash understood the full impact of Makkhan's words.

The coach was indeed dangerous. He felt choked by the heat and the lack of air. He regretted wearing a terry-wool suit that was suitable only when the room temperature was set to 18 degrees. He despaired at the full Windsor knot, but it was impossible to loosen his tie by freeing his arms and stretching them upwards. Luckily, he'd left his sheepskin briefcase in the car, which would've drawn more than a few curses. He understood now that the real value of dressing down didn't have as much to do with style as with comfort, understood why employees showed up in half-sleeves—which he detested—round-neck T-shirts that resembled *baniyans* and shoes without socks.

'Come, Uncle!' A voice rang out from the crowd. A young man stood up and invited Abhilash to take his seat.

'Let Uncle sit properly. Otherwise, his suit will be crushed, and his boss will fire him from his job.' A roll of laughter followed the wisecrack. Sitting down, Abhilash glanced at the young men around him, travelling together in a bunch, paying no heed to the crowd or the heat.

Rumi—the boy who'd given up his seat to Abhilash—seemed the most cheerful of the lot and wasn't shy cracking jokes about Uncle. 'We don't want him to suffer like Dev, do we?'

Daku—another one of their friends with a ferocious moustache that had in all likelihood merited him that name—didn't know about Dev's suffering and thought Rumi was lying. 'How can a singer suffer? All he needs to do is sing to forget his suffering!'

At everyone's insistence, Dev was forced to retell his story. The passengers—both standing and seated—leaned forward to catch his words over the gnashing sound made by the bogies as they went through the shunting.

'My friend gave me the contact of a music arranger. He was medium-sized in the industry but could get me an audition with a music director. He would ask for no favour, I was promised.'

'He must've asked for 5000 no less!' Daku showed his paan-stained teeth. 'They all say no favours required, but demand anyway.'

'No, no, Murari didn't want money,' Dev put the record straight. 'He said, come next Wednesday, and I'll take you to a music director. This week I am busy because my brother is having a hernia operation. So, I returned next week.'

'Then?' a passenger asked.

'He told me to come back the following week on Friday, because his mother had been taken sick with heart problems, and he had to take her to see a specialist and get her admitted to a hospital.'

'*Bechari!*' someone whispered.

'That's what I thought too,' Dev continued. 'The following week his wife was diagnosed with diabetes, and he had to take her to her hometown to stay a few days with her family.'

'It was his sister the week after, wasn't it?' Laughter bubbled in Rumi's throat.

'Sister, then cousin, then back to his brother again who fell sick with malaria.'

'So, what will you do now?' a middle-aged passenger who sported six rings on his fingers asked, clearly wanting to hear the end of the story.

'Keep meeting Murari and giving him some money for treating his relatives, what else can he do!' Daku spat out paan juice from the window.

Amidst the laughter and curses, Abhilash cleared his throat and spoke quietly. 'He should forget about Murari. Once and for all.'

'What did you say, Uncle?' Rumi craned his neck.

'He should stop. What good will come from running after someone who doesn't respect you?' Quite suddenly, a couplet he'd written when he was young came to mind, and he recited them for the passengers.

> *Why wait for rain when the sun rules the sky*
> *Better to wait for tears when the heart lies.*

Abhilash Shukla found himself surrounded by the young men when he got off at his station.

'Wah, Uncle!' Rumi patted him on the shoulder. 'What a couplet. Which film did you get it from?'

'Let me guess.' Manu, for Manjit, answered before Abhilash could say anything. 'It's from *Mughal-E-Azam*. The scene where Anarkali is waiting for Salim in her palace.'

'Give Uncle your special tea,' Rumi commanded Dev, who brought out a flask and poured Abhilash a cup. He shook his head and refused, but the boys kept on insisting. Daku threatened to open his mouth and pour down the tea saying, 'Drink, Uncle, it'll bring us luck. We strugglers need every drop of it!'

The tea—generously sweetened and mixed with milk—went against his constitution as he was both borderline diabetic and lactose intolerant. By the time he had managed to finish the cup, the boys were gone waving at him and screaming, 'See you next time, Uncle!'

When Abhilash Shukla reached his office, a whole delegation was waiting for him outside. There was Makkhan, bent over in remorse, his secretary Mrs Gupta, the doorman and a few others he couldn't recognize. Abhilash raised his hand before Makkhan could launch into his apology, and reached his office in a few quick strides. Mrs Gupta brought in his customary cup of the day—first flush Darjeeling tea from the Makaibari estate, brewed for exactly 3 minutes.

'Tell me, Mrs Gupta, do you take the suburban train to come to office?' Abhilash asked.

'Yes, Sir,' she appeared surprised by the question. 'I've been taking the Vasai Road line for the past 15 years.'

How do you manage to keep your sari uncrumpled in that crowd, he wished to ask but then held himself back thinking it'd be an inappropriate question.

Sipping from his porcelain cup, Abhilash Shukla considered the boys. 'Strugglers'—the name fascinated him. Those who fight against the odds. The dreamers. The world might write them off, but they keep on going, refuse to be cowered by fate. They manage to laugh and crack jokes while the rest perspire and curse and wish their world—like the suburban trains—would stop tossing them around.

Travelling back with Makkhan, he asked him—indirectly—about those who come to Bombay hoping to become film stars. His driver, who was a man of the world, would know, he was certain.

'They are fools, Sir. Like moths, they rush towards the flame only to burn.'

'What's wrong with having an ambition?' Abhilash pushed him gently.

'Ambition is good,' Makkhan nodded wisely. 'But not madness.' He took a quick turn into a quieter street and kept up his commentary. 'If you go to Victoria Terminus, you'll see long-distance trains arriving. From Punjab, Chennai, Kolkata—every part of the country, carrying hundreds of boys and girls. Some want to become actors or singers or writers or dancers. They live, five or six to a room, borrow money from friends and neighbours, hang around the studios hoping to meet someone important.' Makkhan sighed.

'And?' Abhilash probed further.

'Most have to take the train back home after a few years. Those who remain here suffer. Many of them have to do bad things just to eat.'

Parking the car in the driveway, Makkhan provided his closing statement, 'Not everyone is lucky like Mithun Chakraborty or Shah Rukh Khan, Sir. Most people are born to be unlucky.'

The Strugglers stayed on Abhilash's mind the whole week. It made him forgetful and make mistakes signing cheques. Rumi, Daku, Dev and Manu visited him when he sat alone in the balcony, cracked jokes with him, implored him to share another couplet with them. *Come on, Uncle, you must know hundreds of them!* The following week, he decided to act on his impulse and set out with Makkhan to meet them again.

'Listen carefully,' he told Makkhan, telling him to take him to the railway station where his car had broken down the last time.

'You will drop me here and go to the office. You are to tell no one where I've gone. If someone asks, say Sir has gone to a bookshop to buy a present for his wife. Do you understand?'

Perplexed, Makkhan nodded.

Then he strode into the station and boarded the very same train that he had last time and purely by chance found the boys.

'Uncle is here!' they roared. This time, Daku gave up his seat and given his broad girth, Abhilash had more space to make himself comfortable. The joke this time, as he found out in minutes, wasn't on Dev but Daku.

'He'll remain a bachelor all his life!' Manu teased him. 'He'll show up late for his wedding, and Damini will get mad and marry someone else.' Daku, as the others filled in, was late for everything, and it was a miracle that he'd somehow held on to his job assisting a set designer.

'If he became the head designer, the film would take 3 years to complete!'

The latest crisis was caused by his late arrival to the bus stop where Damini met him every morning to evade her brothers who'd warned her to break it off with Daku, who belonged to a lower caste. 'The bus stop is their set for romantic drama. Miss it and you've missed the whole movie!' Everyone in the compartment laughed.

'But his lateness may well be Daku's strength.' Everyone fell silent when Abhilash spoke. 'When they are married, Damini will know her husband to be calm and unhurried. He'll never take a decision in haste. Like a statesman, he'll act only at the right time.'

The passengers heard in amazement as Daku's fault turned into his virtue by the gift of Abhilash's words. Daku gave him a high five.

'Rumi is down, Uncle,' Manu whispered into Abhilash's ear when they got off at their station. 'It's a big day for him. He has an audition with a casting director in the afternoon, but he thinks he has no chance of landing the role.' He gave Abhilash a pleading look, 'Please cheer him up; tell him a couplet that'll bring his smile back.'

Following the boys, Abhilash went to Easy Café—a basic joint for cheap food and refreshments. It was a regular haunt for those who wished to be in films, as the studios were close by and there was a chance of bumping into someone important. Youngsters hogged the tables. Smoke rose like volcanoes. Pulling up a few chairs, Manu ordered one extra-large tea and five small glasses. As the tea arrived, he poured it into the five glasses in equal amounts, with a larger share for Abhilash. Then he comforted Rumi.

'Look, it's not as if you'll be appearing in a crowd scene, where no one will ever notice you and you'll leave with Rs 200 at the end of the shoot.'

'Also, it's a film by an A-list director,' Dev joined Manu.

A man, a bit older than them, waved at Rumi from a neighbouring table, and he waved back.

'Don't pay any attention to Jash,' Dev shook Rumi's shoulder. 'Nothing like what's happened to him will happen to you.'

'What happened to Jash?' Abhilash asked cautiously. Straightening up, Rumi answered, 'He's Jaslok Bhatti. His film name is Jash. He comes from my hometown. I had lived with him for a year after I came to Bombay. He helped me. But he couldn't get any roles for himself. He tried for 3 to 4 years. Now he supplies girls for parties.'

'It's getting tougher, Uncle,' Manu explained. 'Nowadays, even engineers and MBAs are becoming strugglers. They speak good English, wear nice clothes and treat the studio people to expensive meals. They can walk into any party they want, while we have to bribe the bouncers to get a peek even.'

Manu and Dev had to leave to meet their contacts. Even Daku was in a rush to reach the set where shooting would start soon. Leaving Easy Café, Abhilash and Rumi walked along towards Jubilee Park—a tiny patch of green boxed in amidst the concrete.

'Tell me about your audition today,' Abhilash asked Rumi as they sat down on a bench.

Rumi pursed his lips, 'It's just one line, which a man will say to a journalist who has come to cover a story about a market that has been burnt down in a riot.'

'What is that line?' Abhilash nudged Rumi. 'Tell me.'

'*I have lost everything.*'

Both kept silent for a moment or two, then Abhilash began to speak, almost to himself, starting in mid-sentence: '. . . she was the only one who cared for my poetry. I'd read everything to my mother before showing them to anyone. Her eyes would fill with joy. One day, I won a big prize for my poem in my college. Rushing home, I dashed into my parents' bedroom. My mother was sleeping, her face turned away towards the wall. I told her the good news and recited the poem for her once again. But she didn't move, didn't say a word. I became impatient and shook her by the shoulder. She was still unmoved. It took me some time to realize that she had passed away in her sleep. My mother was dead. I had lost everything.'

Abhilash passed Rumi his handkerchief to wipe his eyes. Then he told him to tuck in his shirt, polish his shoes with a piece of tissue, and comb his hair before going for his audition.

'Why have you stopped wearing a suit?' Sreya asked Abhilash one morning, after she had finished her yoga. 'Is it because the old ones don't fit you anymore and you need to have a new set tailored?'

Abhilash had to think hard and quickly to come up with a good excuse. 'Smart casual is the new style. It's popular all over the West. Why should people come to work wearing a costume? They must wear what's comfortable.'

'And as the company's president you are setting an example.'

'Yes!' Privately, he let out a sigh of relief. The real reason was to hide his identity from the Strugglers. Whose uncle took the train wearing a Savile Row suit and silk tie? Maybe they took him for a retiree with time on his hands to kill. Or someone suffering from loneliness. His friends shared each other's clothes—the best set worn by the one who had a meeting with a hot contact. 'Should I wear a tie?' Manu had asked him one day. As a scriptwriter, he had to meet a famous author who had come from the UK to Bombay. He didn't have a tie, but Daku had borrowed a scarf from Damini and tied it in a knot to look like one. Abhilash had to bite his tongue before he could blurt out, 'I have a collection of fifty ties at home. I'll happily gift you one.' They mustn't see him as a man of means. That could ruin their friendship.

There was a moment that came close to blowing his cover. 'Do you always eat all your meals at Easy Café?' he'd asked Dev once.

'Lunch by the road, dinner by the road, only Old Monk at home!' he had replied with a flourish.

His friends had piled pressure on him to join their Old Monk party one evening.

'But I don't drink,' Abhilash had lied.

'Just watch Daku drink, and you'll get drunk!'

Four to five strugglers in a one-BHK flat—that was the norm. Abhilash told Makkhan to park the car at least a mile away and wait for him. Covering his nostrils with a handkerchief, he picked his way past the richest assortment of garbage he'd seen in his whole life. 'Why do you make bathrooms?' an NRI friend had once pulled his leg. 'All of Bombay is a bathroom!'

The rooftop party was already under way when Abhilash arrived.

'Welcome, Uncle!' they shouted in a chorus. 'You've come at the right time. Daku is just one drink away from puking!' Manu, who was pouring the drinks, brought over a glass of Fanta for Abhilash.

'He is allowed to be drunk,' Rumi came to Daku's defence. 'Today's party is for him.' Damini has agreed to marry him, he explained to Abhilash. 'She has decided to take the risk. Her brothers might try to bash Daku up, but we'll be there for him.'

'You will be there for him too, won't you, Uncle?'

'Sure.' Abhilash nodded vigorously.

Soon, Manu ganged up with Rumi and demanded a poem. 'Recite something special, just like the one on the train.'

It was a hard task. The new setting—unlike any he'd ever been in—distracted Abhilash from his thoughts. The jumbled landscape of ugly houses, the maze of antennas resembling the devil's tentacles, the blinding floodlight that friends had installed to set the roof ablaze on Daku's special day, the breeze that seemed as hesitant as an innocent lover and the distant horn of the suburban trains set his mind racing. Like an unexpected ripple—the gentlest of them all—it turned the jaws of a rusty valve and released a trapped reservoir.

There was once a bird named hope
It sat on my arm, pecked at the seeds then flew away.

'Wah, Uncle!' Daku raised his glass and swayed on his feet. The boys looked at Abhilash in admiration. Once he'd made a start, the words flowed. Abhilash Shukla had no trouble recalling the lines he'd written a good 25 years ago. Unlike Chowpatty, the roof drew them out with gusto and startled him.

'Another one, Uncle!' the boys shouted in a chorus.

Like a performer on stage—just as he'd hold his audience in awe as a young man in Raipur—he launched into his poems, reciting them one after another, throwing his arms aloft like a troubadour, blew kisses at the crescent moon.

'Which films are they from?' Daku asked.

'These are mine,' wetting his lips, Abhilash replied shyly. 'Poems I'd written many years ago, when I was about your age.'

'Our Uncle is a poet!' Daku screamed and would've toppled over had Rumi not caught him just in time.

'He's a budding lyricist,' Manu nodded wisely.

'He's a struggler, like us,' Daku said and passed him another glass of Fanta.

The applause drew onlookers from neighbouring roofs, and Dev gave him a bear hug and refused to let him go although it was getting late. 'If I ever get a chance to sing in a film, I'll convince the music composer to use your poems for lyrics. That's a promise, boss.'

His hosts crowded around Abhilash as the party ended. Rumi, who'd drunk the least of the lot, spoke to him confidentially.

'Look, Uncle, you have done so much for us. We have left our parents behind, but you have been our guardian. You have held us up when we were about to fall.' He stopped to take in a deep breath, 'Now it's time for us to help you. Tell us what your problem is, and we'll fix it.'

Everybody nodded, Dev joining up with Rumi, 'If someone in your family is bothering you or your neighbour.'

Abhilash shook his head, 'I don't have any problem, believe me.' He tried to smile and bring the topic to an end. But Manu wasn't the one to let go, 'Everyone has a problem. Even SRK.'

Then Rumi went into details, 'We know the place where you catch the train to join us. Daku used to live there once. He knows all the criminals from that area. They can give some pain to whoever is troubling you.'

'There's no need for pain,' Abhilash Shukla said, before extracting himself from his friends and heading back. A nervous Makkhan was waiting with an ashen face and drove back home without a word.

Over the next weeks and months, Abhilash Shukla met frequently with the Strugglers. Once the precautions had become a habit, Makkhan didn't bat an eyelid when he changed course on his way to the office to meet his friends. 'Shall we go to Easy Café, Sir?' he'd ask. Or drop him off at the Marine Drive if his friends had a day off meeting their contacts and simply wished to enjoy the breeze. Daku took him to Chor Bazaar, where he had to hunt for a prop for his set, and Abhilash bought a carved bookend for Manisha. He should stop this lying business and confide in her. She'll catch him one day, he was certain—if his burp smelled of spicy samosas or by the smell of cigarette on his clothes. Why should she mind if he told her that he'd met some new friends and enjoyed spending time with them? She too had changed her group of friends—from those who practised Ikebana to Art of Life. But something held him back. A successful man made friends with successful men. That was the unwritten rule of friendship. Crossing the line invited risks, and she might fear for her husband's safety. *These boys are out to fleece you*, she might say. *You might think friendship, while they might think business.*

Only Makkhan understood. Driving his master, he'd come up with startling observations. Like when he told Abhilash, 'Manu will go far. He doesn't speak much. He observes everything, listens to everyone, like a true writer.' His comment about Daku was even more revealing: 'He isn't lazy. He waits for the right moment to make a move, like a driver must wait to overtake a car safely.' Makkhan brought him disturbing news one morning as Abhilash Shukla had finished signing the salary cheques in his office.

'Your friends are in danger, Sir.'

Abhilash stood up from his chair.

'The landlord of their flat has brought some goons to throw them out of the flat.'

'But they had rented it from the landlord, hadn't they?'

Makkhan nodded. 'The man is saying that they're using the flat for bad things.'

'What bad things?' Abhilash stepped out of his desk.

Makkhan kept silent. Abhilash repeated his question, which was now a command, 'Tell me.'

'He's saying Daku has brought a street girl to the flat.'

'But that must be Damini, his wife to be.'

'It's a lie, Sir. Everyone knows. It's a trick he is using to throw your friends out.'

Giving the excuse of urgent bank work, Abhilash left the office with Makkhan to reach the dirty neighbourhood. A crowd had formed around the house, and Makkhan stopped his master from going any farther. Standing behind the crowd, Abhilash observed the action.

Daku was screaming at the goons. Rumi and Manu held him back. He could see a young woman—Damini? He wondered. She was cowering at the back. Dev was talking to a portly man with a broken face who appeared to be the landlord. Words flew all around—curses, jeers, catcalls.

'What will happen now?' Abhilash asked his driver.

'The police will come and settle the matter against a bribe,' Makkhan sighed.

Abhilash Shukla was distracted by the unsettling events on his way back to the office, his mind unable to focus on the passing scenery. Once again, it was Makkhan who broke into his thoughts.

'There is only one solution to your friends' problems, Sir.'

'Solution?' Recovering his business mind, he asked Makkhan to spell it out.

'Why don't you give a job to one of them in your company? Then he'll be able to afford the rent of a proper flat that was big enough for all his friends.'

'You mean a job in my office?'

'No, Sir,' Makkhan shook his head wisely. 'Then everyone will find out the real story. Give him a job in the factory. That way no one will come to know.'

Getting off at the office, Abhilash admitted his mistake to himself: He should've sacked Makkhan as his driver and given him an executive's job at Shukla & Sons, Bathroom Supplies.

Enjoying the evening breeze in his balcony, Abhilash Shukla thought how much better it would've been if he had owned a film studio rather than a bathroom supplies company. At the snap of his fingers, he could've found jobs for all four. But there'd be hundreds of strugglers still, waiting for a hot contact—he recalled Makkhan's account in the car.

Sagar thought his father had summoned him to enquire about the Mauritius project—their first venture outside India. He'd come prepared with notes to justify the expenses of parts that'd have to be outsourced rather than shipped from Bombay.

'I have received the details of a bright boy from a friend. I want you to employ him in our factory.' Abhilash spoke with his eye on the peacock cage. It was mating season, and the birds were active.

Sagar frowned at the unexpected proposal. 'But we are cutting down costs at the factory,' he spoke hesitantly, 'shedding personnel, offering VRS to the older employees.'

'I know,' Abhilash Shukla nodded. Then he turned his gaze to Sagar, 'But we must also provide jobs to our young people. It is our national duty.'

Sagar held his silence.

'You must arrange everything with the foreman and issue the employment letter.' He called Sagar back as he was about to leave the balcony. 'And remember, if anyone—including your brother—asks you about this decision, you must say it is yours and yours only. Understood?'

Sagar left with a quick nod.

When he called Manu to give him the news, he was overjoyed. But a shade of doubt showed in his voice: 'But Uncle, will I be able to write given the full-time job? What will happen to my dream?'

Abhilash reassured him. 'Think about the great Kalidasa. Didn't he have a family to support?' Then he added his warning to Manu, 'The company belongs to a friend of mine. He has agreed to employ you. But you mustn't mention my name—ever—to anyone over there. Understood?'

Employees of Shukla & Sons were taken aback by the resurgence of their president as the true helmsman of the company that he once was. Now he didn't hide in the president's suite, with occasional trips to the executive toilet. He paced the floors, checked blueprints, made enquiries about inventory and the progress of the projects. He restrained Sumit if he appeared overconfident selling to a big client; terrorized the accountant, appearing to have all the numbers inside his head. 'He has become the Abhilash Shukla we knew,' Mrs Gupta heaved with pride. 'He is dreaming again!'

For a whole week following the roof party, Abhilash had no time for his friends or work. Sagar's engagement took up the energy of the entire household. His fiancée, Rukmini's parents were due to arrive from Delhi, and a meeting of the two families was set for afternoon tea on 15 August.

'It'll be the day of his independence from his mother and the beginning of his dependence on his wife!' Abhilash joked with Sreya, the designated master of ceremonies.

'Lord Krishna had to fight a duel with Rukmini's brother to marry her,' Sreya joked back. 'Whereas our Sagar might have to fight off her favourite Doberman to win her over.'

'We can't have dogs in this house; they'll spoil the lawn,' Manisha struck a discordant note.

'And scare the peacocks,' Sreya concurred.

'Wait, we must first make the Mehras comfortable, discuss the wedding details and then bring up dogs,' Abhilash restored calm. When Rumi tried reaching his private number, he disconnected the call as he was on his way to receive his prospective in-laws from the airport and deposit them in Bombay's best hotel. As a businessman, he was used to frenzy, but the first meeting with people who might become relatives for life set off a flicker in his hardened temper.

'It's urgent, Uncle, please listen for a minute; don't hang up,' Rumi pleaded when he finally took his call.

'Manu has some big news to share, and we're holding a party at Jubilee Park tonight at 9. You *have* to come.'

'Tonight? That's impossible.' Abhilash stopped giving out the reason to Rumi. But he was insistent, 'Please, Uncle. If you don't come, the party will be called off.'

The Mehras were vegetarians. Warned, Sreya had laid out a full spread catered by the city's best-known delicatessen. Abhilash blinked when he saw the waiters bring in the platters: sun-blushed tomato quiche, Roquefort and caramelized onion tart, cauliflower gratin, garlic mushroom, spinach soufflé and tofu with Italian herbs.

'The Mehras know that we make bathrooms, but they must also know that we understand what happens inside the kitchen!' Sreya quipped. Sagar, everyone could see, was nervous. He had worn his watch upside down.

When their guests arrived, more than a half hour late owing to traffic, Sunidhi Mehra went straight for the dessert, letting Sreya serve her a generous helping of chocolate banana crêpes.

'Happy occasions should begin with sweets, isn't it?' she said and wouldn't have minded a second helping, before Rukmini moved the platter away from her reach. 'My mother is diabetic,' she smiled in a way that was far more confident than Sagar. 'Sweets are her poison.'

'That's a tragedy, isn't it?' Sunidhi sighed, her eyes still dwelling on the desserts. 'You spend most of your life struggling to achieve everything. But when you've got them all, you are only allowed to eat boiled green papaya!'

Abhilash laughed heartily. 'Absolutely! There's no greater truth than this. I was once a long-distance runner but couldn't afford to buy running shoes to enter the state competition. And now, I am not allowed to even walk briskly, let alone jog, as it might increase my heart rate.'

'In Punjab, where I grew up, everyone was a sportsman.' Apurv Mehra spoke for the first time. He was a slow eater and was making his way gradually through the quiche. 'I too wanted to represent my country in the Olympics, but my father forced me to enter the steel business.'

The opening of the high tea was meant for chit-chat, to get everyone relaxed, but the main course took a long time to come as Sunidhi went into a lengthy travelogue. The couple had just returned from their Char Dham pilgrimage. 'I don't believe in these modern-day gurus and their mumbo jumbo about inner joy. Our family guruji told us that to be close to the gods, we must go where they live—the Himalayas.'

Abhilash glanced quickly at Manisha. She had already bitten her tongue and filled her mouth with tofu. His phone—set on buzzer mode—buzzed inside his pocket, and Abhilash knew it was Rumi calling or Manu or Dev. It was 7.45 p.m.

It took another 15 minutes for Sunidhi to go from Yamunotri to Gangotri, describing all the snacks they'd had during that stretch. Rukmini, who must've heard the story a hundred times, tried unsuccessfully to rush her mother along, saying, 'But you enjoyed the pony ride to Kedarnath most, didn't you?'

'Yes,' Sunidhi nodded. 'But before that, there were stops in Uttarkashi and Guptkashi. Your father felt dizzy.'

Finished with the quiche, Apurv attacked the cauliflower with the gusto of a discus thrower that he was in his youth. 'It was altitude sickness; it happens to the fittest of men.'

Abhilash despaired. There were still two more stops to Char Dham, and the time was 8.20 p.m. He pushed the baby pink macaroons towards Sunidhi and assumed an executive demeanour to come to the point.

'We've known Rukmini for some time now and come to love her. It'll be our pleasure to . . .'

Turning away towards Manisha and Sreya, Sunidhi sought to create the classic Indian diversion—men talking to men, women to women. 'Pilgrims talk about Kedarnath, but it was Badri that stole my heart.'

Sumit, who'd stayed quiet all this time, seemed suddenly interested. 'Why Badri?'

'Because of the divine setting. If you stand at the temple and look downwards, you'll see the Alakananda River. Look up, and you'll find the Nilkantha Peak gazing down!'

His phone buzzed again, and Abhilash knew this was the final call. It was well past 9 p.m. when the wedding matter was settled, rather swiftly, by the three women huddling together in the kitchen. All of them emerged beaming, and Manisha gently reproached her husband, 'Aren't you going to offer Mr Mehra a drink?'

Abhilash panicked. A drink would mean 30 more minutes. Two drinks an hour. Fortunately, Sunidhi intervened saying, 'Our guruji has forbidden any drinking-shrinking for a month after the pilgrimage. It will cancel out the boons.'

The wrapping up was pleasant, and Rukmini gave hugs to both Manisha and Abhilash before leaving with her parents.

'Thank God they've left on time!' Manisha breathed a sigh of relief. She had promised to attend a seance with her fellow Lifers at a friend's house. Sumit and Sreya had shopping plans and Sagar for a final blast of a party before his wedding. Quite suddenly, the house was empty of residents and guests.

Changing into smart casuals, Abhilash left in an auto for Jubilee Park. It was 9.30 p.m. He felt a rare thrill, like stealing out of his home in Raipur to watch an adults-only film with friends. He was late, and the show would've started already, but there might still be time to catch the juicy bits.

'Uncle!' the Strugglers greeted Abhilash Shukla raucously when he arrived. They were in high mood. Daku had taken off his shirt and was drinking heavily. Rumi had set his boom speaker at a high volume, blasting off their favourite numbers. Before Dev could offer Abhilash a Fanta, Rumi switched off the music and asked everyone to be silent.

'Manu has something to say, Uncle,' he said.

Kneeling down in front of Abhilash, Manu brought out a packet and presented it to him.

'What is it?' Abhilash asked.

'Open it, Uncle!' his friends spoke in chorus.

Unwrapping the case, Abhilash found a watch. It was a cheap Chinese-made digital watch with a black plastic band.

'It's both analogue and digital. You can press a button, and it'll even play you a little song!' Dev sounded excited. 'It's time to take off your HMT Janata!'

'Why are you giving me this watch?' Abhilash asked, still unable to comprehend.

Rumi answered for Manu, 'Because you've found him a good job. Now all of us can live in a decent place. One must pay respect to one's elders when they enter the workforce—it's our culture.'

Before Abhilash could recover from the surprise, Dev dragged him by the arm to a small table made from bricks. It had its own spread of drinks plus kebabs and tandoori chicken. The music resumed, and this time, Rumi made his pitch to Abhilash: 'We've heard your poems, Uncle; now you must show us how you dance.'

'Dance, Uncle!' The roar grew. 'Play Dev Anand songs!' Manu knew his favourites. One after another, the booming speaker blasted out hits from *Prem Pujari*, *Des Pardes*, *Shareef Badmash*, *Heera Panna*, *Johny Mera Naam*. Perhaps it was the release he felt from the Mehras, perhaps it was the Old Monk that Manu had mixed with the Fanta, perhaps it was the joy of the unexpected gift that made Abhilash Shukla dance like he'd never danced before—arms aloft, waist wriggling, shoulders arching back and forth, winking to his friends and laughing his head off.

That was the very moment when Sumit, out with Sreya for shopping, drew close to Jubilee Park. The traffic was bumper-to-bumper on Independence Day, and they inched forward at snail's pace.

'Look!' Sreya pointed towards the park. There was a look of shock and disbelief in her eyes.

'Look at what?' Sumit took his eye off the road to follow Sreya's.

'Papa!'

Furrowing his brows, Sumit looked closely, 'It can't be him. He's at home.'

'Maybe he too left after all of us did.'

'But what's he doing here?' Sumit rolled down the window and stuck his neck out. Cars honked, urging him to move on. 'Who are these people? They look like . . .'

'Thugs.' Sreya voiced his suspicion.

The boys settled down on the grass after the bout of dancing. Sweating profusely, Abhilash took out his handkerchief, embossed with his name, to wipe his face. Then passed it on to Rumi who asked for it. Dev was humming a song, while Daku buttoned up his shirt.

'We know who you are, Uncle,' Rumi spoke quietly.

'I'm Dev Anand!' Abhilash laughed, 'Don't you know that already?'

'You are Mr Abhilash Shukla.' Rumi's voice was even. 'President of Shukla & Sons Bathroom Supplies. Over 100 people work for you in your office, and you have a factory where Manu is an employee. You had told us your name, but nothing else about you.'

'You live in a mansion. It's bigger than Shah Rukh Khan's house.' Now it was Dev's turn. 'You have a Mercedes and three other foreign cars.'

'And you keep peacocks.' Daku barely whispered.

'You've been playing a game with us, Uncle,' Rumi brought his face close to Abhilash's. 'We found out who you really are, but thought we'd play the same game with you. The game of secrets.'

'But why, Uncle?' Daku sounded as innocent as a child. 'Why did you have to leave your Mercedes to ride the train with us? Forget about your office to sit in Easy Café? Why did you have to listen to us, to our stupid problems when you have everything already?' He stopped, then gazed plaintively at Abhilash, 'Why did you fool us, Uncle?'

'No . . .' Abhilash whispered.

'What could we have given you that you didn't have?' Manu kept shaking his head. 'We couldn't figure out the reason why you spend time with us. It didn't make any sense, unless . . .'

The air had turned still, as still as the world around them.

'Unless you just wanted to be our friend. Unless you loved us.' Rumi shrugged, 'That's the only reason we could come up with.'

The entire neighbourhood, including the Shukla residence, was quiet when Abhilash Shukla returned home in an auto. The gate was locked. He didn't wish to shout and wake up the *durwan* and went around the back to the part of the boundary wall that was low in height and which he could still scale. He landed on the lawn with a thud, then picked himself up and made his way over to the house. The door to his wife's bedroom was shut and bolted from inside. He sat in the balcony and gazed at his neighbours' homes. There was no sign of Kukreja, Balbir or Johnny Walker. Where is everybody, he wondered. Did they all die while he was in Jubilee Park?

Abhilash woke next morning to the sound of weeping. He followed the sound to the servants' quarter and found Makkhan. He was crying. A half-packed suitcase lay before him. Seeing his master, he hung his head in shame.

'Where are you going?' Abhilash asked.

'Home,' he answered between sobs.

'Has something happened there? Is your father ill?'

Makkhan shook his head. Then, at Abhilash's urging, was forced to reveal the truth.

'I have betrayed you, Master. I didn't know that you had gone to Jubilee Park last night, because you hadn't asked for the car.'

'So what?' Abhilash couldn't follow.

'Sumit and Sreya saw you there. Then came back and told Madam and Sagar. They couldn't understand what you were doing there. Sumit said those men must be criminals. They must've blackmailed you. Maybe you had done something with a girl. Sagar thought you were into drugs, and the boys were peddlers. 'You must know everything,' Madam told me, because I take you everywhere. Sumit said I am part of the gang, and they'd hand me over to the police. He slapped me, Sir.' Makkhan covered his face with both hands. 'They forced me to tell the truth.'

Abhilash Shukla clenched his teeth as he sat down with his family for breakfast. Everyone had their gazes fixed on their plates. Normally, there'd be talk about the Mehras and the wedding, but tongues remained firmly locked inside jowls. When the puris arrived from the kitchen, Manisha didn't serve the first one, as was the custom, to her husband. Like actors, they waited for a command from some invisible source to begin. Then Abhilash cleared his throat.

'I must tell you where I went last evening.'

Manisha stirred on her seat.

'I went to Jubilee Park.' Picking up a piece of ripe papaya in his fork, he continued, 'There's nothing to see there. No flowers, not even a pond. Just an ugly patch of grass. I went there to meet my friends.'

'Those thugs are your friends?' Sumit looked up and spoke angrily.

Raising his left palm, Abhilash calmed him. 'Not thugs. They are a group of boys, who are known as Strugglers.' Over the next 15 minutes, relying on his great ability to make lucid the most complex of subjects to his employees and clients alike and marshalling the resources of a leader used to dealing with dissent, he spoke about his friends. He told his family about their accidental meeting in the train, the occasional rendezvous in Easy Café and the visit to the rooftop party. He'd learnt of their dreams and their struggles. It had reminded him of his days in Raipur when he too had dreamt of a life in films. He'd felt close to them because—he paused to look around the table before continuing—he had nothing to give or take from them. Except friendship. 'And I realized,' he said, fighting back his emotion that threatened to choke his voice, 'that I may no longer be useful to my company, but I am still useful to some people. It gave me a reason to keep on living.' Then he held up his right hand to show everyone the cheap plastic watch that Manu had given him as a gift. 'Look what my friend gave me. A watch for his first job.'

Sreya stifled a sob, 'Sorry, Papa . . .' Ignoring her, Abhilash turned to Sumit.

'You have slapped Makkhan. Consider the fact that you've slapped your uncle, for Makkhan is my brother. When your mother had collapsed on the verge of delivering you, and I was busy doing business in Pune, he had picked her up in his arms and rushed her to the hospital. Without him, you wouldn't even be here.'

Sumit rose and stood with his head down.

'Sit down,' Abhilash said, speaking in his president's voice. 'I have taken the decision to introduce my family to my friends. You will see with your own eyes who they are. They may not be like us, but they surely aren't unlike us.'

The boys loved Chinese food, which prompted Abhilash to invite everyone to Dragon's Cave. It was neither too fancy, nor a hole in the wall. Arriving with his family, he sat at the round table with a revolving Lazy Susan in the middle. The Strugglers were late for their appointment, and they finished a pot of green tea. Abhilash checked his watch. He had told Rumi to bring everyone over by 8 p.m.

'Maybe they are shy to meet us,' Sreya ventured. Sagar thought they might've made a mistake and landed up at Dragon House on the other end of town. Abhilash called Daku. However late he was for appointments, he always answered promptly. His phone was switched off. Manu and Dev's rang through. Rumi was busy on another line. He wondered if 'hot contacts' had popped up all too suddenly for them all at once.

At 8.45 p.m., Manisha suggested they leave and schedule another appointment, maybe at their home. 'We can cater in Chinese food if that's what they like.'

There was some commotion at the door, and then Rumi rushed in looking dishevelled. 'Uncle, let's go,' he shrieked, spotting Abhilash.

'Go where?' He tried to calm Rumi down.

'Daku's down. They've thrashed him. He was alone in the flat after we'd all gone out for work.' They—Rumi explained, once he'd drunk a full glass of water—were Damini's brothers and their friends. 'They hate Daku and had warned Damini that they won't tolerate a low-caste boy marrying their sister. She had tried in vain to reason with them.'

'Where is Daku now?' Abhilash rose from the table.

'At the Motilal Jain Hospital. He's in a coma, but they won't treat him at the ICU because he has no money.'

'Come.' Leaving his family behind in Dragon's Cave, Abhilash dashed out of the restaurant and jumped into the car with Rumi. Manu and Dev were at the local police station, pleading to have the culprits arrested. But the station chief didn't believe their story; he was calling it gang warfare.

At Motilal, the superintendent stood up from his chair when Abhilash arrived. He was a big donor, and the newly opened cardiology ward was named after his mother.

'I want my patient to be moved from the corridor, where he's lying unattended, to the ICU. Immediately.'

'Yes, Sir,' the superintendent rushed down the hospital corridor. Returning to the car, he made three quick calls to his neurologist, trauma expert and cardiologist, asking them to make private visits to Motilal. Then, with Rumi in tow, he left for the police station.

The SI was known to Abhilash. He had saved his skin in a bribery scandal involving property sharks. Manu and Dev were sitting on a crowded bench when he arrived, waiting for the SI to listen to their complaint.

'How do you know Mr Daman Pandey?' the officer asked.

'Daman?' Abhilash didn't have a clue.

'That's our Daku,' Manu whispered.

'He's my . . .' Abhilash checked himself in the last moment, calling him 'my employee' rather than my friend.

'It's a clear case of Section 153A of the Indian Penal Code,' he told the SI. 'Promoting enmity on the basis of caste, religion, etc. And I shall take it up with the police commissioner if you don't act to arrest the culprits immediately.'

After the police party had left for Damini's home, Abhilash dropped Rumi, Daku and Dev back at Motilal and set out for Bombay's best private hospital. He needed to make arrangements before shifting Daku over. The call from Rumi came when he was already halfway there.

'He's gone, Uncle.' He heard Rumi break down over the phone.

'I'm sending Makkhan to the house. I want you to give him Rs 10,000 and send him back to the crematorium.' Abhilash called Manisha once arrangements had been made to inform Daku's relatives in Patna. It would be too messy to transport the body back, and his elder brother had given consent for the last rights to be performed in Bombay.

The queue for the furnace was short. They didn't have to wait long before Daku went in. His friends sat in the waiting hall for the three-quarters of an hour that he'd spend inside. The wind had stopped, and the lone standing fan turned its head in jerky movements like a busy traffic cop. Dogs barked in the grounds outside. Temple bells rang whenever a party arrived with their corpse. A tea seller scolded his boy who'd forgotten to rinse the dirty glasses. Parking the car a few metres from the gate, Makkhan accompanied Manisha as she made her way into the crematorium. It was her first visit, and Makkhan led her past the furnace into the waiting hall. She searched for her husband among the mourners and then spotted him huddled with his friends in a tight circle. Their eyes met. She saw his face broken by the tragedy.

By all accounts of gossip, Rukmini and Sagar's wedding was a grand success. Following the tradition of the Shukla household, giving alms to the poor ushered in the festivities. Sumit and Sreya kept a close eye on hospitalities. The Strugglers too were invited alongside the city's elite and made a grand entrance wearing tuxedos hired from a company that supplied costumes for films. 'We've come to take part in the crowd scene, Uncle!' Manu joked. But as the evening progressed, they ended up captivating the crowd—Dev by his singing and Rumi by performing a one-man comedy act written by Manu. They managed to charm even Sunidhi Mehra, and Sreya introduced them to everyone as Papa's young friends.

'Don't forget to come to Easy Café Saturday morning at 10 sharp,' Dev whispered into Abhilash's ear before leaving.

'What's happening then?'

'You'll have your audition. It'll be your first.'

'What audition?' Abhilash was confused.

'Remember the poem you'd recited on our roof? The one about the bird?' Dev's eyes twinkled. 'I'd written it down and showed it to a music director, who has become my friend. He's willing to record me singing it.'

Abhilash's mouth fell open in wonder.

'Didn't I promise I'll make your dream of becoming a lyricist come true?'

The recording studio resembled a glass cage with stacks of equipment jumbled up inside. The doorman took Abhilash to be a producer and gave a big salute. Manu whisked him in, made him sit inside the cage and strapped a pair of large headphones around his ears.

'Who's he?' the music director, who was busy chatting with the instrumentalists, asked Dev pointing at Abhilash.

'He's the lyricist I'd told you about,' Dev answered and winked at Abhilash. 'This will be his debut.'

'Him!' The music director paused to examine Abhilash—an elderly man with greying hair. 'I thought he was your friend!'

'He *is* my friend.' Dev joined the musicians, and soon they were speaking in a language Abhilash couldn't comprehend. He spotted Rumi through the glass pane, who'd come to join Manu. Then, the conductor made a curt announcement, and everyone fell silent. The music started on cue, and Dev's voice floated in through the earphones.

I once knew a bird named hope . . .

Abhilash watched Manu and Rumi's eyes shining. They were happy for their Uncle, he could see, for the struggler among them who was at last making his debut. He searched for a third face, the one who was always late for their meetings. His eyes started to well, and he closed them and listened to the song. It was his sacred moment.

The wedding canopy had been taken down, and the lawn was back to its full glory. There was a nip in the air, and the gulmohar had started to shed. The neighbours' homes were silent, and sitting in the balcony, Abhilash gazed up at the clear sky that revealed a dazzling constellation. He heard the door between his and Manisha's bedrooms open. She came into the balcony and sat beside him, a withered notebook on her lap. It was his book of poems from Raipur. When she spoke, her voice was as clear as a bird's night call.

'I too once had a dream. I dreamt I'd marry a poet. Not a rich man, but one who'd write me poems for love letters. They'd be my only treasure.' Then, gazing up at the sky like Abhilash, she recited the poem her husband had written for her when they were yet unmarried, when he'd still dreamt of becoming nothing else but a poet. Listening to her, Abhilash knew these lines to be true, the truest he'd ever written in his whole life.

They sat late into the night in the balcony, eyes burning in the darkness like the peacocks'.

OXBLOOD

It was unclear who found the corpse first. Was it the honeymooning couple, up early after a night of frolicking, come for a dip in the sea? Perhaps it was the English boy, building sandcastles while his parents lounged on recliners, happy to have escaped to Goa from the rotten English spring. Or was it the petty thief who wished to steal the man's watch while he was still asleep—or so he thought—until he'd touched the icy-cold wrist and fled in terror?

The police had to ring-fence the corpse once the hordes descended after the news had spread. It wasn't unusual to find a body on the beach—mostly ravers who'd died of an overdose or drowned fishermen washed up ashore. But this one was curious, or 'too much' as Inspector Vandana Sathe remarked, arriving at the scene. She wasn't far off in her comment as the corpse was remarkable to say the least.

Surrounded by the moat that the boy had dug around it, the man lay dressed in an immaculate suit, a double-knotted silk tie around the collar of a hand-stitched shirt and matching pocket square barely peeking out. Outstretched legs sported tailored trousers, held at the waist by a crocodile leather belt, while Burberry-striped socks brought up the lower extremities tucked into Italian Brogues. A half-smoked cigarette dangled from the lips. He was lying on his back, face up towards the sun that gleamed on a pair of dark glasses. A single bullet had pierced his temple, releasing blood, which had dried in the sun. It didn't look like a wound, but a kiss.

'Take it all off,' Inspector Sathe ordered the morgue attendants, who went about the painstaking task of denuding a rigid frame. Every item was labelled and put away to help with the investigation, but other than the clothes, nothing was found on the man. No wallet, no pen, no comb, no cigarette pack or lighter—absolutely nothing that might supply a lead or two. Even the maker's label of the suit had been carefully snipped off. It was a clue-less corpse.

The police made their round of the resorts, but none could recognize the dead man. Road cameras in nearby locations failed to spot anything more than a trickle of members of the beach yoga club arriving for their morning workout. Newspaper ads were the last resort, but they too failed to bring forward a next of kin. After a month, the file was shut and stacked away in a rack that had gathered the dust of 30 years of unsolved cases.

That month brought about a major change in Inspector Vandana Sathe's life, caused by her marriage to biology professor Neeraj Paranjpe. After the couple had returned from their honeymoon in the mountains, she reported to her station and attended to pressing matters such as an ugly property dispute between two developers and an unnecessary riot caused by fake news. But the beach corpse remained stuck in her mind, pricked her conscience as an unsolved mystery. On a relaxed Friday, she visited the station's storeroom and asked for the box of contents to be brought out.

'For the suited corpse, Ma'am?'

Helped by the attendant, she went through each item of clothing yet again. Her eyes scanned every inch of the remains and zeroed in on a secret pocket stitched into the trousers' waistband. Delicately slipping her finger in, she prised out a visiting card printed on high-quality paper with a name embossed on it. Martin Long—it read. Turning it over, she found a single word scribbled in red—Oxblood.

Later—after concluding 2 years of enquiry—she presented her full evidence on the case to the state's prosecuting attorney. Relying on her superior investigative skills, she was able to establish without doubt that the dead man in a suit was none other than Manohar Lele, and his killer was his lover cum business partner, Jyoti Singh.

Manohar Lele met Jyoti Singh at Kathmandu's largest casino that drew big spenders from India, where gambling was banned by law. Mr Lee, the Korean floor manager, spotted the young recruit walking around the tables, observing both the staff and the players. He liked what he saw. Boys who learnt by themselves were better than those who waited to be trained. In less than a month, he graduated from being a simple croupier—spinning the roulette wheel—to being the Boxman who handled the chips in a game of craps to the stickman, moving the dice across the table with a wooden stick.

'Give me a chance to be the dealer, Sir.' Manohar requested his boss when he was sipping a drink in a relaxed mood.

Lee frowned. 'The blackjack takes at least a year to master. It'll come to you in time.'

'Let me challenge you, Sir, to bust me if you can.'

The floor manager burst out laughing, the drink spilling from the glass. 'You mean . . .?'

'Yes, Sir. Bring your friends and let me deal you a game of blackjack.'

It took less than an hour for the casino managers to learn that not only did young Manohar know how to deal cards but also knew if it'd be better to hit or stand on soft 17. Then, showing supreme confidence, he ejected Mr Lee from the game, accusing him, rightly, of the grave sin of card counting that was prohibited.

Like a rising star, he rose quickly, impressing too by his manners. He was friendly but not overfriendly. Players cosied up to him to get a helpful tip but ended up giving him a tip about their betting plans. Just to be safe, Lee told his guards to keep an eye on his recruit, to examine the closed-circuit TV tapes and to walk around the secret catwalks in the ceiling and look down at him through the one-way glass. Smart boys could cheat better than the smartest guests, and he wanted to be absolutely sure.

Manohar passed all the tests successfully and became a trusted casino man in no time. His knack, which was a vital asset to any casino, was to read a player's personality. His eyes pierced each guest, and he knew who was a novice, who was a seasoned gambler who knew his limits, who were the habitual cheats and the pathological ones, who couldn't stop and had to be escorted out by guards after they'd lost their shirts. His roving eye caught everything, including Jyoti Singh—the casino's other great asset.

If Manohar was the plane's pilot, Jyoti was the engineer who made it possible for him to fly. Invisible at the gaming floor, she ruled over a small office that kept track of the players' profiles, spending habits, the daily profit and loss of the casino. The House always wins—every employee knew that; the games were designed such that the odds of winning were stacked against the player. Still, there were days when the odds were upset. Like the arrival of one Mr Zhou from Macau. Before the portly Chinese gentleman could make a move towards the Baccarat table, Manohar dashed into Jyoti's office.

'The whale's here,' was all he said, but she understood him instantly. Like James Bond, Mr Zhou favoured Baccarat. He dealt only in large bets, knowing full well that it was a game of 100 per cent luck and zero skill. He'd won some serious money during his last visit, and the House management wished to avoid a repeat.

'I've tried to offer him complimentary chips for craps, but he refused.'

'Wait,' Jyoti interrupted Manohar. 'I'll give him a better game to play.' She'd called a special number and summoned a 'special' attendant to accompany Mr Zhou to his hotel suite for a little massage before the Baccarat. 'He'll have no time for the casino tonight. Even if he does,' she'd given Manohar an even stare, 'we'll have his photographs, which will discourage him from Baccarat.'

They shared a smoke on the casino's open terrace, which offered a view of snow-capped Himalayan peaks on a clear day. Co-workers used their breaks to worship at the Swayambhunath Temple or join the hippies to smoke some weed. Jyoti and Manohar chewed over their business. 'There's one thing that the casino teaches,' Jyoti said, reaching for a drag, speaking in riddles, which was her style. 'Luck is variable, but life is fixed.'

'How so?' Manohar didn't follow.

'Just think of your life. So far it has been a mix of odds and ends, hasn't it?'

Manohar agreed. He had told Jyoti about the twists and turns of his 20-something years, starting in his hometown Gaya; the accidents that had landed him in tight corners and his run-ins with the law. From being a morgue attendant to mountain guide, he'd adopted the only pattern life had allowed him to follow to land at the blackjack table.

'Even if you were to win a million bucks at the casino, you'd still be doing the same—just bigger odds and sadder ends.'

Jyoti was right. They'd all seen an ending—a pathetic one—that very afternoon. A man was gambling wildly at a slot machine and drinking heavily. Casino staff knew who he was—a bank robber who came to Kathmandu to blow off the loot. Jyoti had increased the scent that's piped into the hall—the scent of women. It was an aphrodisiac; it made men aggressive, made them gamble harder. The police must've been on his trail, and he was picked up at the casino following a tip-off.

'Poor guy,' Manohar mused.

'Not poor. Stupid,' Jyoti disagreed with him.

'Bad luck he got caught this time, although it was bound to happen sooner or later.'

'Not if he turned into someone else, into a man the police wouldn't have recognized as the bank robber.' Stubbing out the cigarette, Jyoti waited for Manohar to get her point.

'Do you mean if he assumed a disguise?'

'More than a disguise. If he did an Adolf Eichmann.'

Manohar didn't know who Eichmann was, and when he asked Jyoti to explain during their next break, she spoke tersely, 'Adolf

Hitler's deputy. He was a mass murderer. A war criminal. The allied forces were searching all over Europe for him, but he escaped to Argentina and lived undercover as an auto mechanic. No one there had the faintest suspicion who he really was.'

'So, he erased his past?'

'Yes! Precisely. He became a different person.'

'But can that be done so easily?'

'Not easily,' Jyoti said, straightening her jacket as the break was nearing an end. 'But only if there was help available. If some people—a company say—took charge to give him new papers, destroyed all past traces, got him into a different profession, changed his looks even.'

'For which he should be ready to spend money,' Manohar started to catch on. Jyoti smiled, 'Yes, lots of it. Only people of means can afford it, not your common criminal.'

'The company offering such a service would also make lots, wouldn't it?'

Jyoti smiled. After a moment or two, Manohar smiled back. They left it at that.

An opportunity—if one can describe it as such—arose in less than a month. A gang leader who specialized in kidnapping for ransom had taken shelter in the casino. He was shifty at the card table, and it didn't take much for Manohar to prise out his story.

'It all went wrong because the fellow tried to run away when I'd parked the jeep to take a piss. I caught him, but he wriggled himself free, and I had no choice but to shoot him.' The master kidnapper sounded vexed.

'Is he dead?' Manohar asked cautiously.

'Of course,' Rajesh Chauhan snorted. 'Who can escape my bullet?' Then he turned instantly remorseful. 'His father is a state minister. He would've happily paid the ransom. But now he'll come for my throat. They'll take me back to India and hang me.'

Jyoti's words came to Manohar's mind, and along with it a sudden inspiration. 'We can help you stay alive,' he told Rajesh. 'But it'll cost you money.'

The kidnapper's eyes lit up; he grasped Manohar's hand. 'I have a suitcase full of cash. It's in my room.'

Jyoti smoked two full cigarettes after she'd heard Manohar's proposal. Then she started to walk down to her office.

'Wait! Aren't you going to try an Eichmann with him?' Manohar called after her.

'Not before I've done my research,' she said, before disappearing.

'He's a fool,' she told Manohar when they met later in her office. 'Which is a good thing. Because no one will expect him to behave smartly. The police will set a simple trap and hope he'll fall into it.'

'But how can we turn him intelligent overnight?'

Picking up a file from her table, she ushered Manohar out and spoke in a low voice as they marched down to Rajesh's room, 'Let me explain that to him and to you at the same time.'

Rajesh, as they found out, was unused to five-star etiquette. He'd been taking his meals indoors but hadn't asked the room service staff to remove the plates. The room stank. His clothes lay in a heap on the floor. He was dressed in a bathrobe.

Jyoti called housekeeping to clean the room and waited outside with Manohar till the job was done. Then, she sat down with the two men and started her briefing.

'Give me your phone, and everything you've brought with you, including all the cash.'

Rajesh looked bewildered.

'We'll give you a dumb phone, which you must use on pay-as-you-go basis only. And a small amount of cash to use as needed.' She brought out a pad and pencil and asked for the name and password of his email and social media accounts, if he had any. Then screwed up her face writing down the details, as Manohar relayed the obscene words to her, which Rajesh had sheepishly whispered into his ear.

'Are you married?' she asked next. Rajesh shook his head.

'You mustn't call anybody—nobody at all. Understood?'

Manohar marvelled at the manner Jyoti conducted the meeting, sounding like the casino's boss.

'What will I wear, Ma'am, if I give you all my clothes?' Rajesh asked, sounding like a child who'd received a scolding from his teacher.

'Manohar will bring you a fresh set.' Then, she put her papers away and came to the hardest bits. 'From now on, you are no longer Rajesh from Bihar but a mountain guide named . . .' She looked enquiringly at Manohar.

'Batsa.' Manohar spoke on cue, remembering his friend and fellow guide Batsa Thapa, who'd died, tragically, during a landslide.

Before leaving, she looked Rajesh in the eye and said, 'You'll have to take a little bit of pain, not much. Tonight, my partner here will come and take you to a doctor's chamber. Tomorrow you'll leave the casino and go with him to your new home.'

Then, between the two of them, Jyoti and Manohar dragged Rajesh's suitcase to a storeroom, which was outside the casino's CCTV coverage. There were banknotes worth 25 lakh inside, some gold bars and jewellery and a kilogram of heroin.

After Mr Lee had cut the cake at his farewell dinner, followed by clapping, whistling and singing, Jyoti and Manohar withdrew to their favourite terrace. The night was calm, and the moon glimmered on the snowy peaks.

'Did you do what we needed to with Batsa before you deposited him in the mountains?' Jyoti asked.

Sipping his drink, Manohar nodded. Rajesh, now Batsa, had screamed like a child when Dr Lobo, whom Manohar had known from his days as a morgue assistant, slashed a cut on his right cheek, like a master sculptor, with a scalpel. It was meant to heal quickly and become a permanent facial feature. It'd fool a detective attempting a pictorial match.

That was their first success, if one can call it that. But since every business venture comes with its fair share of doubt, Manohar voiced his to Jyoti.

'How long do you think our Batsa will be able to keep up his cover?'

Jyoti shrugged. 'A year, at the most.'

'Then?'

'Then, he'll get drunk and brag to the whole village what a great sharpshooter he was, how he'd gone about his business and collected suitcases of cash.'

'So, the police will catch him, and he'll tell them everything. Including . . .'

'About us,' Jyoti completed Manohar's suspicion.

Gazing down at the dark city, he brooded. One more 'odd' in his life will then have yet another unhappy end. Jyoti laid a hand on his face, drew him closer to plant a kiss before bringing out her phone and scrolling down to a page.

Manohar saw the picture of a giant cruise ship. It was advertising to hire staff for its impending voyage. Jyoti lit a cigarette and passed it on to Manohar. Then let out her words like the curling smoke from her lips, 'Then we'll both become Eichmann.'

The *Silver Cloud* docked in Fort-de-France on the day of Vaval, the famous carnival of Martinique. It was the third stop of the luxury cruise ship, following a successful visit to Jamaica's Falmouth port and Nassau in the Bahamas. The mostly American passengers—retired, obese and rich—were just as eager to join the festivities on shore as the ship's staff. So far, it had been an enjoyable ride with plenty of on-board activities, such as water sliding, go-karting, aerobics and Zumba, plus time spent at the spa. Like all luxury liners, the *Silver Cloud* offered a grand spread of world cuisine, leaning towards the heavy southern style given its clientele. Nights were meant for dancing in the company of an expert and exquisite partner employed by the ship. Plus, magic shows, pantomimes, clowns—for there was a child in every adult—and a casino.

An official part of France, the island parade was known for its blatantly exhibitionist dancers. Dressed up as he- and she-devils, they performed devilish acts on the gaudily decorated floats, scandalizing the American tourists. The year's Beaujolais Nouveau flowed freely, and by the time everyone was drunk, no one noticed the costumes, just the gyrating bodies enacting the most primal of moves.

'That's one of our gals, isn't she?'

Stan or Dick or Joe, whatever his name was, noticed a she-devil and drew the attention of others. He meant the ship's dance instructor, who took the morning Zumba class with the ladies, and danced with the men at night.

'It's Selena Sanchez,' Martha said. She was once a schoolteacher and had the ability to memorize every student's name.

'She's hot!' Martha's husband quipped and invited a glare from Martha.

No one noticed the he-devil who was dancing alongside Selena, Manuel Lazaro, the ship's magician.

Late afternoon the following day, the *Silver Cloud* left French shores for Spanish San Juan, Puerto Rico, giving her passengers the chance to recover from an exhausting night. It was time for some magic.

Magician Manuel Lazaro opened with the amazing aces trick, asking a spectator to take a pack of cards and deal them into four piles. After he'd finished, Manuel, wearing a magician's top hat, turned the face of the top card of each pile revealing them all to be aces. Finding his guests to be bored, he went through the rest of the tricks, from pick a card to the blind three-card Monte.

'We've seen these before, young man,' an elderly grandmother patted Manuel on the back. 'My grandson learnt them from the internet.'

The dance floor, by contrast, was livelier. Cha-cha-cha was popular with the ladies who'd grown up performing it in high school proms. Those with knee problems preferred the easier Cupid Shuffle. 'Y.M.C.A' was the all-time favourite, closely followed by 'Macarena'. The men preferred dancing the tango with Selena, their lady instructor, standing in queue for a one-on-one.

'Yours is the more difficult job,' Manuel teased Selena when they relaxed in the pool way past midnight after the guests had retired.

'Why difficult?' She winked at the barman who'd brought them complimentary drinks.

'With all those men slipping their leg between yours, waiting for the moment when you'd stand on one foot and wrap the other around their waist.'

'You mean, like this?' She wrapped her foot around Manuel's under the water. Then took a sip of her drink. 'For men, dancing is the same as gambling. It's all about fucking.'

Night-time was reserved for themselves—to drop the guard of all-day geniality that was on permanent display towards guests and be rude about them behind their backs, to do rude things to each other. It was also the hour for business.

'There's someone dangerous on the *Silver Cloud*,' Manuel reported to Selena one day.

'Dangerous as a bank robber? A jewel thief?'

'Worse.'

He had worn his black Houdini cloak and was on his way to the deck, Manuel said, when a man resembling the Incredible Hulk bumped into him in the corridor. 'Miroslav Babić fell on his knees, taking me for a priest. He needed to confess urgently, and I invited him to my room for a tête-à-tête.'

'What has he done?' Selena massaged her ankle, sore from tango.

'He is a mass murderer, a general who took part in the Yugoslav genocide. He has killed, raped, looted and has burnt down entire villages.'

'So he should be put away, shouldn't he? I bet the Interpol has a lookout notice with his name on it.'

Manuel nodded. 'He is a wanted man. He is our Eichmann.'

Selena stopped massaging and looked up at Manuel, 'You mean . . .?'

'He fits our business perfectly. We erase a man's past and give him a future, don't we?' Leaving the pool, Manuel towelled himself. 'I thought that's our mission.'

Floating on her back, Selena took in the weight of Manuel's words. When she finally spoke, she sounded well aligned with his thinking, 'That's all well and good, but can he pay?'

'He has diamonds, he has confessed.'

'The trick is to find a hiding place where no one would suspect you to be in.' Selena spoke wisely when they met in the employees' locker room in the afternoon between their shifts. 'Just think of Adolf Eichmann. Who'd think that he could become a car mechanic? The rich are expected to hide among the rich, the poor among the poor.'

'So where should Miroslav hide?'

'Here,' a bolt from the blue seemed to strike Selena as she answered Manuel, 'in the cruise ship!'

'Why here?' Manuel failed to understand, taking her answer to be yet another riddle.

'He'd be expected to be on the run. But not to be somewhere that keeps changing location and for a perfectly good reason.'

'But what would he be doing here? He can't simply remain as a permanent guest. It will raise eyebrows.'

'No, he can't. He must have a job.'

That was when Manohar, now Manuel, given his sharp eye, spotted a quality that his client possessed that could be put to good use. Miroslav, he found, was a regular at the ship's jazz bar. Tapping his legs and miming the musicians, he appeared to be a real aficionado with a knack for the music.

'Do you know how to play any instrument?' he asked the Yugoslav when he found him alone.

'Sax.' The hulk of a man mimed blowing through his mouth and tapping the keys with his fingers. The rest was easy: convincing a band that played its routine on a sister ship to take on Miroslav Babić as a saxophonist as a favour to be duly returned in not-too-distant a future.

Like Rajesh, aka Batsa Thapa, Miroslav too was puzzled when he heard of the arrangements from Selena and Manuel.

'I'll have to spend my whole life on a ship!' he asked, not believing the two.

'You don't really need to, do you?' Selena answered back. 'Not unless you want to stand trial at the Human Rights Court and spend the rest of your life in jail.'

'You'll have fun, you'll see!' Manuel tried to cheer him up. 'What a life it'll be, going from Jamaica to the Bahamas to St Maarten and Puerto Rico and Barbados and . . .'

It was all too much for Dhyanesh Mirdha, the state prosecutor, when Vandana Sathe, now Vandana Paranjpe, began debriefing him on her investigation.

'You mean the casino led you to the cruise ship?'

Vandana was used to slow-witted attorneys. Mr Mirdha carried the reputation of honesty and the additional burden of being a nitpicker.

'Yes, Sir. It started with a routine arrest of one Batsa Thapa from Nepal who'd stolen a car and crossed over our border in Raxaul. The BSF was about to hand him back to the Nepali side when he got into a needless argument with an officer.'

'So, he was beaten up?'

Vandana evaded answering directly. 'He was brought to Patna for cross-examination when his real name, Rajesh Chauhan, was revealed. It turned out that he was a wanted man, a gang leader on the run after he'd murdered an MLA's son. Rajesh told us about a couple of casino employees in Kathmandu who'd helped him escape.'

Mirdha had to ask her to slow down because he relied still on the old-fashioned way of taking notes by hand, but the details of the case set his ageing fingers racing. Taken to the Kathmandu casino,

Rajesh had identified a Jyoti Singh and Manohar Lele from their photographs as his accomplices, both of whom had left the casino together a couple of months after his disappearance.

'And, so, you sent out an appeal to Interpol to check casinos worldwide.'

Vandana nodded. 'But they couldn't find them anywhere . . . Las Vegas, Monte Carlo, Macau. The investigation reached a dead end.'

'And then?' Dhyanesh Mirdha poked his right ear with the blunt end of his pencil, expecting a breakthrough.

'The breakthrough came from an unexpected source. An alleged war criminal from Bosnia was arrested from a cruise ship in St Kitts. Miroslav Babić had confessed his crimes to a guest who was a southern Baptist evangelist. Babić told them about a dancer Selena Sanchez and the magician Manuel Lazaro, both of whom worked on the *Silver Cloud*.'

'Wait!' Mirdha raised his hand to stop Vandana from getting carried away. 'Neither of them worked as casino staff on the ship, did they?'

'No, sir. But they worked on the same business they'd started in Kathmandu, creating cover for criminals. Jyoti's and Selena's photographs matched, as did Manohar's and Manuel's. The trap was set to arrest them on the *Silver Cloud*.'

The ship would only make a night stop at St Maarten, a protectorate of the Kingdom of the Netherlands in the Caribbean. The guests could spend an hour on the Philipsburg pier to watch the sunrise before they set sail, but the staff were told to hold their stations on board.

Manohar was the first to spot the ocean blue uniform of the St Maarten's policemen who'd gathered at the landing docks. He ran to wake Selena up, told her what they'd suspected all along: Babić has cracked. He was no Eichmann. Given the extradition treaty that was already in place, the Dutch would hand them over to the Indians, and the game would be over. Escaping on the speedboats reserved for giving rides to the guests was the only way out, and by the time their rooms were raided, all that the police found were a pair of tango heels and a pack of cards.

It was unclear to the investigators, by now spread over several countries, how they'd managed to navigate the Caribbean Sea, helped perhaps by Cubans crossing over illegally on home-made boats from Punta de Judas to the Florida Keys. Some recalled the two of them jumping into the sea to evade the coastguards and swimming towards the sandy Cuban beaches, looking like a pair of dolphins.

Life in Havana might've been easier, without the police on their heels, but they'd have known of the other danger: being watched 24/7 by the state as possible spies of the big bad West. Plus, with all criminals locked away, there was no chance to carry on their business. For a whole year, they held hands and strolled on the Malecon, which reminded them of Bombay's Marine Drive, watching the amateur anglers. They haggled for crabs with fishermen, then came back to their flat in upscale Miramar to cook, eat, make love and sleep. They danced at the Tropicana bar, and everyone took them for light-skinned mulattos from one of the slave islands. It didn't take them long to get bored with life. Then, Selena hatched a plan.

Agostino Rossi from Ferrara, the city of the Italian Renaissance, had taken the most adventurous trip of his life and come to Havana looking for a little brown bride. He was nearing 50, a widower without children, an actuary with a comfortable but solitary life. Like fellow lovelorn tourists, he stayed at the Havana Hilton and hung around the city's bars. He'd drunk quite a few mojitos with quite a few prospects, including Selena.

'Your boyfriend belches badly and has bad breath,' Manuel teased Selena. 'He's a scrooge and won't even buy you a wedding dress. You'll have to walk the aisle in rented whites.'

'Who's talking about a wedding?' Selena pouted. 'We're talking about a spousal visa to the European Union. And one for you as the wife's brother.'

There were days when he grew bored watching Agostino and Selena lounge on the beach—he snoring and she painting her nails. There were nights when he felt like loading the gun that he'd bought in the black market and finishing off the fat Italian. Waiting for Selena at the foyer of the Hilton, he felt like a pimp. He hated her, hated himself.

'I'm doing this for our business,' she'd say, when the matter came up.

'I thought you were doing this for us,' he'd say, breaking the crab claws before setting them to boil in hot water.

'Do we want to rot in Havana then, as *señor* and *señora*?'

'Must you spend all day and half the night with that oaf?' He peeled the onions with a venom.

'He sleeps most of the day and night anyway. I think he suffers from sleep apnoea.'

'Would you have liked him to be roaring like an Italian stallion?' He stopped, arm raised with knife in hand.

'Don't show me your knife,' she barked back. 'I'm not afraid of it.'

When they fought, the house shook as if there was a cyclone.

In the end, Selena kept her word. There was no formal wedding, but a deed was drawn up at the Italian Embassy where both she and Agostino promised under oath to obtain a valid marriage licence once they reached Ferrara. The ambassador blessed the couple, toasted them with imported grappa, then patted Manuel on the arm. 'Your sister will give you a nephew soon!'

He gritted his teeth.

The rest was easy. At Rome airport, she desperately needed to visit the toilet and left her husband-to-be to collect their baggage. By the time he'd pushed the trolley out into the arrivals hall, she was gone, travelling in a Fiat taxi with Manuel, beyond anyone's reach.

'Their European crimes are well documented,' Dhyanesh Mirdha weighed the heavy Interpol file, then scolded his office boy for bringing milk tea when it was well known that he was allergic to milk.

'Yes,' Vandana looked up from her notes, 'but only after they'd been committed and the culprits had gotten away.'

She read through the section that described how the two—who by now were being referred to as Make-up Artists, given their knack for altering reality—had 'dressed up' a West African smuggler of blood diamonds as a minor-league footballer in Turkey. How they'd passed off an Afghan terrorist as a specialist in Dari language and found him a job in a reputable university. How they'd whitewashed the corporate crimes of a rogue trader from Hong Kong who'd sent millions down a sinkhole.

'How could they have done all this?' Mirdha asked in amazement.

'Because they possess an exceptional amount of common sense, which is the basic requirement for committing any crime,' Vandana replied, quoting from her detective's manual.

'What then explains their return to India?'

A call came from Mr Paranjpe, and Vandana excused herself to step out of the office for a few minutes. When she returned, she hesitated before answering the prosecutor's question.

'It could be just boredom, Sir. Or as my husband says . . .' she stopped in mid-sentence.

'What does he say?' Mirdha persisted, like a good prosecutor.

'He says, all species have a biological instinct to return to their origin where they were born. Sea turtles swim thousands of kilometres back to the shores where they'd hatched out of their mother's eggs. Snowbirds do the same. Elephants return to the bush where they were born to die.'

Europe or India? They debated which was better for business.

'I'd say Europe because it gives us more options,' Manuel, who was now privately back to Manohar, opined.

'I'd say India,' Jyoti disagreed. 'It has more crooks per square mile than any other country. Plus, the police aren't interested in catching criminals any more than taking bribes.'

When a business came up, the choice was made automatically. An American marine who'd deserted the Afghan war was holed up somewhere in Kashmir. His wealthy parents wanted to have him moved to Russia, where he'd be beyond the reach of American law. The multi-country operation demanded collaborating with other make-up artists and took a whole year to execute successfully. From Kashmir, our lovely pair came to Goa for a bit of a breather. The homing instinct took root there.

'I won't go under the knife,' Jyoti announced on their way over. The police would be on their lookout, but a plastic surgery was out of bounds for her.

Manohar agreed. They'd do the usual erasure trick—digital death, coupled with inventing a new persona. The middle class in India was the least suspected, they understood, given their utterly unspectacular lives and general absence of tragedy that afflicted the poor, bringing them into the limelight of newspaper headlines. Jyoti would become Urvashi, it was agreed between them. They'd live in a housing colony in a 2-BHK flat with a little balcony. She'd work from home as a hairdresser, doing manicure and pedicure for extra fees. She was trying to conceive, she'd tell nosy neighbours, which would invariably draw sympathy.

Manohar, now Martin Long, would pass himself off as her Anglo-Indian husband, a wedding photographer. Once they'd settled in, he left every morning in normal clothes carrying a bag with a suit and tie and fashionable shoes. He dressed respectably only if he managed to land a job, changing his clothes in an abandoned beach shack; the suited Martin bearing little resemblance to Urvashi's middle-class husband. He prowled the hotels, while she gossiped with the ladies indoors.

Perhaps it was no wonder that given her superior acting skills, Urvashi fitted into her role with minimum effort. An ordinary hairdresser, her business grew by leaps and bounds as the ladies enjoyed the time they spent chatting with her. She listened, never interrupting their agitation as they complained about wayward children, demanding in-laws and unfaithful husbands. The plainness of their lives brought out her dormant sentiments buried under layers of gloss. She felt sad and joyous for her friends, revelled in petty backbiting, felt truly blessed by their blessings for a child that might soon arrive.

Manohar fretted. Demand had fallen for wedding photographers with every bloke who owned an expensive camera taking himself for a Cartier-Bresson. Giving up on his daily routine, he'd sit at the beach and dream about the casino and the cruise ship. He heard the ringing of coins dropping from the slot machines, smelled the maddening scent of women, sensed the thrill of masked parties at the Venice Carnival and the glamorous walks on Milan's Via Monte Napoleone. Jyoti, he could sense, had come home, while he was still in flight.

'I thought we've come to India for business,' he complained.

'We have,' she answered from the kitchen. 'You are doing your business; I am doing mine.'

'I meant our joint business.'

'Oh, that!' she didn't utter a word the whole evening, then propped herself up on a pillow at night to express herself. 'All businesses, even successful ones, must end some day. Think about the Ambassador car that we grew up with. It has vanished from the roads. Or the HMT watch.'

'Yes, but they've been replaced by better things. While we have slipped back, further back than even Havana.'

Increasing the fan's speed, she returned to slump down beside him. 'Here, I have friends, whereas out there, I only knew crooks and fellow employees who didn't care if I lived or died as long as I could party hard with them. Here, I can spend months without having to plan an Eichmann.' She paused, then added, 'By the way, Eichmann did get caught in the end. As do all our clients—sooner or later.'

'So, what do you want?' Manohar wanted to get the words right out of her. Was she quitting their business once and for all or simply taking a vacation?

'We'll get caught too.' She sighed, turning her face to the window, which showed stormy clouds. 'It's a matter of time. Then we'll end up in jail—you in the male ward and I in the female. I knew it the day we packed off Rajesh Chauhan to the mountains. Even smart people get caught; that's the plain truth.' She turned around to kiss Manohar, but he moved away from her. 'Why not use a bit of warmth before we enter those cold cells?'

He hated Jyoti when she spoke like that. 'You don't shut down a successful business while it's still profitable,' he told her. 'If it goes bust, then it's just bad luck. Meanwhile you keep going.' Back on the prowl, he thought about blackjack—the trick of making players believe that you're about to quit when you aren't.

Then one day, he met Nusrat Khan on the beach.

Nusrat was her real name. Manohar found out after a determined effort when he finally got her to talk. Was she quiet by nature or quiet because she had a secret to hide, he wondered as she sipped pina colada at her hotel bar. She'd taken Manohar to be a hanger-on who sopped off drinks from tourists. Once he'd found out that she hailed from London, he offloaded his London logbook, which relaxed her considerably.

'You're the only one in India who knows about the Dogston bar,' she broke into a little laugh. 'Few know about it even in London.'

'You go there for the cocktails but stay for the company,' Manohar played her along.

'The very best people,' Nusrat nodded, taking a longer sip this time. 'Full of loving.'

Whom did she go to Dogston with? In the heart of Brixton, it was Black Britain at its best and rawest.

'My boyfriend loved it too,' she said and fell silent.

Looking around the bar, Manohar couldn't spot an obvious boyfriend. 'Is he here?' he asked.

'No,' she answered curtly and then remained silent for the rest of her drink.

Next day, it was the same story. Laughs over London, silence over boyfriend and family. It became a game with no winners until he decided to change tack and asked when she'd had her child and if the baby was here with her.

'How do you know I've had a child?' she appeared stung by a scorpion.

'By the stretch marks,' he pointed towards her tummy exposed by the bikini.

'Do you have a nanny who takes care of her while you are at the beach?' Manohar asked, sensing an opening.

She kept mum for a full minute, and then the words came tumbling out. She'd had the baby when she really shouldn't have. Her boyfriend Rex was against it too, but she'd always wanted to have a baby. Her family didn't know that she and Rex had married secretly in Minorca during a weekend trip that she'd hidden from the Khan clan because he was black. 'But my best friend betrayed me.' She looked downcast, and Manohar ordered her another drink.

'My brothers would've forced me to abort. They've taken the child away, given it up for adoption. Now they are after me. They will work with the Indian police to get me back to the UK.'

'What do you mean after you? To do what?'

Nusrat made the sign of a knife slicing her neck. 'Haven't you heard of honour killing?'

'So, you are on the run?' he ventured softly.

'You can say so,' Nusrat let her words drift after her as she left their table.

Manohar wanted to grab her right there but held himself back. *I am in business!* he told himself, and his heart skipped a beat.

Back home, he pretended to watch Jyoti's favourite soap opera with her, joined her friend Ranjita and her husband Jiten for dinner, took part in boring talk about housing society matters. His mind worked overtime. *Goa is the last place she should be in if she was hiding. Loads of gangsters get busted here. Wasn't Charles Sobhraj arrested in the infamous O'Coquerio restaurant? She should be in Gaya, not here.*

Jyoti's sharp eye caught his wandering. 'Are you thinking about business, dear?' she asked him in bed. 'This isn't the wedding season, but you can do family portraits right here in the society.'

He hated her for suggesting that he—the master of blackjack, the magician, the businessman—should take pictures of bored couples, toothless grandparents and rowdy children. Unknown to her, he had quit the wedding business months back although he still left home with his suit bag. It was simply his cover to fool Jyoti.

'I can save you from your brothers, but you have to trust me,' he told Nusrat the very next day. Then he read out the riot act to her, just as Jyoti and he had done to Rajesh Chauhan. Because the rich must hide among the poor, she ought to check out of her resort at once and move to a hostel he'd already rented in her name. Found her a job too.

'What job?' Nusrat sounded alarmed.

'As a warehouse worker, stuffing packages for home delivery.' He took his time to explain, 'The indoors job will keep you away from public sight. The police won't think to search for you there.'

'How long must I stay there?' she asked Manohar meekly.

'As long as it takes before we can find you a safer place to hide.'

Over the next two weeks, Manohar planned Nusrat's cover, relying on his vast experience. He went about building a new past for her, working out the details of family, education, hobbies and profession, keeping in mind her exquisite Indo-Persian look. She could be passed off either as a Lebanese now living in the Gulf or even a Greek Cypriot in Canada. He started working his string of contacts, making sure that the lines didn't get crossed with Jyoti's.

'You'll have a new name,' he told Nusrat, lounging on her narrow sofa in the rented hostel. 'You can choose from Aleyna, Leyla or Sonia.'

'Why can't I just be Nusrat?' she made a face. Then cradled Manohar and planted a kiss on his forehead.

By then they'd become close, closer than with any of his clients that he'd ever been. She'd wept over her strict upbringing in London— free on the outside but stifling inside. Her brothers kept a close watch on her; she was expected to marry within the clan—another Khan from somewhere in Pakistan or India. 'My brothers dated white girls before they married our own type, but it was different with me.' She told him, shaking all over while Manohar held her steady, about her cousin Rumi who was bumped off in Guildford because she had a child with a black man. 'They'll do the same to me. It's better that I die in Goa than at home.'

He comforted her. In a way, she comforted him too. For the very first time, he could see what his business really meant to his clients. Beyond the thrill of risky makeovers, he sensed something bigger, close to a divine truth: the ordainment of a second life, bestowed upon those who'd suffered in their first.

Once he'd removed all stains of intimacy from his bearings, they sipped the light tea that Nusrat preferred over the stronger variety that was to Manohar's taste. She seemed to be thinking deeply about something, then confided in him, 'There is a place we could go to where I won't have to change my name, change anything.'

She's fantasizing, he thought, and raised an eyebrow.

'Waverly, Iowa. It's a small town in the Midwest. My godmother lives with her American husband in a farm over there. She loves me like her own child, a child she never managed to have. She'll have us live with them forever.'

'But your brothers will know where you are.'

'They would, but they wouldn't be able to catch me there. They got mixed up in some police trouble in London and won't get American visas.'

Manohar drank two more cups of the light tea, then asked Nusrat, 'We?'

'Yes, we.' She answered, as if it was a foregone conclusion. Then mused, 'I wish I'd met someone like you before I met Rex. With him, it was always about him. With you, it's about me.'

Jyoti watched him closely. Observed the way he spoke: if he changed the subject or took his time answering what he'd done during the day. She waited for his comments when they sat down to eat: if he'd notice the extra chillies she'd put in the curry, which he disliked. Or when she made a light cup of tea. She went through his clothes, checked his fingernails when he was asleep to discover traces of intimacy. She asked her friends to spy on her husband, just like all of them spied on each other's. At night, she waited for him to make the moves when they made love. She would know if he'd been with another woman from the way his body accommodated hers. The body would give away the mind's secrets, she was certain.

Nusrat took to her warehouse job surprisingly well. Co-workers loved her for her generosity—willingly covering for their absence or agreeing to stay back and finish their jobs for them. She gave them vague answers when asked about her life, and they took her to be one of those 'foreign types' who get lost from time to time in Goa.

She met Manohar for a quick smoke after work, and then they returned together to her hostel. The plan was progressing swiftly, but he had to rework the original one. Now, she wouldn't need the standard 'erasure' method—no name or appearance change, not even that of her digital self. She'd simply need to board a flight from India to the US. There was no lookout notice in her name yet at the airports, his sources had confirmed to him. It was just a matter of picking a date, buying a ticket with cash and walking through the gates.

'What about you? Shall we travel together as a couple or separately?'

America! he marvelled. *Manhattan! The White House! Golden Gate Bridge! The Grand Canyon!* The real trick would be to keep it a secret from Jyoti. She should simply discover that he's gone when he's gone. Otherwise, she might pull one of her own tricks to keep him as prisoner in the housing society.

He'd picked a date, he told Nusrat. They'd travel by the same plane but check in separately. Once their flight had left, they could exchange seats and be together.

'Lovely!' she squealed in her girlish voice. 'We can snuggle up all the way over to America!'

'I saw your husband smoking with a lady who was also smoking.' A housing society friend brought in news, as Jyoti was painting Ranjita's nails.

'Did you see him near a hotel?' She wondered if Manohar had a wedding job and was killing time with an event management girl before things started.

'No, in front of the big warehouse,' she said.

'Was he wearing his suit?'

'No.' Her friend shook her head. Then she started telling the tale of another husband who'd lied to his wife about going to play cards with his friends but was caught smooching his girlfriend in a cinema hall.

Jyoti's eyes wavered off Ranjita's nails, smearing her fingertips by accident. 'Sorry,' she said, and brought out the nail polish remover.

'Have you gone back to business?' she asked Manohar in the evening, sounding casual.

He yawned, lounging in the balcony. 'What business! Young people aren't getting married these days; they are living together. At this rate, there won't be any weddings in the future.'

'I meant our kind of business.'

'I thought you weren't interested anymore,' he tried to shift the whole thing back to her. 'You are happy being a housewife.'

'So, have you decided to leave me out and do the business yourself?' she came out into the balcony and took his cup away.

He laughed or tried to. 'Show me a criminal and I might try. Goa is tame nowadays!'

'I'll kill you if you do. Remember that.' Her voice came from the kitchen accompanied with the sizzle of fresh fish frying in oil.

The noose is tightening around his neck, he felt lying beside Jyoti. She was smart, smarter than him. She was the brain behind their business. She'd know if her partner was moonlighting behind her back. She had become more than his partner now. Her new disguise as the wife has gotten stuck to her; she has become her disguise. And she was afraid now of her own trick—the trick of erasure; she didn't want to become anybody else anymore, not a partner or lover. She wanted to remain as his wife, like so many wives of so many husbands of the housing society. What if he told her about Nusrat? *Let the bitch go to hell!* He could hear her almost.

'I have set the date for our departure,' Manohar told Nusrat and showed her the tickets. 'It's tomorrow. You'll keep yours, and I'll keep mine.' With an eye on the watch, he hurried through the details: 'I'll come to pick you up in a hired car at 9 a.m. sharp from the warehouse at the end of your night shift. You'll change in the car. Carry no more than a small cabin bag.'

'Wait, don't go just yet!' she took a selfie of the two of them. 'This is the "before" picture. The "after" will be after our wedding in Waverly. It'll be in a church, and I'll be dressed in a white gown. My godmother will throw a feast afterwards.' She smothered him with kisses and whispered into his ear, 'You'll give me more stretch marks. Lots more!'

'It's our anniversary,' Jyoti said when Manohar asked why she'd cooked so many items for their dinner.

'Anniversary how?' He was surprised to hear.

'It's 7 years from that day when we sent Rajesh Chauhan off to the mountains. That was the day we got together.'

After many months, they had a surprisingly cheerful dinner, full of laughs, going all the way back to the comedy of Miroslav Babić's arrest. The poor guy had a thing about priests, felt an urge to confess when he met one! They giggled remembering the Hong Kong rogue trader, whose favourite dish was the snake-head soup. How he'd raided the eateries of Venice, where he was hiding and confided to a chef that he'd die if he couldn't eat a snake! The chef, unfortunately, was an informer, employed by the Italian Intelligence Service to rat out the mafia.

'I wonder sometimes who the real fools were—our clients or us!' Jyoti sighed as she cleared out the dishes.

That night was special. As they made love, Manohar couldn't help but notice Jyoti's fury, wringing out every ounce of pain that seemed to have invaded her unnoticed by him. As if her spirit had broken up into many parts, some that were loving, others bent on erasing herself along with her husband. Her soul was dying one breath at a time, urging itself on towards a total annihilation. He felt scared of her, grabbed her with all his might, found himself sinking in the memory of loss.

She knew where Manohar kept the gun that he'd bought off a foolish rich boy from Bombay. It was a sharpshooter's weapon. It took her less than a few minutes to assemble the parts, and then she was off following Manohar, who'd given the excuse of an early morning wedding job. Ranjita asked her where she was going with her shopping bag as the markets were yet to open. 'To the beach,' she answered, 'to get fresh crabs from the fishermen bringing in their nets, before they sell them to the fishmongers at double the price.'

'Your hubby must be loving you extra these days if you're feeding him crabs!' Ranjita smiled.

She knew Manohar's secret beach hut. It was abandoned after a cyclone and barely held on to its reed roof. They had made love there once, one full moon night. That's where he'd go to change his clothes before leaving her for good.

He took extra care to tie the double Windsor knot, because a clumsy one always gave a pretender away. His suit, which he had ironed himself, was in a satisfactory condition. He wetted his handkerchief to add a final gleam to the brogues. Out in the sun, he felt the urge for a smoke and a lie down on the cool beach to take in the sun—the Indian sun before he met the American one. He heard the clamour of fishermen bringing in the day's catch, the cackle of a boy building sandcastles, the splashing sound made by lovers testing the waves. He wouldn't have heard the crack of the gun that had followed him from the shack and was trained on his temple. The shot that killed him left him with no final thought except that of freedom.

Clearing his throat, Dhyanesh Mirdha asked an attendant to reduce the fan's speed as he was on the verge of catching a cold.

'What happened to Nusrat?' he asked Vandana, who was tiring after her long report. 'Did she manage to escape to Iowa or wherever she wanted to go?'

'No, Sir,' Vandana shook her head. 'Jyoti had already tracked her down to the warehouse based on her friend's tip-off. She had caught her chatting with Manohar. She had visited her hostel secretly and entered her room when she was out. She had smelled Manohar's presence there.'

'So, she must've . . .' Mirdha looked her in the eye.

'After she had shot and killed Manohar, she went to the warehouse and waited for Nusrat. When she left as planned, she killed her too. Then dumped the body in the used packing bins outside. The warehouse didn't lodge a police complaint when she didn't report for duty, taking her for a floater who'd left Goa. The garbage handlers found the body. We did our routine forensic and document checks to establish that she was Nusrat Khan, a tourist from the UK, visiting India on a 3-month visa.'

'That explains how the two murders were committed,' the prosecutor cleared his blocked throat, before asking the harder question. 'But how did you know that Jyoti was the killer?'

Vandana Paranjpe paused for a few minutes before answering. Reaching inside her file, she took out something and placed it on the desk. 'By this, Sir.'

'What is it?' Mirdha frowned.

It was the visiting card she had prised out of Manohar's waistband. Turning it over, she showed the word scribbled on it—Oxblood.

'We sent it for forensic examination where it was revealed that the word had been written very recently with the tip of a lipstick, the colour of Oxblood red. It's a rare colour, not many women use it generally. A dark shade of red—it looks like burgundy with brown and purple undertones.'

'And so?' Dhyanesh Mirdha, a lifelong bachelor, didn't understand too much about lipsticks.

'We matched the colour to Jyoti Singh's casino photos and those of Selena Sanchez from the *Silver Cloud*. They matched. It was her favourite colour. She was here in Goa we knew and must've asked Manohar to get one for her.'

Vandana described the routine police procedures that had been followed: 'We checked all the shops. Only a high-end boutique had that shade. We staked it out, hoping she'd come to buy her favourite lipstick. Policewomen were trained to serve as shop girls. I pretended to be a shopper. It took a few days, but our hunch proved to be right.'

'When she finally came, looking like an ordinary lady, we couldn't believe we were looking at an internationally wanted criminal!' One of Vandana's young assistants couldn't resist, and blurted out the operation's details. 'I was one of the shop girls. I showed her many shades. She was only interested in the darker reds. I offered her a Dior 999, Hot Mama, Dragon Red and Ruby Woo worn by Rihanna. But she wasn't happy and kept asking for Oxblood. That's when Vandana Ma'am came up to her and took out the lipstick from her own purse and showed it to her.'

'I've got Oxblood,' I told Jyoti. 'Do you want it?' Vandana let out a rare smile. 'She knew her game was up. On interrogation, she confessed to both the murders.'

Resting his temple on his palm, Mirdha asked, 'So the motive was?'

'Jealousy, Sir.'

'Was it?' the elderly man pondered over the matter. Then he muttered to himself, 'Or was it sacrifice?'

Returning to his prosecutor self, Dhyanesh Mirdha asked Vandana how the victim should be named. 'Should we call him Manohar Lele or Manuel Lazaro or Martin Long?'

No one knew the answer to that question. Exhausted by now after the rather long session, Vandana rose to leave, saying, 'Let's just call him the Dead Man in a Suit.'

PATNA

As he sat on the bus travelling from the city's western suburb to the airport, the morning's events flashed through Rishi's mind like the madly spinning reel of a film. Like all days that spelt chaos, the morning had been deceptively calm. He had risen to the sing-song of his neighbour's bird, jumped the queue to the communal toilet complaining of an upset stomach and then secured a seat, miraculously, on the congested local train on his way to work. Haste was a common refrain in the life of Bombay residents, and his morning was no different from that of millions who found peace in the daily hassle of the city. On that day though he was doubly keen to reach his office before the padlock had been opened by the talkative security guard, ever ready to offer a rundown of noteworthy events—from bank heist to waterlogging. It was Rosy's, Rosalind Yasmin de Rosario's, birthday, and Rishi wished to reach her cubicle next to their boss's plush office before the employees arrived. He had spent a whole week scouting for a proper birthday card and struck gold with one shaped like a pink rose that allowed the petals to be opened to pen one's greetings inside. *May you always feel happy and never sad*, he wrote, signing off with *your loyal friend Rishi*.

Most of the day was spent waiting, Rishi recalled, while travelling on the airport bus. From his own cubicle, a good 50 yards away from Rosy's, her face was visible only in profile. True to Monday morning rush, she could be seen stacking up files for the boss to sign, taking calls, reaching inside her purse for a breath freshener after her tea. Had she dropped the card, left by Rishi on her table, into the wastepaper bin, mistaking it for junk mail? He sat through the whole morning, forfeiting a cigarette break, just to keep an eye on her. By noon, waiting had turned to despair. His thoughts strayed over to several birthday cards he'd left for female colleagues in the past, hoping for a favourable outcome. For an out-of-state person like him, who hailed from a city far from Bombay, without family or friends who might assume the task of matchmaking, he saw the birthday card as his only hope. A card followed by an invitation to tea, a stroll in the nearby park, trips to the mall in the guise of shopping, ending with the final arrangement.

By 3 in the afternoon, he had given up on his prospect and returned to the thorny business of balancing the firm's monthly ledger when Rosy walked down those fifty yards to his cubicle. Taking just a moment to recover, Rishi was about to wish her on her special day, when she cut him short.

'Mr Manjrekar is waiting to speak with you. He has asked you to come at once.'

'Me?' Rishi stuttered.

'Yes, you,' Rosy answered in a matter-of-fact way and walked a step ahead of him to the boss's office.

Like all employees, past and present, Rishi feared his boss. He had the habit of asking awkward questions, giving his employees no time to think before providing the answer himself with an air of disdain. As an MBA, he assumed a rightful superiority over his graduate employees and fell into lecturing them on topics that had nothing to do with their daily business. Normally, he allotted no more than 3 minutes to Rishi whenever he was summoned to his office, but on that day, he asked him to take a seat and came around to lay a hand on his shoulder.

He will fire me, Rishi thought, offer some kind of business logic that was beyond his comprehension. Maybe he's found out about the birthday card and the several before this one and concluded that he was a threat to his female staff.

'Word has come from our Patna office about your mother,' Mr Manjrekar paused, rubbing his hand on Rishi's shoulder blade by way of a massage. 'Your uncle has been trying to contact you by phone from your hometown, but something appears to be wrong with your number. He is trying to pass on an urgent message to you.'

'What message, Sir?' Rishi managed to ask.

'Your mother is sick,' Mr Manjrekar's voice turned a touch gentler. 'She has been taken to the hospital. Maybe it's nothing very serious. Could be the pathogenesis of a condition beyond the patient's bandwidth.'

Rishi's eyes widened, unable to follow what Mr Manjrekar meant. Standing beside him, he could sense Rosy nodding her head in agreement.

Returning to his seat, Mr Manjrekar adjusted his tie and spoke calmly. 'No matter her condition, you must go to Patna and assess the situation first-hand. Rosy has already bought your ticket, and you can leave now to collect your things from home and head off to the airport.'

'The flight leaves at 7.45 p.m. It's the only one to Patna from Bombay this evening.' On cue, Rosy handed Rishi his ticket and turned on her heels to return to her cubicle.

'I'm sure things will be fine back home,' Mr Manjrekar concluded his 5-minute meeting with Rishi, adding, 'We'll consider your absence as a casual leave.'

Dazed by the event, Rishi took the wrong turn as he left Mr Manjrekar's office, reaching the staff toilet at the end of the corridor, which was shut for cleaning. Then he retraced his steps back to his seat, passing by Rosy's desk. The birthday card, he found to be still sitting at the exact spot he'd left it, yet unopened.

Rapid Air's counter was busy when Rishi arrived, and a family of ten had engaged the staff in a lengthy discussion on allowable weight of their many suitcases. A young boy had climbed atop the luggage piled high on the trollies and was hanging upside down like a monkey. Fortunately, there was still time at hand before the boarding call, and Rishi could afford to wait. He had packed a small suitcase—the only one he possessed and had come to Bombay with a year back—with a change of clothes, his favourite book of Hindi film lyrics that he'd bought second-hand from a Flora Fountain pavement stall and a torch that he carried with him on all occasions. Together, they weighed no more than 9 kilograms, well below the 25-kilogram bar.

The electronic board announcing arrivals and departures was busy, flights rolling over every second showing their status. It made Rishi nervous. Used to the leisurely passage of trains in his younger days, when he'd go on holiday with his parents or visit his grandparents in Gaya, he preferred the unhurried shuffle of the lumbering giants leaving the platform at snail's pace, allowing a laggard or two to jump in safely. Airports filled him with unease, made him consult his watch frequently for no reason.

Luckily, a new counter opened as the family lay embroiled at the existing one, and a young lady waved Rishi over.

'Where are we going today?' she asked, smiling at Rishi in the exact manner they'd been taught to smile: showing a hint of teeth but not the molars. 'Ah, Patna! That's my husband's hometown.'

Rishi's heart sank. All eligible women had already been snared by Patna men, except him.

'Do you prefer a window or an aisle?'

Normally, he preferred a window. It gave him a view of the world one couldn't recognize with one's feet on the ground. Also, seeing the clouds close-up made him happy, reminded him of songs sung by lovers in films before they were drenched by the rain.

This time, he preferred an aisle seat, just so he could leave the aircraft quickly and join the queue for a shared taxi ride home.

'No problem,' the counter lady smiled again. 'We have lots of seats available.'

RA 333 to Patna would board from Gate 11B, and he should be there 20 minutes before departure time. 'You can have a snack while you wait,' the smiling lady handed him a boarding pass and wished him a safe flight.

Rishi avoided eating at airport restaurants, which ripped you off and gave no satisfaction. A sandwich might cost Rs 350. Rs 200 for a plain dosa was more than excessive. Teabag tea tasted like drain water. Plus, he wasn't hungry. Sudhakar Apte's wife, who shared the room next to his, had fed him a healthy meal of rice, lentil and vegetable fries and offered to pack some fruits for his journey. He had refused, uncertain of what view airport security staff might take of bananas.

Descending via the escalator to the gate area, he found the hall packed with passengers waiting for their flights. Gate 11B was at the far end of the hall, with just two more beyond it. A slither of space was free on the lounge seats with frayed Rexine covers and, settling down, Rishi asked the man next to him.

'Travelling to Patna?'

'No, Amritsar.' The man pointed to the board above the counter. RA 332 to Amritsar, it read.

'But I was told to come to 11B,' Rishi was confused.

'It must be the next flight after Amritsar.' The man answered and went back to reading a slim pamphlet.

Passengers milled aimlessly around, waiting for their gates to open and secure an advanced position in the queue. Unnecessary congestion along the corridor led to frayed tempers. Children pestered their parents for ice cream, and the seller of bottled water made brisk business. The assorted chaos allowed Rishi to think about his mother.

'You must go to Bombay and take up your job,' his mother, Mandira Aunty to all concerned, had told him when Rishi had showed her the appointment letter for the office accountant's job. 'Your friends are all leaving. Mukesh is off to Bangalore and Suman to Kolkata, where he'll put criminals in jail working as a law clerk. Boys are going to Dubai and returning with gold bars.'

'But who'll take care of you?' Rishi had asked, remembering the promise he'd made to his dying father.

'You will,' his mother had replied in a flash. 'One phone call, and you'll come to Patna if anything bad happens to me.'

Swatting a fly that was drawn to Gate 11B by the smell of fruits from someone's hand luggage, Rishi rued the mishap that had smashed up his phone, dropping it by accident from his balcony as he was trying to catch a kite that was flying by, its string cut by a rival in a kite fight. Not only did the screen crack but the logic board inside also suffered some damage, and the repair shop mechanic told him to leave it behind for a week at least.

In the absence of his phone, Rishi fidgeted with the boarding pass and regretted not being able to look up 'pathogenesis' in Google. Maybe it had something to do with the heart? Or her knees, which swelled up during winter. His grandmother had died of cancer and the thought of a congenital inheritance made him shudder. The man sitting beside him shuddered too as he scanned the pamphlet of horse-racing odds.

Sharp at 6.45 p.m., an army of primly dressed airline staff arrived at the departure hall and took up position behind the counters. The air rang with their shrill announcements. RA 412 would be leaving from Gate 3A for Jabalpur, RA 666 from Gate 4B to Guwahati, RA 1091 from Gate 10A to Madurai. RA 457 to Lucknow was running late, and passengers were told to keep their eye on the electronic screen. Passengers of gates 3A, 4B and 10A jostled to form queues despite repeated pleas by the staff to hold still until their seat numbers were called.

'Amritsar always leaves on time,' the man next to Rishi sounded smug. 'It's not a hopping flight, accumulating delays by stopping and picking up passengers from different cities like a local bus.'

'And Patna?' Rishi hesitated before asking. Maybe the man who seemed to be a veteran flier would know.

Returning to the pamphlet, the man shrugged, 'Never been there. It's out of my circuit.'

A young lady had arrived with her baby in a stroller, and Rishi gave up his seat to her. Then went to the gent's toilet between

Gates 7 and 8. He waited for his turn at the urinal and stared hard at the mirror after washing his hands. His mother would find him unchanged from the time he left Patna a year back. His cheeks were yet to turn puffy from the fatty snacks that Bombay people enjoyed. A darkish circle had formed under his eyes, which was a result, he knew, of watching too many late-night movies. Other than that, his haircut was the only change she'd see—the taper-and-fade Virat Kohli style, close-trimmed at the bottom, blending into a generous crop at the top of the head.

A cleaner came into the toilet pushing his cart—an elderly man with a pair of droopy, sad eyes. Rishi left to return to the departure hall.

He found Gate 11B empty. Within minutes, all passengers had disappeared, including the man with the horse racing pamphlet. The sign announcing the Amritsar flight was gone too. How could so many have boarded the flight so quickly while he was in the toilet? There wasn't a single laggard in sight, which was unusual and contrary to the Indian way of being late for appointments. It was nothing short of a miracle! A lady sweeping the debris of empty chips packets, newspapers and candy wrappers pointed towards the airplane on the tarmac outside the glass pane when he asked where everybody had gone.

Traffic was moving at the other gates, with more shrill announcements. An airline staff was striding down the hall warning all passengers for Guwahati to board immediately without delay. Making his way up to the counter of Gate 10A, Rishi asked the ground staff about the Patna flight.

'He's jumping the queue!' a young man who also sported a taper-and-fade complained. Shaking his head vigorously, Rishi tried explaining, 'I'm not travelling to Madurai, Sir, I only came to ask . . .'

'The Patna flight, RA 333 has been delayed,' the counter lady checked her departure chit and asked him to wait for further announcements. This time she didn't offer a smile, refusing to answer any more questions.

Returning to Gate 11B, Rishi slumped on a seat and put his carry-on beside him as there was no shortage of space. Had the flight left on time, he'd have reached Patna by 10.15 p.m. as it took just under two and a half hours to cover the distance. It would've been easy to get a shared taxi at that hour, even a bus that'd take him within a mile of his home. Now, he didn't know. After midnight, it'd be hard to find any transport whatsoever. He might have to call his friend Atul to fetch him on his bike. But how would he call his friend without his phone?

By then it was 7.20 p.m. The sun had set and the tarmac outside the hall's glass window was lit by the runways' floodlights and the blinking strips that led an aircraft to its bay. Exhausted by the day's events, Rishi peered out at the bustle of activities: workers in overalls were loading an airplane, chatting happily among themselves. A couple of pilots inspected the aircraft, walking around its wings and gazing up. A bus was inching its way towards the plane's ladder carrying the stewardesses, and he saw them wearing the prim maroon uniform of Rapid Air.

He was in the wrong job, Rishi concluded. Not an office accountant, he should've become an airline mechanic. That way, he wouldn't have had to spend his days cooped up inside an office, but out on the tarmac in the company of these giant birds. Perhaps he'd have become friends with one of the stewardesses on her way to Bhubaneshwar or Coimbatore, even Patna, and offered her a birthday card. The romance of the airline job lulled him into a snooze, and he woke with a start at the announcement: *All passengers are advised to keep their luggage with them at all times, and report any suspicious item to the airport authorities.*

Rishi found the departure hall deserted. Gates 1 to 13 didn't have any staff or passengers. The boards that featured the destinations had been taken down. Nagpur, Cochin, Kolkata, Gwalior, Hyderabad, Lucknow—each and every one of them. The electronic departure screen had gone blank. The ice cream stall had shut, and the bottled water seller had vanished too. Jumping up, Rishi scanned from right to left to spot a living soul. Only the cleaning lady, bent waist downwards, was sweeping the boarding area between Gates 2 and 3. Leaving his hand luggage on the lounge seat, he ran the length of the hall towards the far end, zigzagging past the cleaning trollies left behind by bathroom attendants. 'Listen!' he shouted at the lady, but by the time he reached Gate 3, she seemed to have disappeared into thin air.

Rishi checked his watch. It was 7.40 p.m. Just 5 minutes before the scheduled departure time to Patna. Surely, they couldn't have cancelled the flight without informing the passengers. Nor those of the other flights, all of which couldn't have left at the same time! He recalled seeing departure times on the screen as late as 9 or 10 p.m., even midnight. Bombay airport never sleeps, he'd been told by friends; it was the busiest in the country.

He felt disoriented for a few moments, till he sensed the lift's light blinking, on its way up from the departure area to the main hall. He made a dash towards it, but just then—at that very moment— the lights went out, plunging the entire departure hall into darkness.

Blinded, Rishi caught himself just in the nick of time before colliding against a row of lounge chairs. Cold sweat ran down his spine. Strobe light from a plane's signal filtered in through the panes and ran a ghostly pattern on the wall. Unlike the interiors, life on the tarmac seemed to proceed just as before with aircrafts taxiing down the runway and men loading the holds of the stationary ones.

'Hello!' Rishi shouted, hoping to catch someone's ear. 'Patna passenger here!' The echo of his voice beamed back from the glass panes.

Wild thoughts ran through his mind. Maybe they've shut down the airport due to a bomb threat. Perhaps a team of detectives will arrive soon with sniffer dogs, go from gate to gate, check the toilets even. But why didn't anyone wake him up as they must've dashed out of the hall? He was more than visible, he was certain, in his orange and black chequered shirt, and his carry-on—a fake Adidas kitbag— in electric blue, the colour of Chelsea Football Club. In the few moments that he needed to recover his mind, Rishi thought of the escalator. That would be his escape route, the path that had brought him down would take him up to the main hall. But he needed to recover his carry-on first. As he made his way back towards Gate 11B, there seemed to be more cleaning trollies haphazardly parked along the corridor. Someone had upturned a bucket of water on the floor, and he had to tread cautiously to avoid slipping. Finding his gate in the dark was no easy matter, and he made several false moves, scanning the lounge chairs before finally spotting his Chelsea Football Club kitbag.

The escalator's switch was turned off, and Rishi started to climb up the steel-plated steps. It felt better with each step, as if he was rising up from an abyss into the living lights. About halfway up, he felt something move underneath his feet—at first slowly, then picking up speed like a sleeping beast coming to life. It was the escalator. It had started to move, activated somehow by a switch. But it was moving in the wrong direction—downwards instead of up. The force of gravity pulled him back and threatened to buckle his knees, forcing him to grab on to the rails. Turning back somehow, he sprinted down, stumbling as he fell in a heap at the bottom of the escalator. Like a man gazing up from the bottom of a well, Rishi saw a shadowy figure at the top of the escalator. It was the cleaner he'd seen at the toilet—the elderly man with a pair of sad, droopy eyes pushing his cleaning cart.

His life flashed before Rishi's eyes as he lay on the floor of the departure hall. A life shrouded in darkness, dreaming of a grand illumination. From the hovel of a room in Bombay that he had managed to rent with his meagre salary to the tiny cubicle of his office, he'd lived in confinement. The darkness had closed in on him every time he'd wished to escape. He felt jealous of the betting man who must have reached his home in Amritsar. Of the passengers enjoying the company of friends and relatives in Madurai, Guwahati, Cochin and Kolkata, dining out in restaurants, strolling in parks or simply enjoying the breeze from their balconies. And here he was, cloistered in a dark hall, cut off from everyone—Mr Manjrekar and Rosy, Sudhakar Apte and his wife and his mother. None could ever imagine that he might have to spend a very long time, a whole night even, in the prison of the departure hall. His stomach growled with the distant memory of Mrs Apte's meal.

On the verge of giving up to his fate, Rishi saw the light. He'd simply have to walk all the way back to Gate 11B, then climb up the stairs adjacent to it to the main hall. It'd be safer than the temperamental escalator or the lift, which might trap him inside and suffocate him to death. His steps rang loud in echo as he traipsed through the hall and held firmly on to the rails, managing to reach the top of the stairs. There he was, finally, where he had started, lining up at the Rapid Air counter and receiving his boarding pass from the smiling lady.

'Mr Rishi Sarin?' A ground staff from Rapid Air stood at the top of the stairs, clipboard in hand, as if waiting for Rishi.

'You are late, your flight is about to close,' she spoke impatiently. 'You must go to Gate 57 on the upper floor immediately if you want to board your flight. Otherwise, your baggage will be offloaded.' Pointing up and away to the left, she made a gesture with her arm implying a rapid transit. Then she disappeared just as suddenly as she'd appeared.

Rishi ran. Dashed rather, bounding through the main hall. He passed the check-in counters of all the airlines serving domestic routes, swerved his way past the showroom for athletic ware, the leather goods boutique, the glass cases full of 18-carat gold jewellery. The food court was on his way, but he didn't think to stop for a quick bite or even drink from the water fountain. Although it was barely 8 p.m., he didn't notice too many passengers or security guards, just legions of cleaners sweeping the floors and making their way in and out of toilets.

Gate 57, at the end of a passage that bore no signage, was the best kept secret of the airport and reaching it finally, Rishi found a pair of ground staff waiting at the entrance of the sky bridge. Neither

of them smiled at him; they checked his boarding pass, eyed his hand
luggage for size restriction and then waved him on. Heart pounding,
he reached the aircraft just before the hatches were firmly shut.

'Seat 14C will be to your right, Sir,' the maroon-uniformed
attendant pointed Rishi to his aisle seat. Thrusting his kitbag into the
overhead bin, he collapsed in his seat and heaved the heaviest sigh
of relief in his life.

'You must fasten your seat belt and keep your seat upright
for take-off.' He could barely hear the instructions clearly and
followed them in a trance. As the aircraft began to taxi down the
bay, he collected himself, wiping off the sweat from his face with
his handkerchief, and breathed normally. The ordeal was finally
over, and he praised his luck for making the flight in the nick of
time. Then, he looked around, left to right, to check up on fellow
passengers, craned his neck backwards to the far end of the plane,
examined every aisle, middle and window seat. He was alone, he
realized, absolutely alone—the sole passenger of flight RA 333 from
Bombay to Patna.

'You must sit down, Sir. Immediately!' The stewardess poked her
head out of the galley as Rishi stood up in agitation. 'We are about
to take off.'

'Where are the passengers?' he managed to shout through the
roar of the engines before the forward thrust jolted him back on
his seat. *We have lots of seats available*—the Rapid Air counter lady
had told him during check-in. Did she mean *all* seats were available,
that not a single soul wished to fly from Bombay to his hometown?
Even for someone unversed in worldly matters, the whole thing
seemed incredulous. As the state capital, the city of his birth boasted
trading firms and big companies with head offices in Bombay. There
were more than two dozen daily flights between the two cities.
Workers came to do menial jobs; the streets of Bombay were full of

policemen, electricians, auto drivers and even executives and film stars who greeted each other in the favourite dialect of their much-beloved Patna. He had expected a crowded cabin, with little room in the overhead compartments to stow his kitbag, not 200 seats all to himself and row upon row of empty lockers.

'We are experiencing some unexpected turbulence, and all passengers are requested to keep their seat belts fastened and refrain from using the toilets. Cabin service will begin once we reach cruising altitude.' The captain's voice came from the cockpit. Rishi gazed out of the window into a dark, cloudless sky. Used to joyrides on the giant wheel as a child, turbulence didn't worry him. He enjoyed the bumps and sudden lurches, took it as a joyous part of flying. But now, the dark exterior filled him with foreboding. It reminded him of the airport's departure hall, the sudden blackout and his solitary confinement within it. Used to a busy city with bustling bodies all around, he craved for the crowds, the rude shoving of elbows on local trains, the unwelcome breath of a stranger packed tightly close to him. Most of all, he worried how long the flight would last. He was afraid to check his watch. On a day when nothing had gone to plan—from the birthday card to the airport saga—he shuddered to foresee what the night had in store.

When the stewardess brought him a snack, Rishi was still stuck in his stupor and couldn't manage to ask the question that clawed at his throat. 'We shall be landing shortly,' the stewardess, who was smiling now, said and applied a gentle push on the backrest of his chair to set it upright.

Landing in Patna made all the difference to Rishi's mood.

As the sole passenger, deplaning was easy, and he rushed out of the aircraft without even a nod of thank you to the stewardess. Freshly painted white walls welcomed him into the terminal building. Sparkling new glass windows sported stickers with the name of their manufacturer. The smell of paint was suffocating, but Rishi felt proud. There was talk about building a new terminal to replace the old one, but he hadn't expected it to be ready so soon.

People are quick to blame the government but slow to praise its good work, he mused, striding quickly to reach the baggage claim area. A lady, wearing a brand new uniform, pointed to the left as signs hadn't been put up yet on the walls. Turning left led to a large door that was shut. Retracing his steps, he found the lady gone and climbed up a set of stairs to a hall with a sign that read 'Danger Area'. Without any fellow passengers, there were none to guide him through the new terminal, not even the crew of RA 333. It must've been a hopping flight, Rishi surmised, which had left Patna already for some onward destination. By the time he managed to reach the baggage area and collect his suitcase turning circles on the conveyor belt like a lost orphan, it was already 11.30 p.m.

The prepaid taxi counter was vacant, just as he had expected. There were no signs of private cars that fleeced unsuspecting passengers. The last airport shuttle had left according to the posted schedule. Not even a beggar was in sight as Rishi stepped out of the airport. He felt desperate having travelled for so long and so far, only to be thwarted at the doorstep of his destination. The thought of going back into the terminal to look for a phone booth to call Atul made him nervous, the prospect of getting lost, yet again, too large a risk to venture. He must wait six more hours till daybreak to resume his journey; he felt resigned to search for a bench to stretch his legs.

Barely had he closed his eyes for a snooze when a three-wheeler rambled into the pick-up zone, its engine sputtering to a stop. An elderly man with a broken face and sad eyes stuck his head out of the driver's seat. 'Patna?' the man asked Rishi.

'How far is it from here?' Rishi asked back. The man scratched the stubble on his chin before replying, '17 kilometres. Rs 150.'

'100.' Rishi tossed his bag into the auto and jumped in.

Later, he didn't recall much of the journey, except that it was conducted mostly through a roll of mist that enveloped the highway. The auto's feeble headlamp barely lit up a dozen feet of asphalt, showing an occasional tail light of a car that had overtaken them. Buses sped past in either direction—interstate carriers with passengers sleeping on reclining seats and their luggage riding on the roof, secured firmly by nylon rope. He wished he'd returned the Rapid Air ticket to Rosy and taken the bus. The journey would've taken longer, but he would be in the company of fellow passengers. If he was lucky, there might've been a doctor among them who could've explained to him the meaning of pathogenesis. Once or twice, he tried engaging his driver in small talk but failed to catch his replies in the whizzing breeze. *When was the new terminal built? How far is it from the old one? How much time did they have remaining before they reached Frazer Road in the heart of Patna?* It seemed pointless asking questions.

Leaving the highway, the auto bounced over a dirt track and came to a stop before a villa. Nestled among woods, it was too well appointed for its out-of-the-way location. A driveway led to an enormous door. It seemed like the home of a plantation owner or an opium baron from British times. The auto driver cut the engine and demanded Rs 100.

'But this isn't Patna!' Rishi protested.

The man shook his head. 'It is transit house. Passengers come here to wait for their next destination. They are given food and a place to rest.'

'Do you mean this is Rapid Air's hotel for those who've missed their connections?'

The auto driver didn't have an answer to Rishi's question. Counting the money, he gave Rishi a sad stare then restarted his engine and left.

It was better to spend the night at transit house than on a bench outside the airport, Rishi thought. The maroon-uniformed ground staff will surely help him reach Patna next morning and he'd visit his mother at the hospital. Dragging his suitcase, he went up to the door and rang the bell. It was already quarter past midnight.

The man who opened the door didn't seem upset at Rishi's late arrival. Scratching his arms, itchy from mosquito bites, he asked for his flight number.

'Ah, RA 333? For Patna from Bombay. It had departed late owing to delayed arrival of the aircraft.' He seemed to know the details of the flight, which reassured Rishi. Then, consulting some imaginary ledger, he pointed upwards, 'The third room upstairs is for Patna passengers.' Refusing the man's offer to carry his suitcase, Rishi trudged up the stairs, entered through the unlocked door of the assigned room and crashed on the bed. Exhausted by the day, he fell instantly into a deep and dreamless sleep.

Rishi woke next morning to the singing of Bhairav from the adjoining balcony. It was a morning raga, the purest of the pure, as his father used to say. Ramu, the man who'd showed him into the house last night, came to the room with bed tea and told him all about the singer.

'It's Chandrakanth Mishra. He's a famous singer of the Benaras *gharana*. He is travelling from Varanasi to Delhi to attend the thread ceremony of his grandson.' Swaying his head to the music, he added, 'He wakes everyone up and puts them to sleep with his singing. But you must be careful with him.'

'Why careful?' Rishi sipped his tea.

'Because he is an astrologer as well and a terrible one at that! He'll ask about your birth details and cast your horoscope. Then he'll tell everyone in the house all about your bad qualities.'

The rest of the passengers were waiting to meet Rishi, Ramu said, and announced that breakfast would be served soon downstairs.

Throughout the morning, Rishi met the passengers one by one. There was Mrs Purnima Sen from Kolkata, who sat next to him at breakfast and brightened up at the mention of Patna. 'I have two nieces and a cousin who are married to Patna men. Their husbands are solid and take very good care of their families.' She asked Rishi if he was married, then squinted her eyes as if performing a rapid calculation.

'Are you going to Patna too?' Rishi felt relieved having found a co-traveller.

'No, no. I'm off to Ahmedabad and would've reached there by now if I hadn't missed the flight connection. I have important business there,' she pursed her lips and smiled impishly. 'If I don't reach Ahmedabad, a poor boy and a poor girl may remain unmarried for life!'

Rohit, the magician, leaned over to Rishi overhearing their conversation. 'Mrs Sen is an expert matchmaker. Her mission in life is to get everyone married!'

'Really!' A load started to lift off Rishi's chest.

'You mustn't trust everything Rohit Shetty says,' Ramu drew Rishi aside after breakfast and gave him the low-down on the magician. 'His job is to fool others. Like drawing a rabbit out of a hat. Or changing a shoe into a sparrow.'

'What is he doing in transit house?' Rishi quizzed Ramu. He gave a broad smile. 'He may be a magician but is quite foolish really. He was travelling to Kathmandu, where he claims to have a regular gig entertaining hotel guests but forgot that there are no daily connections through the airline hub. He is waiting for the next available flight.' Mrs Sen, apparently, had almost finalized a match for him, but he turned out to be a playboy. 'He has his eye on our dancer,' Ramu said and ran for his errands before Rishi could probe further.

Rishi spent the large part of the day trying to call his mother and his uncle. Mrs Sen offered him her phone but, sadly, their house in the woods was beyond any network connection. Catching hold of Ramu, he requested to fetch him an auto, a taxi even. With Patna just a few kilometres away, he should be able to reach home in an hour. 'Don't worry about transport,' Ramu assured him. 'Rapid Air will take care of everything.' A journey that was to take no more than a few hours was taking him more than a day. Rishi fretted. At this rate, he'd run out of casual leave, and Mr Manjrekar would deduct a good part of his salary for his absence. Just as he was about to throw a fit and march out with his suitcase, Mrs Purnima Sen called him over to her room reserved for Kolkata passengers.

'Listen, Rishi, you're upset, and you should be.' She patted her bed and asked him to sit next to her. 'Things don't turn out the way we want 90 per cent of the time. No, 99 per cent,' she corrected herself. 'Our plans have a habit of failing when we least expect. That is an unwritten rule of our life. You might think you're driving along on a smooth road, but little do you know that a banyan tree has been felled by a storm and lies across your path. The trick is not to look for things you don't have, but to enjoy what you already do.'

'Like what?' Rishi was exasperated by the speech and felt doubly restless.

'Like the dancer. She lives not far, just two doors beyond you. And she hasn't set her mind on any of her suitors yet.'

The room next to Rishi's was vacant. It was the Chennai room. It was waiting for its passenger to arrive. The one beside it had its door painted pink, while the rest were the colour of wood. It was reserved for Bombay passengers. Passing the door, Rishi heard music coming from inside. It was film music from the 80s, and it took him less than a minute to name the film, the composer, the singer, the hero and the heroine. Ramu saw him lingering in front of the room and smirked.

'That makes three of you. Rohit Shetty, Shashank Dwivedi and now you!'

Rashmi Sethi didn't like mixing with the other passengers, he said. 'She is rehearsing for her big performance. It could make her famous, turn her into a star.'

'What's a star doing in transit house?' Rishi asked.

'She is travelling from Gwalior to Bombay to take part in the Dance India show. She's a fantastic dancer and has a great chance of winning.'

True to Ramu's words, Rishi didn't find Rashmi during dinner time. The rest had gathered around the table, and Mr Chandrakanth

Mishra was conducting an examination of the sixth passenger of the house, Shashank Dwivedi, who hailed from Ranchi.

'Name all the prime ministers of India from 1947 up until now.' Reaching across the table, he drew the bowl of eggplant curry towards him, and fixed Shashank with an examiner's stare.

'Jawaharlal Nehru, Gulzarilal Nanda, Lal Bahadur Shastri, Indira Gandhi, Morarji Desai, Rajiv Gandhi, Vishwanath Pratap Singh.' Shashank recited in his bird-like voice.

'Wrong.' Chandrakanth Mishra spat out a piece of green chilli that didn't agree with his stomach. 'You forgot Chaudhury Charan Singh, who hailed from Balia, only 150 kilometres from Varanasi in my home state.'

Shashank, bony and clean-shaven, was preparing for his senior clerk's exam that he'd have to take soon, for which he was travelling from Ranchi to Bhopal. He was nervous on both counts: reaching his examination centre on the due date and memorizing the *Indian Book of General Knowledge*.

The day passed quicker than he thought, and by the time dinner ended and Mr Mishra had struck the first notes of Raga Khamaj, Rishi felt sleepy just like the others.

'You have Taurus ascendant in your chart, which means you are headstrong and prone to rash judgements.' Chandrakanth Mishra peered at Rishi's horoscope that he'd cast, having inveigled his birth facts out of him while he was still sleepy. 'It shows you're ambitious, but unable to achieve your dreams.'

Rishi nodded, agreeing with Mr Mishra.

'Your wife, if you manage to have one, will control you, like a farmer controls his bullock.'

Luckily, Rohit arrived, to save Rishi from further despair, looking for a torch.

'Why do you need a torch during daytime?' Mr Mishra enquired.

'Rashmi wants it. She's dropped her contact lens and can't spot them without one.'

Rishi waited for the commotion over the torch to subside, and then knocked on the Bombay door. It was open, and he could see Rashmi sprawled on the floor, searching for her lens.

'Oh, you . . .' she said, spotting Rishi. 'I've heard someone from Bombay has come. I love your city although I've never been there.'

Rishi didn't waste time and, flashing his torch under Rashmi's bed, managed to find her lens. He waited for her to put it on, making a face in the mirror and batting her eyelids several times before she focused back on Rishi.

'Are you working in the film industry?'

Rishi shook his head.

'In music, modelling or . . .'

Rashmi looked disappointed. 'I thought Bombay people did.'

It was a weak beginning, but Rishi sought to recover the situation by holding out—what Bombay people were masters of—a promise. 'I can still help you.'

Fiddling with her earphones, Rashmi appeared half interested.

'I've watched all seven seasons of Dance India and can tell you which songs have received the best ratings from the judges.'

On the verge of dismissing Rishi, Rashmi didn't appear too convinced. 'Even if I knew that and chose my numbers, I'd still have to memorize the lyrics to lip them while dancing. I'll have to listen to those songs a hundred times to get the words right.'

Lifting up his forefinger to draw her attention, Rishi bounded back to Patna and emerged with his book of lyrics and re-entered Bombay. Laying it down before Rashmi, he spoke as calmly as he was capable of, 'You have all of them printed here, and I can help you memorize them just like Mr Mishra helps Shashank memorize general knowledge.' To further convince her, he turned the pages rapidly, 'Here you have all of Lata Mangeshkar, Geeta Dutt, Suman Kalyanpur, Asha Bhosle, down to Alka Yagnik.'

'Really!' Rashmi watched in amazement as her face broke out into the amazing glow of a virtuoso dancer. Then, quickly recovering her composure, she bade him to leave. 'I must do my practice now. Let's meet at 6 p.m. in the balcony.'

Bathed in excitement, Rishi paced his room. This was the closest he'd come to a date, that too initiated by a girl. Ramu entered without knocking and winked at him.

'She's given you almost 15 minutes. That's more than Rohit and Shashank put together! Now you are Number 1 in the rankings.' Then, bumming a cigarette from Rishi's pack, he lowered his voice. 'Did you see the photographs on her wall?'

The Bombay room was unusual, Rishi agreed with Ramu. Its walls were painted pink, with photographs stuck all over them forming a collage.

'It's called the honeymoon room.'

'Why honeymoon?'

'Because,' Ramu took a long drag and let out the smoke slowly. 'A couple from Mysore was travelling to Goa for their honeymoon when their plane developed engine trouble. They had to spend the night here in transit house; their very first night together. There have been other couples afterwards also.'

With every passing hour, Rishi worried about his date with Rashmi. What if Mr Chandrakanth Mishra was there in the balcony, singing Raga Hamsadhwani, which was like the cry of a swan returning home at dusk. Shashank could be there as well, pestering Rohit to quiz him from the general knowledge book. Most of all, he worried about Purnima Sen. Catching them together could have her unleash her mission. From what he'd gathered about Rashmi, she didn't appear to Rishi as being one amenable to matchmaking but one who'd make her own match.

'I have considered your suggestion,' Rashmi said when they met at 6. 'But you have to shortlist a few songs for me. Then I can decide if I'd like to include them in my routine.'

Rishi was overjoyed. There couldn't be a better suggestion than that. He was about to start right away, but Rashmi stopped him. 'First, you must watch my show reel. Then you'll know my style.

No point choosing songs that clash with my strengths.' Turning her phone to landscape view, she played recordings of her shows, from the qualifying rounds of Dance India.

Just one glance at the show reel was enough to convince Rishi that he was in the presence of a champion. He saw her as a dolphin cavorting on a stage that resembled the blue ocean, as a bird of prey flying high in the sky and swooping down as music reached a crescendo. She showed no stiffness that might've betrayed her upbringing in a small town or a lack of training. Like molten metal, she was ready to assume any form she wished.

Making a quick note of her style, Rishi flipped through the book of lyrics and folded the edges of half a dozen pages. Rashmi would need to find the songs on her playlist, and he started to hum a few of them.

'You have a good voice,' Rashmi observed him closely. 'Have you considered becoming a professional singer?'

Rishi laughed. His father called him a donkey whenever he sang in the bathroom. His son's voice had neither the range nor the cadence for classical music, he'd say.

Rashmi made a face when he mentioned his father. 'Forget parents. They never see anything good in their kids. My mother wanted to marry me off when I was 16. My father thought I should become an accountant.' She knitted her brows, as if struck by a thought. 'I think we can work together while we are here. It's hard to practise without an audience. You can be my audience. Maybe I'll take up some of your favourite songs.'

Overwhelmed, Rishi was unable to answer. Rashmi went on, 'This balcony is too small. We can go down to the garden,' she pointed to the patch of green at the back of the villa, 'and have our sessions there. Too bad we won't have any stage lights at night, but . . .'

'But we can imagine they are there,' Rishi completed the sentence for Rashmi.

That night, lying in bed, Rishi thought again about his mother. Purnima Sen was right. Life was unexpected. And who would know best all about that than his mother? She'd lost her second baby after Rishi—as he'd come to learn much later—due to an unexpected fall inside the toilet of their home. She'd lost her husband, unexpectedly, to a heart attack when he was barely 50. Lost her job when her school was shut down to build a shopping complex. She'd had to deal with the unexpected ups and downs of her only son's life who'd passed his entrance to the defence academy only to be rejected for being flat-footed, his government job application also rejected because he'd missed the deadline by just a day.

Whatever her sickness, she must've dealt with it by now. She'd have raised her delicate form over the fallen banyan tree and reached home safely.

Staying awake, he thought too of the passengers of transit house. They didn't appear anxious or angry with Rapid Air over the delay in reaching their destination, at peace at the mere possibility of their departure, confident that they'd all leave some day on a hopping flight. Their pending tasks didn't trouble them too much; transit house had frozen them in the present. Each of the six had discovered one of life's vital tricks—to live without the fear of a pressing future.

That thought calmed Rishi. He smelled cigarette smoke rising from below his window and coming down found Ramu and Rohit sharing a smoke. Both were unusually quiet and motioned Rishi to hold his silence. They heard the sound of crying from the Kolkata room. It's Mrs Sen, he was told.

'She lost her husband to an accident barely a year into their marriage. She refused to marry again and devoted her life to getting others married,' Rohit whispered. 'But she still misses her dead husband.'

'Mishra has read her chart,' Ramu added. 'He has predicted that in her next life, she'll be born as a moth, which is both male and female, with no need to marry.'

Breaking his silence, Rohit cursed Chandrakanth Mishra. 'He's a piece of fraud. He's even predicted his own death to occur on the night of a lunar eclipse.'

Rashmi and Rishi rehearsed her dance routine every afternoon in the garden till it was dusk and the mosquitos troubled them far too much to remain outdoors. He stopped the number if she made a false step, then resumed the song when she was ready. He counted the seconds before she changed her routine from one dance piece to another. He poured her water from a jug after she'd finished for the day.

During intervals, they exchanged stories about their lives. Once she'd let down her guard with Rishi, she told him about her dream of a career in showbiz and her fear of returning to Gwalior with nothing to show. He too had nothing to show, Rishi told her, except an accountant's job. Nor did any of the passengers of transit house, they agreed.

'Rohit thinks I'm a snob because I don't like magic,' Rashmi said.

'Mr Mishra thinks I am a failure,' Rishi confided in her.

'Mrs Sen has told me I'll never get married because I'm afraid of boys,' Rashmi giggled.

'She told me to look for a Patna girl.'

'Why Patna?' Rashmi was curious.

'Because they are solid, like Patna men.'

'Do you really like solid people?' Rashmi looked at him quizzically. Rishi didn't wish to answer, didn't want her to know that he preferred a dancer much more.

Unknown to themselves, they left the garden one night, crossed the driveway and reached the highway that had brought them to transit house.

'This is much better than the lawn,' Rashmi struck the asphalt with her heels and twirled like a ballerina. 'Let's dance together,' she said. 'Imagine you're my partner in the show.'

Holding up his arms, Rishi shook his head. 'I may sing like a donkey, but I dance like a mule!'

'You must still try,' Rashmi was adamant. She put on a number from her playlist, then stretched out her hand towards Rishi, 'Let me show you.'

'This is the classic Kathak, popular among the 40s and 50s' courtroom dancers.' She frowned, stopping the music. 'Maybe it's too hard for you. You can try disco, which is all about hanging loose and shaking every part of your body.'

Rishi tried, then stopped feeling embarrassed.

One by one, she took him, reluctantly, through flamenco and swing, tango and hip-hop, till he'd broken out in a sweat.

'Wait, let's try one last time. This one will be easy.' She put on a slow and swaying melody and drew Rishi close to her. 'It's the ballroom dance. It takes very little effort, except to hold your partner really close and follow each other's steps.'

Gingerly at first, Rishi held Rashmi by the waist. 'That's good.' She closed her eyes and led him on. 'Remember, just go slow and sexy.'

Slow and sexy! Rishi loved that.

At the end of the piece, she played it again and then again as they continued dancing. Quite amazingly, they kept going, unmindful of the time as the mist blew in and passed over them, making them seem like a pair of ghosts. It was the night of a lunar eclipse.

The sputtering sound of an auto broke into the music, and they saw a three-wheeler racing down the highway. It took a sudden turn towards their villa and braked to a stop beside them. The driver, an elderly man with droopy eyes, poked his head out of the driver's seat.

'Patna?' the man asked, his voice barely audible.

Rishi didn't answer.

'Only 10 kilometres. Rs 75.'

Then he turned to Rashmi and spoke to her, 'Bombay? Rs 350.'

The two remained silent as the driver kept repeating, 'Patna, Rs 75. Bombay, Rs 350.'

'He's the one who'd brought me here,' Rishi whispered.

'Me too,' Rashmi whispered back. Then they looked each other in the eye and waved the auto away to go bounding back on the highway.

Transit house was unusually quiet when they returned. The table had been set for dinner, and everyone was present. Mr Chandrakanth Mishra sat at his usual seat at the head of the table. But his head had dropped down to his plate. His body was as still as a rock.

'He suffered a heart attack while eating,' Ramu whispered.

All of them lent a hand as they carried the body upstairs to his favourite balcony and laid him down on the floor. Shashank changed his clothes to a pair of milk-white kurta pyjama. Purnima Sen laid her palm on his forehead. Rohit lit a candle, and Ramu could be heard weeping.

Rashmi and Rishi took their seats at Mr Mishra's feet. At her urging, Rishi sang a short refrain from Malkauns, which was the raga of mourning.

A black van arrived at transit house early next morning to take Mr Mishra away. The passengers assembled at the gate to send off his corpse—Kolkata, Ranchi, Bombay, Gwalior and Patna bade farewell to their friend from Varanasi. Everyone returned to their rooms and spent a quiet day by themselves, and the only event of note was the arrival of a limousine carrying a new passenger. He was Mr Manoj Tukaram, whose flight had been diverted due to bad weather on its way to Delhi. He had an urgent connection to catch for New York and could be heard arguing all day on the phone with the ground staff of Rapid Air, demanding a full refund of his business class ticket.

Catching Rishi making tea in the kitchen, Ramu smiled, 'Give him a week, he'll forget New York and become comfortable here!'

Later that night, Rishi went to Rashmi's room and found it lit up with candles. She had dressed in a prim pink skirt and a cake sat on the table by her bed.

'It's my birthday today,' Rashmi said, sounding a bit shy.

Rishi felt even more shy, as he didn't have a present for her and didn't know from where he could get one.

'If you like, I'd like to give you my book of lyrics as a present,' he managed to say.

Rashmi shook her head and lit the sparkler on the cake and beamed at him, 'You can give me a birthday card when we are together in Bombay.' Then she shut the door, leaving the two of them alone inside the honeymoon room of transit house.

His mother had recovered from her stroke, and returned home after a few days at the hospital. She was already up on her feet by the time Rishi arrived, and the delight on her face was enough to banish the guilt he felt for coming over much later than planned. True to character, Patna neighbours had thrown a ring around Mandira Aunty during the difficult days, and his uncle too had risen to the challenge. Rishi felt relieved. It seemed like a normal homecoming, with the comforting chatter of visitors and familiar kitchen smell. The sighting of the Rapid Air shuttle in their neighbourhood had drawn curious onlookers, and before long he was flooded with questions about the City of Dreams.

'At first, we were worried because we couldn't reach you on your phone.' Recalling the crisis, Rishi's uncle offered him a cigarette in a mark of respect for his nephew who was now an employed adult. 'But we knew you'd come soon, once Mr Manjrekar called and assured us that you were on your way.'

'You are lucky to have such a kind boss,' his mother joined in and reminded Rishi's uncle to mention 'that girl, who was kind too'.

'Which girl?' Rishi was curious.

'I think her name is Rosy. She said she works in your office and is your friend. You were calm when you received the news about your mother, she told me. You knew what exactly needed to be done.' There was a hint of pride in his uncle's voice.

Was that before she'd read the birthday card or after? Rishi wondered.

'Then there was this other lady,' his mother filled in more details. 'Purnima Sen, a Bengali who called from Ahmedabad. You had met her in the airport or somewhere. Rishi is steady, she told your uncle. He sleeps well and has a good appetite. He's among friends.'

'What else did she say?' Rishi held his breath.

'Nothing,' Rishi's mother seemed tired after the recent ordeal. 'I knew all along that you'd keep your promise to your father . . . to come over if something bad happened to me. With so many kind people around, you couldn't fail.'

Over the next couple of days, as his mother's medical matters gradually took a back seat to planning about the family's future, he was repeatedly asked if there was any prospect that he could be transferred to Patna. 'Why not find a job here?' his friend Atul asked him. That way he could still go for swims in the Ganga like they did when they were younger. His uncle offered to accompany his mother to Bombay to see first-hand how he was faring in his adopted dwellings, and if arrangements needed to be made to find someone local who could cook for him like his mother. Waking early on the day of his departure from Patna, his mother asked Rishi the question all mothers ask their sons once they've settled in their jobs.

'When will you marry?' She told him about a Jamshedpur girl who was related to one of her dear friends. 'She can come to Patna to meet you, if you wish, or you can go from Bombay to Jamshedpur.'

Rishi was tempted to tell his mother about the transit house, about his friends there and the special Gwalior girl who was already in Bombay waiting for him, but held back wondering what she'd make of their honeymoon before the wedding. We shall both come to Patna to give her the good news, he resolved in his mind before saying his goodbyes.

It was easier to take an auto to the airport, splitting the cost between him and a neighbourhood boy, Jamil, who was going to Bombay to take up his first job as a ship's electrician. His vessel was due to leave from Mazagaon Docks in a couple of days. An elderly man drove them at snail's pace to the old airport, as the new airport was yet to be inaugurated by some dignitary. Covering the 10-kilometre stretch, they arrived at the Rapid Air counter bustling with passengers. Flight 334 to Bombay was fully booked, they were told, and the counter girls were far too busy to smile. His 9-kilogram bag had grown in weight to 14 with his mother's contribution of his favourite sweets, and Rishi had to carry it to the gate as there were no escalators. Barring a few minor altercations with queue jumpers, the boarding went smoothly, and soon he had 16C all to himself with Jamil beside him on 16D. The flight was full.

The roaring of the engines signalled the start of their journey, with the aircraft backing out of the parking bay and moving gently along the tarmac. Passengers had started to settle down, and several could be seen saying their prayers with eyes closed. The customary safety announcements started as the plane reached the runway and then came to a halt. Everyone waited for the big thrust forward.

After what seemed like an unusually long wait, the pilot's voice came from the cockpit. There would be a delay to their departure, it was announced. The air traffic controllers had stopped all flights till the Prime Minister's plane landed safely in Patna. It was a routine procedure that was conducted for safety. Passengers were told to be patient and wait for the next announcement.

There was commotion inside the aircraft as travellers let out their collective exasperation. Those praying, opened their eyes and looked around bewildered. Several could be seen arguing with the stewardesses over the unnecessary harassment meted out to ordinary citizens. Bells rang, with calls for water. Jamil was tense, Rishi could sense. He must be worrying about reaching Bombay on time and the docks to board his ship. As a first-time employee, he'd be anxious, afraid of missing his chance. Someone behind them cursed Rapid Air for failing to inform passengers about the delay before the boarding.

Rishi felt calm. Gazing out of the window, he saw the airport terminal, the passengers waiting for their flights, the attendants pushing carts in and out of toilets, the airline's crew loading holds and buses carrying stewardesses in maroon uniforms criss-crossing the tarmac. A wave of kindness spread from everything around him. The static plane relaxed his senses, he felt grateful for the stillness.

Stewardesses went around the cabin handing out packets of peanuts to the passengers. Rishi collected his and then passed it on to Jamil to enjoy and calm his nerves.

FAKE

Blood had stained the floor, like the veins of Carrara marble. Jagannath took it to be wine, spilt at the party the night before. Stepping gingerly, he looked for broken glass, for remnants of the buffet or a nose ring lost in a moment of heat. Nobody had told him about the party, not the security guard or the girl who bolted the locks after visitors and staff left *Gallery Hormone*. Had he known, he would've arrived an hour early. *Saali!*—he cursed Lady Luck for dashing all hope of finishing quickly and catching a train back to his sick mother. Luck was Jagannath's enemy, indeed of all those destined by fate to clean up a city as dirty as Mumbai.

It was his job to keep the gallery spotless. When you enter, it must feel like entering paradise—he was told when he had joined and was reminded often. Not a speck of dust must irritate the visitors' nostrils; the clear glass door offers a perfect reflection, and feet slide over the floor like a skater on ice.

Paradise! Jagannath scoffed every morning. Whoever had thought to lay a white marble floor in paradise? Like the devil, it spoiled the party—the white floor and white walls, all too ready to capture the delinquent dirt of this earth. The purpose—as he understood—was to display the paintings, hanging them under the spotlights for the visitors, after they'd been chosen from the stacks of the storage room. He was warned never to touch the paintings and to use a feather duster to brush the canvases lightly, as gently as a lover. Only the staff were allowed to handle the gallery's treasure— the three angels of paradise.

Of them, Ronnie Sen, was the dirtiest, his desk littered with visiting cards of clients and some from Juhu's massage parlours. He expected a salaam from the gallery's sweeper whenever his eyes fell on him, and Jagannath obliged, pocketing his tip. Privately, he and Rahman, the guard, joked about Ronnie who arrived in an auto but pretended to own a Mercedes.

Atiya's corner was the cleanest of the three. 'She's not Chinese; she's from Manipur.' Rahman had corrected Jagannath, who didn't know where Manipur was. Like a dutiful maid, she cleaned up her mess before leaving. There were no girlie things in her trash, like hairbands or an empty bottle of nail polish. And then, there was the *chutiya*—the boy who was just as lowly as Jagannath but had managed to become the boss's pet. Kamlesh Kumar or KK, as everyone called him, even had his own visiting card, came to work suited-booted and handled clients all by himself. 'He's a prankster,' Rahman said of KK, and Jagannath agreed with him. 'He's the mongrel who's sneaked into paradise while the gods were sleeping.'

Fetching a pail and mop, Jagannath paused before the boss's office, partitioned off by walls. He was permitted to enter before Ishvat Irani arrived at noon. Everyone called him Sir. Clients called him Ish. There were cameras inside the gallery, but none inside the boss's chamber. 'His eyes are better than any camera,' Jagannath was warned. 'He'll know if something has moved an inch.' In his 2 years at the gallery, Sir had spoken to him just once, to ask if he could read English. 'No, Sir,' he had smiled shyly, 'only a little bit of Odia.' Collecting his files from the table, their boss had smiled back, 'Good!'

Jagannath wasn't allowed to enter the antechamber attached to Sir's office, which was permanently locked. Whatever was inside required no dusting. The most precious of the gallery's treasures were kept in the antechamber, he had heard rumours, and only the choicest of clients allowed to take a peek inside. Even Rahman, with his prying ways, didn't know anything about it. The stain on the marble had its origin inside the locked room, Jagannath was certain. Squatting, he put his nose to the floor.

Over the years spent as a sweeper, he had developed a special quality that made it possible for him to trace the exact source of an odour and its true nature. Shifts at a hospital had taught him the difference between urine and watery discharge. During his brief sojourn at a nightclub, he'd become an expert on vomit. The city's conservancy had marked his senses, indelibly, with myriad varieties of waste. But this, as Jagannath concluded, still squatting, was neither urine nor vomit or waste. Furthermore, spared by the cool gallery air, the thin stream was still viscous, bubbling with a faint vitality. He hesitated before touching the stained floor with the tip of his little finger and taking a proper sniff.

It was blood. Leaping up, Jagannath started to shake. He knew it from the hospital and the nightclub, from his mother who coughed it up from her dying lungs. Teeth chattering, he prayed to Jagannath— Lord of the Universe. What followed next could only be classed as an act of misdemeanour on the part of the sweeper. Casting off all warnings, he pushed against the antechamber's door and found it to be unlocked. The air was just as warm inside as street air and smelled of dry paint. Barely able to see in the darkness, Jagannath spotted his Sir among a jumble of canvases, collapsed and emanating the stream that had stained the Carrara marble floor.

Then, without a look back, he bounded out of the gallery, leaving behind ugly marks of red on the precious white.

Kamlesh Kumar was broke when he arrived at *Gallery Hormone*. Out of rent and knee-deep in debt, he had woken up that morning, cursing the fourteen missed chances that could've saved him from his plight. Mornings took him back half a dozen years when he'd boarded the train from Jabalpur to Mumbai. At each of the fourteen stops, he'd weighed his odds, kept a foot hanging on the platform, ready to jump off and go back with his tail curled between his legs. Hope stood in the way—that motherfucker whose aim is to turn men into losers. The train whistled its tune . . . you'll be a star one day! The greatest of greats among artists! You'll be the pride of

Jabalpur! He had heard the voice of his dead mother—'Go.' She was the only one he trusted.

Hope had kept her word. In the early years, he'd breezed his way through art academy, wowed teachers, charmed friends and seduced a great many of them. The next Hussein, he was called. Next Raza, next Souza—all those young men who'd come to Mumbai in trains and left in limousines. The Arabian Sea sent a tidal wave to wash away Jabalpur; he was now KK from Mumbai. When the dream started to die, he learnt lessons of life that were more valuable than his art lessons. Among throngs of 'new masters' jostling for space among 'old masters', he ran a poor race. He missed the connections that might've spun him into overnight fame. A bad ear made him follow wrong advice. Called names behind his back, he fought back, only to be called more names. He lost friends; those that remained considered him spent. When the balloon burst and the market crashed, he felt the chill of the sea. There was drink, of course, and at each dead end it told him the truth: he'd missed the train of hope and taken the train to hell.

Then he was handed a ticket to the last chance saloon by a friend: 'Go to Ishvat; he'll show you the way.' He learnt the meaning of that name—*desire*—and knew it to be the purest of words and the dirtiest.

Gallery Hormone was about to open its doors, welcoming visitors to its annual show, when KK arrived. It was a much-anticipated event, a notable date on the city's art calendar. Barely out of its cradle, *Hormone* was a brash intruder and every gallerist's nightmare—an enfant terrible. And its reputation was equal to its founder, Ishvat Irani. It was unclear where the man had come from. In a business where pedigree was as important as profit, none knew the name of his father or grandfather. City sleuths had failed to pin down his address in the Malabar Hills or among the gorgeous ruins of

Parsee Colony, and he looked distinctly Indian, not like one of those hybrids with a tinge of Western blood. Rumours had him as an ace punter, an ex-banker, even the frontman for a sheikh. In a city where reputations are built on rumours, he had beaten the odds.

'An art gallery must signify emptiness,' Ishvat, or Ish, had said in a rare interview. 'It must be characterless unlike a designer boutique.' To prove his point, he had built a white box inside an abandoned textile mill, with his collection as the centrepiece. It was as spectacular as a blank sheet. Entering, gallery visitors felt a rush of hormones, a sensation both mental and physical.

A show opening at *Gallery Hormone* attracted old and new collectors, the buyers kept in suspense till the very end. It wasn't simply a matter of who he will show, but what. Whatever it was, *Hormone* wasn't a mortuary of dead masters, sold and resold a hundred times. The secondary market was meant for cowards; Ish traded in risk. The chatterati never failed to bring up the fact that on its very first show, the gallery had exhibited a garbage vat overflowing with rubbish inside a glass case. And a dead foetus, preserved in formaldehyde. 'He is ruining art,' senior artists griped in private, then thought nothing of offering their new work to *Gallery Hormone*.

The guests were gathered outside, with the sun casting the mill in a startling silhouette. Very rich people rubbed shoulders with poor artists, served with tea from a street stall. It was Ish's idea of a pre-show bash—equalizing buyers and sellers. The gallery staff could be seen poking their heads out of the windows, measuring up the crowd to report to their boss.

He'd come on the wrong day to visit Ish, KK thought, clutching his portfolio. It was the occasion to show off the works acquired by the gallery, not entertain hopefuls. Busy selling, Ish and his staff might not even notice KK. For a moment, he had the crazy idea of taking his paintings out and hawking them right there and then like a street peddler. That'd create a stir, for sure. Guests might even take it to be Ish's novel idea—holding a sale before the show! Following the crowd into the gallery, he slipped past the guard. In truth, he didn't mind being caught, getting into a fracas and thrown out in front of a bevy of reporters. That'd get him attention, which was exactly what he, along with the rest of the world, wanted.

The white box put everyone in a trance. Clever lighting made the guests seem like ocean weed, coalesced and floating languidly like a blob from wall to wall, nodding at the paintings as if they were living things waiting to be acknowledged. No one coughed although it was the season of catching colds. Just the nervous breathing of an anxious collector or two.

Art wasn't the only exhibit, attendees eagerly sought out fellow visitors—the first movers and the late arrivals—making a mental note of surprise absentees.

KK spotted the Khemkas. They were old money. Gallery owners treated them like royalty, eager to arrange private viewings, although Madhu and Raj didn't mind the company of fellow buyers, always ready to offer a tip. If a work of art is 'priceless', then any price you pay for it is a bargain—that was their motto. The Khemkas loved dangling carrots in front of gallerists, but few risked offending them with a false claim.

From the gossip among artists, KK knew the Dirty Couple. Dressed in hoodies and ripped jeans, they resembled ravers, rather than hedge fund owners. It was all about price with them—the price they'd fetch when reselling the art they'd picked up on behalf of rich investors. They were known to squeeze gallery owners and artists, but sellers loved them because they bought in bulk.

He noticed a visitor waving at the smartly dressed gallery girl, who stood at a corner, clipboard in hand. She had the price list. The buyer was likely to cast a discreet eye over her list, then instruct her to place a red dot next to a painting. Other guests observed the two conferring. A red dot would signify the beginning. With the game under way, more would wave, more red dots flock towards the walls.

Looking around the room, KK couldn't spot Ish. 'He's a big man,' he'd been told by his friend. 'Unmissable, but with the voice of a bird.' Animated visitors had split into clumps around each wall, a pot-bellied man with a pallid face answering their questions like a tour guide. He avoided the handful of artists milling around like lost souls. His presence in *Hormone* would spread rumours. Poor fellow, his ex-friends would say, the desperate fool who'd lost his way to the whorehouse and ended up at the butcher's. He felt hungry and looked around for waiters serving refreshments to the guests, spotting Leena—one half of the Dirty Couple—sticking out her tongue at the painting of an apple dropping like a bomb from a skyscraper. Was she hungry like him too?

Waiters poured champagne at the drinks table. It was Dom Perignon, he was certain, from the golden crest on the green bottle. His bartender friend Govind had told him the names of drinks he might be lucky to afford in his next life. At Rs 17,000 a bottle, a glass would be worth about Rs 4000. KK hesitated to pick up a glass. The champagne might misbehave inside his empty stomach. It might fight a war with last night's drink—the local hooch guarding its turf against the foreign invader—have him rush to the toilet. Then there was the gallery's guard to consider. He had kept his eye on KK. He'd be aware that the young man with a portfolio wasn't a buyer or a gallery artist who'd be known to him. His stocky gait and devilish eyes reminded KK of a bus conductor who'd catch him whenever he travelled ticketless in Jabalpur.

Khemkas held court among committed collectors. KK overheard Madhu describe how they'd met an artist and acquired his work when he was a struggler. 'No gallery was prepared to accept him, he was a nobody,' Madhu drew a big circle with her hand, 'a zero.'

'Now, that piece must be worth 100 times what you paid!' Leena's partner Tushar salivated openly.

'More!' Raj drew admiration from the group. 'He was avant-garde, and nobody wanted him on their wall. We saw the talent. You people call it investing in an undervalued asset. We call it respect.'

Bakwas! KK growled under his breath. Everyone had a story about artists going from strugglers to stars. It kept buyers hopeful. Maybe they too might get lucky, multiply their money 100 times. Look at me! He was tempted to scream . . . You can get twenty times more if you put a red dot on my portfolio.

There was a commotion at the door, but the guests didn't pay much attention. Serious looking was about to begin before serious buying, and the gallery staff were on their toes. Someone was arguing with the guard, and a few of the employees rushed over. The waiters darted glances but didn't spill a drop pouring drinks with their white-gloved hands. The light seemed to dim, casting unwanted shadows on the exhibits.

Must be a local *neta*, KK thought, making his rounds before the election, arrived with his goons at *Gallery Hormone*. Or a mafia lord, out to stuff the lot of collectors and decamp with the loot. The visitors' book at the entrance landed on the floor with a thud, and the guard could be heard swearing loudly. The gallery girl with the clipboard waved her hands frantically to catch the attention of the pot-bellied employee. A sharp cry escaped the lips of a guest, and then the bedlam started.

A young man could be seen dashing into the hall, evading the guard and screaming wildly. Like an arrow seeking its target, he went straight for the group gathered around Madhu and Raj, scattering the guests. He was holding something in his hand, which looked like an artist's scalpel. The rush of bodies towards the exit made it impossible to keep track of what was exactly happening. Glasses crashed to the floor; the gallery's alarm wailed. Sensing imminent danger, the waiters formed a wall around the Dom Perignon.

The man froze in front of the painting for a moment, then shouted, 'It's a fake!' He slashed the canvas with his scalpel, making a diagonal cut through the middle. Then he dropped his weapon and dashed out, leaving everyone in a state of shock.

The hall fell silent, with the guests cowering. Then the Khemkas, who'd stood still amidst the chaos, started to clap, beaming from ear to ear. 'Brilliant!' Madhu's voice rang across the room. The bewildered guests rose to their feet, slowly gathered their wits and joined them, till the gallery resounded with the sound of applause. A rather large man emerged from a small office, came up to the scene of assault and bowed lavishly like a ballerina.

'Oh, Ish!' the visitors gasped and squealed.

In the humming that resumed, those assembled were all praise for the master gallerist fooling everyone with a grand performance. 'It was a bloody show!' Tushar picked himself up from his foetal posture. Several guests went up to congratulate the young actor, who'd changed back into his regular clothes, for giving them such a unique treat.

'Was it a fake really?' someone asked Raj Khemka.

He nodded. 'We have the original at home. When Ish came to us with this idea, we thought it'd be marvellous!'

In the aftermath, *Gallery Hormone* resumed its show, with visitors admiring the exhibits and calling the gallery girl over to them. Now Ish could be seen mingling, drawing as much praise from the guests as the paintings. KK found himself before a largish canvas in the company of a lady who had drifted apart from the rest. She held a glass in her hand, and the spotlights left her mostly in shadow. Only her lips were clearly visible.

'You aren't drinking?' the lips asked KK.

He smiled shyly.

'It's rude to refrain from wine while keeping the company of an indulgent woman.' She waited for an answer, then went on, 'Don't tell me you were part of the performance?'

He shook his head. The lady kept talking, but he was distracted by the lips, painted Oxblood Red. Given up with small talk, his company turned towards the painting on the wall and frowned, 'What on earth is this? Can you tell me?'

He saw a burnt sienna spot on a white canvas, slightly off centre, a fine grey line radiating out from it. It was an example of conceptual art, practised by the New Mumbai School. He knew the artist, who'd recently returned from a fellowship in London and bragged about Charles Saatchi—the god of contemporary art—picking up his work and sending them to a Sotheby's auction.

'He's a fraud, just like his art,' friends said whenever his name came up. 'One of those who dresses up his canvases with words, not with paint.'

'Basant Adiga.' The lady read from the catalogue. 'What can you tell me about Mr Adiga's painting?'

'It's a journey into the unknown . . .' KK recovered his tongue. Why not play the word game? That's what that *behenchod* Adiga would've done if he was here. The lips, turned up towards him, gave him confidence.

'It shows the impossibility of knowing where we are. The dot searching for another dot—a twin, a lover, a friend—who might be nowhere,' he traced the grey line with his forefinger. 'Like . . .'

'Like what?' the lips whispered.

'My mother.' The image of his mother lying in the hospital bed before her death came to KK's mind.

'Your mother?'

'Yes. It's unknown where she has gone after leaving this world.' He added after a pause, 'This painting is about the impossibility of knowing, knowing anything.'

His company searched for words, then the lips closed. Moving away from KK, she ushered the gallery girl over and gave her consent to purchase the Adiga.

Relieved, KK was about to move away and take a brave sip of the champagne, when he felt a hand on his shoulder. It was Ish. Unknown to the two of them, he was watching the scene as it unfolded. 'Do you know what you've just done?' The gallery owner brought his gaze down to KK. 'You've just persuaded the famously tight-fisted Lalita Raghavan into buying an unsellable painting!' Leading KK towards the champagne table, he kept on speaking, 'You aren't an invitee, are you? You came to pitch your work to me, isn't it? A struggling artist? Our profitable gatecrasher!' He laughed. 'I like that.' Handing him a drink, the big man spoke like a bird, 'Come see me tomorrow at the gallery.'

KK gulped down his glass.

Recently employed at *Gallery Hormone*, KK sat in his cubicle and scrutinized the other occupants of the desks. The pallid-faced man reminded him of an Albrecht Dürer portrait. 'If you can copy the master, you can copy anything,' Roshan Lal, his drawing teacher, would tell students. Given a chance, he could've done a perfect portrait of the fat boy buried under a mountain of files: Chubby cheeks, eyes bulging out of a pudgy face and uncombed tufts to hide premature balding. He'd have taken artistic licence and added a goatee to balance the absurdly conical skull.

Looking up from his files, Ronnie Sen rested his gaze on KK. He seemed to measure him up, then raised half an eyebrow. Was he an artist like him? KK recalled more gossip: Gallery workers dress up the bride and groom, arrange bouquets, usher in guests at the wedding, keep a count of gifts received and steal some if they can! Jealous of the newly-weds, failed artists make the worst gallerists. The rest are riff-raff, a gallery no better or worse to them than a factory.

The gallery girl, now out of her costume, wasn't riff-raff, KK concluded. Unlike Ronnie, she didn't make eye contact, but he was aware that she was watching him. She'd be a hard portrait to paint. Absolutely nothing about her suggested what he had learnt to call 'expressed character'. The foul-mouthed Roshan Lal had once thrown out a nude model from his class. 'All flesh, no character! Like a Chinese panda.' Atiya Angom offered him a well-lit profile, a full face even. But she hid her character. His gaze stopped at her pale skin, couldn't penetrate any farther. Busy drafting a brochure, she took even breaths with an occasional break to sip water from her bottle.

The boss's office was empty. He didn't hear the squeal of a chair or a yawn. Will this be his routine if he became Ishvat Irani's staff? Mornings spent twiddling his thumbs in *Gallery Hormone*?

'You must never bring street food or tiffin from home,' Rahman warned him once Ronnie and Atiya had left for lunch. 'You can come down and eat with me. But from tomorrow, you must pay me to share my lunch.'

'Tomorrow?' KK squinted at Rahman.

'Tomorrow after tomorrow after tomorrow . . . till Sir throws you out like he threw out Patkar.'

Rahman was the gallery's designated storyteller. In the 30 minutes of lunch break, he told six stories, beginning to end, describing character, plot and conclusion. They were all tragedies. Patkar, the hyena, was fired because he was stealing from the lion, selling off the gallery's collection on the sly and pocketing the profit. Then, the fox—Charu Behl. He was planted by Sir's rival to collect information about how much was being paid to the gallery's artists. Munching stale parathas, Rahman told stories about the turtle, who sat idle all day and twiddled his thumbs; the ass who sold a master for the price of a novice; and the peacock who thought he was Picasso. Then, there was the dog who was caught screwing his girlfriend inside the storage room during office time.

'Why does Sir want me to work for him?' KK asked Rahman.

'Because you are a wolf, not afraid to fight the lion.'

'Why would an artist like me waste his time here?' KK asked, when they finished eating. Rahman belched, then replied like a wise saint, 'Because no one except Sir can make you an artist.'

Called finally to Ish's office, a rush of warmth spread over KK. *He's going to ask to see my work!* There was no need to use fancy words to describe them, not like that bastard Adiga. Ish will cut through the bullshit and judge them for their worth.

'You must know Kabir Shah's work?' Ish stopped turning in his chair and levelled with KK.

He smirked, 'Like a Mumbaikar knows rain!'

Who didn't! He, and fellow students, had been lucky to catch a glimpse of the great Kabir Shah, father of Indian modernism, obscenely wealthy and a darling of the press, when he had come to their academy and shook hands with the principal. The college had organized a memorial after his death.

'Then you must know that he'd gone into exile in the mid-90s?'

'He was rumoured, Sir, to have moved to France to be with a French lady,' KK expounded cautiously on the rumour that was considered as good as truth.

Ish pursed his lips in a gesture of mockery. 'No, he was very much in Mumbai with his Indian lover Varun Joshi.' Turning around to face the masks adorning his wall, he offered them a concise lecture on Kabir Shah's absence from the art scene that was once a topic of heated conjecture.

'After climbing the Everest of fame, Kabir felt bored. He needed to reinvent himself. What's better than love to get a fresh start? He and Varun found each other. It was tumultuous and messy. They couldn't bear to live apart yet came close to killing each other. Their affair was classical, like a grand Renaissance painting. Before he died, he left Varun a great gift.'

'What?' KK could barely ask.

'He'd painted a series of nudes with Varun posing as his model. He called them Mad Nudes. Never shown before, they capture what Kabir truly was—as mad as God.'

An African mask, its head the shape of a gazelle, squinted at KK. They sat silently, then Ish spoke, turning back from the wall.

'I want you to go with Ronnie and bring the Mad Nudes to the gallery.'

In the moments that followed, KK pondered over the assignment. If theft was what was asked of him, he must know the details. Some private collector, such as the Khemkas, must have the Mad Nudes in their vault; he must've refused Ish's advances to have them exhibited at *Gallery Hormone*. He'd have to do detective work to spot their exact location, devise a grand plan. He'd have to fool a lot more people than he'd ever before. He wondered too about his partner in crime. How might a pompous Ronnie Sen help in the heist?

'What if I get caught, Sir?' KK managed to ask Ish.

'You must catch Varun Joshi before he does something stupid,' Ish kept his gaze fixed on KK. 'The man is dying of terminal cancer. So far, he has resisted making the paintings public, fearing that they might tarnish Kabir's reputation. He might decide to burn them before he dies.' He gave a short laugh, 'Purifying love with fire!'

'How much will we offer him, Sir?' KK took a deep breath, waiting to hear a sum that could buy up half of Mumbai.

'Leave that to Ronnie,' Ish was ready to wrap up their meeting. 'You must make the parting sweet for him.'

Afterwards, KK settled back at his desk and went over Kabir Shah. What would make an artist hide his work? The very thought made him sick. Here he was, dying to exhibit, ready to gatecrash or grovel at the feet of gallerists, and there you have the star stashing away his jewels like the Kohinoor. It was the perfect opening he needed to approach Atiya Angom.

'What can you tell me about the Mad Nudes?' KK didn't bother dropping his voice. 'I need to know how many paintings, what sizes, which medium. Everything.'

Atiya brought her measured gaze up to KK. Her voice sounded huskier than he'd expected, 'No one keeps count of the disappeared. You'll know when you find them.'

That was heavy stuff. But how was he to know if Varun Joshi was lying about his treasure? If he even had them anymore. KK decided to press Atiya again. 'But someone must know, otherwise it could all be a lie.'

Seeing his despair, she parted with a little secret, 'Varun Joshi had played a hand behind Kabir's fame. As an influential art critic, he was the first to champion his work. He was the one Kabir went to whenever he was wounded by critics. But he was unhappy with Kabir's many loves.'

'Jealous?'

She nodded, 'As lovers are.'

KK left Atiya's desk with gratitude.

'Beware of Ronnie,' Rahman parted with his saintly advice to KK over lunch. 'He was once as powerful as Sir but lost it all. Used to being the master, he is unhappy as an employee.'

'Why hasn't Sir fired Ronnie, like he had fired Patkar, Charu and others?'

'Because,' Rahman smirked, half revealing the mystery to KK, 'he still owes Sir something. He'll be released once he's paid his debt.'

Ronnie kept his face averted, gazing out of the taxi, as they rode together in silence. Their eyes met for the first time for a brief moment, once they'd reached, before they heard footsteps approaching the door.

'Don't expect too much from Mumbai homes,' KK was told by a Jabalpur friend who knew the city. 'They are like Mumbai people. Their insides don't match their outsides.'

KK shivered, ushered into Varun Joshi's presence. Propped up by cushions, he sat like a living ghost on a leather chaise longue. The glass door to the garden and a giant glass mirror reflected his face—there seemed to be not one but many Varuns in the room. Frilly wallpaper, in the raging style of the 70s, had left no space for a painting, not even for a Kabir Shah. A Venetian glass lamp glowed on a side table, adding nothing to the bright sunlight. The heady aroma of lilies scented the interiors, masking the wisps of smoke that bubbled out of the art critic's lips.

Ronnie surprised KK. Courteous and restrained, he had an entire script rehearsed in his mind and trod a cautious path, beginning with his father, the late Abhilash Sen. Varun Joshi nodded at the mention.

'I knew him to be a kind man. Far too kind to be in this rotten business.' His eyes drifted towards the window, and he drew in his breath deeply as if to smell the garden outside.

'Papa made some mistakes,' Ronnie spoke with his head lowered.

'Not mistakes,' Varun turned his gaze back. 'He didn't know the difference between art and business. Spent far too much time with artists, felt their pain when he should've given them more pain!' He let out a laugh and went on. 'That's what gallerists do, the successful ones at least. He was both mother and father to his lot. And when the time came, they forgot about him, like we forget our parents.'

'He had a high regard for Kabir Shah,' Ronnie ventured carefully. 'He believed in your words and ran a full show with his works.'

Varun Joshi checked the brew in the teapot, then poured a cup each for KK and Ronnie. Addressing KK for the first time, he asked, 'I hope you don't take milk with your tea? It's a ghastly practice Indians have inherited from the British.' Returning to Abhilash, he made a face. 'He shouldn't have drawn you into his business, made you inherit his liabilities. Sons end up failing their fathers. Just look at the Gandhis . . .'

This is his game plan, KK surmised, as Varun Joshi went over progenies of famous men and their litany of failures. *He has lived an entire life by deflecting attention from what he is; his craft is that of a sophist. Ish has given him the job of finding a way to shatter the glass and arrest Varun Joshi from his myriad reflections.*

With Ronnie becalmed, Varun felt pity for his friend's son and offered the opening himself.

'You haven't come to drink tea with a family friend, have you?'

Gathering himself up, Ronnie showed a semblance of his gallerist self. 'We've come for the Mad Nudes that you have in your possession. I hope we can interest you with a deal, the deal of a lifetime.'

'Deal of a lifetime!'

KK expected Varun Joshi to chuckle. *What does lifetime mean to a man who was at the end of his life?*

'Whose lifetime? Yours or mine?' Varun kept a dead face.

Caught up in his rehearsed pitch, Ronnie was unstoppable. 'You can turn the paintings into liquid assets. They'd certainly be worth more than this home.' Rising, he walked over to the garden window and made an expansive gesture, 'More than all of this.'

He'll play with Ronnie now! KK wanted to shut his ears.

'You silly goat!' This time, Varun Joshi let out a snort. He raised his voice a touch. 'This house and the garden belong to Kabir Shah's trust. After me, it'll go to Mumbai's street children. I have all the liquid I want, right here,' he raised his teacup in a mock toast before delivering the final punch. 'You are just like Abhilash. All heart and no brain. Fancy leaving your son in bondage to Ishvat Irani! How many more years do you have left to slave it out for him?'

During the intermission, as Ronnie excused himself to smoke in the garden, KK drew up his chair to the chaise longue. Pouring himself some cold tea from the pot, he pretended he hadn't been a party to the previous round.

'You can keep the Mad Nudes, but there is someone else who's decided to exhibit the special paintings gifted secretly to her by Kabir. They are known to be brilliant and scandalous—the kinkiest Kabir. She claims they were inspired by their . . .'

'Bitch!' Varun cut KK off. 'I'd say . . .'

'Exactly.' It was KK's turn to cut Varun off. 'She wants the world to know that she was Kabir Shah's only love. The rest of his affairs were simply that—affairs.'

A cushion or two fell off the longue as Varun Joshi rose from his regal posture. The tea service rattled on the side table. He cleared his voice, his quivering lips trying unsuccessfully to form words as KK twisted the knife.

'She is going ahead with her plan to sell her Kabirs directly to Sotheby's.'

Grabbing KK's arm, Varun recovered himself. 'She was a stop-gap arrangement, nothing more. She let him use her farmhouse when he had trouble with his wife and had to move out. He gave her a few sketches that he'd made of her in return. Sketches of her powder-puff face. No nudes.'

'Still, they will be shown, while yours will remain hidden. The world will believe her story, not yours.'

Ronnie gazed wide-eyed as Varun Joshi tottered past them and down the corridor to a dungeon, flapping his arms and gesturing at them to follow him. Entering, KK saw Varun's vault. Canvases lay stacked up along the walls. Coiled up reams of handmade paper occupied the corners like snakes. The alabaster bust of a demon graced a table. Panting, Varun's eyes glowed at his treasure.

'Find your Mad Nudes here. Good luck!' Turning his back to the two, Varun stumbled to the living room aided by his maid.

Later, twilight turned Varun from a critic to a lover once KK had laid out the paintings on the floor in front of him. 'There you see love,' he whispered, 'not the cheap love of a powerful man, but of a wandering saint. His brush strokes aren't those of an assured hand, but the quivering fingers of a lovesick boy. Do you know why he called them Mad Nudes?'

KK held his tongue.

'Because an artist becomes truly mad when he's naked. These paintings are of his naked soul not my naked body.'

'Why eleven of them?' KK managed to ask.

Varun gave a dry laugh, 'A dozen would signify the end of a series. He didn't want it to end.'

Ish called KK over to his office after he had helped Atiya store Kabir's portfolio safely.

'You were Roshan Lal's favourite student at the academy, I am told,' Ish spoke evenly. 'He has a poison tongue, but for you, it is coated with honey. He gave you the toughest of subjects, like Dürer, but you copied them with ease. You understand light and angle better than the best. And mood. You are a natural.'

KK felt blood gather speed in the veins. Ish has done his homework! He has gone to the source to verify the worth of a new artist.

'You are brash—reports claim. Headstrong, unscrupulous, delinquent when it comes to repaying loans and a lecher.' The elephant-headed mask trumpeted gleefully, swaying its trunk in agreement with Ish. 'But your work is good. That's all that matters.'

He's going to offer me a show! KK wanted to give Ish a hug. Maybe he'll exhibit my drawings and warm up his clients to the Mad Nudes.

Rising from his chair, Ish went inside the antechamber attached to his office to retrieve a largish canvas. Standing it up against a wall, he stood back to observe it closely. It was a Kabir Shah, painted at a time when he was at the pinnacle of his fame. It was part of a series he'd done to depict his pain after the Mumbai bomb blasts had killed 257 innocents. Each showed a disfigured face, framed by the architecture of ruin. Critics had compared them to Goya's *Massacre of May 3rd* and Picasso's *Guernica*.

'I want you to copy this painting,' Ish spoke in a whisper.

He had misheard what Sir just said. KK leaned forward to catch his words, 'Copy what, Sir?'

He waited to hear Ish's reply. The masks waited with bated breath.

'This masterpiece. Copy it exactly.'

Was his boss verifying Roshan Lal's account of his skill by giving him a test? Still unclear of the assignment, KK pressed Ish, 'What would be the point of copying it, Sir? It'd be no more than a fake.'

Ish shook his head. His voice dropped a further notch, straining KK's ears.

'Not a fake. I want a twin. An identical twin.'

In the tussle between good and bad luck, bad holds the upper hand. Securing a foot in the door didn't lead KK to stardom on the gallery floor but to *Hormone's* attic, his lodge and very own studio for fakes. 'I don't want you to be a jack of all trades but the ghost of Kabir Shah,' Ish had approved KK's faithful copy of the Mumbai blast, then given him a stack of Kabirs—drawings, canvases, nudes. 'You must inhabit his soul.'

Alone and drunk in the attic, KK cursed Ish, condemned Kabir to a thousand seasons in hell. Roshan Lal's praise haunted him . . . 'Copying is your second nature, but don't let it become your first.' His mood darkened like the storm clouds over Mumbai, but the downpours failed to relieve a scorched soul. The attic reeked of liquor mixed with the smell of pigment, and the rancid remains of the meals brought over by Rahman. Like a divine visitor to his private hell, he brought him news of the living.

'Mr Ludovico will be visiting our gallery; he'll spend a lot of money this time.'

Rahman took KK's silence to be ignorance and filled him in with the details. 'He is Russian but lives in London and has galleries all over the world. Rich people come in private jets to buy from him. He can speak Chinese and spends half the year in Shanghai. Sir trusts him like the right hand trusts the left.'

'What'll he do in dirty Mumbai?' KK spoke gruffly.

'He's coming to buy your paintings; I mean the things you do here,' Rahman corrected himself, casting a sideways glance at the original on the wall and its copy on KK's easel. He had overheard Ronnie making plans with Atiya to arrange a private viewing of the Kabir Shah fakes produced by KK.

'It's illegal to sell the "things" I make here,' KK didn't bother with the meal and kept mixing paint in the palette. 'Your Sir can go to jail if he's caught.'

Munching a juicy piece of tandoori stolen from KK's lunch, Rahman laughed. 'No, he won't. If he's caught, he'll simply say you, Kamlesh Kumar, have copied the paintings and unknown to him put them up in the place of the originals. You'll get screwed, not him!'

'But Ludovico must know he's buying fakes?' KK persisted. Rahman nodded, 'Probably. Which is why, he'll ask for a big discount.'

'And the buyers? What if they find out the truth?'

Polishing off the tandoori, Rahman scoffed. 'What do the Chinese know about Kabir Shah? They'll believe whatever Ludovico tells them. Buyers buy with their ears not eyes.'

KK cursed Rahman for finishing off his meal and slurped on the chutney that came with the tandoori. 'But what if they find out later that they've bought a Kabir Shah fake. What then?'

Rahman brushed aside KK's doubt. 'Rich people are used to fakes. They live with fake wives, fake lovers and friends. They don't mind hanging a few fakes on their walls.'

'Half the paintings displayed in galleries and in people's homes are fakes,' KK recalled one of his art teachers telling his students. 'They are easier to catch in the West, with the help of technology, but here, we go by the judgement of experts who are paid to lie.' Drinking on an empty stomach, he felt a strange exhilaration. Once Ludovico buys his fakes and sells them to a Chinese tycoon, a Chinese artist may fake them and sell them back as original Kabir Shah paintings to some rich idiot in Mumbai. The fakes will multiply and keep circulating, like a swarm of locusts, feasting on the rich. He was tempted to alter the copies, just a tiny bit, to make them his own fakes, turn them into Kabir–KK originals. Like adding male genitals to a female nude! Then watch the shock on Ish's face.

'Ronnie is close to a nervous breakdown,' Rahman brought KK fresh gossip from the gallery. 'He will either hang himself or kill Sir.'

KK ignored Rahman. With Ludovico set to arrive soon, Ish had flooded him with commissions. He had asked him to be extra careful. 'The Mongoose will be sniping at our heels.' Suppie Sarkar, the holier-than-thou art critic, was on the prowl for cheats. She was

known to raid shows and shred gallerists to bits for displaying fakes
or gouging buyers. 'She's the Mother Teresa of the arts.'

'Ronnie fears Sir will offer him to Ludovico.'

KK frowned. It was early in the day for Rahman to be drunk, and
in any event, he abstained from haram on Fridays. 'You mean a fake
Ronnie to go with the fake Kabirs.'

It was a national holiday, and an empty gallery gave Rahman full
scope to tell Ronnie's story. He started with Abhilash Sen, Ronnie's
father, and jumped early to the conclusion to hold KK's attention.
'Everyone hates Ronnie, but you'd feel sad for him once you know
everything.' Ronnie's father had taught Ish the ropes, made him
a junior partner of his gallery. But he double-crossed his mentor,
caused him to go bankrupt and surrender his share to Ish. 'Mr Sen
hung himself right here in this attic. But his loans from Sir hadn't
been fully paid, and so he took over the son, our Ronnie, as well.'

'How can you take over a person?' KK wasn't prepared to
believe Rahman.

'By turning him into a slave,' Rahman gazed meaningfully at KK.
'You can hear them if you go down to Sir's office on certain nights
and press your ear to the door. Hear poor Ronnie cry, begging Sir to
release him.' He made a crude gesture, of a bull riding a cow. 'You
can see the misery on his face next morning at his desk.'

KK couldn't fall asleep on his bunk bed in the attic. Abhilash Sen
hung from the ceiling above his head. He imagined hearing cries
coming from downstairs. Like Ronnie, has Ish turned him into a
slave, a fake artist unable to escape from Kabir Shah? He too had
wished to kill Ishvat Irani after their last meeting, after he'd turned
down, yet again, KK's request to show his work in the gallery.

'The press might do a special story on a Jabalpur boy making it
to the greatest gallery in India. It'll create a stir,' he'd tried tickling
Ish's ego. The large bird-like man had squeaked through his beaks
and scotched KK's dream, 'You must be patient and wait for the
right moment. It takes years to turn an artist into a brand. Or you
can leave now and show your work at a garage.' He had scoffed at

the 'rags to riches' story, 'Show me an artist who isn't poor. Poor artists get no press. It needs something more . . .' he'd searched for a word and come up with 'kinky'.

The hanging man troubled KK more than the slave in Ish's office. Going down the stairs, he steeled himself against an unexpected encounter with Sir. He was going out for some fresh air, not to look for a girl and bring her into the attic. He'd tell Ish so if he caught him loitering in the dark and empty gallery.

His foot caught in the steps, made him tumble and grab the rails. The clash of metals set off by his armband echoed on the walls. Ish's door was locked. Like a blind man, he made his way through the gallery by instinct. The vault of paintings was protected by an alarm, he knew. The wailing would turn him deaf if he happened to touch the metal door by accident. Rahman would be dead asleep in his hovel at this hour, and by the time he scrambled up bleary-eyed, the entire neighbourhood would've crowded around the mill.

KK heard the sound of sobbing. Not a whimpering or a moan, but a heartbroken lament. In the darkness, he saw Atiya, head buried on her desk. Sensing his presence, she jerked her face up, giving him, for the very first time, a clear view of her character.

In the weeks that followed, KK forced himself to stay sober, worked on his commissions all night and hovered around Atiya's cubicle during the day under some pretext or the other. Not the one to dither, he asked her for precise reports on paper and pigments used by Kabir Shah, information that'd help him make flawless fakes. With each encounter, he zeroed in on Atiya. His sharp eyes added layers to the portrait he had started to paint in his mind. Their gallery girl was an artist, faking her way through *Hormone* just like him. Like countless others, she too would've taken the train to Mumbai before she was tricked by the city. 'She's a clean girl,' Rahman had told him. He hadn't seen her getting off a swanky car or arrive at the gallery with late-night circles under her eyes. 'Don't mess with her,' Rahman had warned him. 'She may look like a cat, but, inside, she's a leopard.'

Atiya was following him too, KK could sense, with her leopard eyes. It wasn't the gaze of a predator but one that was openly curious. Having revealed her character to him by accident, perhaps she wished him to return the favour or wished to reveal even more of herself. Words thrown across the office to Ronnie appeared destined for him; packages meant for clients landed, by mistake, on his desk. KK was on her mind; it seemed to be a matter of time before she invited him into her cubicle.

Rahman picked up the lightning streaks and teased KK over their meals. 'You can forget all about tandoori; she'll feed you stinky fish if you marry her!' He warned KK not to get mixed up with Manipuri business, with, 'the troubles over there with rebels fighting the army, guns, kidnapping and what not'. Narrowing his eyes, he added a postscript, 'No one knows Atiya, who she really is, not even Sir.'

Lightning turned to thunder the day Ish hauled up all employees to gather in front of his office before he called them in one by one. A miniature painting by a modern master had gone missing from the gallery's storeroom, and the faulty CCTV didn't offer a recording of the theft. As part of a consignment to a foreign buyer, it was a costly loss.

'Must be an inside job,' Ronnie muttered under his breath. His absence on sick leave from the gallery made him less of a suspect than the others. Jagannath, the sweeper, went in and left shivering. Rahman fared worse than him. Ish's squeak was audible through the door, berating him for 'jerking off while on duty'. Breaking the pattern, KK and Atiya were called in together, to stand the interrogation jointly.

'I won't ask who paid you how much for the monkey business but will ask you to explain why the two of you were hovering inside the gallery so late.' He pointed to old CCTV footage playing on the monitor, showing the ghost-like pair of KK and a sobbing Atiya at her cubicle. To break the silence, he threatened to have the two arrested, calling KK, 'a lousy faker', and Atiya, a terrorist.

KK shifted on his feet as Ish kept up his glare. 'I heard a sound . . .' he started to say before Atiya drowned his voice under hers.

'He came down to take me to his attic. We left the gallery together.'

'To the attic for what?' Ish sounded puzzled.

'To do our monkey business,' Atiya answered calmly.

Even after it was established without a hint of doubt that Ludovico was the culprit, seizing his chance to snitch the miniature during the special viewing, the mystery of Atiya's words haunted KK. Now, when they strolled on the Marine Drive or gave themselves treats at the beach shacks, he brought up the 'monkey business' hoping for an honest answer.

'I had to give him a joint excuse. Otherwise, he'd want two separate ones. One lie is better than two.'

KK searched for the truth hiding beneath Atiya's answer. Did she expect him to invite her to the attic? Was the lie a hint or just a clever ploy to throw Ish off guard? She was the cleverer of the two, providing him with the vital lead to fox Varun Joshi and now this. Ish was dead right branding him a faker; KK wondered if he was right about Atiya.

With an eye on the receding sea, he spoke to her about Jabalpur, the low tide laying bare all the refuse: the accident that'd killed his father, the scraps he'd gotten into from the time he could understand the dirty things friends said about his mother and the fourteen missed chances that'd landed him in Mumbai. Art was his friend and now his enemy. Hand brushing against her hand, he confessed that Kabir Shah, having taken possession of his brush, was now threatening to take over his soul. From making duplicates, he had become a duplicate, a cheap and disposable one.

Atiya spoke with her eyes, hardly through her lips. No stinky fish, no guns or bombs. KK accused Rahman of spreading lies: 'She hears everything I say but gives nothing back.'

His wise friend grimaced. 'Her tongue has receded into her heart. It happens to those who have learnt to live with wounds.'

The leopard made her appearance whenever KK brought up *Gallery Hormone*. Ronnie was her friend. 'A weak man has just as much right to live his life as a monster does,' she bristled if he made fun of Ronnie's mistakes. In the office, she guarded her friend from callous slips, even took blame if a client's folder had gone missing from his desk. With time, KK understood. She defended all of Mumbai—Jagannath and Rahman, Ronnie and him—the ugly waste floating unnoticed on the seabed.

Then lightning became light, abundant and alluring, when she began coming up to KK's attic to enact her lie. The hanging man didn't trouble them, nor Rahman's gluttony, polishing off KK's meal with an ear to his door.

'What will you do when you run out of Kabir Shah, when there's none left to fake?' Atiya asked on her way out of the attic.

He tried, without luck, to grab her and pin her down. Sizing up his subject from the floor, he offered her the next course of action: 'I'll bring out your paintings from the vault, every one of them.'

'Mine? Why?' She stopped brushing down her hair. 'They aren't in the vault anyway. Ish has a few from the time I was foolish enough to show them to him. But he's forgotten all about them. What good will they be to you?'

'I want to fake them.'

Checking her laugh, Atiya stilled her gaze on KK. 'I can suggest doing something better with your time.'

He raised his brows, half expecting her to say something worthless like doing his own artwork, besides slaving away on the fakes.

'Taking over *Gallery Hormone*.'

'How?' KK shook his head. 'Isn't that impossible?'

'By getting rid of Ishvat Irani.'

The plan came in two parts. 'The fakes are key,' Atiya whispered to KK although none could catch their voices in the crowded tea stall. 'Once they are discovered, everyone feels cheated. They can devastate a gallery like a bombshell. It's impossible for the owner to make a comeback like a failed actor.'

'My fakes, do you mean?' KK recoiled at Atiya's plan. That would make him a criminal too.

'No. We must prove the gallery's originals to be fake.'

Ish was planning the mother of all events—holding the first-ever art auction at the gallery. It'd demolish his rivals; he'd become the last word when it came to Indian art. Ronnie was in charge. He had attended a New York auction with his father and understood the bidding game. 'He's working on a list of paintings to be approved by Ish,' he'd confided in Atiya. 'The lesser works will be put up first, building up the crescendo to the crowning pieces, which would lead to war with blood on the floor.'

'The Mad Nudes?' KK ventured cautiously.

Atiya gave him a thoughtful stare. 'They are valuable and scandalous. Tongues will wag for years to come; critics will feed on them like hyenas on rotten flesh. The Khemkas might gobble them up or the Coffee King, the Chutney King, the Tyre Prince . . .'

'And who will claim the Mad Nudes to be fakes?' KK smashed his earthen teacup, more than ready to dismiss Atiya's wild plan.

'Varun Joshi. Who else?'

KK started to cough, drawing the attention of the tea drinkers. Recovering his voice, he spoke gruffly, 'Why would he cut his neck with his own hand? It was he, after all, who'd sold Ish the paintings for a sky-high fee.'

Giving KK time to cool down, Atiya assumed a conspirator's tone, 'You will convince him. He knows you. You'd managed to get under his skin. This time, you must get inside his bones.'

Part two of the plan fell within Atiya's purview. 'I'll convince Ronnie to grab the reins once Ish is arrested on the charge of auctioning off fake paintings. Ronnie will call a press conference and tell the whole story of *Gallery Hormone*, beginning with his father. He'll become the custodian of the place while legal things are sorted out.' She took KK's frown to be doubt and hastened to reassure him, 'You should trust Ronnie. He's a loser like us.'

'An auction is like a fashion parade within a gambling casino,' Ronnie smirked when KK asked him the reason behind Jagannath and Rahman marking out the floor with a tape measure to fit in the maximum number of chairs. A long table came in on the shoulders of workers, to set up the bank of telephones to receive phone bids. The electrician and his assistant struggled to instal a giant screen on the wall that'd display the bids in real time.

'Like cocaine and sex,' KK smirked back. Ronnie, in charge of arrangements, seemed friendlier and relaxed. *He's already smelling his freedom* . . . KK thought and threw him a gentle barb, 'What if the chairs go empty?'

'They won't,' Ronnie was buoyant. 'The rotten cream of Mumbai won't miss the chance to smell the perfume, starting with tycoons and film stars, models, gigolos posing as art critics, whores as consultants.'

Madmen paint and madmen buy, KK mused, sitting alone in the attic. Only the likes of Ish were sane—jailers of a mad world. Rahman arrived with his meal, saw him brooding and cheered him up, 'When I came here, I didn't understand what was going on. Why people pay money to buy these things. Why beautify a world that has already been beautified by Allah? Afterwards, I understood. All this is needed to remind us that we'll soon be dead, and our lives will never be as beautiful as the paintings and nowhere close to what He intended them to be.'

KK gaped in wonder listening to his friend. Was Rahman the only true artist in *Gallery Hormone*?

The gallery opened its doors to the auction at 6.30 p.m., letting in collectors who'd arrived much earlier to beat the crowd and were waiting in their cars. Men grasped elbows of friends in greeting, ladies pressed lightly against each other to preserve the ironing of their dresses. Smartly dressed girls in black pantsuits handed out paddles to the guests, to be used by the auctioneer to mark their bids. Clerks hired by the gallery manned the phones. Ronnie's voice conducting a soundcheck resounded on the walls.

KK expected all the usual suspects to be present and occupying the best seats in the front, leaving the back row to the reporters. He smiled politely at Lalita Raghavan, waving her paddle to attract a friend's attention. 'I wish I could remember your name . . .' she returned KK's smile. Suppie Sarkar, the mongoose, was there, eyeing everyone around with suspicion. And Radhika Singh, the queen of daytime soap. 'She's plastic,' hustling by, Ronnie whispered into KK's ear. He meant implants, seventy-two going merrily on to twenty-two. With the room filling up, he searched for a face, the most important one.

The sound of the gavel silenced the din and drew attention to the lectern and the auctioneer. Dressed in a zebra suit, Ish hung over the crowd like an oversized balloon. 'We must start at 7 p.m. sharp,' he'd warned his staff against desi-style delays. Ronnie handed him the list of works, lots 1 to 69, approved by Ish to go under the hammer.

Raj Khemka emerged as the winner in the early rounds. His aggressive bidding aimed to establish the fact that he was still the king among buyers. With each work displayed on an easel as well as on the giant screen, Ish squeaked his commentary on its worth, then announced the bids . . . '15 lakh . . . 15 lakh 20 . . . 15 lakh 40 . . . Do I hear a 15 lakh 50?'

The lots were disappearing quickly, and KK sweated despite the gallery temperature set at a freezing 18 degrees. He recalled some Western idiot claiming that lower temperatures heated up an auction and spurred on muscular bidding. He saw Ronnie sweating too. Across the room, Atiya, dressed in a Manipuri sarong and a colourful Inaphi shawl, raised a brow to ask him the very same question that was clawing at his throat.

The thirties lot passed in the blink of an eye, the game getting hot and hotter, inching up to the hottest.

An anonymous phone bid halted proceedings at Lot 44. A fashion designer with outlets in India and Europe was on the verge of making a winning bid when a higher offer came through. 'It's a chandelier bid,' Ronnie whispered to KK, explaining that it was a fictitious offer, meant to push up the price. 'There isn't anyone on the other end of the line.'

Hedge funder Tushar Deshpande, who'd been unusually quiet all evening, wanted the identity of the phone bidder revealed, but Ish put his foot down. 'It's against auction rules,' he lectured Tushar before a recess was announced to allow guests to have a taste of the canapés and sparkling water.

'Why no champagne?' KK asked Ronnie.

'It's prohibited during an auction. Guests might turn unruly.'

As the action resumed, KK breathed a sigh of relief. An attendant pushed a wheelchair through the back, the guests respectfully giving way to Varun Joshi. Greeting him, Ish gestured his staff to seat him in the front row.

Lot 60. Sweat ran down KK's spine. Only eight lots stood between what had so far been a successful auction and the moment that'd change everything. He tried, unsuccessfully, to catch Varun Joshi's eye. 'Why should I commit hara-kiri at your gallery?' he'd asked KK, when he'd gone to him following Atiya's plan. 'Why should I profess the real to be fake?'

'Because only life is real,' KK took a lofty tone. 'Art is fake.' He'd offered the deal of a lifetime to Varun Joshi, 'Once the Mad Nudes are claimed as fakes by none other than you, the world will know Kabir Shah wasn't your lover, that he never painted you nude. His reputation will remain intact. The paintings will be returned to you by the gallery. The money that Ish has paid for them will go to the street children.'

'And that woman?' Varun eyed him searchingly.

He had seized the moment to undo a lie with another, 'Sadly, she's in coma following a stroke. No chance of her messing any more with Kabir Shah.'

Searching for words, the aged critic had blurted out, 'And what's in it for you?' Then reprimanded himself quickly, 'Silly me! When you've got nothing, you have nothing to lose. You want to get rid of Ish and grab *Hormone*, don't you?' He laughed, 'Didn't I tell Ronnie that only crooks can ever hope to win this game?'

With the auction under way, Ronnie drummed his fingers on the black folder of winning bids, opening and shutting the last page. 'Sixty-nine is the grandest of numbers, and the dirtiest!' KK recalled his words. 'It'll be Ish's trump card, and his guillotine!'

Leaning forward on the lectern, Ish breathed in deeply, then breathed out to the count of 10. His bird-like squeak grated like a crow's call. Heart pounding, KK could barely hear the opening words for Lot 69.

'Our final lot is the anticlimax. It's like nothing you've seen before. The freshest piece of art from the freshest of artists.' Keeping the audience in suspense, he raised an arm to call Atiya over to join him. Seeing her hesitate, he hurried her along, 'Come!' Walking gingerly through the aisle, she tripped then gathered herself to stand beside Ish as he announced, 'Atiya Angom, the artist of our final piece.'

KK cursed, barely keeping down his voice. Ish went on, 'To know who she is, you must know her father.' On cue, the projectionist put up a black-and-white photograph on the giant screen—the face of a dead man, bearing the marks of violent torture. Ish resumed, 'He is Lingjen Angom, a terrorist belonging to the People's Liberation Army of Manipur, a militant, an enemy of the state. He had evaded arrest for more than a decade by sneaking into China. Finally, our jawans caught him and served him justice. Our artist is the living soul of her dead father.'

A gallery attendant brought over a smallish painting and set in on the easel. It was a village scene—vibrant and innocent, the artist holding back her skills to convey her world through the eyes of a child.

'This is real art,' recovering his voice, Ish trumpeted, 'not tortured, requiring no explanation, beyond dispute, as terminal as the dead. Not fake.'

KK watched Atiya standing under the spotlight, framed by her dead father. Her eyes didn't waiver; she seemed like a doll, gaze spread across the gallery far and beyond.

'Fifty lakh . . . Do we have a taker?'

Raj Khemka raised his paddle, then Tushar Deshpande. Radhika Singh let out a sigh and raised hers. Paddles jumped up and down the aisles, giving Ish no chance to acknowledge the bids. Quite suddenly, a pack of mad bulls seemed to rush towards the lectern, mowing down all obstacles on their path, the guests jostling with one another, roaring drunk on sparkling water.

Dropping the file on the floor with a thud, Ronnie bolted out of the room.

Drinking from the bottle straight up, KK waited at the attic late into the night. The days of back-stabbing were over; it was the hour for front stabbing. *Ronnie! What'll he do now? Kill himself or kill Ish?* Laughing aloud, he agreed with Varun Joshi. Losers will lose, always; that's how the game has been played forever. They'd been screwed by the fakes, by their fake plans. Only the traps were real, those that Ish had set for them. And Atiya? Was she fake too, the queen of Lot 69, the leopard who'd played with the Jabalpur goat before mauling him with her paws?

KK saw an auto limping its way towards the mill and coming to a sputtering stop. Stumbling out of the gallery, Ronnie managed to crawl his way into it, the driver kick-starting the reluctant engine to life.

Coward! All great acts needed madness. To kill, he'd have had to bring down his hanging father at the attic and seek his blessings for the revenge. Drinking some more, KK searched for the missing scalpel. He must do what Ronnie had failed to do, release the curse of Abhilash Sen and set *Gallery Hormone* free. Perhaps he'd have to release Atiya too, send her to her father. Then the gallery's white walls would belong to none but him, to leave blank or piss on if he wished.

Steadying himself on top of the stairs, he inched his way down, afraid of falling. His eyes were used to the darkness when he arrived at the main floor, now empty of chairs. The row of telephones set up for the bidding was the only reminder of the evening's event. And the lectern, standing like an errant student, punished for his mischief. The sound of angry words drew him towards Ish's office.

The antechamber's door was open. Peeking through, KK caught Ish and Atiya arguing. She had his missing scalpel in her hand and was threatening to slash Lot 69, her painting that had fetched the auction's highest bid. 'You have defiled my father's memory,' she growled, 'used your dirty mind to spoil his sacrifice.' He heard Ish reasoning with her, trying to make her understand that displaying her dead father's photo was nothing more than a smart trick, an innocent gimmick, to turn her from a nobody into a somebody, the hottest name in Mumbai. It was every artist's dream. Evading his grasp, she lunged again at the painting, catching Ish with her scalpel. A fine red line appeared on the zebra suit, but she didn't stop, kept on lunging and slashing him, painting her revenge against her father's tormentors with her own brush.

Following the routine of the past 6 years, Rahman brought tandoori for KK to share at the visitors' shed of the prison. Unlike at the attic, his friend gobbled up the pieces, hardly leaving any morsels for him. Fingers had been pointed at KK following Ish's murder, his hot temper blamed for the crime of involuntary manslaughter. He had escaped a life sentence for lack of adequate proof and was due for early parole given his good conduct in jail.

Only a little encouragement was needed for KK to teach inmates to draw and paint, and he'd pleased the jailer who relied on his superior skills to help his son score highly on his homework. He had helped too to paint over the ugly walls of the compound with colourful designs and decorate the offices during yearly celebrations. All in all, he was a good prisoner, well adjusted to his confinement and given to writing richly illustrated letters to his dead mother.

Rahman brought him news of the world—the world of the shopping mall where he now worked as night guard. It had its own Ish and Ronnie and stories not dissimilar to that of *Gallery Hormone*, which had to close its doors after the tragedy. For the most part, KK listened in silence, didn't show much interest, not even when he learnt of Varun Joshi's death.

'Where will you go when you are free?' Rahman asked him.

KK stopped munching to gaze at the frozen arms of the clock of the jail's watchtower.

'I'll go to Manipur.'

'And then?' Rahman probed.

'Find Atiya and ask for her hand.'

Rahman went over KK's words on the long auto ride home. He understood his friend. Just as the Arabian Sea had washed away Jabalpur, the prison had washed away Mumbai. He was now Kamlesh Kumar, the artist.

PASSPORT WALLAH

Rakesh Mundra had decided to shut down his ancestral business, but Montek Singh arrived at his shop and changed his mind. Neelam, his wife of 11 years, had read the writing on the wall much before Rakesh. 'Computers can do better than rubber, ink and a piece of wood,' she had made a face when her husband complained about the dwindling number of customers at Mundra & Son Rubber Stamp Makers. 'These days, shops simply print out a slip. They don't bother to stamp PAID on the receipt.' Rajesh sighed, agreeing with her. No one believed in paper anymore. Even Billu's school insisted that he pay his son's monthly fees through the phone and wait for a beep to confirm that money had been transferred from his account. He knew what Neelam would say next: 'It's time to close down the shop and start something new.'

The thought of shutting down made Rakesh sad. He remembered his father's pride—the failed artist who'd exchanged his passion for the profit that came from making rubber stamps. Vinod Mundra considered his workshop to be an artist's studio, his thick glasses lovingly bent over soft wood held firmly in an iron vice. Nothing was beyond his chisel—patterns or letters that his clients demanded—be it the name of the district collector stamped on a land lease or the drawing of a woman with tresses down to her knees, to be stuck on a bottle of hair oil. But animals were his favourite. Senior Mundra fondly recollected the day the superintendent of Lucknow's Prince of Wales Zoo had called him over to commission rubber stamps bearing the images of its prized collection—lions, elephants, hyenas and wild buffalos—to stamp on the orders for procuring rations for the beasts. As a child, Rakesh loved the animal stamps and begged his father to make some for him. But his class teacher had taken a different view of the monkey stamp on his homework, fetching him a juicy slap.

Of all the rubber stamps that his father considered precious enough to store inside a locked box, the simplest bore just a word: CENSORED. The warden of Naini jail had gifted it to him out of friendship. It was used to approve letters that freedom fighters wrote and received from their families during the British Raj, the bold red stamp ensuring they posed no danger to the state.

On the day he had resolved to shut down the stamp-making workshop, his thoughts hovered around Sanju, his one and only loyal assistant. Born with his right leg thinner than his left, the boy had more than made up for his defect with a brain that took in more and worked a lot faster than Rakesh's. Perched on a tall stool at the workshop, he laid out the stamp designs on graph paper, corrected spellings, kept the books and aired his views on the state of the world, which he'd acquired surfing the net in his spare time. With two good legs, Sanju could've found work as a sorter at the post office, in a company even, but what use will he be to the developer who'd offered to buy the premises of Mundra & Son to turn it into a block of 2 BHK flats?

'We have a visitor,' Sanju bellowed from his stool. 'He's getting off a Toyota land cruiser, which is frequently used in desert safaris given its superior traction on sand.'

Rakesh took the man to be a chartered surveyor, come to measure up the land. The hour was approaching when he'd have to break the news to Sanju, whose superior brain might come to the obvious conclusion even before the measuring tape had made its appearance.

'He's wearing a designer suit and carrying an imported leather portmanteau.'

'Portmanteau?'

'It's a bag larger than a briefcase but smaller than a suitcase,' Sanju explained.

All that Rakesh would remember after his visitor had left was how tall the man was, ducking his head under the door to enter the shop, the wonderful smell of his perfume and the pocket-sized notebooks he took out of his portmanteau.

And the most soothing voice he'd heard in his entire life.

Unused to keeping secrets, he decided to reveal a part of Montek Singh's proposal to Neelam, lest she should catch him lying later and give him the silent treatment. In any case, she frowned when she saw him returning empty-handed, without the box of his father's treasured rubber stamps that he had resolved to save as a keepsake. He pre-empted her by giving her the good news.

'We have a big order now, which'll keep the shop running for a few more months. Then, we'll see.'

Neelam didn't believe him when he said it was a foreign order. 'What do foreigners want from you?'

Rakesh gave her a big smile, 'Rubber stamps!'

He knew he'd have to keep the whole matter secret from his dearest friend and neighbour Jitu, Jitendra Kumar, who smelled a story under every leaf and stone. As a freelance crime reporter for the local paper, finding the mother of all scoops was his life's mission, one that'd propel him from the lowly status of a stringer to that of a full-time employee, maybe even an assistant editor. Small towns, such as theirs, were worthless when it came to big crime, he'd complain to Rakesh, as they shared their nightly smoke on the common terrace. 'How can you have a real story without a proper mafia, film stars and businessmen?' He'd throw his hands up in the air, sneering at the petty fist fights among shopkeepers, which were the staple of his daily rounds.

Jitu, Rakesh was sure, would leap up into the dark sky if he heard Montek Singh's proposal. He'd have to fox the crime reporter with a lie if he sensed something was cooking with his friend, something even hotter than the naughty MMS clips they shared between them during their nightly smoke.

The proposal, as he recalled while tossing and turning in bed that night, was innocent at first sight. With pleasantries out of the way, his visitor had snapped open the gleaming brass buckle of his portmanteau and taken out, as far as Rakesh could fathom, a set of notebooks, small enough to fit into one's palm. 'Take a look,' Montek said and pushed the lot over to him across the table. 'Do you know what these are?'

Holding up one of them—a dark-blue notebook with the Ashoka Pillar embossed in gold on its soft cover—he replied quietly, 'It's an Indian passport, Sir.'

'Good.' Montek took the lot back and shuffled them like a pack of cards before laying them out before Rakesh. 'And this one is from Bangladesh, while these three are Nepali.' Picking one of them up randomly, he flipped through the pages and stopped to show Rakesh the markings.

'What can you tell me about these?'

'They are rubber stamp marks,' Rakesh answered, feeling a ripple of warmth recognizing the handiwork of a familiar craft.

Stacking up the passports in one pile, Montek spoke in the well-modulated voice of a yoga teacher, 'Precisely. This is what you do, don't you? Make rubber stamps?'

Rakesh was confused. 'Yes, Sir, we've been making rubber stamps for the past 40 years. My father was a master, and I have learnt a little bit from him. But we have never made rubber stamps to put inside a passport.'

His visitor's perfume—more fragrant but a lot milder than Neelam's attar, which gave him a headache—struck his nostrils as Montek Singh leaned forward. 'Never doesn't mean ever, does it?' Smiling, Montek drummed his fingers on the table, 'What if I placed an order with you to make me rubber stamps that will produce exact copies of the markings that are there inside the passports? Do you think you will be able to do that?'

'You mean . . .' Rakesh felt at a loss for words.

'I mean when someone stamps a passport with the rubber stamp that you will make for me, no one will be able to look at that marking and tell the real one from yours.'

Never say no to a customer. His father's words flashed through Rakesh's mind. *Even if he asks you to make a rubber stamp that weighs a ton!*

'I shall give you an advance and pay the rest when the job is done.'

Montek took his silence as an agreement, then spent the next few minutes pointing out the markings he wished Rakesh to copy and create rubber stamps of. Without bothering to ask for a price, his visitor had left an envelope of cash on the table along with the passports.

Once the Toyota land cruiser had left the narrow lane leading up to his shop, Rakesh sat silently by himself. Shadows had gathered inside, and it was time for Sanju to switch on the lights and bring him his evening tea. He wondered what his loyal assistant would make of the unexpected order and the more than generous advance. It occurred to him that he was on the verge of a new business, even before he'd shut down the old one.

Normally, he spent an hour buying vegetables after he had locked up his shop, taking his time in the narrow market lanes to avoid returning home early. He was afraid of Billu, rather, his incessant prodding for help in finishing his homework. No sooner had he reached home and handed over the shopping to Neelam than was he confronted by the trickiest of riddles.

'If a train leaves a station at 10 p.m., travels at 30 kilometres per hour and covers 120 kilometres, what would the time be?' Billu asked him one day.

'It depends,' he answered, wearily.

'Depends on what?' Billu stared sternly through glasses that were too big for his face.

'On if he'd had to stop to let a mail train pass by, or taken a tiffin break.'

'You are confusing your son,' Neelam overheard them and drew Billu away, cursing the 'useless rubber stamp maker' under her breath.

Rakesh spent more than an hour in the shop following Montek Singh's visit, joined by Sanju who sat across from him, occupying the visitor's seat. His employee had overheard everything and appeared deep in thought. Opening and closing the passports, which had been left on the table, he offered the first of the riddles to Rakesh.

'Do you know what these stampings mean?'

It was a hard question to answer, harder than any posed by Billu. The square, rectangular or circular stamps with non-English words written in them didn't offer any clue. A few had the outline of an airplane and dates imprinted in smudged ink. Rakesh could imagine his father's reaction if he'd examined them; he'd have passed them off as child's play, not worth the master's chisel.

'They are entry and exit stamps, indicating that the passport holder has entered and exited a country on such-and-such date through such-and-such airport.' Sanju's cousin, who worked as a chef for a foreign service officer, had many such stamps in his passport, accompanying his boss during his frequent transfers from one country to another.

The riddle was yet unresolved in Rakesh's mind, as he kept turning more pages and inspected more stampings.

'Do you know who are authorized to stamp a person's passport in an airport?' Sanju posed the next riddle.

This one was even more difficult. Neither Rakesh nor his father worried about the users of the rubber stamps, not unless the customer complained of the wood splitting at the edges or the knob coming off the block.

'Only immigration officers, those with the power to admit or deny a person permission from entering or leaving a country.' Sanju sounded smug, having floored his boss with the riddles. Then, his voice took on a grave tone, 'But Montek Singh didn't appear to be an immigration officer. Even if he is one, why would he want to have entry and exit stamps for all these countries? Unless . . .'

'Unless he wanted to give the holder of the passport the appearance of a much-travelled person.'

'Yes!' Sanju was overjoyed at Rakesh solving the most critical piece of the puzzle. 'If he was someone adding fake visas with entry and exit stamps in passports in order to fool foreign immigration officers.'

Both sat silently with the passports between them, then Sanju spoke softly, 'That would make Montek Singh a criminal.'

Tossing and turning in bed, Rakesh found the riddles multiplying, each leading to a chain of others, till he was too exhausted to keep awake. By the time he'd whipped up enough courage to lie to Neelam next morning about leaving early to buy stamp pads from the hardware shop a few kilometres away, his heart had started to pound. In all his years, he'd considered his business to be nothing but innocent, a far cry from makers of spurious medicines or adulterated liquor, even fireworks. Senior Mundra made it a point of reminding his family of the virtue of honesty every time his wife complained of a shrinking household budget. 'A rubber stamp is a mark of honesty and trust, just like us, their makers.'

Sanju was ready with more worrisome facts and even more riddles when he reached his shop. His eyes, bloodshot from a night spent browsing the net, were as threatening as those of Billu's headmaster.

'Our visitor is a people smuggler. Someone who illegally transports humans across borders, like smuggling drugs.' He waited to see Rakesh's reaction, then charged ahead. 'There was a case in Delhi last year, involving someone just like him. The man fooled some poor boys from the slums, with the promise of sending them to

Canada to work as lumberjacks. He dressed up their passports with fake Canadian visas and those of Western countries printed in local presses and fake entry–exit stamps to make it seem as if they were seasoned travellers, workers who'd legally undertaken many foreign assignments in the past. It fooled the Canadian immigration people in Toronto, and they were let in. Do you know what happened next?'

Given up on riddles by then, Rakesh shrugged.

'They lived happily ever after in Canada till one of them, Sukhbinder Singh, wanted to come home and marry his sweetheart. After the singing and dancing was over in Punjab, he set out to return to Canada when he was arrested at the Indira Gandhi International Airport in Delhi.'

'Why?'

'Indian immigration officers found his original Canadian visa to be fake. The newly-wed Sukhbinder broke down under questioning and told the police everything. In the end, all the Indian lumberjacks were deported from Canada.' Sanju shifted his weight from the right to the left leg, then smirked, 'All those rubber stamps couldn't save them!'

'What happened to Montek . . . I mean the people smuggler?' Rakesh asked his employee cautiously.

Sanju gave him a know-all look, 'He's in prison, convicted of Section 420 of the Indian Penal Code for cheating, Section 468 for forgery and Section 471 for using as genuine a forged document.'

He must return the passports to Montek Singh, Rakesh resolved, and called his visitor, taking the number from his ivory-toned, gold-embossed card that didn't carry an address. The phone rang through, and he hesitated to leave a message, deciding against it. Worried about Sections 420, 468 and 471, he toyed with the idea of confiding to Jitu during their nightly rendezvous and asking him to call Montek on his behalf. Reporters were smarter than shop owners, and perhaps his friend could even pass himself off as Rakesh Mundra on the phone. He decided to carry the passports safely back home inside his VIP suitcase, given to him by Neelam's father as a wedding gift. No one, not even his wife, knew the combination lock, which was the only secret he'd allowed himself in their more than a decade-long marriage.

'It's the right decision, Sir,' Sanju nodded after Rakesh had hung up. 'Don't worry about what'd happen to me once the business is sold. The developer has offered me something.'

'What?' Rakesh was startled by the revelation.

'He has promised to give me a small space in the new building at a low rent if I can adjust the numbers in his books to show that his company has been running at a loss, making him eligible for a cheap bank loan.'

'And what will you do with the small space?' Rakesh asked, once he had digested the offer.

Sanju gave him a sheepish look, 'Maybe I'll make rubber stamps, Sir, since you have decided to withdraw from the business.'

Rakesh felt a tinge of envy. But before he could indulge his employee to reveal more secrets and riddles, he remembered Neelam warning him not to be late returning home, and buying a toy as a birthday gift for Jitu's son Mahi, who was Billu's best friend.

A night of bafflement and a day of worries had tired him to the point of a late afternoon nap, and by the time Rakesh woke, the house was silent. With Neelam away to her friend's needlework exhibition and Billu at the birthday party next door, he felt calm after the unexpected upheaval at the shop, his mind turning away from the rubber stamps inside the passports to their owners. He recalled the names and details of some of the men. There was a Ranjit Kumar, born in Azamgarh on 7 May 1997. A mole on his forehead was his distinguishing mark. Then there was Imtiaz Khan, an early-thirtyish man, who looked baffled by the photographer's flash. Shakun Anand, Prithvi Khanna and Amar Pradhan, who looked barely older than Billu. He felt sad for these boys who were hardly men. How hard it must be for them to go from Azamgarh and Balia, Lucknow and Gazipur to as far as Canada, if that was where Montek Singh was taking them. They must feel homesick when they reached there, and their families back home would miss them terribly. He tried, unsuccessfully, to recall if Billu had ever asked him about lumberjacks. Unexpectedly, Jitu summoned him upstairs to the terrace much before dinner time, calling him on his mobile instead of hollering from the balcony of his flat. Rakesh sensed an urgency in his friend's voice, wondered if he wished to share something special with him, a hot clip perhaps, that couldn't wait till later.

'Let me show you the present that Billu has brought for Mahi on his birthday,' Jitu held up something before Rakesh's eyes under the terrace's naked light bulb. It was a notebook, small enough to fit into one's palm, blue with the Ashoka Pillar embossed in gold: a passport. Opening the cover, he started to read: 'This passport is the property of the Government of India. It should be in the custody either of the holder or of a person authorized by the holder. It should not be allowed to pass into the possession of any unauthorized person.' With a quick look at Rakesh, Jitu flipped over to the first page. 'It belongs to one Uddhav Pande, born in Hissar. Both his parents are deceased, and he sports a diagonal cut on his neck as a distinguishing mark.' Still holding up the passport, he asked Rakesh in a serious voice, 'May I ask how Billu came to be in possession of Mr Pande's passport?'

Stupefied, Rakesh failed to answer Jitu.

'And that's not all,' Jitu went on. 'Billu has brought over six more passports to the birthday party to offer to his friends, against some suitable item of exchange. Of these, three are Indian passports, two Nepali and one Bangladeshi, which is of the highest demand given its bright green colour.'

'They were inside my VIP attaché. No one knows the combination lock. I don't know how Billu managed to open it,' Rakesh managed to say.

'Hah!' Jitu snorted. 'Our sons know the combination locks of all briefcases in the house. They are like cats, pretending to scratch themselves while keeping an eye on everything that goes on. Your wife may not know about your secrets, but your son, most certainly, does.'

Seeing the distress on Rakesh's face, Jitu laid a comforting hand on his arm. 'Don't worry, I have collected all the passports, threatening to withhold the birthday cake till they are returned to me. Now, may I ask how the passports got inside your attaché?'

Then, Rakesh had no choice but to tell Jitu about Montek Singh—the strange and unexpected proposal, about the advance, down to the exceptional fragrance that he carried on his being. He took pains to lay out Sanju's opinion about his visitor's motive and the cunning schemes of people smugglers. Jitu took in everything, then grimaced, 'That would make you, not him, a criminal.'

'But I haven't yet made any rubber stamps for him,' Rakesh protested.

'No. But you have the passports that none but these men should have in their possession. Montek could easily deny he'd passed them on to you.' He chuckled, then blurted out, 'How wrong I was about small towns! They may lack a mafia, but criminals do their small crimes here in order to commit big crimes elsewhere. I'd say hats off to Montek Singh! He's turned a God- and wife-fearing rubber stamp maker into a criminal.'

Rakesh could hear Neelam calling him over for dinner, but for once he didn't answer her immediately. 'What should I do now?' he implored Jitu to save him from the mess he found himself sinking into.

Back to his reporter self, Jitu didn't take more than a moment to answer, 'Carry on making the stamps as per the order. But first, call him up and ask him for a favour.'

'What favour?' Confused, Rakesh thought Jitu was telling him to double the price.

'Ask him if he can get a fake visa on the passport of your dearest friend using whichever stamp he finds suitable.'

Neelam called again, and breaking away, Rakesh asked, 'Which friend?'

'Your dearest friend, Jitendra Kumar, of course!' Jitu answered with a flourish.

The plan, as Jitu explained to Rakesh later, was to save oneself by catching the criminal and taking the credit for it.

'It is dangerous to go to the police now,' he looked Rakesh in the eye. 'They don't know about Montek and have no reason to believe your story. They might take you to be a thief, who'd stolen the passports or picked them up from a bag left behind accidentally in a rickshaw.'

'Why don't you write a story in your paper then?' Rakesh was ready to plead with Jitu. But his friend shook his head.

'What will I tell my editor? That there is one Montek Singh, who doesn't answer his phone and doesn't have an address, has plans to hoodwink immigration departments across the world? He'll want proof.'

'What if I simply return the passports to him and refuse to do the job?' Rakesh made the gesture of washing his hands of the matter.

'Then he'll have to wash you off too, because no criminal wants to keep a trace of his crime. He'll think you'll betray him to the police sooner or later.'

'So, I'll drown one way or the other!'

'Yes!' Jitu appeared to relish Rakesh's despair. It was way past the hour for the two of them to finish their nightly smoke, but Kusum, Jitu's wife, was already asleep, exhausted from the birthday party, and Neelam was far too absorbed in her favourite television saga to miss her husband.

'We must do a sting operation,' Jitu said, oozing the confidence of a crime reporter. Taking pity on Rakesh, he explained simply, 'Think of an undercover agent, someone who pretends to be one of those men, who wishes to travel abroad using Montek's fake visa. He has paid full fees for his service. He gives the appearance that he trusts Montek completely, just as the people smuggler trusts him too with his evil plan. Then, at the moment when he's caught while he is about to slip through the ring of immigration, he spills the beans.'

'Caught?' Rakesh frowned. 'Why will he be caught if he has a visa and the stamps in his passport?'

Jitu smiled at Rakesh's ignorance. 'Because, the immigration officers are smarter than Montek. They are trained to spot fake passports and visas. They have eyes like X-rays.'

'What happens to the boy who's caught?' Rakesh sensed his normally high BP inching upwards. But Jitu's seemed cheerily staid.

'When challenged, the undercover agent will announce himself to be a reporter conducting a sting operation and confess to having a fake visa. He will reveal the identity of the criminal mastermind, and Montek will be nabbed by the police.'

'And then?'

'He'll become a celebrity overnight. The press will be all over him.' Appearing to lift off towards an overcast sky, Jitu exulted, 'The stinger will become a star!'

The rains failed to distract Rakesh from his anxiety. Normally, he'd worry about moisture seeping through the shed of his workshop and softening up the wood, making it impossible to carve it into rubber stamps. He might have to discard the whole lot, inviting another outburst from Neelam over the foolishness of buying new supplies and carrying on, as useless as giving vitamins to a dying man. 'Take off Son from Mundra & Son,' she'd screeched during a flare-up. 'My son will not touch your chisel. He'll become a software engineer and work in Canada. He'll take his mummy with him.'

Rakesh worried about Montek. What if he demanded the rubber stamps or demanded that he return the advance? It'd be hard to explain to Neelam the sudden disappearance of the foreign business. The thought of landing up in jail scared him, the prospect of spending days and nights with hardened criminals. Not a single convict could be found on the Mundra family tree, and it troubled him to consider the pain it'd inflict on poor Billu.

'Who was Noor Jahan's father?' Billu asked him the night before his exams.

'Noor?' Rakesh felt confused. He recalled that name from the lone Bangladeshi passport. It was for one Noor Mohammad. Both his parents were dead. Billu frowned and took off his glasses to give him an even sterner stare than before when he told his son that the person concerned didn't have a father.

'How can someone not have a father!'

The matter would be reported instantly to Neelam, he knew, and that night, his wife assumed an unusually kind tone, as she brought up Mundra & Son.

'You should close the shop and join my brother. He'll help you make some money.'

Neelam's brother, Bunty, sold organic manure to farmers and owned a decent-sized cattle farm. Everyone teased him for smelling like his product, but his business was booming as upper-class families preferred their food to be grown with cow dung rather than chemicals.

'You can leave the cattle to him and manage the office.'

Next morning, as he sat in his shop listening to the sound of rain, he weighed up rubber stamps against manure, and decided to give Montek a call. It was better to get to the heart of the matter instead of swallowing up Sanju and Jitu's stories.

'No need to trouble yourself; my office will come to your door,' Montek Singh sounded even more soothing than before, picking up the phone after the first ring. 'I am dying to see your rubber stamps,' he said before signing off with, 'I am sure they'll be excellent like those made by your father.'

Having made the first move, Rakesh pondered his next. What would he say to his client? Asking him to reveal the purpose of the rubber stamps would go against his father's dictate never to poke one's nose into other people's business. And it would be downright rude to ask if he was a criminal. He could, of course, make up the excuse that the wood had rotted in the rains, making it impossible for him to carve them to the desired specifications. He might even suggest his rival Jyoti Prakash & Son to Montek although neither Jyoti nor his son knew how to hold a real chisel in their hands, let alone carve.

Sanju came with more disturbing news. Montek had called the shop while Rakesh was away and asked to speak to him.

'Why you?' Rakesh was surprised.

'He wants me to do some background research for him,' Sanju answered smugly.

'Did he ask to see our balance sheet from last year?' Rakesh felt his BP spiking. There was a small error in the calculations. It had escaped Sanju's sharp eye. If caught, he might have to pay a fine.

'No, no,' Sanju corrected him quickly. 'He wants me to check online the images of immigration stamps from a list of countries. Both arrival and departure ones. If they have changed over time. What would an Ankara stamp have looked like if the visitor had gone there in 2010, things like that.'

'Ankara?'

'It's the capital of Turkey,' Sanju replied confidently, going on to fill in the blanks for Rakesh, 'He asked me what I do here when I had escorted him back to the land cruiser. I told him I cruise the net in my spare time. He wants to use me as his back office.'

Rakesh felt encircled. Not only did he owe money to a criminal—if indeed Montek was one—but from now on he would also be under close watch by his accomplice. Sanju's face brightened up at the sound of a heavy vehicle grinding its way over their bumpy alley. 'Now Montek Sir will invite you to his office.'

It took Rakesh a few minutes to realize that his car was Montek's office. Inside, it felt like the lounge of a five-star hotel. A far cry from his shop, the leather-covered seats accepted his posterior like a gentle lover, making him relax instantly. Soft bounced lighting cast an intimate halo inside the tinted-glass windows, shutting out the harsh exteriors. Strains of sitar came from well-concealed speakers. He noticed a coffee machine, the likes of which are given away to winners of a TV quiz contest.

'Would you like a cappuccino or a double espresso?' Montek asked. Rakesh shook his head. Neelam had forbidden him from drinking coffee, which kept him awake at night and suffer her loud snoring. The driver served him a cup of tea, and Montek gently cleared his throat.

Rakesh felt at a loss for words. What do you say to someone who'd brought his plush office to his humble shop? He lost the lines he'd rehearsed all morning.

'Did you want to discuss the advance payment?'

Rakesh shook his head. After a suitable interlude, Montek probed again, 'Or the volume of business I can bring to you? If this is a one-shot order or part of a bulk?'

'Bulk?' Rakesh gulped hard. Did he have more passports—Indian, Nepali and Bangladeshi?

'Our clients travel to countries all over the globe. We need to prepare their passports for them. The stamps change constantly, and we must keep making them, update our stock.'

In the midst of Montek's long account of tourist, medical, business and student visas, entry exemptions and bans and travel histories of applicants, Rakesh remembered the line supplied to him by his friend Jitu. Interrupting Montek, he blurted out, 'I want to request you to prepare my friend's passport.'

Montek fell silent. A line appeared above his trimmed brows.

'He wants to go to some good country, like America or Canada, maybe Germany. But he has no job there. He has no visa in his passport.'

After the line had disappeared from his forehead, Montek resumed speaking in his soothing tone, 'What does your friend do?'

Words came to Rakesh's mouth, but he gulped them down. It'd be a mistake to say Jitu was a reporter. Nobody he knew trusted reporters for the lies they wrote in the papers. Plus, if indeed Montek was a criminal, he'd shy away from the press. Unused to lying, he made an indeterminate gesture.

'So, he is unemployed? Maybe he's tired of his job and is looking for a better one.' Montek thought aloud, then finished his cappuccino before speaking. 'We have a package for people just like him. We find them jobs, secure work permits then process their visas.'

'Package?' Rakesh ventured cautiously. Sanju had mentioned that word, urging him to buy the full package of data plus Neelam's favourite TV programmes from a new mobile phone company that was all set to take over India.

'We don't charge our clients separately for each service. They give us a lump sum, we deliver them everything all together. For 10 lakh, they achieve their dream.'

Rakesh's face fell. Ten lakh! That was more than Jitu's annual income from the paper plus his side business of selling insurance. He could imagine his friend's disappointment, missing his chance to be a stinger.

'But for you, we are prepared to give him a discount.' Montek looked kindly at Rakesh and asked if he wanted a refill of his tea.

'How much?' Rakesh asked abruptly, forgetting that he was in Montek's office, taking the tone he used to haggle with his supplier over the price of wood. Leading him out of the land cruiser, Montek Singh walked him down to his shop with an arm over his shoulder, assuring him that he'd find a way to help his friend, just as Rakesh would be helping him by making rubber stamps.

After he'd broken the news to Jitu during their evening chit-chat, Rakesh left the terrace to walk the deserted alleys of the neighbourhood. He'd taken a momentous decision, he realized, one that'd change his life forever. Jitu hid nothing from his wife, sharing the naughty MMSs even with Kusum, who in turn hid nothing from Neelam. Now his wife would know everything about the 'foreign order' and the matter of Jitu's 'package'.

Unexpectedly, Neelam served bed tea next morning, with a plate of freshly made jalebis. It reminded Rakesh of their honeymoon a dozen years back. His parents were still alive, and the two of them had to escape to a hotel by the Ganges to do their newly married business. She seemed as light-hearted as she was then—teasing and a touch mischievous.

'So, you are sending your friend to Canada,' she poured him a cup and knitted her brows in a show of false anger, 'while forgetting about your own son!'

Rakesh stuttered, unable to say anything; the teacup rattled on the plate. Breaking off a piece of the jalebi, she fed Rakesh then returned to her usual practical self. 'It's better that way. Billu is too young to go to a foreign country. Let Jitu and his family settle there first, then our son can go to stay with them and complete his studies.'

Jitu must've misunderstood him, Rakesh thought. Montek Singh had promised a discount for his friend, but there was no mention of his family.

'Kusum has started to make her plans. She has asked for my help in settling everything here before they leave.' Neelam slapped her husband playfully, 'You shouldn't have hidden such good news from me. I had to lie when Kusum told me.'

'But it is supposed to be a sting operation,' Rakesh managed to say.

'Sting? Like bees? Who will sting who?'

The tea turned cold as Rakesh told Neelam the whole story, starting with Montek Singh's visit to the shop. Leaving nothing out, he went over the people-smuggling business described by Sanju and confided his fear of being branded a criminal. 'Just think of those boys,' he recited the names on the passports, 'what suffering they must endure, stranded far from home, forced to spend months in jail if they are caught, plus their families losing 10 lakh!'

Neelam didn't interrupt him even once, heard Rakesh out in silence before removing the half-eaten jalebis. Then, she changed the subject.

'Do you remember the boy who polished shoes at the market?' She waited for Rakesh to nod, then went on, 'He was studying commerce. His parents had died in the floods, and he lived with his uncle who was poor. There were days when he slept in the streets. He couldn't find a proper job that'd help him complete his studies although he was a hard-working boy. Then, one day, a car ran him over. He died on the spot.'

Neelam sighed, then stroked Rakesh's arm, 'He would be alive today if he could escape to a foreign country. Maybe he would've completed his studies there and got a proper job. Become rich.' A look of pride shone in her eyes as she kept stroking, 'You are helping poor boys like him fulfil their dreams. With your stamps, they can escape the suffering. They can save their families.' She sounded melodramatic like her favourite soap actor, 'What will they do here? Die?'

'But it is illegal.' Rakesh tried dampening her emotion without success. Neelam brushed aside his worries.

'A little bit of shady business doesn't do anybody any harm. Just think of your father. Didn't he increase your age by a year on your birth certificate to get you admitted to school early? Kusum doesn't mind Jitu taking the risk; plus, Montek Singh will make sure everything happens smoothly.' She had signed off with a line worthy of any TV drama, 'Life is more important than laws.'

Kusum came with a bowl of laddus, which was Rakesh's favourite. She was laughing and crying at the same time. The young Mahi gave him a handmade card with *Thank You, Uncle Rakesh* scrawled on it. Jitu sounded unusually philosophical when they met at the terrace at night.

'Opportunities are like sunrises,' he glanced eastward, 'if you wait too long, you miss them.'

Rakesh hesitated directly raising the matter of his family joining Jitu once he had settled down abroad. Instead, he relied on Kusum's plans about renting out their flat following their departure from India.

Jitu gave him the sly look of an undercover reporter. 'I had to tell a story to my family—about us migrating to Canada. Otherwise, they'd begin to suspect me. What would they think if I packed my bags one day and left for Delhi airport? I am not a businessman like your Montek. In any case, migration is a better story than a sting operation.'

'But won't they be disappointed when you do your stinging, and return from the airport without setting foot on foreign soil?'

Jitu let out a deep breath, 'We shall think about that when the time comes.'

Suddenly, as if by some miracle, the secret matter of rubber stamps turned into an open and joyous affair. Instead of pestering Rakesh over the loss-making business, Neelam showed a newly awakened interest, learning the intricacies of designing the blocks, chiselling wood and gluing a stamp to its handle. 'It's as hard as making embroidery,' she massaged Rakesh's fingers on his return from the workshop. 'No wonder they are sore and feel rough on my skin.' When not busy with housework, she and Kusum spent afternoons deciding which clothes would find space inside the suitcases and which should be left behind to give away to relatives. Billu tormented them both with riddles, 'What is the minimum temperature reached during a Canadian winter?' The ladies were stupefied by the answer, which was printed in Billu's book titled World Geography. 'How can one live in minus 40 degrees!'

Kusum was ready to plead with Jitu to select a warmer country, but Neelam dissuaded her saying, 'Your body will adjust faster than your mind.'

Sanju too went into overdrive, tracing the designs and checking spellings of foreign names, like Zagreb and Venezia, Sao Paulo and Macau. A few with Arabic markings required examining the letters under a magnifying glass. Luckily, the wood had dried and yielded willingly to Rakesh's chisel. Carving the stamps made his mind fly; he imagined presenting his non-existent passport to officers and receiving a well-inked impression on the page. Then, leaving the airport and striding into a foreign land. He felt envious of Jitu, although he'd never make it that far. He even envied the lumberjack boys.

On his next visit, Montek Singh took out a small eyeglass from his portmanteau and examined the stamps closely, comparing them to the markings on the passports he'd left with Rakesh. He resembled a jeweller, checking if a shining stone was indeed a diamond, not some piece of useless glass. Rakesh held his breath. In the end, the tall man smiled and collected the newly made stamps into a cigar box. 'You've made your father proud, Mr Mundra,' he said, and handed over the balance of the payment. After he'd instructed Sanju to dig up images of entry–exit stamps from a dozen more countries, he assured Rakesh of the promised 'bulk order' and added a subtle warning.

'I must advise you to destroy all the stamps that might have come out defective. Or any duplicates. Nothing at all from this order must remain in your shop.'

Rakesh remembered his father's animal stamps and nodded. Montek's deep voice deepened a touch when he delivered his final and firmer warning, 'And there's no need to tell the world what you've done for me.'

Accompanying Montek back to the land cruiser, Rakesh brought up the discount for Jitu. His client smiled, 'I shall prepare something special for your friend. He shall never forget the journey I've planned for him.'

With Jitu busy with his family, Rakesh strolled alone on the terrace at night. The monsoon had taken a breather, and overhead clouds promised no immediate relief from the heat. Given the whirlwind of the past few weeks, he recalled his father's wisdom in the face of domestic calamities. It was better to be weak than cruel, senior Mundra would remind his son, reciting from the Mahabharata, and trust in friends was superior to trust in God. Finishing the last of his daily quota of cigarettes, he dwelt over these words, wondering which of Jitu's stories to trust.

The first of the hurdles appeared when Kusum accidentally discovered a slip in Jitu's pocket, with the name and address of a foreign lady scribbled on it. She let out a cry and left the washing to report the disturbing matter to Neelam. After an afternoon of commiserations, Neelam showed her true colours when Rakesh returned from the shop.

'So, you've planned to send your friend to his lover in Canada!' She took her husband's bafflement as admission of guilt. 'How could you not think about poor Kusum and Mahi?' she hissed, 'making up stories about stinging, to let Jitu escape from his family.' Because guilt comes wrapped in conspiracy, she traced the mischief back to the evening chit-chats on the terrace. 'That's where you go to make your evil plans about how to fool your wives. Maybe you've planned to join him later, to be with your own lover.'

The dramatic change in mood in the house discouraged Rakesh from going up to the terrace to meet Jitu, but when they finally met late into the evening, he confronted his friend about the slip. Jitu, as usual, appeared calm in the face of calamity.

'A reporter must be prepared for every situation. If Montek does his job well, I might just sail through immigration in Delhi and Toronto. What will happen to stinging then? I have to find another target.'

'Who?' Rakesh didn't follow him.

'Someone who'll be interested in the passport fraud story and consider it newsworthy. My "lover" is a brave reporter of *Toronto Star*. I've found her details from the net and shall approach her to tell my story—your story.'

Rakesh frowned, 'What if she's not interested?'

'Then,' Jitu shrugged and threw away his cigarette butt, 'I'll simply have to catch a return flight and go back to reporting fist fights in the market.'

Kusum, Neelam told Rakesh over tea next morning, has told her husband that she won't let him go to Canada unless they all went together—all three of them.

'But they don't have passports and visas.' Rakesh interrupted her.

'Exactly.' Neelam eyed him sternly, like a customer demanding a refund for a faulty product. 'You must ask Montek to prepare Kusum and Mahi's documents too.'

'But that's impossible!' Rakesh tried to reason with her, explain why it was a problem asking his client for three favours in exchange of half a dozen rubber stamps, but Neelam gave him the look of an ultimatum. 'That's what men say when they want to shirk responsibility.'

Sanju was sceptical as well. 'Sending women over to foreign countries with fake documents is riskier than sending men. It's called trafficking. The UN forbids it. And underage children too, who might be taken to be illegal adoptees.' Montek, he thought, was already taking enough risk, and was certain to turn down Rakesh's request for a family migration.

'He'll ask your friend to settle down in Canada and then bring over his family legally in a year or two.'

Year or two! Rakesh despaired. Would he be able to withstand the combined pressure of Kusum and Neelam for 2 years till the reunion?

Luckily, the next hurdle arrived before the fallout from the first one could get worse. As promised, Montek delivered Jitu's passport, the driver of the land cruiser bringing over a fancy parchment-paper envelope to Rakesh, embossed with the words Dream Merchants, the name of Montek's company. Rakesh handed it to Jitu, and the whole family gathered around him when he opened it. Mahi let out a squeal at the sighting of the passport. Kusum slapped the boy's palm, stopping him from grabbing it. Even Jitu, Rakesh could see, was nervous, as he kept wiping his hands on his shirt to stop the sweat from spoiling the passport. Then, he carefully turned the pages to find the visa. Everyone held their breath, till he stopped on a page with a colourful sticker pasted on it.

'What is it?' Rakesh could barely conceal his excitement.

Jitu kept staring at the page for what seemed to be an eternity, then spoke, whispered almost, 'It's a tourist visa for the Republic of Kazakhstan, valid for 90 days from the date of entry.'

'Kaz . . .!' The word stuck in Billu's throat, before he rushed off to consult his copy of *World Geography*.

'I thought we were going to Canada!' Kusum looked accusingly at Rakesh. He dropped his gaze.

Neelam hugged Kusum in an embrace of grief, then the two women left the room.

'It must be a mistake,' Jitu kept looking at the passport and turning pages to see if there was another visa sticker hiding somewhere. 'Why would someone pay 10 lakh to go to Kazakhstan?'

Once he had recovered from the shock, Rakesh probed his friend cautiously, 'Does it matter where the passport takes you? To which country? You will go only as far as the immigration counter of Delhi airport, won't you? That's where you'll play your undercover reporter act. You'll have your story, be it Canada or Kazakhstan.'

Jitu heard him out, then shook his head, 'It does matter. Readers will pay attention only if it is a place they too want to go to but can't. They'll get angry because someone just like them has been caught cheating the system. Then the whole thing will become news.' He dropped his reporter's hat to wear that of a philosopher's, 'People want to go to paradise when they die, not to any old guest house.'

The air of confusion that reigned following the rapid mood swings of the past week, left everyone drained except Billu and Mahi, who vigorously scoured the pages of *World Geography* to supply juicy tidbits. Kazakhstan was the ninth largest country in the world, but only six people lived there per square kilometre—

Billu read aloud from the fat book, but Neelam didn't believe him. 'It must be a printing mistake,' she said, 'our small town has more than 5000.' It was a land that nomads shared with wolves and snow leopards, but the favourite food was horse meat and favourite drink horse milk.

'It's better than Canada,' Mahi said, and drew an angry glare from Kusum. 'The minimum temperature reached is minus 18 degrees, not minus 40!' Even the description of the steppes and mountains, the rivers and lakes—comparing Kazakhstan with Switzerland—did nothing to soothe Neelam, who cornered Rakesh, coming up to the terrace in the evening and serving the final ultimatum, 'You must threaten Montek Singh, and tell him you will go to the police and tell them everything. You must tell him to stop this monkey business and send our Jitu to Canada.'

Montek laughed when Rakesh complained to him about Kazakhstan. Like a raga, the chuckle at the base of his throat rose gradually to a hearty and sonorous laughter, forcing Rakesh to hold the phone away from his ear.

'Didn't I say, I'll send your friend on a journey he'll never forget!' Regaining composure, he explained, taking the tone one assumes with children, 'To reach Canada he must go through Kazakhstan. Otherwise, he'll be in trouble.'

Rakesh hung on firmly to every word.

'Toronto is suspicious of Indians these days. Maybe it has something to do with bad things done by our people there. Maybe it's racism. But we have no problems with the Kazakhs. They give us oil, aluminium and visas. When your friend lands in Astana, they might not even check his passport. *Ündilerdi jaqsi ködi*—we love Indians, they say. My Kazakh friend will take Mr Jitendra Kumar to Turkey by land.'

'Then he must need a Turkish visa as well?'

Rakesh imagined Montek Singh sipping coffee in his land cruiser. Saying something inaudible to his driver, he resumed, 'That will not be necessary. He'll be accompanied to the coast where he'll take a boat to cross the Mediterranean to Europe.'

'Boat!' Rakesh exclaimed.

'Then fly from Europe to Canada.' Montek Singh didn't allow Rakesh to exclaim any further, ending their conversation with his reassuring baritone, 'Your friend will travel by air, sea and land, and reach his destination in the end.'

Later, Rakesh sat stupefied, while Sanju pored over his computer. It took him less than an hour to map out Jitu's journey, but his report did nothing to brighten Rakesh's mood.

'It's a dangerous route that is increasingly favoured by people smugglers,' Sanju made a face. 'In the past, they'd take the men on a dhow from the Gujarat coast to Aden across the Arabian Sea. Once in the Middle East, they'd be given false passports of Gulf states and flown over to Europe to work in Italian or Spanish farms. Over time, they became EU citizens. But now, European laws have tightened; plus there is the threat of pirates hijacking the dhows at sea.'

'And Kazakhstan?' Rakesh wondered how anything could be more dangerous than pirates.

'Bandits extort money from travellers crossing the Central Asian plains, and several have disappeared on that 4611-kilometre stretch. Once in Russia, the mafia kidnap them to work as slaves in the Siberian mines. But the riskiest of them all is the Mediterranean. The inflatable dinghies are overloaded with migrants, many of whom drown during the passage.'

Bandits, the mafia and pirates. Rakesh's head swirled with the portfolio of criminals. He worried for the boys whose passports were filled with markings of his rubber stamps and recoiled from the guilt of abetting their tragedies. He imagined Jitu facing the bandits' knives and drowning in the sea, then managed somehow to keep distress at bay knowing that his friend would encounter an angry immigration officer at best.

Over the next week, the two families were caught up in the whirlwind of Jitu's impending departure. Each undertook a sacrifice to honour the occasion. Billu and Mahi readily agreed not to whisper a word about the journey to their friends and keep their mouths firmly shut. Neelam forbade Kusum from crying in her husband's presence as it might dampen his spirit besides bringing bad luck. Offerings were made at the local temple and alms given to a blind beggar who sang hymns in his unmusical voice. Neelam, quite out of character, kept her voice down, to prevent the domestics from overhearing the 'secret' and spreading it like wildfire. 'We don't want the entire neighbourhood knocking on our door to plead with you to get them Canadian visas.'

Up on the terrace, the two friends smoked in silence. Sharing naughty clips on their phones seemed like a thing of the past. Neither Jitu nor Rakesh brought up the journey or the stinging plan.

'I wonder what Montek is thinking now,' Jitu spoke absent-mindedly, gazing at a family of crows busy building their nest. 'Is he as anxious as us and worried about the future?'

Rakesh sniggered, 'I bet he is busy counting up the cash extracted from fake visa holders.'

'Maybe he is,' Jitu kept on musing, 'or perhaps, he's thinking about how his business will shape this world; if the forged visa stickers and rubber stamps are the real agents that will change who we are.'

Rakesh felt puzzled and upset with Jitu. Is he now trying to portray Montek as a hero? The man who was sending a bunch of innocent boys to their deaths? How could he say such things about someone he'd be stinging in just a few hours from now? Or was he privately grateful to Montek for giving him the chance to escape?

'Sometimes even criminals can be useful. Like pollen, they can plant seeds in a barren land.' Sighing, Jitu flicked away his cigarette.

It was decided that the two families would travel together in a hired van to Delhi's international airport for Jitu to catch his flight. The matter of preparing packed meals was the subject of much cogitation as the journey could take a few hours. They set off in a buoyant mood, but soon everyone fell silent appearing to withdraw into their shells. Rakesh observed Jitu closely. His friend watched the passing scenery intently. His eyelids didn't flicker, even though a stiff wind blew in through the windows. He has left already—Rakesh thought; in his mind, he is elsewhere. To distract the children, he played the game of 'name the car that'll pass us next, coming from the opposite direction'. The boys were smarter than him, winning on more occasions than Rakesh, although he caught them cheating by poking their heads out of the window. 'It'll be a BMW for sure!' Billu squealed. Mahi smacked him playfully, 'You'll find BMWs in Canada, not here.'

Family and friends weren't allowed to enter the terminal and gathered around the entrance to bid farewell to the travellers. The pain of parting tinged all those who were touching the feet of elderly relatives or grabbing close ones in a tight embrace. A few had garlands around their necks. Rakesh noticed someone who reminded him of Ranjit Kumar from one of the passports he'd received from Montek. His face bore a baffled expression, and the mole on his forehead, which was declared to be his distinguishing mark, seemed to have grown in size since the taking of the photograph. Rakesh leaned over the swarming heads to catch others—Imtiaz, Shakun, Prithvi or Amar—who might be there too.

'Are you looking for Montek Singh?' Neelam whispered into his ear. 'If you see him, tell him to take good care of Jitu, to give him a comfortable seat on the plane.'

'He won't be here,' Rakesh mumbled. 'His job is done now.'

The line to enter the terminal was unruly, with a lot of pushing and shoving. When it was time for Jitu to say his farewells, he picked up Mahi and Billu on both arms and kissed them on their cheeks, then gave Neelam a mock salute. The rest of the group hung back when he held Kusum close, and she fought hard to hold back her tears. At Rakesh's turn, his friend hugged him and whispered 'Thank You' into his ear.

Rakesh made mental calculations on how long it might take Jitu to check in his luggage and present himself at the immigration counter. The airport was busy, and the queues were likely to be long. There might be delays at the airline desk, with haggling over heavy bags. In any case, the stinging business could be lengthy. After his visa is found to be faulty, Jitu would be taken off from the queue of passengers, led into a room and grilled by a senior officer. They might check his handbag to see if he was carrying gold or drugs. Rakesh shivered thinking what Jitu could be facing any minute from now. Convincing the men in uniform that he was an undercover reporter would be tricky; they might not believe his story and throw him in jail.

Rakesh felt a tug on his arm. Neelam urged him to leave, as they'd have to travel back on a highway that was notorious for accidents at night. Plus, the boys would be hungry soon. The crowd at the departure gate was thinning, with the passengers having made their way in.

Travelling in the van, Rakesh kept up a close watch on news portals on his phone. The tantalizing news of a sting operation might break any minute now, with Jitu seen speaking to reporters. The flashing cameras would focus on his passport and the fake Kazakh visa. Jitu, he was certain, would tell them all about Montek Singh who sent young men to their deaths in exchange for 10 lakh. His BP, already running high, threatened to break the dam with every passing hour.

It was quiet on the terrace, when Rakesh came up, the house heaving with the tired breath of the sleeping residents, exhausted by the airport trip. Neelam was snoring, and he wished to stay up as long as possible till he was sleepy enough not to be disturbed by the high peaks. His mind worked overtime. He missed Jitu—missed the last of the day's smokes that they shared, and the naughty videos.

The 'Thank You' at the departure gate troubled him. For what? He should've asked Jitu. For agreeing to the sting operation, or was it to give him the chance to make a dangerous journey? He regretted not asking Jitu that question, which was now choking him. Most of all, he regretted getting entangled with Montek Singh's business, putting his dear friend at risk for the sake of a few rubber stamps. It had made him distrust Jitu, suspicious of his true motive. Smoking more than his daily quota of cigarettes, he felt suddenly emboldened. Sting or no sting, if needed, he'd tell the police the true story—that he wished to save his business without upsetting Neelam. He had simply fallen into a trap, which only innocent men are capable of falling into.

There was still no news of his friend on the channels, and as he retired to the bedroom to make an effort to fall asleep, his phone rang. It was Jitu on the line.

'Are you already in Kazakhstan?' Rakesh could barely conceal his excitement.

'No,' Jitu sounded calm.

Maybe his flight had been delayed, and he was still in India. Rakesh was overjoyed. There was still a chance then to call off this crazy plan. 'Are you in Delhi?' he asked his friend. There was silence on the line, then Jitu replied, 'I have taken the night bus from Delhi and come back. It's late now and I don't want to wake Kusum and Mahi up. I am staying at a lodge overnight and shall come home tomorrow morning.'

'So, the stinging worked!' Rakesh was breathless.

'No,' Jitu answered. The line went quiet for a few moments.

'Then why have you come back?' Rakesh managed to ask.

Jitu seemed tired, his voice dropping from time to time, 'I was on the verge of committing a grave sin and checked myself at the last moment.'

'What sin?' Rakesh whispered back.

'I hadn't told you everything about Article 420, the penal code for committing or abetting the crime of cheating. It carries a maximum penalty of a 7-year imprisonment. My sting would've led to Montek's arrest. The police investigation would then reveal all those who helped him forge the passports—the printing presses and rubber stamp makers. Along with Montek, they, his accomplices, too would be treated as criminals. And so . . .' Jitu paused for Rakesh's reaction, 'I would've become a celebrated reporter, but you, my friend, would've ended up in jail.'

Rakesh was speechless.

'Just imagine what it'd do to Neelam and Billu,' Jitu said before Rakesh could ask, 'So what did you do at the airport?'

'I didn't check in my suitcase. Sat in the toilet and kept thinking. Then left once the crowd had cleared.'

Finishing the last of the cigarettes, Rakesh felt calm. His dark mood lifted off into the night sky, carrying away the madness of the past month. Everything about his life seemed to return to where they were before Montek Singh visited his shop. He'd have to look into the manure business seriously, he knew, to prevent any recurrence of the drama. As an innocent man, he must live innocently—his thoughts returned to his father's words: trust in friends was superior to trust in God. He understood the wisdom of the Mahabharata.

THE ENEMY

It was a disfigured face. The bullet, which appeared to have been fired from close range, had split the skull open. The impact had dislodged the right eye from its socket, giving the face the appearance of a one-eyed demon.

Manisha looked intensely, then dropped her gaze.

'Here's another one,' Piyush Chowdhury, dressed impeccably in a suit and sweating under a listless fan, placed another dead man's photo on the table in front of her.

This one showed no wounds, just a gaping mouth with smashed molars and tongue cut in half.

Wincing, she shut her eyes.

'Sorry,' the IPS officer sounded sympathetic but firm. His office, cramped for space in the Criminal Investigation Department, sported the usual jumble of files and a dusty photo of the Mahatma on the wall. A naked bulb blinked in the outer passage flooded by the summer sun.

'This is the last one.'

The last victim was free of blemish, almost serene in the way the eyes were shut. Was it a natural death? Manisha wondered.

Putting the file of photographs away, Piyush Chowdhury peered into his own jottings, offered some tea to Manisha and continued with his interrogation.

'When did you see your father last?'

'Three years back.'

'That long ago?' The officer raised an eyebrow.

'Could have been longer,' Manisha took her time before answering. 'If it hadn't been for the death of my brother, my only sibling, he would've remained out of touch with his family for at least 5.'

'So, he came from Chhattisgarh to Delhi when that tragedy occurred?' Chowdhury sipped his tea.

Manisha shook her head. 'No, I went over there to give him the news. He was busy with his work and couldn't find the time to visit me or my mother.'

'You mean he dropped his family,' Piyush Chowdhury made an expansive gesture with his hand, 'just like that?'

'Yes, just like that.' Falling silent, she pushed her cold tea away.

In the pause that followed, Manisha Gupta slipped back into her professional role as reporter, accustomed to asking questions rather than answering them.

'Why did you call me over to look at these photos?'

'Because,' Piyush Chowdhury shut his file and rose from his desk to gaze thoughtfully at the Mahatma, 'Bharat Coal Mines has reported the disappearance of their medical officer Dr Prahlad Gupta from their Chhattisgarh operations. The area is known for Maoist activities. It is feared that he has been kidnapped for ransom. The local police are considering several possibilities . . . even torture or murder. We have recently recovered corpses from the neighbouring forest and want to rule out that Dr Gupta, your father, is one of them.'

'But he could've simply disappeared, couldn't he?' Manisha followed up with her next question. 'It might've had nothing to do with Maoists. He could've decided to break off all contact with his company, just as he had with his family.'

Returning to his seat, Piyush sighed. 'Yes, he could have. But now at least we know that he might still be alive.'

Still alive. The words kept ringing in Manisha's ear as she drove to work after the morning summons. For all purposes, Prahlad Gupta had died soon after she'd come to Delhi to attend college, accompanied by her mother Madhvi. Her brother had stayed back for a year more, and then he too was sent over to finish school here in the capital. It was the enactment of an old routine: fathers minding their jobs in the inhospitable mines, while the children chased their dreams in cities. They'd expected the Delhi–Raipur corridor to be busy, but Madhvi was first to sense her husband's withdrawal.

'His work means more to him than us,' she'd told Manisha one Diwali, when neighbours' families came from far and wide to assemble under one roof. Except the Guptas. 'He knows we are safe here, and that's all that matters to him.' Their letters fetched replies after months. After some years, the tragedy of Chhattisgarh drowned under a greater tragedy—the death of Mrinal in a mindless accident, racing bikes with friends on the Jaipur highway. From a family of four, mother and daughter became a twosome. Then she became the last of the Guptas as Madhvi began losing her mind to dementia, losing all traces of husband, son and daughter.

Taking a sharp turn into her office complex, Manisha recalled Rohit, her husband, dismissing Manisha's pet theories and offering his own.

'It had nothing to do with marital discord. From all I've known about him, your father wasn't the roving type. Your mother didn't leave him.'

'Then why?' she'd persisted, after her visit to Madhvi's care home.

'Because some men are like that. They care only about their mission, nothing else. Like Alexander's soldiers who left their families behind or Chengis Khan's.'

Her colleague Sumit ambushed her as she headed for her cubicle.

'A morning delay can only mean a juicy story or a bad hangover!'

She had half a mind to confess to Sumit about the interrogation but held back. Instead, true to her features editor self, she set him down on a wild goose chase.

'See what you can dig up on Chhattisgarh Maoists.'

'Are you planning a photo feature?' Sumit's eyes lit up. Manisha knew her protégé's appetite for adventure. Office work bored him;

he thirsted for conflict: Nagaland, Kashmir, Sri Lanka, anywhere. She was the switch that he flicked to flee into danger. He was her secret weapon to ambush her boss.

'Not yet. Let's get the facts first.'

All day, she thought about the three dead men. Maybe they were warriors too—on the wrong side—or simply unlucky. Their masters could've abandoned them, refused to pay ransom. Might they be Maoists, tortured to confess, then shot?

Back home, Rohit gave her a glare. Her daughter Rimi's class teacher had identified her lingual strength and numerical weakness, prompting her parents to adopt the Kumon method for both enrichment and remedial action. Rohit dealt with remedies and Manisha with enrichment. Leaving father and daughter alone, she stepped into the balcony for a smoke.

Even after 2 decades, Delhi felt strange. Once a mining child, always a mining adult—she remembered her father's friend, Shashank Srivastav, who was now their neighbour, telling her once. 'As a child, you learn to train your eyes to recognize form by gazing at the men toiling away in the open pits. At night, you hear their camp songs, which teach you music. You smell . . .' She smelled their guard Rammadhav, her fellow native from Chhattisgarh, cooking his night meal, the breeze floating up the aroma from the clay pot. She smelled the mines.

'You were late taking Rimi to school this morning,' Rohit came into the balcony to put words to his glare. 'Her teacher has sent a complaint note. Thank God she didn't have a test during the first period. Otherwise, she'd have been in trouble.'

'I had to go to the Criminal Investigation Department,' Manisha spoke, holding her gaze towards the night sky.

'But I thought you've given up crime reporting; you're into features now, into films, fashion and all that.'

'I was asked to identify my father from photos of corpses.'

'And?'

Manisha shook her head. 'He wasn't one of them.'

She expected Rohit to ask for details, but he moved on to Rimi's school matters, satisfied with the excuse, 'So it was an unwanted distraction. I'll explain all that when I write my guardian's note to her teacher.' Then added before leaving, 'Don't worry, I won't mention the corpse bit.'

'Your father was always the one to help you with studies at home,' Manisha remembered Uncle Shashank telling her. She could still glimpse her father in her mind's eye—half reclining on the sofa, the newspaper covering his face while she sat on the bed reading. *On 15 August 1947, India became free.* She could hear her girlish voice reading from the history textbook. Her father had corrected her from behind the papers. *No, Munni, on 15 August 1947, India became independent but not free. When will she become free?* She had pestered her father for an answer, but the phone in their staff quarter had rung just then. Her mother had answered it and then passed on the receiver to her husband. Her face had become tense. Dr Prahlad Gupta, the mine's medical officer, had left on his scooter before she could pester him anymore.

'You've come just in time for the morning cuppa!' Shashank Srivastav's cheerful voice rang out as he rolled in on his wheelchair when Manisha visited her neighbour's flat on Saturday morning.

'How did you know it was me?'

'From your footsteps. The way you part the door in one clean sweep and slam the bolt shut from inside.'

Manisha laughed. 'What if I was a burglar? An open door would be a welcome invitation, wouldn't it?'

'Then I'd be dead by now.'

They went through the usual routine with Manisha smiling to herself inside the kitchen as Shashank instructed her about the tea, the sugar and the milk. She knew exactly where his maid had kept them, expecting her visit.

'Have you had a fight with Rohit?' Shashank inspected Manisha's face closely. She shook her head.

'Has Rimi's class teacher complained again?'

'No.'

It was her old sadness, he knew, the one that brought her over to listen to him tell stories about her father, stories she'd heard many times over.

'Prahlad was a strange man,' Shashank Srivastav wet his lips with tea. 'He didn't fit in with the other officers. No one could figure out why a gold medallist medical graduate would leave a lucrative practice in the city to come to a godforsaken mine. He didn't play bridge on Sundays or tennis in the evenings. Our management subsidized good Indian whisky, but Prahlad was a teetotaller.'

'So, what did he do when he wasn't treating patients in the mine's clinic?'

Shashank Srivastav squinted his eyes, as if trying to imagine his friend. 'He visited the workers' colonies. Saw more patients, taught the kids, learnt their language. We thought he'd gone native.'

'And his family?' Manisha asked, her voice down to a whisper. 'Did he ever speak about them?'

'In the beginning, we took him to be a bachelor. He never brought Madhvi to our parties to play bingo with the ladies. By the time we found out about you and Mrinal, you'd both grown out of your nappies!'

His pet mynah whistled from its cage, and Shashank threw a piece of biscuit, landing it at the bird's feet. 'He worried about Mrinal, told me once that his boy was a dreamer. About you . . .'

'About me, what?' Manisha spoke up.

'His Munni was the only sign that he was human like us. He didn't say much, but his eyes spoke when he watched you play with the workers' children in the pits.'

Manisha told Shashank about the three dead men. He listened carefully, then shook his head. 'Why would Maoists harm him? They need him as much as the miners. He never chose his patients—whom to treat and whom not to—which made him so special. There must be another reason, a different mystery.'

'Which is why it's so upsetting.' Manisha rose to leave but was held back by Shashank's question, 'Why upsetting?'

'Because it's better to know that he's dead than the possibility that he might still be alive and is about to die.'

Piyush Chowdhury called when Manisha and Sumit sat down with coffee for their weekly office gossip.

'We have news of your father from the field,' he sounded urgent. 'There are reports of his sighting but no clues about what his captors want.' He cleared his throat, 'Have you received a call from anyone about Prahlad Gupta?'

'No.' She added some more sugar to her coffee.

'You might. Sometimes kidnappers make direct contact with the family and express their demand.'

'But how would the Maoists know I was his daughter?'

Piyush didn't answer directly but took a slightly different line, 'In fact, you have a better chance of contacting him than the police. Who knows what might happen if you were on the ground in Chhattisgarh. Dr Gupta's captors might prefer to do a private deal with his daughter than with the coal company or the Indian state.'

Manisha took a large sip, then turned her face away from Sumit before speaking, 'Are you asking me to go to Chhattisgarh?'

The IPS man was direct in his reply, 'That's your choice, Mrs Gupta. We'll have some safety briefings for you if you do decide to go.'

They finished their office gossip, taking their time over an intern who'd ratted out a staff member to the boss to get a permanent job. Reporting isn't what it used to be, they commiserated. Now, it's a cut-and-paste job. Gone are the heydays when a *Time Life* photographer was the toast of the town.

Her mind worked overtime as Manisha chatted with Sumit. She recalled the last time she'd brought up her father with Madhvi. Her mother's mind had seemed like an intricate tapestry with some of the threads missing. She believed the whole family—all four of them—were still living in the mine's staff quarter. She worried that Prahlad's scooter might be stolen if it was left outside at night but didn't want Mrinal to push it indoors as it might topple over and break his leg.

Did her father know the threads were breaking? As a gold medallist doctor, had he spotted the early signs and simply stepped out of the way?

'Get ready for Chhattisgarh,' Manisha told Sumit, bringing on a huge rush and inviting a big hug.

'I'll do a Nick Ut, you'll see!' He meant the Vietnamese–American photographer whose image of a 9-year-old naked girl burnt by napalm had caught the world's eye.

'*We'll* do a whatever his name is,' Manisha corrected Sumit. 'I'll come with you. You have to give me a list of things to carry along, such as insect repellents.'

'You'll need a green plastic sheet more than any repellent,' Sumit smirked.

'Why?'

'For camouflage, to cover yourself, head to toe, when you go to the fields for your bodily functions!'

It'd be hard breaking the news of her absence from Delhi to Rohit. He'd bring up Rimi's end-of-term exams and lecture her about a child's need for motherly comfort during stressful times. He'd advice Manisha to postpone her business trip without upsetting her boss. He'd take an even more negative view if she revealed the real purpose. 'I thought you'd written off Dr Gupta after he abandoned you and your mother,' he might say. 'He's in the midst of a crisis now,' she might argue back. 'Why worry about his crisis when he'd paid no heed to the crisis suffered by his family?' They'd go back and forth. 'He could die unless I do something.' Manisha might throw in her last dice. 'But isn't he dead already, for all practical purposes?' She could imagine the sarcasm in his voice.

'No one's dead unless they are dead,' she'd have to bring down the curtain, then leave Delhi with a pouting husband and a sulking child back home.

'I am going to Chhattisgarh to find my father,' she spoke quietly, sitting beside Madhvi on a wicker chair. She didn't expect her mother to respond. 'I'll see if I can free him from his captors. He'll need help if he is sick or wounded, and I might have to find him a doctor, take him to a hospital even. If he is already . . .' she stopped herself from speaking the words that could upset her mother even though she might not understand what they meant.

'She's smiling a lot these days,' Madhvi's attendant told Manisha, 'at the birds that perch on the nearby trees and the visitors.'

She touched her mother's face and kissed her lightly on the cheeks. Then picked up her things. 'I'm going to try one last time,' she told Madhvi before leaving the care home.

Moving away from Sumit at the airport check-in counter, Manisha left the queue to speak with Piyush Chowdhury. No longer in his suit, he appeared businesslike as before and handed her a package.

'This is your satellite phone,' he said, looking around him to avoid being overheard. 'Carry it at all times. It'll give us your exact location when you call.' Changing his tone, he spoke like an officer advising a new recruit, 'As a reporter, you are trained to ask questions. I'll ask you to speak less, observe more. Do not trust anyone—your driver, hotel manager or teaboy. They might be Maoists in disguise. Everybody will want something from you. Money, information or whatever.' He looked at her meaningfully. 'We've informed the local police to provide backup in case you get into trouble. In case . . .'

'What happens when I find him?' Manisha interrupted him.

Piyush seemed at a loss for words.

'I mean if my father flees from his captors and we are somehow able to meet?'

'Then,' Piyush grit his teeth, 'you must call me immediately.'

Manisha stood in the balcony of their lodge in the outskirts of Raipur that evening and recalled Piyush's briefing. *I'll ask you to observe more.* What was there to observe in this dusty outpost by the highway? 'That road will take us to the forest,' Sumit had said. Checking in, the lodge's sleepy manager had handed them keys to two separate rooms. The narrow staircase allowed only a single person to pass through. Smell of oil fries came from the kitchen downstairs and the smell of manure from the adjoining fields. A truck came sputtering into the petrol station visible from her balcony. The driver jumped down from the cabin and got into a lengthy chat with the pump attendant. The night magnified their voices.

'He had refused a promotion to our head office in Bombay,' Shashank Srivastav spoke into her ear. 'He wasn't ambitious like the other officers. He wanted to remain in the field.'

Sumit came in after knocking on the door and held up a bottle of rum. She was sleepy, Manisha told him, and promised a proper party the next day to flag off their mission.

Next day they were gone, cruising effortlessly along the national highway in their rented gypsy with a marginally deaf Kishen as driver. Vast tracks of barren land broken by fledgling social forestry reminded Manisha of a childhood spent amidst trees, tall enough to shroud the sky. Dirt roads criss-crossed forest dwellings of the locals. A whistling bus overtook them, inviting curses from Kishen. Launching into his research, Sumit recited his homework on the Maoists. 'They're running a parallel state to counter the government, which has sided with the mining companies. Villagers have been given arms to defend their land. It is nothing short of a war.'

A group of marchers passed by, forcing the gypsy to slow down. Men carried goats on their shoulders, led bullocks by the rein. The elderly lay on coir beds, ferried by carriers. Women brought up the rear, children bundled on their backs. They seemed to be on a long journey, treading silently along in an unbroken order, gazing vacantly ahead.

'They've been evicted from their homes,' Sumit reported back to Manisha after conferring with Kishen. 'The police are conducting an operation to flush out Maoists, and these villagers are suspected of harbouring them. The truth is different though according to our friend here.'

'What's untrue?' Manisha asked, keeping an eye on the marchers.

'He blames the mining companies. They are robbing peasants of their land, converting them into mines. The government has turned a blind eye and has raised the bogey of Maoists.'

'These are the Badlands'—Manisha recalled reports from journalist friends who'd covered the region. Here private armies mete out justice in favour of landlords: villages are gutted and men hunted down for going against powerful men, their wives and daughters raped, widows tortured, children orphaned in the name of upholding the law. 'Delhi is as far as the moon from here,' she'd heard her friends quip.

'For some, the Maoists are saviours. To others, they're no better than their tormentors,' Sumit kept up his commentary as they stopped at a village for a long-awaited tea break.

'Speak little, observe more,' Manisha repeated Piyush's advice to Sumit. By then, the group of elderly men lounging about had fixed their gaze on them.

'They must think we are journalists or NGO people,' Sumit whispered. 'There's no reason for outsiders to visit this damn place or pass through.' He snatched the cigarette pack from Manisha's hand, 'Don't smoke. Women here aren't expected to.'

The oldest of the elderly men called Sumit over and pointed at his camera. Then took off his turban with deliberate ease and exposed his bald head. 'Take a photo,' he pointed with his forefinger.

The scar seemed fresh, raw and angry, a crusty red question mark carved on the bare skull with a sharp knife. He gestured again.

'Who has done this?' Sumit asked, Manisha coming up to join them. The man didn't answer, starting to tie back the turban.

'Go back now,' the elderly village head waved his hand towards the gypsy. 'You've seen enough. What else is there to see?' Turning to Manisha, he spoke gruffly, in a way that was almost taunting, 'How much will your newspaper pay if you are kidnapped? One lakh? Two?' He let out a guttural laugh. 'They'll want 20.' He spat out tobacco, and made a lewd sign with his fingers, 'What will you do if they want this?'

Back in the gypsy, Kishen started up the engine before Manisha asked him to wait a little longer. She strode back to the man and showed him a photo, bringing it out of her purse. It was a portrait of Dr Prahlad Gupta. Taken at a younger age, it was one of the few she had in her family album. Shot on Mrinal's 5th birthday, it was a strong face, turned away from the camera, as if in defiance of the photographer's gaze.

'Do you know him?' Manisha asked the village head. He took a good look, then stared back at Manisha and shook his head.

'Everybody knows everything here,' Sumit complained as they got going again. 'It's the same old story as in Kashmir. No one's prepared to volunteer information and run the risk of getting killed as a traitor.'

Why did he choose to stay back among the tormentors, the victims and those complicit in the crimes? Manisha wondered. Why did the village head hold back? Was it her father who'd treated his wound?

'We must find the Maoists if we wish to do a story,' Sumit began laying out his plans. 'Conflict reporting works only when one meets the real actors.'

'What can they bring to the story?' Manisha asked, half listening to Sumit.

'Drama!' He gave her a quick look. 'Gun-toting young men and women in battle fatigues conducting a 'people's' trial of a police informer, followed by a public execution.'

'Why will they let us rub shoulders with them? Aren't we the enemy?'

'We are the soft enemy. The bigger enemy is the state. They'd want us to carry their message to the people.' Sumit would've said more, giving the example of the Lankan LTTE or the jihadists of Kashmir, but stopped as Manisha had dozed off.

At the next stop, Sumit went into a hut and emerged triumphant with a plastic bottle filled with a dark liquid. 'This'll help our evening celebration!'

'I thought you'd brought rum,' Manisha yawned.

'I have, but who cares for the fancy stuff when you have hooch!'

Getting off at their lodge, which was even smaller than their previous one, they made a discovery. Leaning against the gypsy, Kishen was reading a newspaper while they were kept busy filling up the register at the reception desk.

'It's an English paper,' Manisha whispered to Sumit. 'Which means he has followed our conversation fully.'

Sumit, who'd rented car and driver at Raipur's bus stand, didn't look too worried. 'He has, but we shouldn't worry about that too much. Our Kishen is a good chap!'

The hooch loosened knots, and Manisha felt better after she'd called Rimi. Her elocution competition was due next week, and she'd been rehearsing Walt Whitman's 'Song of Myself'. Her father has promised her a movie and ice cream if she won.

Sound of Kishen's singing came from below and, leaning over the parapet, they saw him dancing around the gypsy, serenading it like a lover in a drunken jive.

'It's good to see there's still some fun left here,' Manisha mused. The bright light of approaching vehicles blinded them for a few moments, their grinding noise drowning out Kishen's song, leading up to the lodge. Leaving their jeeps, the policemen surrounded Kishen, barking out curses. One of them grabbed him by the collar and landed a hard slap.

'What's he done? Why are they doing this!' Manisha gasped.

The assault turned savage as Kishen fought back. The uniformed men descended upon him, bashing his head against the car, beating him with rods till he couldn't hold his ground and fell.

'Stop!' Manisha screamed.

Boots rushing up alerted her to danger and grabbing her satellite phone, she pressed the alert button. Reaching the roof, the policemen armlocked the two of them, dragged them down and landed them at the officer's feet. Forced into a jeep, the convoy crunched its wheels over the gravelly road and headed towards the police station.

'Point of origin?' the officer barked out.

'Delhi,' Manisha answered, recovering from shock. The reporter's manual of police harassment ran through her mind.

'Write down,' the medium-built man with a pronounced double chin ordered the station clerk to begin typing the FIR. 'Two Maoists from JNU were arrested. They had come to the state to foment unrest among the Adivasis.'

'I went to Kirori Mal College, not JNU,' Sumit spoke up from the squatting position at Manisha's feet, that he'd been ordered to hold.

'Shut up!' the officer turned towards him. 'Are you her husband?'

'No,' Manisha answered for Sumit.

'Then what? Lover?'

Sniggering came from the other policemen. Encouraged, the officer expanded on his question: 'Did you come all the way from Delhi just to fuck in Chhattisgarh? Couldn't you find a lodge over there?'

Hold your tongue. Manisha recalled the reporter's manual. *An argument will only inflame the situation further. Let the insults flow till they are exhausted. Then offer a compromise.*

'We are reporters,' Sumit held up his press card. 'We've come to do a story here. You can check with our Delhi office if you wish.'

'They all claim to be reporters!' another man commented from the back. Everyone laughed. 'If you catch them with a gun, they'll say they are NGO workers!'

'They were caught with explosives, and . . .' the officer ordered the clerk to hurry up typing.

'Wait!' Sumit raised his voice. 'You can't simply file false charges and throw us in jail. You must produce us before a magistrate; that's what the law says.'

'*Motherchod!*' the portly man exploded. Then, rising from his chair, rushed over to Sumit to kick him with his boots, 'I'll take you to the magistrate after I've smashed your balls. Your lover won't have any use for you afterwards.'

Manisha fell on the ground, covering Sumit with her body. The phone rang just then. An orderly cupped his hand on the speaker and whispered to the officer, 'It's CID, Delhi, Sir.'

It took an hour after Piyush Chowdhury's call for the matter to be formally closed and the FIR cancelled. By dawn, they were back at the lodge. Sumit went down to the gypsy with his first-aid kit to attend to Kishen. On the verge of sleep, a beep from her purse made Manisha reach for the satellite phone. It was a message from the IPS officer. 'Sorry'—it read.

The gypsy had broken down, leaving Kishen no choice but to walk to the nearest village to look for help. Coming up to Sumit, Manisha lay a hand on his shoulder. He was cleaning his camera lens and didn't look up.

'You can leave if you don't want to go any further,' she said.

Sumit shook his head. 'This is routine, nothing more. When you become a field reporter, you know you'll be thrashed, your camera broken to bits; you'll be thrown into jail with common criminals. Killed even.' He looked up at Manisha, 'Our story makes the real story meaningful.'

Slipping his camera back into the bag, Sumit turned to face Manisha. He looked puzzled. 'Why did you come to Chhattisgarh when you could've simply given me the assignment? Feature editors don't normally go to the field. Did you want to meet the Maoists?'

A scene played out before Manisha's eyes. She could see in minute detail the room where her brother's corpse had been laid after it was released from the morgue. Madhvi sat at the boy's feet, her face expressionless. Neighbours had gathered. Whispers came from those arriving after the news of the tragedy had spread in their Delhi colony. A telegram had been sent out to the mining company for Prahlad Gupta, and an answer was awaited. Maybe he'd call. Come over even, taking the afternoon flight from Raipur. She could see herself glancing out of the window every now and then. The whole afternoon had passed. Then a neighbour spoke up asking if they should wait any longer. The body might decompose if it was left exposed to the heat. Everyone looked towards Madhvi. She had shaken her head and asked for the last rights to proceed.

Manisha sighed before answering Sumit's question.

'I came to look for my father.'

With Kishen still missing, they wandered into the forest, trampling on the dry Peepal leaves. A whistling bird led the way, tempting them to leave the dirt path and stomp through overgrown bush. A million insects slithered away under their feet; a cool breeze came from nowhere and hurried them on towards its source.

They found a lake—clean like a mirror—and a canopy of trees hiding it from the forest. It was a world within. Stripping off his clothes, Sumit jumped into the water, sending ripples to meet Manisha at the shore. She sat admiring the stillness. Saw her face reflected like a solitary leaf on a branch stooped low, almost touching the lake. Sumit's voice broke the silence of their world.

'Have you told Rohit you have come here?'

She shook her head. 'He wouldn't have understood. Would've seen it as an unwanted distraction. I am running away, he'd have thought.'

Wading towards her through the water hyacinth, Sumit wanted to hear more.

'Running away from Rimi before her term exams. Not applying myself in the office and win a promotion. Driven by nothing but a whim.'

She saw the question written plainly on Sumit's face and took her time answering before he could ask, 'My father was the reason why I agreed to marry Rohit. His absence rather. I was tired of waiting, afraid that the man I would be with might also disappear some day. Wanted someone solid, an ordinary man.'

They heard a splash—a frog jumping in, followed by an army of tadpoles.

'And I couldn't leave because of Rimi. Didn't want her to grow up like me, having one parent but not the other.'

Extending his arm, Sumit invited her to jump in. She stripped off like him and slid into the water, the two of them joining the frog and the tadpoles, the hyacinth and all the mysterious creatures of the lake.

The sound of women singing drew Manisha and Sumit towards the village that was close by. Making their way in cautiously, they peered into the thatched dwellings through bamboo shutters. The huts were empty. Not a soul gazed back, not even a shadow of a passing form caught their eye. Piles of paddy sat in empty courtyards waiting to be husked. They strained their ears to catch children crying or the bleating of a goat.

Like the silent marchers, have these villagers too been flushed out of their homes in the hunt for Maoists? Manisha wondered. 'At this rate, what will happen to all the forest people?'

'They'll live in miners' camps,' Sumit muttered. On the verge of giving up, they found an old, toothless woman sleeping on the floor of her hut. She didn't mind the two of them stepping in and rose to offer water from an earthen pitcher. 'The men have gone to the forest,' she told Sumit. 'Only the women have stayed back with the children.'

'When will they return?' he asked her and received an incoherent answer.

The singing drew them to a largish enclosure fenced on all sides. The village women had gathered inside. Manisha watched through a split in the reed wall. It seemed like a celebration. A young woman lay on the floor in the middle, surrounded by the rest. She was heaving, her breathing rising as high as the singing. It didn't take long for Manisha to realize that she was in labour, and the rest of the women had assembled to comfort her by their singing. The moment was fast arriving she sensed, then parted the reeds as best as she could for a proper look.

'What is it?' Sumit was impatient. She hushed him. The expectant mother was screaming now, her mouth frothing. A pair of male hands—powerful and gnarled—held the baby's head and eased it out of its mother.

As agreed, Manisha called Piyush to report their visit to the village. He heard in silence as she described the strange absence of men. Then conveyed his instruction: 'Listen carefully. You must leave this place as soon as possible without delay.'

Sumit was opposed to the idea of leaving as darkness had fallen. They might get lost in the forest. With Kishen gone, it'd be risky to spend the night in the gypsy parked by the road. 'Let's wait here till sunrise,' he managed to convince Manisha. Later, riding in the gypsy without Sumit, blindfolded and held firmly on both sides, she regretted not having overridden that decision. Appearing out of thin air, Kishen had locked her hands behind her back after she'd taken off the green plastic sheet in the fields. His accomplices stuffed her mouth with a piece of cloth and carried her back to the car. Leaving the highway, they'd set off over bumpy roads, and after a while, she had given up struggling.

Just as sleep erases the memory of the waking hours, the journey had wiped her slate clean of thoughts, setting her mind free among her captors, till noon when they arrived at the Maoists' camp.

'Sit down, Munni.' The voice came to her across an ocean. Manisha shivered. She'd have recognized it even in her sleep. The white overalls that he wore did give him the appearance of a doctor, but his face had changed from the one on Manisha's photograph. Weather-beaten like a miner's, it was notable for the eyes that glowed from within a pair of deep sockets. He looked strained, and the stubble made him seem older than he was.

'Give me what you've been carrying in your bag,' he stretched out his hand across the doctor's table inside the camp's clinic. He gazed steadily at her, 'Give me the satellite phone.'

She had spent the day inside a hut that resembled a prison, hardly able to catch a wink on the camp bed. A guard stood outside the door, and she had had to bang hard to be let out and accompanied to the makeshift toilet. She had asked the youngish man for a cigarette and received a hand-rolled *biri*. A woman, barely older than her, had brought in a bowl of food, and she'd eaten hungrily. She'd spent the day observing: chicken being slaughtered and the bustle of a gruel kitchen. A group of recruits whistled as they dug a trench. She heard the sound of a drill at a distance.

'Whoever you called last night found out your location. That village has now been surrounded by the state's armed forces. They are conducting a raid. By this evening, they would've killed and wounded scores, burnt down the huts.' He paused, 'The young mother and her child might still survive, but we don't know for sure.'

'And . . .?' Manisha felt a surge of anxiety.

'There's no news about your friend.'

'But why would anybody attack a harmless village?' Manisha ran through a frantic list of possibilities in her mind. That voice, quiet but definitive, spoke to her again.

'A village without men suggests it's a Maoist base. The able-bodied have gone to conduct an operation to blow up a bridge or lay landmines against the security forces. That's why I left right after the childbirth when I should've stayed longer to care for the mother as it was a complicated case.' The sun fell on Prahlad Gupta's face. 'I decided to remove you as well before it was too late.'

For the first time, she looked around the room. It was spacious and airy, a white curtain hung across, cutting it into two. She saw a hospital bed on the other side and a man lying on it, and smelled ether and blood. A nurse, whom she recognized as the woman who'd brought her food, carried a tray of surgical instruments out of the room and threw them a casual glance.

'So, you knew I was there at the village.'

'Kishen is one of them,' Prahlad took a quick look out of the window. 'He knew you and your friend were after Maoists. And you were looking for me, showing my photo to people all along your journey.'

The shock had passed, and now Manisha faced him squarely as her father took on a harder tone: 'Who has sent you, Munni?'

She took in a deep breath.

'Is it the police? Have they sent a message through you asking me to surrender? Are you carrying a mercy package that'll tell me all about the deal? Have they given you this satellite phone to track your movements and to alert them if I agree?'

'No,' Manisha barely whispered.

Sliding back on his chair, Prahlad waited for Manisha to say more, then mused, 'It couldn't have been Madhvi. She wouldn't have allowed you to take on the risk.'

Tears welled in Manisha's eyes. She could barely speak. Then she fought back the pain of that many years to say what she'd come say, 'My mother doesn't remember her husband anymore.'

She was allowed to roam freely inside the camp, treated more like a visitor than a prisoner. Her guard accompanied her to a hut at the edge of the camp after sundown, and she was greeted by the nurse named Akka. She was busy in the kitchen, preparing a feast. She spoke to her rapidly in a tongue Manisha couldn't fully understand and fell silent as she eyed Prahlad's clothes hanging from a hook. His watch lay on a stool, alongside a surgical box. Is this her father's dwelling? Why has he abandoned his staff quarters to move into a Maoist camp? Was he a Maoist? Had he always been one and hidden the fact from his family?

Akka opened a small suitcase, taking out Prahlad's things to reach for a decaying envelope of photos. Thumbing through them, she brought out one and passed it on to Manisha. It was of her with her father, taken on her sixth birthday. He looked relaxed in it, gazing fondly at his Munni blowing out the candles. A small group of company officers had gathered in the back, including Shashank Uncle standing assuredly on his feet before he was crippled by a mining accident.

Cosying up to her, Akka too peered at the photo, then traced the contours of Manisha's face with the tip of her finger. You're a copy of your father, she seemed to say, a glow of motherly affection in her eyes.

Who is she? Dr Prahlad Gupta's medical assistant and fellow Maoist? Was she his woman?

You can keep the photo, Akka seemed to say to her, dropping it into her bag.

When Prahlad returned, he sat down to eat with the two of them, but not before he'd washed his hands thoroughly just as Manisha remembered him doing when she was young.

'The forest isn't as friendly a place as people think,' he started on a long monologue after gulping down a mouthful. 'There are snakes that will bite, poisonous scorpions, fruits that can kill if swallowed. Gangrene can set into wounds in the absence of proper care—as was the case with the man you saw in the clinic, part of whose leg I had to amputate.'

Akka hushed him. They kept on eating.

'Is it worse than the mines?' Manisha asked out of curiosity.

Dr Gupta shook his head, 'Mines are death traps.' Taking a quick glance at his watch, he went on, 'For years, I'd begged the company for a proper hospital to treat victims of pulmonary diseases caused by coal dust and exposure to poisonous gases. For proper care of trauma recovery in case of mine disaster, dealing with silicosis and much more.' He broke off. Akka egged him on to keep eating, but he pointed at his full stomach. Manisha could hear a barely audible sigh when he spoke, 'Nobody cares if they live or die. They care about coal, copper, iron, mica—about profits.'

'And so, you waged your one-man war!' Manisha quipped.

'What else can a doctor do?' Prahlad shot back. 'Miners, forest dwellers, peasants, shopkeepers . . . fight for each and every one of them.'

'Even Maoists?'

Akka stiffened. Rinsing his hand, Prahlad returned to sit across from Manisha. He stared long into the night before answering. 'Yes, even them. They have their reason to fight, and I have mine.'

'Which is to do what?'

'Save a person from death. To stop the pain. A blocked artery is a blocked artery, no matter who that person is—rich or poor, Maoist or not. You use the same forceps to extract a bullet as you do to ease out a breach baby. I fight for the body that knows only suffering; it cares for neither good nor bad. The state may call me an enemy, but I am just a doctor.'

The food went slowly down her throat as Manisha listened.

'Which is why the police have been hunting for me. Turned me into a marked man, keeping a tab on which patients I see, if I secretly visit the Maoists to treat their comrades. I had to leave my staff quarters; otherwise I couldn't be with those who need me most.'

'So, the police know you are alive?'

A smile passed over his face as he answered Manisha, 'Why do you think they have sent you here!'

Prahlad left with Manisha for the clinic. The amputated man needed a painkiller shot. Driving out of the camp, he stopped on a hillock and sat motionless. His mind seemed far away. Beside him, Manisha lived moment to moment. How long since she'd been this close to him? Smelled his fatherly smell, heard his breathing? A dead man has come alive, her mind felt trapped in a maze, conflicted yet numb.

'Remember Pande?' Prahlad asked Manisha.

'The magician?'

'The one who forgot his trick in the middle of a show!' Both laughed remembering their neighbour.

'And Badshah? I wonder if he's still alive.'

The mongrel they'd adopted and named Badshah had died after Mrinal had brought him over to Delhi, Manisha told Prahlad. 'He had a tumour in his stomach.'

After the tense meal, they seemed relaxed. When will he break—Manisha waited—and ask about his family? How could she tell him Mrinal's story—about all that speeding, always in a mad rush for no reason, desperate to reach the unreachable? And her mother—gone beyond the reach of painkillers, to erase the source of pain. She waited for her father to ask about Munni. It'd be hard to put into words why she was still searching and for what.

Dropping Manisha back at the camp, Prahlad left for the clinic. The place had fallen silent, and she heard Akka snoring. A bed had been laid out beside her, with a blanket folded neatly at the foot. Will the Maoists consider her an ally, like her father? Or hostile, given her links with the police? What if they decided to hold her at the camp even after the doctor had left, demanding ransom for her release? Cold sweat ran down her spine at the thought of being separated from Rimi. Might she too disappear into the forest, like her father? Inside the hut, she searched for the object that could set her free. Spotting the satellite phone under Akka's bed, she switched it on, bringing the dead instrument to life.

Woken up by Prahlad, as dawn was about to break, Manisha panicked. There could be some bad news about Sumit. Her father told her to get ready. 'You must go now,' he spoke under his breath and helped her gather her things. 'The Maoists have detected a convoy of security forces nearby, and an attack on the camp is imminent.' He hurried her on and marched ahead, leaving the clump of huts behind. Manisha struggled to keep pace with him. They took a shortcut to avoid crossing through the heart of the forest, the dense foliage that blocked passage like a wall. The highway was close by, she sensed, from the roving headlights of trucks that flashed beams, lighting up the forest like torches.

'I'll take you to a petrol pump. Long-distance buses stop there. You can take one of these to Raipur then fly back to Delhi,' Prahlad panted, dropping back to tell Manisha.

'Wait!' she held Prahlad by his shirt. 'I have something to show you.'

By then, they'd reached the highway. The mist was yet to lift fully. Buses and trucks dashed madly past them like monsters in the breaking dawn.

Searching inside her bag, Manisha brought out a photograph, shouted at her father to stop. 'Here, I want you to see this.'

Holding it up to the morning light, Prahlad peered at Rimi's photo, dressed up for school and blowing her mother a kiss.

'She's Rimi, my daughter. Your grandchild. The only one. She's never known her grandfather.' She paused to catch her breath. 'Maybe she'll be lucky to meet him on her birthday, on 15 August.'

Standing by the highway, Prahlad took a long and hard look at the photograph before returning it to Manisha. Then pointed at the petrol pump. 'Go, Munni,' he said, before disappearing into the mist like a ghost.

'I thought you two were having an affair,' Rohit fidgeted with the coffee cup. 'When she stopped calling Rimi, I had no choice but to contact her boss and ask where he'd sent my wife. His answer shocked me.'

Sumit listened quietly.

'Manisha has taken a leave of absence, I was told. It wasn't office work, but a personal matter. Your phone was switched off when I called. They have run off on a Roman holiday, I was sure.'

Sumit's Chhattisgarh photos lay on the table, those that he'd shown Rohit after giving him a full account of their trip. There were shots of the burning village where he and Manisha had spent their last night. He'd managed to do his job with the camera and flee purely by chance.

'Manisha has been kidnapped; I was sure when she didn't return from the fields in the morning. With our driver missing as well, there was no way to launch a search.' He waited for Rohit to finish his cup before saying the most important bit. 'She hid her mission from you, because you wouldn't have understood. Her feelings for her absent father are no less than what Rimi has for you. Loss has only made them stronger. She didn't wish to disturb your world as she tried to make sense of her own.'

Rohit drove cautiously after he'd insisted on dropping Sumit home, promising to meet again once Manisha had recovered from her tiring journey back to Delhi. The roads were clogged with traffic, diverted by the Independence Day preparations. Cops had set up barriers and whistled furiously at drivers to change their course. Curses flew back and forth. Workers carried chairs, stacked up on their heads, over to the VIP stand on Rajpath. A deafening sound came from stands being constructed for lay visitors. Metal detectors had cluttered up the footpaths, drawing pedestrians on to the roads. The presence of an armoured truck signified the lurking danger of Independence Day.

He was late picking up Rimi from school. She'd be waiting at the gate, poking her head through the grill looking for him. Rohit felt anxious. Her father was never late, Rimi knew. He'd be there before the final bell had gone off; she was used to seeing him chatting with the school guard as other parents took their time to arrive. Braking abruptly, he took a sharp turn to try a faster route. Her father has forgotten to pick her up, Rimi might think. She might think the unthinkable—her father has forgotten her! Passing a busy junction, he blew his horn, impatient to get the traffic moving. The road was full of lazy parents, in no great rush to reach their wards. Rimi could've given up by now. She might've climbed up to the top of the slide, alone in the schoolyard, looking over and beyond the gates to spot Rohit. Cursing the policeman, he made the risky move to overtake a van and crashed into its side, coming to a sputtering stop.

This time, the maid brought them tea, Shashank listening in silence to Manisha. His eyes mellowed when she told him about Prahlad's final words.

'I told you he's extraordinary. He didn't abandon his family selfishly. He was swept away by a wave.'

'Why did he have to save me then?' Manisha spoke laboriously, trying to make sense of her whirlwind trip. 'Not once, but twice—at the village and at the camp.'

'Because,' Shashank asked for some more tea before picking up the thread, 'he is a deeply moral man. Meeting you brought forth a greater pain than what he'd been used to treating. The pain of hurting those one had dearly loved. He must've realized that he'd made Madhvi, Mrinal and you suffer a deathly disease, the disease called loss. That he'd ruined your lives to save others. And so . . .'

'And so, he must know that the disease will kill his wife and his Munni, just as it had killed his son. The gold medallist doctor will fail to cure us.'

Shashank Srivastav kept staring at the birdcage, as if the mynah understood the weight of his thought. 'He might still try,' he said, as Manisha rose to leave, making her turn around with a frown.

'Keep an extra chair handy for Rimi's birthday party.' Shashank Srivastav beamed a big smile, 'Let's see if he does or doesn't.'

Returning to her flat, Manisha took out the photo that Akka had given her. Did it merit a place in the family album? She wondered if Alexander's soldiers made it safely back to their homes. A phone rang. It was from IPS Piyush Chowdhury. She let it ring till the caller hung up.

At first glance, the petrol pump's shopkeeper didn't recognize the doctor who'd saved his mother's life. He wasn't dressed in his usual loose pants and plain shirt with sleeves rolled up to his elbows. He had shaved off his stubble, shaved his head even. A white turban matched the white cloth tied in the manner of forest people around his waist and a loose vest. He was barefoot. When he asked for a pair of rubber sandals, he recognized the doctor by his voice. He would've offered him tea, but he seemed to be in a hurry and the bus to Raipur terminus was due to arrive any moment. Besides the sandals, he bought a rattle made of bamboo stick and coloured glass that kids played with and reached inside his vest pocket to pay. The shopkeeper joined his palms and shook his head, refusing to accept money, but he insisted.

Prahlad Gupta slept on the bus, resting his face on his elbow pressed against the window. Men pissed by the side of the road when they stopped. Women kept peanut sellers busy. A man seated next to him asked if he knew a good doctor in Raipur. Beside him, his wife showed a swollen face, a gorged eye and lesions on her arms. *Black fungus* . . . he mumbled to himself, then shook his head and looked away.

The driver stopped at a checkpoint. Bayonet-carrying policemen boarded the bus holding up a page of mugshots of wanted men and went down the aisle. The passengers obliged: it was common practice in this troubled region.

At the Raipur rail terminus, he ate a healthy meal and waited under the station clock for the train to Delhi. An AC sleeper would cost Rs 4000. He bought a non-AC unreserved seat for Rs 400. The journey would take 21 hours, but he didn't mind. He had time.

Leaving her office late, Manisha hurried through last-minute shopping for Rimi's birthday. The cake order took longer than expected given the rush of shoppers, and she bumped into Piyush Chowdhury on her way out of the confectionary. Her jaws hardened.

'Why are you chasing me?' Manisha hissed. 'Do you want to show me more corpse photos?'

The officer blocked her path. 'To ask why you haven't reported back to me after your return from Chhattisgarh. That was our deal.'

'What deal?' Manisha shot back. 'We hadn't agreed upon anything. I went there of my free will.'

'We know you met Prahlad Gupta,' Piyush cut her short. 'You stayed with him in the Maoist camp. The phone signal gave your location away. Our forces raided the camp, demolished it. But there were no signs of the doctor there. He'd fled.' He brought his face close to Manisha's, 'Maybe you can tell me where he went, to which terrorist camp.'

Dropping the shopping bags to the floor, Manisha matched his fury. 'You've done more than demolish the Maoist camp. You've gutted an entire village of innocents. That's a crime!'

'We suspected they were more than innocent, much more.' Piyush spoke haughtily, 'You have no idea about these terrorists, how they use the villagers as shields, employ them to do their dirty work.'

'A suspicion is still a suspicion, Mr Chowdhury,' Manisha levelled with him. 'It's not a licence to kill.' Picking up her bags, she started to walk away, with Piyush following her. Now his voice assumed a threatening note, 'Withholding information can land you into trouble, Mrs Gupta. The police will want a full disclosure, nothing short of it.'

Manisha scoffed, 'Isn't it a bit silly to talk about disclosure? You knew all along that my father was alive. But you pretended you didn't know. Made up the kidnapping story, to get my sympathy. You played on the purest of emotions—a daughter's love for her father—didn't you? You used me as bait.'

Piyush Chowdhury smiled wryly, returning to his normal tone. 'Bait? Yes, you can call it that. That's how one lures the enemy out. It's the norm of the forest.'

He shared the compartment with peasants. With more passengers than seats, a good many of them squatted on the floor, stuffing sacks that held their belongings underneath the bunks. The jolting bogey tossed them from side to side, made it seem as if the men, women and children had been moulded into a single ball of flesh. Prahlad curled up on an overhead bunk, taking as little space as possible, wedged between dozing youngsters.

When the peasants offered him food, he ate with them. Shared a smoke, drank water and poured a little over his head to relieve the heat. He spoke in nods and shrugs; nobody took much notice of him, taking him to be a forest man like them, called him Burha—grandfather.

A couple of policemen boarded at a stop and changed the mood of the compartment. Ordering the peasants to vacate their seats, they lounged on the bunks, putting up their feet. They poked the sacks with their sticks and cracked crude jokes about the women. Now the jolting bogey seemed full of colliding rocks.

Following the same routine as in the bus, the policemen started checking the faces around them, matching them to a sheet of mugshots. They didn't bother with the women or the children, and nudged Prahlad with their baton to wake him up. 'Show me your face, Burha,' one of them said and yanked his turban off. The one doing the matching froze when Prahlad yawned, appearing to be bleary-eyed from the heat and lack of sleep. 'Hold still,' the man barked, then snapped his photo on his phone.

He went back to sleep as the policemen got off at the next station. Besides the din of vendors, he heard the crackle of a walkie-talkie. After a longish stop, their journey resumed, but with the compartment's doors chained from the outside and firmly locked.

Manisha found her mother in a cheerful mood at the care home. She's been chatting a lot these days, Madhvi's attendant reported to her. Especially about her wedding. 'She remembers details of every guest and who gave what as gifts.'

Emotional memory lasts longer in dementia patients—Manisha recalled the care home's doctor telling her. They might forget everyday details, like if they'd taken their medicine or not. Forget names of near and dear ones even. But they might remember something joyous like a childbirth or tragic like a death.

'Next time, we'll chat about our time in the mines,' Manisha told her mother. 'About Mr Pande, the magician, about Badshah, about the trees you planted every year to replace the ones brought down by the loggers.'

Madhvi smiled. Encouraged, Manisha divulged her plans for the evening. 'Today is special; it's Rimi's birthday. I'll bring her over when her school vacation begins. I want you to tell her stories, like you used to when I was a little girl.'

Waving goodbye to Madhvi's attendant, Manisha dashed off to fetch Rohit from home and head towards Rimi's school.

Easing Rohit out of the car and steadying him on crutches wasn't easy, and by the time she had helped him hobble over to the school grounds and found a seat among the parents, the band had started to play. Proud parents scanned the march-past to spot their smartly outfitted children. Teachers looked on nervously, hoping for a smooth passage of the Independence Day events without any glitch.

'That's the principal, waiting by the flagstaff to hoist the tricolour,' Rohit nudged Manisha then shook her by the shoulder spotting Rimi among the marchers.

The forest came into view, as Manisha gazed out towards the greens. She saw the cluster of huts by the lake. Heard a solitary bird call. The old, toothless woman handed her water. As the national anthem played on the loudspeakers, the song of the women rose above it, mixed with the heavy breathing of the expectant mother. Images flitted by in quick succession. She sensed the presence of voices around her and the sound of boots.

'Are you all right?' Rohit noticed Manisha's faraway look.

She nodded. Then winced at the loud boom of the gun salute to the nation's martyrs. She could imagine the camp being raided, surrounded on all sides, bullets flying and flames blazing through the huts. Among the bodies trampled over in the rush, she witnessed a corpse and had no trouble recognizing the man. It was Kishen. She searched among the dead for another face. Where was Akka? Had she escaped with her father, or was she still there?

Rimi beamed at her parents as she passed the visitors' stand. Manisha shut her eyes with her palms. Her body shook.

Thirty-one Up Raipur Passenger had turned into an express train, skipping its stops and dashing on to Delhi. The peasants didn't know if they'd missed their destination and dozed on. Those that did know searched for the guard who seemed to have disappeared. Just a bunch of policemen, now glum-faced, guarded the exits, neither cursing nor demanding a bribe. Shown the green flag at passing stations, the express sped on, unchecked by a shunting or a tiresome wait to allow a mail train to overtake it. Dangling his feet from the bunk, Prahlad watched the towns flashing by, men and beasts waiting at level crossings, the endless horizon. He kept an eye too on the policemen.

He found himself inside a staff quarter where celebrations were about to begin. Young children flitted about like birds inside the rooms, while their parents sat on a long bench cracking jokes among themselves. Half a dozen mine officers had come along, among them his friend Shashank Srivastav. His wife had baked a cake and seemed a bit shy bringing it out as the edges had browned, and it wasn't as perfect a cake as one could buy in the shops. His boy had thrown a fit over a broken toy, and he had to take him outside and tell him a story to quieten him down. Gently swaying on his bunk, Prahlad revisited the scene he'd wished to forget all these years: his Munni cutting the birthday cake as he kept her hand steady on the knife.

'How will you identify your man?' the senior officer asked Piyush Chowdhury. 'It isn't enough to rely on a visual match. There must be positive confirmation.' He waited for Piyush to answer before probing further, 'Can your reporter source be of help?'

He shook his head. 'But . . .' he drummed his fingers on the file, and brightened up, 'there may be someone else who could help to do just that.'

Sumit had already dropped by at their flat with his new friend Sweta and unwrapped the party decorations before Manisha reached with Rohit and Rimi. The guests were set to arrive any minute. Settling Rohit down on the couch, Manisha joined in the preparations, darting in and out of the kitchen and hassling her maid to hurry up and finish the cooking. Punctual as ever, Shashank Srivastav rang the bell and came in with his gift for Rimi.

The party games started with Sumit and Sweta in charge as the flat filled up with guests. Kids darted around the rooms for the treasure hunt. Shashank acted as judge for musical chairs.

Manisha sensed her heart pounding as the evening rolled on; with an eye on the window, she strained her ears to catch the sound of a car coming to a stop at their block of flats.

'Where's the gift you promised me?' Rimi tugged on her arm. 'Show me!'

'Calm down! Everything's under control,' Sumit whispered into her ear.

'Shall we have her cut the cake?' Rohit asked Manisha. She felt Shashank Srivastav's eyes on her.

How could she calm down! She dashed into the kitchen to hassle the maid some more.

Prahlad saw the bright lights of the Capital, as the train approached its destination. The illuminations reminded him of the dark forest. The peasants gazed out, uncertain where they'd arrived. As the bogies jumped over the fishplates and slowed down, he saw a deserted platform without a porter or a traveller in sight. A convoy of policemen lined the long concrete stretch on both sides, with officers waving batons, carrying bullhorns and displaying their weapons in plain sight.

The train came to a jolting stop and raised a cheer among the passengers. Men in uniform thwarted them as they dashed towards the exit, allowing them to leave one at a time, counting them like sheep. Prahlad joined the women and children, who'd formed a bunch apart from the men and moved towards the overbridge that'd take them out of the station. The queue for men inched forward at snail's pace, each passenger checked thoroughly by a team of officers—their faces examined and captured on a screen. A policeman poked Prahlad in the gut, ordered him to get back among the men. He lifted up his vest to show his sunken ribs. 'I'm an old man,' he protested, but was pushed out by force.

Wiping his face with the loose end of his turban, he took out the toy rattle and twirled it around awaiting his turn.

Sumit lit the last of the ten candles on the cake and brought everyone over to the dining table. Her friends surrounded Rimi, and Sweta led the birthday song. Rohit gestured at Manisha to help Rimi cut the cake, but she told him to do it instead, 'Let this be a father–daughter thing.'

Standing in the back she watched the two—Rohit's hand guiding Rimi's. She looked away at the dark night, kept on gazing as the candles blew out and the singing stopped.

When his turn came, Prahlad looked the officer in the eye, offered him the gaze of a peasant—uncomprehending and obstinate. Asked to turn his face to one side and then the other, he obliged, then strode right ahead without waiting for the officer's signal. The platform stretched a bare 50 yards before him, before he'd reach the overbridge. The diesel engine blew its horn, drowning out platform noise. He didn't quicken his steps. He walked the last stretch with the languor of a peasant who walks his land at his own pace.

A solitary figure sat on a wheelchair in front of the stairs leading to the overbridge, an officer standing behind her. She blocked his path, and he had to stop and wait for her to move. They were within a few feet of each other—Prahlad and Madhvi. His eyes glowed from within the sockets, his jaw dropped. The rattle fell from his hand, rolled down and came to rest at the foot of the wheelchair.

The broken threads of the tapestry joined up at that very moment as Madhvi laid her eyes on Prahlad. She screamed out his name. Evading her and IPS Piyush Chowdhury, he ran up the stairs and broke free of the cordon, with the entire force giving him chase.

Cars rolled away from Manisha's flat with parents taking their kids home at the end of the party. Ignoring her pleas, Sumit and Sweta took it upon themselves to clear the mess and restore the furniture to its place. They carried the gift boxes too to Rimi's room, who was half asleep by then, resting her head on Rohit's lap. Sumit gave Manisha a big hug before leaving and promised not to be late for work the next day.

She cajoled Rimi to shift over to her bedroom. It was time for the maid to leave. Telling her to keep the front door unlocked, she asked Rohit to put Rimi to bed. Then switched off the living room lights.

Manisha sat in darkness on the couch. The breeze rustled the streamers, made the balloons dance on the ceiling. Taking off her earrings, she unknotted her hair and shut her eyes.

She heard a TV playing in a neighbour's flat and the hum of voices. A car passed by at great speed. A sudden burst of crackers reminded her that it was still the nation's big day. The street dogs were bound to respond, bring up their own jubilation. She felt a stillness within.

Rammadhav was singing, keeping himself awake as the neighbourhood slept. Manisha leaned from her balcony to catch the words she'd heard as a child and her very first melody. She heard the music of the mines.